THE WICKED PRINCE
A ROYAL ENEMIES TO LOVERS ROMANCE

VIVIAN WOOD

Editor: Gemma Wooley

THIS BOOK IS FOR MY READERS — I LOVE YOU ALL. IT'S ALSO BROUGHT TO YOU BECAUSE OF SOME TRULY WONDERFUL ALPHA AND BETA READERS: PATRICIA, KATHY, AND KYM; MICHELLE, ANTJE, PATTI, REBECCA, AND SO MANY OTHERS.

The Wicked Prince Playlist
Ariana Grande — Dangerous Woman
Adele — Lovesong
Billie Eilish — you should see me in a crown
Le Tigre — TKO
Biggie Smalls — Hypnotize
The Hives — Hate To Say I Told You So
Usher — U Got It Bad
The Kooks — Naive
Metric — Gold Girls Guns
Muse — Madness
Scissor Sisters — Take Your Mama
Billie Eilish — everything I wanted
Arctic Monkeys — Do I Wanna Know?
Glen Hansard — My Little Ruin

Neko Case — I Wish I Was The Moon
Run The Jewels — Run The Jewels
Florence + the Machine — Dog Days Are Over
Billie Eilish — No Time To Die
The Sundays — Wild Horses
Shawn Mendes — In My Blood

A NOTE FROM THE AUTHOR

Dear reader,

The Wicked Prince takes place in a unique, glamorous, glitzy world — the world of the Dirty Royals. If you have already been introduced to this world by reading the prequel novella *The Prince and His Rebel*, you may want to skip to Part II: *The Wicked Prince*.

If you haven't read *The Prince and His Rebel* OR you would like a refresher, just turn the page and begin the book.

PART I
THE PRINCE AND HIS REBEL

CHAPTER 1

MARGOT

If you've already read this, you can skip to part II.

"Wait!" I say, crouching down and peering through my camera's viewfinder. We're on a random side street in Brooklyn, so we're not in anybody's way. Both sides of the street are industrial and it's a definite look. It sparks my creativity. "Hold that pose."

Pippa rolls her eyes and grins, freezing in place. "Margot, you had better get a few good photos for Insta, at least. I'm only in New York for the weekend and we have soooo many places to go and things to see... boys to meet..."

Her sleek British accent makes her stand out; her outrageously gorgeous good looks are almost enough to make me envious. She should be on a stage somewhere, performing before an enraptured audience.

Instead, she went to NYU and majored in journalism, just like me.

Shaking my head, I sigh. Pippa is pretty boy crazy. She has been since college. I kneel down and frame my shot carefully. It's late and dark except for the light coming from the streetlamp. But there is something about that light, coming from behind Pippa… illuminating her willowy frame and filtering through her bright red hair…

I take a handful of shots, then stand up. "All right."

Pursing my lips, I press several buttons on the camera and review what I just shot. Pippa comes over to look over my shoulder. She's a good four or five inches taller than me so it works. At five foot one, I'm definitely used to being the shortest chick in the room.

"Scroll to the photos of both of us," she says, nudging me. "The ones that your friend took in the pizza place?"

Bobbing my head, I scroll through the various artsy shots of objects until I get to the pictures she means. The two of us beam at the camera, my petite stature, my black leather jacket, and my shoulder length pink hair seeming silly next to Pippa in her loose white dress.

She doesn't see it that way, though.

"Oh, we look absolutely smashing! Ugh, I just love your whole aesthetic. I'm all soft pinks and flowy garments and you're all like…" She gestures to me.

I look down at my RESIST t-shirt, my super short red tartan skirt, my torn fishnets, and my black Converse. I cock a brow. "I look like I'm either a rich kid from

Columbia University that's experimenting with couch surfing or a genuine street rat with a drug problem. But the trouble is that you can't tell which," I joke.

Pippa rolls her eyes at my comment. "Yeah right. Everyone wishes they had a tenth of the style that you have and you know it."

My face heats. I change the subject as I loop my camera strap around my neck again and start moving down the sidewalk. "We're already going to be arriving at this spot pretty late."

She shrugs. "Who cares?" She looks up at the night sky, sighing. "That's one of the things I miss the most since my move to Copenhagen. People there care if you're late. Here, you just shrug and say that there was a crazy person on the subway. As if that's even a real excuse for anything."

I grin. "That is one of the things that is a unique charm of New York."

She slides me a glance as we hurry across the street and continue down the block. "I guess you'll just have to get used to it when you follow me to Copenhagen. Seriously, I've talked to my editor at *Politiken* and showed her some of your photographs and articles. She is receptive."

"Yeah?" I say, raising my brows. "I've always wanted to move to Europe for a job… It sounds funny though, just saying it aloud." I spot the distinctive bright green door ahead of us, standing out from the dreary surrounding buildings. "Oh, that's the door of the club. They have to move this place pretty often to keep it under wraps, but the door is always a bright color."

Pippa and I jog up to the door. I lean close, pulling out my phone, and knock on it forcefully. A slot slides open and a pair of eyes appear.

"Password?" a feminine voice asks.

I look at the e-vite on my phone, skimming for the password. *"Saluta regi,"* I call out.

The slot slides closed with a metal thunk. A few seconds later the door creaks open, the door woman dressed head to toe in skintight black latex. "Come in."

We step into the tight, dark space. I can hear the thud of music, feel the vibrations coming up through the floor. She opens a second door and we're immersed in raucous sound and a low blue light.

I walk out into the back of the warehouse turned venue, pausing to look around and get my bearings. To my right is a very crowded, very small bar. To my far left is a stage, a cheering and raging crowd swelling around it. Two singers scream into a single microphone while the rest of the band plays loud post-punk music.

The speakers are shitty but loud, which is always a feature of these shows. Pippa leans close to me. "Want to get a drink?"

"God yes." I follow her to stand behind some other girls who are decked out in shiny silver lycra. My eyes wander across the stage and to the audience. I recognize some faces at the back; people that I know from Red-

Green Party meetings, a socially liberal and anti-monarchal political movement.

The Red-Green party started in Copenhagen but it has since blossomed into a genuine political movement, almost anarchist at its core. The same people that used to show up at the Occupy Wall Street and Dakota Access Pipeline meetings often show up in support of the Red-Green party protests.

There is an energy to it, a grassroots anger about the clenched fist of capitalism that seems to drive the whole scene. I respect and admire any kind of rebellion against the system, so… I'm here for it, basically.

Pippa gets us each a beer and a shot of whiskey, as is the usual. We established this pattern in college of taking turns buying rounds for each other. I take the shot, wincing at the burn, and move out of the line.

I glance at Pippa, seeing her brighten. "Hey, I see some people I know. Come on, let's say hi."

She pulls me by the hand toward the opposite wall. There are three extraordinarily tall guys that are propped up against the wall, their heads turned toward the stage. They are probably in their mid twenties, just a few years older than my own twenty three. One of them turns and glances at me briefly. Our gazes snag and hold.

My breath leaves my lungs in a little whoosh. I don't say that lightly, but…

He is *beautiful*. Extremely tall, handsome, dark haired, with cheekbones that look like they could cut steel.

Wearing a dark t-shirt, low-slung jeans, and dark shoes, he looks like he should be on a fashion runway, not in this grimy pop up club.

His eyes are an intense light blue. They skate over me and toward Pippa, but then come back to me. He frowns just a little, like there is something that he should know but can't quite figure out.

I step on a beer can and stumble, breaking my gaze away. When I look up again, I realize that the other guys he's with are equally handsome, one looking so similar to him that I almost can't tell them apart. The third guy has lighter hair and dark brown eyes. Upon looking closely, he's just slightly taller than his two friends.

It's this third guy that catches Pippa's gaze and stands up straighter. He says something to the other two, who nod. Then he pushes himself off the wall and steps out to greet Pippa.

"Pippa, hey," he yells. His accent is strange, Norwegian or Swedish or something. "What are you doing here?"

The band onstage stops playing abruptly and the crowd cheers. Pippa clears her throat, pulling me forward. "Hey. I'm just in town for the weekend. This is my friend, Margot. Margot, this is my friend Erik…"

The lighter haired guy nods at me, taking a second to take me in. "Hey. This is Lars," he points to one brother. "And this is Stellan."

He points to the other, the one I noticed first. The tall one, with the eyes that could melt steel. I blush under their collective inspection, tossing my hair back.

"Hi. I'm Margot." That's all I give them. Luckily Pippa is so extroverted that she just naturally fills in the gaps, making my aloofness seem okay.

God, I've missed her so much since she moved.

"Margot, these guys are from Copenhagen," she says. "They… umm…"

She seems at a loss for how to describe them.

Lars jumps in. "We're Danish. We are enjoying your city, seeing the sights."

Ah. I was close when I guessed at their accents, but not quite there. I sip my beer and keep watching all three of the men.

Stellan is silent and still, but I can tell from his keen gaze that he's drawing all kinds of conclusions. I just don't know what they might be…

Loud pre-recorded music comes over the speakers. Pippa looks around. "We should go dance!"

She heads off without so much as a glance back, just expecting that we will all follow her. Or maybe it's not that, maybe it's just that she knows she will find someone to dance with in the crush of the crowd.

Knowing Pippa, she is probably correct in that assumption.

"Are you staying here?" Erik asks Stellan.

"*Ja.*" Stellan nods. Erik glances at the dance floor. He clearly wants to go out there. Stellan jerks his head toward where Pippa went. "Go dance."

"*Jeg er lige i nærheden,*" Erik says quickly. He looks at me briefly, his gaze narrowing for a second. But then he heads out into the throng, bobbing his head to the music.

I sidle up to the wall beside Stellan, sliding him a gaze as I lean against it. He looks at me too, then shakes his head and looks away.

"What?" I ask. I take a sip of beer.

He shrugs. "I have to go to the bar." He pauses. "Do you like aquavit?"

I wrinkle my nose. "I have no idea what that is."

The corners of his lips lift ever so slightly. "It's like gin, a little."

His accent makes the way he pronounces the word gin a little funny.

I smirk. "Then I guess so."

Stellan pushes off the wall and heads toward the momentarily empty bar. "Come on. You'll like it, I think."

What makes him think that I, a person that he doesn't know from Adam, will like it… I do not know. But I follow him, my wariness of him easing for some reason.

It turns out, I don't hate aquavit. In fact, I kind of like it.

For the next hour we mostly drink and talk a little. We dance at one point. We flirt shamelessly. We dance some more, moving closer and closer together on the dance floor.

"You like this music?" he asks, getting closer to be heard over the music. I inhale his scent; most of the guys I encounter don't smell incredible like he does. Fresh bread and clean soap mixed with a certain maleness. It's kind of addictive. It's also unfair, when you add it to his height, his broad shoulders, his intense blue gaze, and his cheekbones.

I grin up at him, well aware that he's almost a foot and a half taller than I am. Leaning in so my lips brush his ear, I whisper. "Yes."

"It sounds like noise," he says. "There is a melody that is there, but it is under all these… other sounds. Does that make sense?"

My eyes twinkle. "Yes."

He chuckles. "I'm having a good time."

"Me too."

I realize that I'm working up the courage to ask him to come home with me. I have a little sixth floor walkup not far from here. I am drunk and having a good time. And I want to know what his body looks like without those clothes that cling to his muscular frame.

All night the pressure has been building inside me.

Just ask.

He can only say no.

The way he's looking at me, he won't say no.

I'm almost drunk enough to loosen my tongue. *Is that a good thing?* I wonder.

But suddenly Erik appears, whispering intently in Stellan's ear. Stellan frowns and whispers something back. Then he pulls a pen from the pocket of his jeans.

He grabs my arm, the first time we actually touch. It's erotic; for a second, I am aware only of the feeling of the current passing between us, of the goosebumps the electricity leaves in its wake.

He scribbles something on my arm, then points to it. "That is my number this weekend. Call us if you get up to anything fun before Sunday, *ja?*"

Looking up at him with wide eyes, I nod. He releases my arm and turns, following Erik as he heads to the door.

Pippa comes up behind me, a tiny wrinkle of worry set in her brow. "Where are they going?"

Shaking my head, I raise my arm. "I don't know. But I did get Stellan's phone number."

Pippa's brows jump up almost comically. "Really?"

I nod. "Yeah. He said to let him know what we get up to tomorrow night."

Her lips twitch. "Well, well. I guess we are going out tomorrow then, huh?"

I roll my eyes. "We'll see."

"Come on, let's get one more drink before we call it a night." She grabs my arm and steers me away from the door, changing the subject.

My arm still tingles faintly where Stellan touched it.

All right, I can admit it… I'm excited about possibly seeing him tomorrow. And curious about where he went tonight…

Sighing, I stand in line and listen to Pippa talk, only partially paying attention.

CHAPTER 2

STELLAN

"So, Stellan... what is it like to be the future king of Denmark?" the reporter asks, holding his pen at the ready. His American accent is bland and unremarkable.

I shift in my seat, glancing off the balcony of the Four Seasons. The skyline from the vantage point is absolutely stunning... but the afternoon heat is starting to get to me.

That and the fact that being interviewed by a nosy reporter is the very last thing I want to be doing right now. the reporter from the New York Times is named Mark; he and I have been working together for several hours today and yet we're still stiff and disjointed whenever we speak.

My head aches dully from too much partying last night. I take a sip of the coffee laid out on the low table that separates us, a silent sigh on my lips. "It's the only life I have ever known. I couldn't begin to guess at what it is like to live any other way." I crook a brow. "Please tell me that you intend to ask me something better than that?"

He looks up from his pad of paper, pushing his glasses up his nose. His cheeks stain just a bit with embarrassment. "Of course. I have a whole list of more in depth questions."

I study him. He's perhaps fifteen years older than my twenty six years, his gray hairs just beginning to overtake his blond ones. He's a little scruffy and dressed moderately hip in a dark gray button up and black jeans.

It's not that I'm usually a jerk to reporters. I don't mean to put this man on his back foot, although that's not out of the ordinary for a first meeting between me and a commoner.

Rather, it is more that I have my guard up as high as possible with anybody that is outside the royal family. Not just now, but always. And *especially* with the press.

My existence — how I live my life — is a source of curiosity for the rest of the world.

"The reason I agreed to this interview with the New York Times is simple. I am growing into my majority; that is to say, I am ready to take the crown in a few years. It will benefit Denmark to have a ruler that is well known to the American people, as my father King Göran has proven."

It's one of the answers that was provided to me in a nice packet of papers that was left on the royal family's private plane. Just one glance at the words, typed on royal stationery, gives off a whiff of my grandmother, the Queen Mother.

It was her idea to set this all up in the first place.

He nods. "*Ja*, King Göran and Queen Thora's love story is quite well known here. They still seem to be very much in love every time they come visit."

A corner of my mouth tips up. "They are quite the pair."

Mark takes a moment to consider his next question. "Your life is one of opulence and luxury. The finest schools, flashy cars, so many castles owned by your family to even name."

I bob my head, sipping my coffee. He licks his lips and continues.

"I think what people would like to know is how growing up in the spotlight with so much wealth and notoriety influenced you. How does it feel to have your life already laid out for you? Does it feel… mmm… restrictive?"

I want to roll my eyes at the question. It seems obvious that being the Royal Prince of Denmark is, in fact, beyond stifling. This golden mantle is heavy and it only grows more weighted the older I get. But I've been trained since birth to repress and hide my emotions.

So I just blink a few times. "It can be. But I choose to look beyond my duties and responsibilities and see it instead as an honor and a privilege."

Another quote that sounds false, mainly because I'm being puppeted by the Queen Mother. Mark narrows his eyes on my face, but I just stare back at him. I am not easy to embarrass and I've spent years learning how to control that response.

My phone vibrates on the table. I sit up, glancing at Mark as I reach forward. "This could be important."

No, it couldn't. Anything that's important passes through my best friend Erik, who is hovering just out of my eye line inside the glass doors that lead into our suite. There is a hierarchy of what information I need to receive.

Judging by the fact that his enormous shoulder isn't busting the door down, I don't think an affair of state is in question. Flipping over my phone, I see a text from an unknown number.

Tonight. After 9. 5930 Palmetto St. See you there?

It's unsigned, but I have no doubt that it's from *her*.

Margot.

Pink hair, a leather jacket, and Converse. So fucking sexy, so vibrant, so exactly the type of girl my grandmother would hate.

I almost took her home with me for the night, but Erik came and forced me to come back to the hotel. He's a bastard, but he was right.

I bite my lip and turn my phone over. I can't text her back right away, because then she will know that I've been waiting to hear from her.

I raise my eyes to the reporter once more. "Can we do the rest of this over email? I have a pressing engagement."

He pauses like I'm actually asking him whether or not it's possible. "I have a few questions that are more delicate in nature— "

I rise from my seat while he fumbles for an answer. The words *we're done here* might not have passed my lips, but I smile and act as though they did.

"It was a pleasure to meet you." Plastering a vague smile on my face, I hold out a hand for him to shake. Mark's brow pulls down but he shakes my hand.

At the same time, Erik steps onto the balcony. "Mark? I'll show you out…"

I keep that same expression until Mark hurries off, then collapse with a groan of aggravation. Throwing my arm over my eyes, I lay on the outdoor sofa until Erik returns from seeing the reporter to the front door.

"Don't be such a baby," Erik says, taking Mark's seat. His voice is low-pitched, almost a rumble. "I told you not to drink too much last night, did I not?"

I glance at him. He's a distant cousin of mine and you can tell by the way we are similarly built broad, tall, hair cropped close to our scalps. You could easily imagine Erik as a Viking warrior; he even has the light hair to pull it off.

"Aren't you supposed to make me more comfortable?" I grouse.

He rolls his eyes and sits back, kicking up his big booted feet. *"Rend mig i røven."*

My lips curl upward. "Telling your crown prince to go fuck himself is not very nice, Erik."

He looks at me blankly. I think I'm pretty hardened and hard to read, but I've got nothing on Erik.

"We should have left that club earlier." His eyes narrow on my face. "But you wouldn't leave Pippa's friend…"

I grin at him. It's nice to be able to actually express myself, even if it's just between us two. "Her name was Margot. And you'll never guess where they've invited us to go tonight…"

The way his face tightens would be imperceptible to most people. But Erik and I have been friends since birth. I know that he is displeased… I just don't care.

After all, he's my keeper, not the other way around.

"Hey, you agreed to this," I say with a grin. "I said I didn't want to come to New York. You were the one who wanted me to comply with my grandmother's insane demand to come here and do a little positive publicity."

"The Queen Mother was not wrong."

I sit up and lean over the table, pouring myself a glass of sparkling water. "She thinks she can run everything for everyone infinitely. I can't wait until I'm not under her thumb anymore."

Erik pours himself a glass of water too, sipping it. "Be glad for these last years of freedom, Stel."

I snort. "*Ja*. I feel super free. Especially since the Queen Mother celebrated my birthday by giving me a list of the girls she considers marriageable." I pull a face. "Like I need to review. The same girls have been paraded in front of me for my whole entire life."

He lifts his shoulders. "You've dated about two thirds of them, too. You already know what they'll be like. If I were you— "

"Which you're not."

He gives me a look. "I would just pick a girl and settle down."

"Ah. If you were in my place, my grandmother would adore that. She'd get the rule follower that she always wanted. And I would be free of the royal curse."

Erik steeples his fingers. "Don't call it that."

"What should I call it, then?" I rise, heading to the balcony's edge. Far below, a small crowd of protestors are gathered. "The Red-Green Party people have followed me here again. Look."

He doesn't move. "I've seen them."

I turn, dangling my glass between two fingers. "They say that I am representative of the old world order and the patriarchy. Do you know that? If I were only allowed to express my true feelings once in a while…"

His expression smooths out and he looks off at the horizon. "You are ready for the crown. I get that. But you haven't done any of the steps that a prince traditionally does to show he's ready…"

"Like marry a good girl and produce a few heirs," I say, wrinkling my nose. "*Ja*, I know."

For just a second, an angry expression crosses his face. "Don't be in such a hurry for something to happen to your father."

For a second, his rebuke actually takes me aback. Erik usually doesn't like to talk about his father's death. My brows rise in surprise. "I'm sorry, Erik. I didn't mean that. My father doesn't actually have to die for me to ascend to the throne. He just has to relinquish the crown. You know that."

Erik shrugs, apparently no longer interested in the topic. He is usually moody, but this is something else altogether. I drain the rest of my water, my mind wandering back to my phone.

"So about tonight…" I say. "We should go party with Pippa."

His cool green gaze finds me. "And Margot?"

A smile curls my lips. "And Margot," I admit. "She had all the qualities that I love. She's young, she's wild, she's unbelievably hot… and there is something especially sexy about a girl who is clearly attracted to you but doesn't ask a lot of questions."

Tiny, with a heart shaped face and the sweetest, hottest little body I've ever seen. She's like a very feisty doll in sexy fishnets and a leather jacket. And that hair… perfect, bouncy curls that just happen to be neon pink.

There is something about her hair alone that makes me fucking hard.

He rolls his eyes briefly. "She was all over you last night, too."

"She seemed like she was absorbing everything around us, like a sponge. She was…" I squint. "*Hun har hovedet skruet godt på*. What is the English word?"

"Mmm…" He thinks for a moment. "Perceptive?"

"*Ja*. Perceptive."

He pushes himself to his feet. "I think I need a shower, a headache powder, and another cup of coffee before I can even think of going out. Christ. Maybe two litres of water, too."

"And ibuprofen," I add, nodding gravely. "Definitely add that to the list."

"Come on," he says, heading inside. "I'll call downstairs to room service. Then we can make a plan for the night."

Squinting into the sunset, I turn around and look off at the skyline once more. "You go ahead. I'll be inside soon."

Erik shrugs and goes in, leaving me to wonder what Margot and Pippa are doing at this very moment.

I pick up my phone and text Margot back.

See you there.

Smiling, I gaze off the rooftop once more.

CHAPTER 3

MARGOT

"I swear, if Jeff shoots down one more of my articles, I'll scream. Just scream, in front of the whole entire office." Griping about my editor may not be the best or most helpful thing in the world, but it is satisfying.

Pippa glances at me, reaching out to straighten my pink and black negligee that I'm wearing over a pair of ripped fishnets. "Jeff is a ghoul. Not only that, but I heard he tried to put the moves on Marie during the staff Christmas party last year."

I grab a fistful of her filmy white dress. "Marie quit in January!"

Her expression turns pained. "I know. Jeff is really, really awful."

"Ugh!" I say. "Just ugh."

Pippa wrinkles her nose at the dank hallway we're in. We're definitely underground and the whole place smells like piss and a million stale cigarettes. "Are you sure we're in the right place?"

"Definitely. I've been here before. Come on." Pulling her down the hallway, I turn the corner and stop at a thick steel vault.

She eyes the doorway uncertainly. "If you're sure…"

Wrenching open the door; I slowly uncover a den of inequities. Loud pop music plays and the bass actually shakes me where I stand. There are few lights, mostly strobes here and there. As we head in, closing the door behind us, it's obvious just how crowded the dance floor is.

Everybody who's anybody is here right now. Excitement hums through my veins.

Pippa smiles at me, holding out a pill and a bottle of water. "Here."

Biting my lip, I giggle. I take the pill, a little MDMA mixed with a tiny bit of powdered mushrooms. Just enough to make everything pretty, shiny, and fun. Swallowing it with water, I pass the water back to her. She takes a pill too, grinning when she's done.

"Ready?" I ask.

"So ready." She grips my hand and pulls me into the crush of people. The song changes and a female singer comes on, her voice like a siren's call, pulling people onto the large dance floor. Around us, gorgeous people dance together and separately, some of them grinding on each other.

I let go and throw my hands in the air, celebrating my freedom and my body. Pippa and I garner male attention immediately. Everything is heady and pretty from the drugs: the lights seem a little brighter, everything much funnier than usual, and the cool beers that someone hands us seem to slide right down our throats.

I don't let anyone get too close, though. One guy in particular keeps trying his luck and putting his hands on me again and again despite the fact that I dance away each time. Finally I've had enough.

I get close to his ear. His arms envelop me. I whisper to him. "I have a knife hidden in my garter. I will cut you if you touch me or my friend again."

His eyes go big and he takes a staggered step back, raising his hands. I make a *go away* gesture with one hand and twirl, my negligee spinning out like a top when I do.

When I stop spinning, giggling and starting to feel the effects and the drugs pulsing their way through my system...

That's the moment that I lock eyes with Stellan. His gaze is smoldering. His eyes are light blue, but they are searingly hot. Possessive, almost.

I shiver as he strides over to me. He doesn't say a word. He just cups my face and pulls me close, leaning in for a kiss.

My breath freezes in my lungs.

My whole body tingles strangely.

It seems as though there is an odd electric current jumping between us, sparking as his lips draw closer to mine.

My eyes sink closed.

I push onto my tiptoes, needing his kiss like I need air to breathe.

Like a river running down to the sea, I rush to press my lips against his. And there is an immediate jolt of sensation. I clutch at Stellan's shirt and his hands tighten on my jaw and hip where they hold me.

It's perfect. A moment in time that is free of flaws.

Stellan crushes me against his body for a split second. I make a muffled sound, unable to speak. But if I could have, I would've said, yes.

More.

Please.

In the next second he seems to realize that he's a giant compared to me. He lets go and steps back, his eyes still shining with intensity. The music pounds in my ears and slides through my veins.

"Hi," he mouths.

I grin at him. "Hi."

He nods toward a side room that Pippa's distinctive red head is moving towards. I nod in agreement and he takes my hand, leading the way. As we sluice through the crowd, I marvel at the difference between our hands. His is a giant's paw; mine looks petite and pretty holding his hand.

Feeling feminine isn't usually something I'm interested in, but there is something about his sheer size that makes me blush. Is there a correlation between his massive height and the size of his cock?

That's really a dirty thing for me to think, but could it not actually be true?

I giggle to myself as Stellan pulls me into a small side room. The first thing I notice is that music is quieter in here; the second thing is that there are a bunch of old bench-style car seats strewn around. Stellan leads me over to where Pippa, Erik, and Lars have already made themselves comfortable.

He releases my hand and sits down. I bite my lip and sit next to him, unable to keep my blush under wraps. Pippa looks at me and flashes me a grin, then leans back against Lars.

Only Erik seems on edge, constantly looking over his shoulder. What he expects to happen, I couldn't say.

When Pippa pulls out her phone to snap a selfie of herself and Lars, Erik's eyes narrow on her. She just rolls her eyes.

"Don't worry," she says. "I know the rules about photos, okay?"

That gives me pause. Why are there rules? What are they protecting, exactly?

I'm not quick enough with my questions, though. I blame the mushrooms. I just feel too good right now to start quizzing anybody.

Stellan clears his throat uncomfortably. "There are a lot of people in this club for a weeknight."

Lars speaks up. "Especially for New York City. It seems like you all live to work."

Bobbing my head, I lay back on the couch. My flop lands my head on his thigh. He tenses beneath me for a second, a little surprised.

"Is this okay?" I ask, peering up at him.

"*Ja*," he says. He clears his throat again. "I thought that you Americans were all prudes, but I suppose I was wrong, eh?"

One corner of my mouth lifts in a mischievous smile. "I suppose you were."

Everyone sits and talks for a little while. I just let the conversation flow around me. At some point Stellan starts stroking my arm.

I butt my head against his chest. "Mmm. I like that. Do it more."

He obliges, running his hand up and down my arm and across my ribs. Somehow or other a beer appears in Stellan's hand, then another when the first is finished.

When I sit up, Pippa, Lars, and Erik are gone. I notice that Stellan is looking at me like I'm a puzzle he can't figure out.

"What?" I ask.

He mouth turns up a fraction and he shrugs. "I am just trying to figure you out."

Pulling the skirt of my negligee down so I'm not flashing anybody, I fold my legs up on the couch. "I'm not that much of a challenge, am I? New York City, born and raised. Put myself through college at NYU, which is how I know Pips." I stop for a second, pushing my cheek out with my tongue. "I'm a Cinderella story, where I'm both Cinderella and the prince." I grin. "I never had much of anything, which gave me a work ethic like no other. With tonight as being the exception, I guess. Pippa is here, so no work tonight."

He smiles at that. "No, I guess that would make you a bad host."

Eyeing him, I cock my head. "I don't know that much about Danish people. But if I had to guess, you've never had to think about where your next meal would come from."

Surprise looks good on Stellan. "*Ja*. You are right, Margot."

I nod my head. "Yeah. That's what I hope for, when I think about having kids someday. That they'll never have to think about finding food or shelter."

He looks a little taken aback, which is the only way I know that I've overshared. My face goes beet red. Before he can say anything, I pull out my phone, a handy distraction.

"Let's take a picture together," I suggest.

To my surprise, he's hesitant. "I don't think that's a very good idea."

I wrinkle my nose. "Come on. Just for me. I want something to remember you by after you go back to Copenhagen. *Ja?*"

I imitate his accent on the last word. He grins at that, rolling his eyes. "Alright. How do you want me to sit? Like this?"

He adopts a silly pose, which makes me dissolve in giggles.

"Wait, just hold that…" Dropping in the frame beside him, I pull a face. "Okay, now a serious one…"

The song shifts, changing to a young pop singer that I unabashedly love. I grin, standing up. "Dance with me."

Stellan stands too, glancing at the dance floor. "Are you sure you want to go out there?"

I step closer and pull at his shirt, looking up at him. "I wanna dance right here. Just the two of us."

He smiles, his hands sliding down to land on my hips. "Okay, Margot." He pulls me against his body, biting his lip as he looks down at me. His gaze is direct and intense; I almost get lost in his ice blue eyes.

"You are very pretty," he says, cupping my cheek. I blush furiously and yet, I can't look away. "Your hair…" His fingers move to stroke my hair. "And the way you dress…" He fingers the bottom of my negligee. "It's perfect. You seem to be put together just to please me. Do you know that?"

I can't even begin to figure out how I should answer that. A smile tugs at my lips. "Then there is just one thing you should do."

One of his hands slips down to my ass. Electricity crackles between us. "What's that, *skatter?*"

Skatter. I don't know what it means exactly, but the way he says it is enchanting. I lean my head back, presenting my mouth to him, whispering my words. "You should kiss me."

A dimple flashes in his cheek. He doesn't say anything, but his hand that's on my ass presses me closer. His cock presses into my belly.

My eyes widen just a bit at the sheer size of it. That can't be real, can it?

At the same time his face lowers, his breath teasing my lips when he stops just a hair's breadth shy of kissing me. It seems like the most natural thing in the world to close that gap, to push up on my toes and press my lips onto his.

His lips are hot and firm. There is an immediate sense of urgency, growing with every second. I curl my hands in his shirt, needing more. I want to sink into his mouth and never return.

I feel the roughness of his stubble against my smooth face. I feel the frantic beat of my heart against the loud bass beat of the club's music. I feel his arms tighten around me, a python with its prey in its grasp.

I feel all of it, and I want *more*.

He deepens the kiss, bending me back a little. His tongue invades the cavity of my mouth, dancing with my tongue. He tastes so good, like mint and beer and male, under it all.

Stellan starts moving with me, swaying against me, dominating my whole body. At the same time he presses his hips into my belly again, grinding. I suddenly have a flash of exactly what Stellan is going to be like when we go to bed together.

Rough. Dominant. Hard. But I have a feeling that he knows exactly how to make me come, how to make me scream his name, over and over again until my voice gives out.

I shiver and crush myself against him.

All my secret cravings for someone like Stellan will be fulfilled. And the best part? After this weekend, he will vanish into thin air.

Poof.

I can be as uninhibited with him as I want. He's the ultimate one night stand.

It's hard not to bite his earlobe when I whisper in his ear.

"Let's go somewhere private."

Stellan smirks, that dimple flashing in his cheek again. "Come on. We should go back to my hotel."

He takes my hand, leading the way. And I follow him, a rush of heady excitement sluicing through my veins.

CHAPTER 4

MARGOT

The Uber ride to his hotel could take forever or it could be just a few short minutes. I don't actually know because Stellan has his tongue down my throat and his hand on my thigh. His fingers brush under my negligee and over my pussy a few times.

I'm in the grip of the mushrooms and the MDMA. But more importantly, I'm into *him*. My hands rove over Stellan's chest and back and clutch at his shirt. My eyes practically roll into the back of my head every time he touches my breasts or teases the silk-covered triangle between my clenched legs.

The lobby of the hotel seems fancy; I glimpse gold and marble as he hustles me to the elevators. Once the elevator doors glide closed, I gasp as he picks me up and backs me against the mirrored wall.

My eyes sink closed. I pant as he leaves hickeys all over my neck and breasts. His hot mouth is everywhere, his hands rucking up my negligee. He pushes my knees apart and presses between them. If it weren't for a little denim and silk, we would be fucking right now.

I wrap my legs around his back as the elevator rises. When the elevator chimes and the doors slide open, he carries me off and walks straight into the penthouse suite. I pause, my eyes opening.

"Holy shit," I say. Stellan doesn't stop moving, but I can't help but notice the floor to ceiling windows with their exquisite view of Manhattan. "Jesus. What are you, rich? Or is it that you're a rebel? Hmm? Did you steal the keys to this place?"

No response to that from him, except for to suck on my neck extra hard. He keeps moving through the space, dodging the low gray modern furniture until he gets to the bedroom. I take that to mean that Stellan somehow *borrowed* the keys to this suite.

I'm not exactly worried about it; I like a little danger mixed with my fucking. As he lays me down on what has to be the softest mattress ever made, I grin. Such opulence should be used and shared by everyone; just a few hours ago I was wearing a ripped t-shirt that declares EAT THE RICH.

He backs off, pulling his dark t-shirt up over his head. My eyes widen at his well-built chest and muscular arms; he even has a taut six pack, which I didn't think actually existed outside of the movies. He's actually a giant, descended from the Vikings… that's what my overheated brain tells me, anyway.

I lean on my elbows, watching him strip his shoes and jeans off, leaving him in nothing but a pair of tight black boxer briefs. My gaze trails up and down his body, ravenous for his touch.

"Fuck. You're *hot*," I say. Tossing my hair, I bite my lush lower lip.

He grins, flashing me that dimple again in his cheek. "I take that as a compliment, coming from you."

I blush. "Thanks."

His eyes glint. "Now for the love of everything holy, get fucking naked. I can't believe I've waited this long to taste you."

My fingers shake as I sit up, pulling my negligee up and over my head. It falls to the side, forgotten. My tits are bare, my chest tightening and lifting under his inspection. Stellan drinks me in, his white teeth sinking into the pink flesh of his lower lip. His ice blue eyes rake over me, making my nipples pebble.

He reaches down and adjusts his cock in his boxer briefs. Then he grates out another command. "Take off your panties."

My lips twitch. I tilt my head. "Why don't you come over here and do it yourself?"

He smirks and then moves onto the bed very, very slowly. "You are defiant."

The breath leaves my lungs as his arms cage me in. "Until my last breath."

He considers me for a second. Then he reaches up and pushes my hair away from one side of my neck, the backs of his fingers touching my neck. "Someone should teach you a lesson, *ja?*"

My heartbeat pounds wildly in my own ears. I lift my head. "I've been waiting for a teacher."

His beautiful blue eyes glitter. He runs a single fingertip down my neck, over my collarbone, tracing a line between my bare breasts. I suck in a breath.

His touch trails down my ribs, across my navel, and ends at the top of my panties. I squeeze my thighs together, feeling myself grow wet, feeling the slide of my body growing ready for him.

Stellan glances at me. "I'm going to fuck you senseless. If you're going to tell me to stop, this is your last chance."

I bite my lip, smothering a grin. I shake my head. "Less talk. More action."

He smiles as he literally rips my panties off of my body. He kisses me on the hip, then on the top of my thigh. I can't hold back the sultry moan that rises in my throat. His fingers walk up to find my nipple and tweak it hard.

Gasping loudly, I arch into his touch.

"Good girl," he purrs. Stellan splays a big hand underneath my belly button, covering my pubic mound. He presses down firmly as he showers little bites and swift nibbles to my thighs, working his way closer and closer to my shaved pussy.

I watch as he runs the tip of one thick finger up the seam of my pussy, just barely touching. A twisted, angry grunt leaves my lips.

"Stellan," I reprimand him.

He looks up at me, grinning devilishly. He places the lightest of butterfly kisses over my pussy, making me writhe.

"Stellan, please!" I beg.

He shakes his head. "I don't think so, *skatter*. I'm not going to let you come just yet."

Instead, he pushes himself up onto his knees and grasps his cock through his boxers briefs. My lungs constrict as I watch him, looking down on me, naked and spread out.

Eyeing me, he bites his lip. "I think you need to taste me, *skatter*. I want to feel the tip of my cock in your fucking throat."

My entire body tightens with need. His lips form a naughty smile.

"Can you control your gag reflex?"

My cheeks color. "A little." I get to my knees, reaching for him, but he sneers at me.

"No. You lie on the edge of the bed, like this." He grabs me, positioning me so that my head is by the foot of the bed, dangling off just a little. "If it's too much, just tap my leg. *Ja?*"

Nodding, I watch as Stellan strips his black boxer briefs off. His cock bounces up, jutting straight out.

"Holy shit," I breathe, my eyes widening. I knew he was well endowed, but… he's absolutely *huge*. His cock is long, thick, and veiny in a way that male porn stars would be jealous of. He's also uncut, which honestly is a little unnerving.

I don't follow Judeo-Christian beliefs or anything, but it reinforces the fact that he is definitely not from here.

Stellan grins, grasping his cock and wiggling his eyebrows. Then he steps forward. "Open your mouth. Cover your teeth for me, *skatter*."

My heart pound in my ears. *Relax*, I tell myself. *Whatever you do, don't gag.*

Licking my lips, I open my mouth. He steps closer and nudges the tip of his cock between my lips. I taste his cock, the deep earthy maleness and manly musk bursting across my tongue like fireworks.

He groans, closing his eyes for a brief moment. "Ah, fuck."

That's fucking sexy. The sound of his rumbled curse makes my breasts tighten. I relax a little, resting my hand on his inner thigh.

Then he starts very slowly working his length in and out of my lips. More rumbles of pleasure leave his lips. Not groans or moans, but *almost*.

Stellan stops and peers down at me after a few seconds. "Good?"

I nod, my mouth still full of his cock. He grips his cock and starts pumping in and out of my mouth, his eyes squeezing shut. I grab him and pull him closer, attempting to work my tongue against his cock.

His reaction is immediate. His whole body seizes up. There is an intense look of concentration on his face. "*Fuck*, Margot."

I slide my hand down to delicately cup his balls. His eyes actually roll back in his head as he starts to move again, jerking in and out of my lips roughly. "Fuck," he breathes. "*Skatter…*"

He stops suddenly, pulling out of my mouth. Before I can even react, he's covering the tip of his cock with his hand, cursing and clenching his eyes shut. He cums, shooting jets of milky white semen into his hand. The look of pleasure on his face, so intense and ecstatic it nearly borders on pain, makes me quiver.

When he's done, Stellan opens his eyes again. "That wasn't quite how I was supposed to finish… but your mouth felt too good. Too hot."

I lick the corner of my mouth. "My pleasure."

He chuckles, reaching across to the bedside table for the tissue box. He wipes his hand off and then pads over to the trashcan, disposing of the tissue. When he comes back, he kneels at the foot of the bed.

"Now it's your turn," he husks. "Come down here."

Feeling a little weird about it, I turn around. Stellan isn't interested in waiting, grabbing my knees and spreading them wide. I feel a little awkward being exposed like that, but he isn't too worried about my emotions just now.

"Cup your breasts," he commands, ducking his head low. I expect him to start flicking his tongue over my clit, but of course he doesn't.

He is always surprising, always keeping me on my toes.

Instead he starts kissing the inside of my thigh. His hands touch my inner thighs, sliding up as he trails his kisses toward my pussy. I moan softly, bucking just a little. He looks up at me, catching my eye.

His dark brow descends and he looks utterly sincere when he utters the next words. "You are so beautiful, Margot."

Then his head lowers again and he licks along my seam, causing my eyes to flutter closed. My brow wrinkles as he teases me, using two fingers to part my lower lips. When he finally seals his lips over my clit, sucking on it gently, a wave of pleasure washes through my whole body, rippling out from my pussy.

I grab my tits, shaping my nipples with hard pulls. He alternates between licking and sucking my clit. Stellan is going to drive me mad. He pulls unintelligible sounds of need from my lips, makes my hips thrust against that magical mouth of his.

When he's good and ready he tests my entrance with the tips of two thick fingers, working them in and out. My pussy is beyond wet and ready for him, but there is still some resistance as he slides his fingers home. I groan, ready to explode.

"Fuck. Fuck, right there," I whisper. "That's so good, Stellan…"

I feel him pause, wetting a finger from his free hand. Then he starts licking my clit again… while he pushes that fingertip against the tight balloon knot of my ass.

My eyes widen, but it doesn't feel bad. Actually, with my clit being stimulated and Stellan working his fingers slowly in and out of my pussy, it feels… naughty. But good.

I whimper, uncertain.

When he actually penetrates my ass with one finger, my eyes roll up in my head. "Oh god," I choke out. "Don't stop, Stellan. God, don't stop…"

For a second, it's quiet, aside from the sound of blood rushing in my head and my heart beating like a drum. I stop trying to breathe and thinking about anything at all.

I only exist for the pleasure that Stellan is giving me, right now, right here.

I come suddenly, the orgasm ripping through me, clenching and spasming. One moment I'm at the top of a cliff, looking down into the looming crevasse. The next I am in free fall, plummeting toward the bottom, praying that there will be a body of water to save me from certain death.

I'm pretty sure I scream. At some point Stellan withdraws, licking at his mouth. When I can focus my eyes and breathe again, I look at him, chuckling because I am so overwhelmed.

"What?" he asks. He lays down on the bed beside me, fisting his cock. He's hard again, which is impressive in itself.

"That was…" I trail off, shaking my head. I try to catch my breath. "Incredible."

"Mmm." He eyes me, carnal interest still lighting a fire in his eyes.

I turn on my side. Should I be this winded after sex? I'm too young for it, I feel like… "What now?"

His lips turn upward. He moves closer, pressing a kiss to my lips. He still tastes like me, a little metallic but also earthy with a hint of sweetness. He cups my tits, renewing my interest.

"*Skatter*… I want to have your mouth again," he whispers against my lips. "Give it to me, Margot."

I lick my lips, looking deep into his eyes. "For tonight… I'm all yours, Stellan."

That apparently amuses him, but he doesn't say anything. Instead he just kisses me again, so deeply that I forget that morning will ever come.

CHAPTER 5

STELLAN

It's early in the morning when I wake. At first, I just open my eyes and stare at the ceiling. It takes my system a minute to boot up, to realize where exactly I am and that I am not alone. I roll over onto my side and see Margot sleeping there, her outrageous pink hair sticking out in every direction.

She sleeps on her side, her face drawn into her chest. It almost looks like she's trying to protect herself, even in her sleep. But from what?

I repress a sigh and look at her lovely face. Her skin is radiant, her cheekbones high, her eyes large and expressive. For Satan, but she is pretty.

There are faint circles under her eyes.

I am actually partially to blame for that. We stayed up most of the night fucking. Well, doing everything but fucking actually... she sucked my cock until my eyes rolled up in my head over and over. I fingered her and licked her until she came screaming. Her taste still lingers faintly on my lips and tongue.

I don't actually mind that. She tasted sweet and musky; there are far worse things to wake up smelling like.

The point is, I was exceedingly careful where my sperm went.

Even drunk, I know better than to actually spend my seed inside of random girls. If I accidentally got a girl pregnant and the press found out about it…

Ah, there it is. The faint pounding of my head, between my eyes. It's funny… for a minute, just brief window of time, I almost forgot that I was a royal.

Almost.

I hear a noise outside of the bedroom door. Cocking my head, I frown. Is that Erik, then? Where did he end up last night?

Pushing myself up into a sitting position, I sigh. I really need a glass of water and a headache powder to even begin dealing with today.

Erik slams the door open, holding up a phone. Margot stirs and panics a little, sitting up too.

"Erik—" I start.

He has eyes only for Margot, though. "You fucking bitch!"

My eyes narrow. Margot looks alarmed. "What? Don't call me a bitch…"

"Erik, don't call her that. What do you want?" My head pounds, less faintly this time and more like a jackhammer.

Erik looks at me, beyond aggravated. "She posted pictures of you two together to fucking Instagram, Stel. *Intimate* photos."

That gets my attention. "What?"

I have a vague memory of Margot snapping a couple of pictures with her phone last night. A cold fist of worry forms in my stomach.

I look at her, clutching the comforter to her chest. Always protecting herself. My eyes narrow.

"Is it true?" I ask.

Her delicate brows descend, making her eyes darker. "Well… yeah… I didn't realize that you guys had a weird hang up about Instagram or whatever…"

I flinch, then look at the ceiling. Scrubbing my hand over my face, I try to think. I want to scream at her. But that won't help anybody.

When I speak, my voice shakes with barely contained fury. "You have to take them down."

Erik hisses. "It's too late for that. Her post went viral."

"What?" Margot says, confused. "Why?" Her gaze darts to me, accusing. "What don't I know?"

I avoid her gaze, looking at Erik instead. "Can we shut it down? Have you already talked to the royal press office?"

"I called them first. They are working on it, but they don't know if they can squelch the info. Once it's out— "

"It's out." I bury my head in my hands. "Fuck."

"I'm sorry. What the fuck are you two talking about?" Margot clutches the comforter to her chest as she rises to stand beside the bed.

I don't fight her for it; I have plenty of things to be embarrassed about, but my body isn't one of them.

Instead I grab my boxer briefs from where they lay on the floor in a discarded heap. Stepping into them with a curse, I turn to Erik. "Grandmother is likely going to have two heart attacks at once when she hears about this. Give me five minutes… I will meet you out in the living room."

Erik gives a curt nod, shooting Margot one last glare before he stalks out of the room. I find a shirt and pull it on. I can't help but feel the dread growing in my belly, threatening to take over everything.

Margot starts putting on her clothes. Her face is drawn and she's muttering a little. "I don't have to stick around for this. You act like I'm not even here!"

I pull on a pair of pants, casting a dark look her way. "You don't even realize the shit storm you have managed to stir up, Margot."

She shoves her hair back out of her face, looking outraged. "Do you want to explain why? Or do you just want to go vent about it to Erik some more?"

I cross my arms. "I'm the crown prince of Denmark, Margot. The heir to the throne. And the last thing I needed was for you to run around telling people on the internet who I hook up with."

Her eyes go wide with shock. "What?"

"Didn't you notice Erik's reaction to having his photo taken? He knows the drill. Nothing on camera, *ever*. Because if it's on film somewhere, someone is going to find it." I spread my hands wide. "And once the press has it, they will run with it. Make up all kinds of things. You should know... aren't you friends with Pippa?"

Her expression is sheepish, but the second I turn it around on her, she glares at me. Going over to her purse, she grabs a laminated badge and waves it in my face.

"I'm member of the press," she says, her voice rising in pitch. "So maybe stop for a hot second before you malign my own organization to me, okay?"

Now it's my turn to be shocked. "*What?*"

I'm vaguely aware of my heart pounding loudly. Oh god.

She's one of *them?*

I really, really fucked up this time.

She stuffs her feet into her heels, glaring at me. Then Margot grabs her purse and tosses her hair. "I'm a photographer. And I think you are overreacting. Just because a couple of people reblogged my Instagram posts…"

I cross the bedroom, grabbing her by the elbow. "You don't understand. I'm a member of the royal family. These jackals have hunted my family down for centuries. And once they scent blood…"

I shudder. But I'm not prepared for the way she looks at me, like I just kicked her puppy or something. She jerks out of my hold.

"We are *human beings*," she grits out. "The only things separating you and your family from the rest of us are a few tiaras and a lot of fucking money. Money you didn't even earn!"

I glare at her. "I knew that you were bad news the second I laid eyes on you."

Margot tosses her hair and heads for the door. "I can't believe I spent the night with you."

"Wait!" I call.

She looks back at me. "I don't have the time or the emotional space for this."

I growl. "You don't want to leave now. Let Erik find a way to smuggle you out of the building. Maybe if we do that and you take your Instagram posts down—"

"You are unbelievable. You know that?"

Erik comes back in, standing in the doorway. He stares Margot. "This is all your fault."

Looking between us, she cocks her hip. "What, are you going to physically keep me here? I'm a hundred percent certain that there isn't any amount of money in the world that will keep me quiet if you resort to false imprisonment."

Erik and I make eye contact. I fidget. He starts toward her, a giant grizzly bear stalking his weak prey.

"Stop!" I call out. They both look at me. I square my jaw. "Let her go, Erik. If the story is out, it's out."

Erik pauses, but doesn't move. "It was only two weeks ago that the royal family was in the news, apologizing about your uncle Heinlein and those call girls of his." He looks back and forth between Margot and me. "The press will rip you both to shreds."

"I'll believe it when I see it," she sasses.

He rolls his eyes and moves clear of the doorway. Margot is out like a shot, not another word to either of us. In a few seconds I hear the elevator chime.

Flinging myself across the bed, I bury my face in the pillows. My whole bed still smells like sex and flowers, a remnant of her perfume maybe.

"Your grandmother is going to have your head on a spike," Erik says, sitting on the end of the bed.

I close my eyes. "I know."

"I told you to be careful with a commoner."

I grit my teeth. "*I know.*"

He sits there for a moment longer, then hoists himself to his feet. "I'm going to start arranging our trip home. I have to figure out where the fuck Lars is at the moment."

I open my eyes and glance at him. "If you can't find him, my brother can figure out how to get home on his own." I repress a sigh. "I think we should leave as soon as possible. Grandmother will want to see me soon, I expect."

He's quiet for a beat. "Maybe it won't be that bad."

Groaning, I roll over. "Have you checked downstairs, then? Are the press not swarming all over every entrance to the hotel?"

He looks away. "They are. I really wish your girl would've let me get her out without a fuss… because they are going to go nuts when they see her."

Shrugging, I think about Margot's soft curves. I think about how she jammed that press pass under my nose, sending me into shock.

God, how stupid could I be? "I have other things to worry about now."

"All right. Get your stuff together. I want to leave in thirty minutes." He heads out of the door, leaving it wide open.

I wallow in bed for another minute, inhaling the smell of our scents mixed together. It's funny; if none of this had happened, I could've really liked Margot.

Not that it would have done either of us much good... I'm still going to be saddled with some long-faced dullard from my grandmother's list. This little event will actually only speed up the process, I fear.

Going to the closet, I start pulling down the suits and jeans hanging inside, my core filling with dread.

CHAPTER 6

MARGOT

I unbolt the door of my tiny Bushwick apartment, opening the door. Instantly there are camera flashes and reporters shouting my name.

"Margot! Margot! Are you and Prince Stellan an item?"

"Do you plan to move into one of his castles?"

"Margot!"

I see a flash of red hair. Pippa edges through the crowd, throwing a few elbows. "Move, please! Move!" Her British accent makes her sound more polite, but I can tell from her expression that she's actually pretty fucking annoyed.

Welcome to my new life, Pippa. It's hell on earth.

She eventually makes it to the door and squeezes herself in. Then she shuts the door behind herself, giving her long mane of red hair a little shake. She smoothes her hands down her pristine pink floral dress and pulls her oversized white leather handbag onto her shoulder.

"That was insane!" she says, looking at me with wide eyes. She jogs a brown paper bag full of groceries on her hip. "I brought you bagels."

My eyes well up. I rush over and give her a tight squeeze, surprising her a little. "I'm so glad you are here."

Pippa hugs me back with her free arm. "I'm just glad I'm in town." She bites her lip, pulling back and looking at me. "Although I have to admit, if I wasn't visiting, you never would have met Stellan."

"None of this is your doing." I tug the paper bag out of her arms, heading over to the kitchen and setting it down on the counter. "It's one part my fault, one part Stellan's. He could've just told me who he was. Or maybe handled the aftermath a little better."

Pippa sighs, brushing a strand of her hair back. "Yeah. But really, it's the American press that's the problem. They're having a field day with the whole situation."

I wrinkle my nose. "I know. The tabloids are running all kinds of headlines about me. Mostly focusing on the idea of a rags to riches story, which is almost completely made up." I wince. "Well, they aren't wrong about where I came from. They're just making up lies about where I'm going."

She looks around my tiny apartment, screwing up her face. Walking over to my sofa, she sits down. "I'm guessing you haven't heard anything from Stellan, then?"

I snort. "No."

Pippa tosses her handbag down. "I think the whole royal family is on lockdown. It's been one scandal after another for them this year."

Sitting beside her on the couch, I look wistfully out my small living room window. "I don't particularly care. I just want the tabloids and the paparazzi to leave me alone." I glance at Pippa. "Did I tell you that I lost my job over this whole thing?"

Her jaw drops. "What?"

"Yep." I make a disgusted sound. "Jeff said that if I didn't come in yesterday, I could consider myself no longer employed. I can't even get out the front door without enacting a mob scene!"

She reaches over, placing a comforting hand on my arm. "I'm so sorry. I wish none of this had happened to you. Really I do."

I sort of shrug off her concern. We have been friends for a long time, but it's just hard for me to let people show concern for me like that. "I'm fine. Or I would be, if some scummy tabloid hadn't dug up a couple of people who knew me in high school. They've been running these clips of different people that say they spend time with me, when in fact I didn't even recognize their names until I looked them up in my yearbook."

Pippa bites her lip. "That sounds like bullshit."

"It is!" I growl.

"Well..." She flashes me a nervous smile. "I actually come bearing news on that front. *Politiken* is still very interested in you, perhaps even more so now that this little fiasco happened."

My eyebrows fly up. "Really?" Then I scowl. "I don't know. I don't want to be headhunted just because I posted some pictures online of myself with Stellan."

She scrunches her face up. "I'm sorry to be the one to tell you this, but... tough shit."

Her pronouncement actually makes me smile. It feels good to express something other than the anger and disappointment that's been consuming me for days. "Yeah?"

"Yeah!" she says. "Stuff happens. This *happened* already. It's sort of shattered your existence. All you can do now is figure out the best way out of this mess." She raises her eyebrows, with a hopeful smile on her face. "Plus, *Politiken* is offering to pay for your flight and basic moving expenses. You are getting an offer to move to Copenhagen, all expenses paid. What could be better than that?"

I bite my lip. "I... I'm not even sure what to say."

Pippa squints, then looks around. "You live in a space where you can almost fry an egg from your bed. Your bathroom is just a shower and a toilet, packed into a few square feet. You don't even own a mirror that I can see…" She makes a face. "So… what? You are afraid to give up all this opulence for a chance at adventure?" she teases me.

I can't help the bark of laughter that escapes my lips. "Hey, at least the heater works." Then I stop, admitting the truth. "Well, it works *sometimes*."

"So come work at *Politiken*. Stay with me. My roommate moved out last month so it's basically perfect." She gives me a cheesy grin. "It'll be like the NYU dorms all over again. But like, less marijuana smoke drifting through the halls."

I glance outside again. "I don't know. I've never lived anywhere that wasn't New York City."

Pippa rolls her eyes. "New York isn't going anywhere anytime soon. It'll still be here when you decide you're tired of Copenhagen. Besides, what will you miss?" She wiggles her brows. "Come on! Say yes!"

Outside, I can hear raised voices. Likely two of the paparazzos are bickering with each other. I release a long-suffering sigh. "You're right. I think I should go. At least for a few months until this whole thing blows over."

Her entire face brightens. "Really? I didn't actually expect you to accept…"

My heart seizes up. "The offer isn't real?"

"It is," she assures me. "*Politiken* definitely asked me to beg you to come. They'll be over the moon that you said yes. I just didn't foresee your answer, that's all."

I bite my lip. "Do you think it's the right choice?"

A loud thump comes from my front door, making us both jump. Pippa's eyes widen.

"Definitely."

I screw up my face. "In for a penny, in for a pound… How soon do you think I can leave?"

She stands up, pulling out her phone. "I can find out with one phone call… just give me a minute…"

She presses the phone to her ear and walks to the other side of my studio apartment, setting the wheels in motion. I start to pull out my two duffel bags, filling them with my clothes.

It doesn't feel real. Then again, nothing really does.

Nothing except for the fact that I'm still angry at Stellan.

It's only the work of an hour for Pippa to get us booked on a flight to Copenhagen. She keeps giving me the same comforting smile while she works on it, checking on me every so often.

But Pippa was right… there isn't anything holding me back. Nothing tying me to New York except that I was born here.

And that just isn't enough.

We pack up everything I could need to take in twenty minutes. Then I open the front door, looking out into the crowd of reporters. There are a million camera flashes and people jockeying to be close enough to me to ask me a question.

"Margot! Margot!"

"Are you joining the prince?"

"Will you become queen, Margot? Is that what this is about?"

I roll my eyes harder than they've ever been rolled in my life. There is a somewhat violent struggle between the paparazzi to get my attention. I stop, giving them the only sound bite that I will ever utter.

"It must be terrible for you to be so bound by the rules of the patriarchy," I tell one woman who keeps shoving her microphone in my face. "You should really work on that."

Pippa locks the door behind us and then steers me through the jostling crowd. We get into the waiting Lyft, jetting off toward Pippa's hotel, our only stop on the way to the airport.

I look out the back window as my flat disappears around a corner. Splaying my hand out against the glass, I say a silent goodbye to my shitty apartment.

Then I turn and face forward, wondering what Copenhagen will be like.

PART II
THE WICKED PRINCE

CHAPTER 7

MARGOT

At twenty three years old, this is definitely not where I saw my life headed.

Exiled from New York.

Running away to Denmark.

Haunted by memories of a man that wasn't at all who I thought him to be.

A man whose fiercely good looks and skills in bed still wake me up at night, panting his name.

Stellan.

I close my eyes and lean my forehead against the smooth off-white plastic surrounding the window of the plane. I let myself drowse and drift. As the plane carries me across the Atlantic, I'm in the elusive space between wakefulness and sleep. My mind wanders, half-formed shapes rising out of the ether to remind me of what I'm running from.

"Margot! Margot!"

Dimly, I am aware of a round black microphone materializing out of the dull gray void, and being pushed toward my face.

"What was it like to sleep with Denmark's future king? Do you have royal aspirations? Are you and Prince Stellan declaring your intentions to marry?"

I flinch away, stirring a little. The microphone is shoved toward my mouth. Everyone is waiting for a response. I have no choice but to answer.

No, I think. *I don't want anything to do with him.*

Stellan's face takes shape in my mind. He is tall and broad, dark-haired with ice blue eyes and cheekbones for days. He is exceptionally gorgeous. It's clear as day that he descended directly from the Vikings and looking at his face makes me feel weak in the knees.

In fact, I would describe his features as being distinctly aristocratic. But along with that comes the aloofness that I have always associated with royalty.

He holds himself apart from everyone else, makes a distinction based solely on how much money his family has. And that makes me wish I had never slept with him, no matter how fuckable I find him.

"Margot!" the reporter says again, jostling me. "Margot?"

Why is the reporter suddenly speaking in a smooth English accent?

I open my eyes to find Pippa peering at me. Pippa is my best friend from college; she is taking me with her back to Copenhagen, to outrun the screaming mob of paparazzi that dogged my every step back in New York.

Well, that explains the accent. Pippa is British.

It takes me a moment to realize that we are still on the plane. Pippa brushes her fiery red hair out of her face and folds up her tray table.

"We're about to land," she says. She nods to something past me. "Look out the window."

I turn and look at the view. It's pitch black out as it is quite late here in Copenhagen. A million tiny points of light shine through the darkness, filtering up to me in the shape of a city. It isn't nearly as huge as New York City, the place that I'm running from.

But it shimmers and twinkles all the same. I place my hand against the glass as we start to descend. Copenhagen will be my home for the next few months.

As the plane lands and I rush to follow Pippa to customs, I am beyond nervous. We line up behind half a dozen other people, all waiting to have their passports examined and stamped. I flip open my brand new passport, creasing the book a bit, and peer at the picture inside.

A tiny, shell-shocked woman with pink hair glares back at me. I'm wearing a leather jacket in the photo and look like more of a badass than I actually feel like. I grew up with less than nothing; not only did I not have any money; I wasn't even sure from night to night where I would sleep or how I would eat.

I've definitely never been out of the country before now. Swallowing, I try to slow my heart rate, which soars higher with every step I take toward the plexiglass security booth.

Pippa leans in close, seeming to tower over me. Pippa is a good six inches taller than me and always dresses impeccably in long, flowy dresses. "Relax." She elbows me. "We'll be through this line in just a minute."

She winks at me. I wrinkle my nose but stay quiet. It's often best to stay silent if you only have negative things to say, I find.

We go through customs and security, arriving outside. New York City is hotter than this in the early summer. It's probably only about seventy five degrees outside right now, just warm enough to not be chilly.

As we get into a cab that Pippa flagged down, she yawns. "This time change thing is going to give me killer jet lag. Tomorrow we should sleep in if we can before we have to be at *Politiken*."

I look out at the blurry cityscape, feeling bleary. "*Politiken* is essentially the New York Times of Copenhagen. It's about as liberal as they come…"

I look at Pippa, who cocks a brow. "I know. You're telling me about a place that I work. And as of tomorrow, we will both work there."

Giving my head a shake, I roll my eyes at myself. "Sorry. I think the jet lag has somehow caught up with me already. I meant to ask whether you think that they'll want me to just write or to take pictures, too. My camera hasn't been used professionally for way too long."

Photography is very much my first love.

She shrugs. "I have no idea. My editor Anna just told me to get your butt to Copenhagen... she didn't say what kind of stuff she'll have you working on."

I lean my head back, closing my eyes. "Maybe this is the launch of my career and I don't even know it. Maybe it's a new opportunity that comes disguised as a torrent of paparazzi screaming questions."

It's true. When I left New York, it was under a black cloud. It seemed like every paparazzo had the same endless strings of questions for me every time I dared to open my door just to check the mail.

Margot, did your affair with Prince Stellan leave you star struck?

Are you going to Copenhagen to be with him?

What is it like being a real life Cinderella?

The last one really stung. The tabloids really concentrated on the rags to riches aspect of the whole salacious affair. Basically I didn't tell them anything, so they just jumped ahead without any kind of factual basis for the entire story.

Stellan has been radio silent ever since I walked out of his hotel to a mob of reporters. I met someone that I thought was my dream guy… tall, handsome, and witty… and then he vanished into a swirl of dust at the first camera flash. A low sinking feeling still lurks in the pit of my stomach a week later.

Pippa chuckles. "I know you must be tired, because that is way more optimistic than you usually are."

I grin. "Yeah, probably. Ask me how I feel tomorrow and I can guarantee it will be different."

The taxi stops downtown in front of a high rise and we get out. I carry my two duffel bags — the sum of all my worldly possessions — up to the fourth floor. Following Pippa into her apartment, I look around.

It's a cozy little apartment; the perfectly white kitchen is to my left, a living room set up to my right. There are stacks of magazines, newspapers, and junk mail piled haphazardly every place I look.

Pippa bares her teeth as she sweeps a pile into her arms and drops her suitcase on the couch. "Sorry it's such a mess. I didn't realize I would be returning from New York with a new roommate." She pauses. "I'll actually have to move some stuff out of your room. And make some room on the counter in the bathroom…" She pulls a face. "And you shouldn't open the refrigerator…"

My lips curl upward. "It's okay, Pips. We lived together during college. I remember it fondly."

She blushes. "I'll get a maid if my mess starts to affect you."

I shrug. "I've literally been homeless before. I'm sure I'll manage."

Pippa shows me down the hallway and into the second bedroom. There's a little futon set up in there that is literally covered with books. Other than a tall IKEA lamp and a mostly empty closet, the room is bare.

"We'll set it up way better," she promises. Then she yawns and stretches. "Come on. Help me get these books off the bed. I think I have some extra sheets in my room…"

Half an hour later I lay down on sheets that only smell like mildew a little bit, sighing as I close my eyes. It's almost two in the morning here now.

I toss and turn for a few minutes before I realize that I am used to a streetlight glowing just outside my window when I'm trying to sleep. My brain is just full of anxieties: my work, my address, and my social status have all changed in the last twenty four hours.

Rolling onto my side, I stare up at the ceiling. In the back of my mind, one paparazzo's question stands out in my mind still.

Margot! Aren't you glad that you won't have to work anymore now that Prince Stellan is your lover?

I grit my teeth. When it comes down do it, that is the problem. These tabloid hacks are allowed to make up whatever they want about my life. Not only that, but they reap rewards from lying.

I would never give up my dreams for a guy, no matter who he is. I don't know how I feel about love in general. Can it be trusted?

It doesn't matter in this case. No amount of insanely chiseled abs or dimples that make me swoon are worth that. Besides, giving up photojournalism for a man would make me extremely vulnerable.

Vulnerability isn't something I can afford, not when Stellan is around. One night together shattered my entire world… I hope I never have to be in that position ever again.

Blech! I make a face in the dark, though no one sees it except for my musty-smelling pillow.

No. No fucking way. I would rather die than be that dependent on any man.

I'm Margot fucking Keane, and I make my own way in the world. For better or for worse, I will always be independent. I've been at the ass end of society: on welfare, my parents MIA, uncertain where my next meal could come from. I've been homeless and I've was even in the foster care system for a while.

What I've learned in all that time is a fiercely held independence and a kind of stubbornness that can shame the devil. And no matter how hard they try, they can't take that away from me.

Rolling over, I bury my face into my pillow with a sigh.

CHAPTER 8

STELLAN

She's so small, her features like that of a doll. Her head doesn't quite come up to my shoulder. Yet she is so... perfect.

Soft pink hair like so much cotton candy, with dark blue eyes that follow me whenever I move. And her body... as she tugs her black negligee over her head, the sight of her full breasts makes my breath leave my lungs. Her nipples are the most alluring color of blush; they make my mouth water.

God damn, she's so beautiful.

I reach down and adjust my cock in my boxer briefs. Then I grate out a command. "Take off your panties."

Margot's gorgeous lips twitch. She tilts her head. "Why don't you come over here and do it yourself?"

I smirk and then move onto the bed very, very slowly. "You are defiant."

The breath leaves her lungs as my arms cage her in. "Until my last breath."

I consider her for a second. Then I reach up and push her hair away from one side of her neck, the backs of my fingers touching the slim white column of her throat. "Someone should teach you a lesson, ja?"

She lifts her head, her eyes full of need and want. "I've been waiting for a teacher."

I can feel her racing pulse. I run a single fingertip down her neck, over her collarbone, tracing a line between her bare breasts. She sucks in a breath.

My touch trails down her ribs, across her navel, and ends at the top of her panties. She squeezes her thighs together, biting her lower lip.

I smirk at her. "I'm going to fuck you senseless. If you're going to tell me to stop, this is your last chance."

Margot bites her lip, smothering a grin. She shakes her head. "Less talk. More action."

I smile as I literally rip her panties off of her body. I kiss her on the hip, then on the top of her thigh. She can't hold back the sultry moan that rises in her throat. My fingers wander up to find her nipple and tweak it hard.

Gasping loudly, she arches into my touch.

"Good girl," *I purr. I splay a big hand underneath her belly button, covering her public mound. Pressing down firmly as I shower little bites and swift nibbles to her thighs, I work my way closer and closer to her shaved pussy.*

She watches as I run the tip of one thick finger up the seam of her pussy, just barely touching. A twisted, angry grunt leaves her lips.

"Stellan!" she reprimands.

I look up at her, grinning devilishly. I place the lightest of butterfly kisses over her pussy, making her writhe.

"Stellan, please!" Margot begs.

I shake my head. "I don't think so, skatter. *I'm not going to let you come just yet."*

Instead, I push myself up onto my knees and grasp my cock through my boxer briefs. Her lungs constrict as she watches me. I'm looking down on her, naked and spread out.

Fuck. She's the most gorgeous little thing I've ever seen.

Eyeing her, I bite my lip. "I think I need to taste you, skatter. *But I also want to feel the tip of my cock in your fucking throat."*

Her entire body tightens with need. My lips twist into a naughty smile.

"Can you control your gag reflex?"

Her cheeks color. "A little." She gets to her knees, reaching for me, but I sneer at her.

"No. You lie on the edge of the bed, like this." I grab her, positioning her so that her head is by the foot of the bed, dangling off just a little. "If it's too much, just tap my leg. Ja?"

Nodding, she watches as I strip my black boxer briefs off. My cock bounces up, jutting straight out.

"Holy shit," she breathes, her eyes widening. My cock is long, thick, and veiny in a way that male porn stars would be jealous of. I'm also uncut, which honestly can be unnerving to the unprepared.

I grin, grasping my cock and wiggling my eyebrows. Then I step forward. "Open your mouth. Cover your teeth for me, skatter."

Licking her lips, she opens her mouth. I step closer and nudge the tip of my cock between her lips. It's hard to be still in that moment. I want to take her mouth, fucking it with abandon, and making myself come in a matter of seconds.

But I don't.

I groan, closing my eyes for a brief moment. "Ah, fuck."

She relaxes a little, resting her hand on my inner thigh.

Then I start to move, very slowly working my length in and out of her lips. A rumble of pleasure leaves my lips. Not groans or moans, but almost.

God, it's hard to be good right now.

I stop and peer down at her after a few seconds. "Good?"

She nods, her mouth still full of my cock. I can feel the slow slide of her tongue against the sensitive underside of the head.

Fuck. I had better start moving before I lose control.

I grip my cock and start pumping in and out of her mouth, my eyes squeezing shut. She grabs me and pulls me closer, attempting to work her tongue against my cock.

My reaction is immediate. My whole body seizes up. It feels so fucking good. "Fuck, Margot."

She slides her hand down to delicately cup my balls. My eyes actually roll back in my head as I start to move again, jerking in and out of her lips roughly.

"Fuck," I breathe. "Skatter…"

I know I'm going to come. There's no stopping it.

I halt suddenly, pulling out of her mouth. Before she can even react, I'm covering the tip of my cock with my hand, cursing and clenching my eyes shut. I come, shooting jets of milky white semen into my hand. The look of pleasure that was on Margot's face when I closed my eyes makes lust slither through my gut.

She likes watching her handiwork.

When I'm done, I open my eyes again. "That wasn't quite how I was supposed to finish… but your mouth felt too good. Too hot."

She lick the corner of her mouth. "My pleasure."

I chuckle, reaching across to the bedside table for the tissue box. I wipe my hand off and then pad over to the trashcan, disposing of the tissue. When I come back, I kneel at the foot of the bed.

Margot looks at me uncertainly, biting her lower lip.

"Now it's your turn," I husk. "Come down here."

She turn around, her movements a little awkward. I'm not interested in waiting, so I grab her knees and spread them wide. Her lower lips spread, giving me unbridled access to her most intimate parts. She squeaks softly, probably feeling a little awkward being exposed like this, but I'm not too worried about her emotions just now.

"Cup your breasts," I command, ducking my head low. She sucks in a breath and does as I ask, mmming at the sensation.

I start kissing my way up her pale, creamy skin, just inside her knee. My hands touch her inner thighs, sliding up as I trail my kisses toward her pussy. She moans softly and shivers, bucking just a little. I look up at her, catching her eye.

My dark brow descends. "You are so beautiful, Margot."

O ne second I'm about to go down on Margot, the next second I am awake and sweating.

Where am I, exactly?

I manage to focus my eyes and see that I'm in my bedroom at the palace, naked against the thousand dollar silk sheets of my bed.

"Fuck."

I close my eyes, trying to recapture the dream. But it's like trying to catch fog in my cupped hands; the dream slips away and I'm left feeling a twisting kind of loneliness.

Margot is gone.

I left her behind in New York.

And I'm here by myself, almost four thousand miles away, the scent of her perfume still teasing my senses. Groaning, I cover my face with a satiny pillow and try to go back to sleep.

CHAPTER 9

STELLAN

Don't react. Just keep your facial expression smooth and untroubled.

I'm sitting at one end of a very long dining room table, looking at the coffee cup in front of me. I am being lectured on responsibility for about the millionth time; I learned as a child to school my expression into a troubled frown and look at some object that's just out of reach.

God. Why am I even here? I know I messed up. But my mother and father, the queen and king of Denmark, are sticking to their world tour. They are busy; my four siblings are off doing god knows what with god knows who.

Why won't my grandmother just let this scandal die?

But I can answer my own question. As the oldest child of Goran and Thora Løve, I should expect to inherit the crown someday. There are endless expectations and responsibilities that I'm responsible for… things that even my closest family and friends don't know about.

"I don't even think he's listening!" Prime Minister Finley, the prime minister of Denmark, growls at me.

He stops to brush a fleck of lint off of his dark gray suit, shaking his head. He tsks and tuts; with his fake blond hair and his preening posture, reminding me of nothing so much as a prized cockatiel.

As of today, he's an angry cockatiel. He puts his hands behind his back, pacing back and forth. Several other members of my private cabinet have been brought to Amalienborg Castle to watch this act of Finley's. To watch and learn as Finley scolds the golden boy prince.

They sit at the opposite end of the table, looking at least as bored as I am. This isn't new, the summoning of multiple people to witness my dressing down.

My grandmother watches everything from her seat by the window, her keen blue eyes picking up on everything she sees. She clears her throat gently and picks at a phantom thread on her pink Chanel suit. A tendril of steel gray hair has escaped from her chignon. No one says anything about it, though. Just like no one is fooled by the fact that she isn't speaking.

We all know who really has the power in this country, and it isn't the absentminded king or the ridiculous prime minister.

"The entire reason you were sent to New York was to do one simple interview. And what do you do instead? You go and cause a scandal!"

He walks over to the table and points a long, pale finger at the tabloids that are spread out over it. My face is splashed on every last one, as is the same shot of a very harassed-looking Margot leaving my hotel.

PRINCE STELLAN HAS ONE NIGHT STAND

ONE MAGICAL NIGHT WITH THE MAN WHO WOULD BE KING

RAGS TO RICHES: BEFORE MARGOT MET STELLAN

And my personal favorite…

SHE'S ALREADY PREGNANT WITH HIS ROYAL BABY

God, even in that picture of her scurrying away from my hotel, her face pinched, Margot looks incredible. She's a tiny person, yes. And she's wearing nothing but a dark-colored negligee and that shocking pink hair… I could've given up everything if only she had let me keep sleeping with her.

Instead, she ran away—

"Stellan!" my grandmother calls. I look up, my cheeks coloring slightly. She nods to Finley. "Prime Minister Finley isn't done."

I crease my brow but my expression stays... not placid, but fixed. Margot reached out to me after she fled my hotel. Several times, actually. I've obsessed over her messages but not returned any of them.

After all, I'm supposed to be on publicity lock down now. The last thing I need in the world is a spotlight.

"You see, that's the problem with your generation..." Finley says, puffing his chest out and pacing again. He pulls out his glasses and puts them on, blinking at me like an owl. "You don't have any privations or restrictions on what you can do. You have so much more freedom than our generation ever had..."

The feral beast inside my chest raises his head at that. He glares at Finley, showing his teeth.

What Finley knows about my personal freedom could fill a thimble. And the fact that he has the audacity to come here to my home and lecture me makes me fucking furious.

But I shove that anger down deep, trying to exude a vaguely repentant air. I want everyone in this room to know that I'm concerned about the scandal, but not *too* concerned. There is an art to wearing the right level of intensity on my face.

My grandmother Ida checks her tiny gold watch, silently sighing. Her gaze rises to take in the whole room with its vaulted ceilings and baby blue walls. Outside the gauzy drapes of immense windows, the summer sun is at its zenith.

Could that mean that Ida expects this to end soon? It's been going on for over an hour and it's the fourth time this week that I've been yelled at for…

Well, an *indiscretion*, to say the least. It's really not even my fault… I just looked into Margot's eyes and saw myself. Or not myself, exactly. But myself if I were not a royal.

If I weren't going to be king, how different my life would have been. How could I be so close to that reflection of my other self and not lean in a little?

She just had this quality that made me forget about everyone else around us, homing in on *her*. What is that, exactly? If I could, I would find out and bottle that essence for the future.

It made me fall for her, at least a little.

Besides, I can guarantee that one glance at Margot's incredible body and her unbelievable ass would have even old Finley howling like a wolf at a cresting moon.

"What do you have to say for yourself?" Finley's smug expression and cocky strut make me fucking angry.

I roll my neck, listening for a loud crack. When I speak, I try to show Finley and his government cronies not an ounce of genuine emotion. "It was a mistake." I grit my teeth. "It won't happen again, obviously."

"You're damned right it won't happen—" Finley starts.

Ida rises from her seat. As soon as she does, the room falls silent. Everyone is extremely afraid of her, the physically weakest one among all of us.

One day, I hope to wield that kind of power.

"I think that's quite enough, don't you?" she says. She gives Finley a smile that is as cool as ice. "As it happens, I have a solution."

Finley looks astonished. "A solution?"

The smirk is in her voice but not on her face. She just appears critical, as usual. "Yes. A solution. You may not be familiar with them as you are only prime minister, but in the royal family we require them from time to time." One of the cabinet members gasps quietly. Ida cocks her head and her lips curl up. "It appears that the girl has already moved here. All the royal family has to do now is find a way to silence her."

My eyebrows rise and I rock backward in my chair. "She moved here?" My brows hunch. "Why?"

My grandmother eyes me for a long moment before walking purposefully over to the table, looking down at the tabloids splashed out there. "It appears that Miss Margot Keane is a journalist. I used a contact at *Politiken* to lure her here." She frowns. "Not that I gather she will miss much about New York. From my understanding she doesn't own anything of value."

She shrugs, the movement barely raising her shoulders. What she isn't saying out loud is the second part of her sentence. *In comparison to us; we have all the castles and all the yachts that anyone could want.*

Ida raises a brow, looking down at me. She's very small and very fierce; she eats lesser men than me for breakfast. That's her unspoken communication sent to me, anyway.

I shift in my seat, struggling to keep my face assembled in a remotely pleasant expression. "And you think that Miss Keane will just... what, sign a nondisclosure agreement? I'm assuming that you believe that she will agree to lie for the royal family."

She scans the room, pretending at being thoughtful. "Prime Minister Finley, cabinet members... would you please leave us? I think my grandson and I should speak in private."

Finley bows, turning to usher the rest of the small group out of the room. Picking up my coffee cup, I take a sip and look at my grandmother. I would guess that she came up with whatever plan she's about to unveil days ago.

She comes up to me, pulling out a chair and sitting down. Ida looks at me, her blue eyes like two frozen pools of ice.

"Now then." She cants her head. "Perhaps we offer Miss Keane something... like an exclusive story with you, close up and personal. We could have her sign documents saying that you were working together in New York... and she won't be able to contradict us, because she will have signed a nondisclosure agreement. We will control the story, not the other way around."

Ida's lips quirk; she looks pleased with herself, from what I can tell. I narrow my eyes at her.

"*Momse*," I say, careful to use her pet name. "I don't think this is a good idea. Will Miss Keane just write an article based on nothing, then?"

My grandmother's lips flatten. "No. She will follow you around for a few weeks or a month to complete the charade."

I shake my head. "People don't like to be led around by the halter, *Momse*. I hate the press as much as anyone. You know that. I don't want or need anyone in my private business. But—"

She pushes herself to her feet with an anger that is born of ruling a kingdom with an iron fist for ages. "Enough! I expect more from you, Stellan. I pulled you out of the fire once already when you were wrapped up in drugs. I stepped in and made sure that other girl and her family stayed quiet." Her expression turns from disappointed to terrifying. My toes curl up in my shoes. Even though she's old and almost a third of my size, she's still domineering. She has been this way since I was born.

I lower my gaze. "I know, *Momse*."

She slams her hand down on the table, startling me. "I was willing to write that off as a youthful failure, *ja*? But this? This could be the end of the monarchy."

I stare at her for a second. Yes, she absolutely did have to save my fucking neck once. And she did so without question. But that was ages ago.

I feel defensive. Rising to my full height, I fold my arms across my chest. "That was a lifetime ago, *Momse*. And this little mistake with Miss Keane? It was just that. Why can't we just let it be?"

When Ida gets angry, she glares at me and her face puckers like a wrinkled apple. Her eyes flash, their blue icy enough to cut fucking steel.

"One day soon, I will be gone. Let's both face it; your father does not have the instincts that my husband had. So I am trying to instill those instincts in you." She pauses. "I think I've done a passable job. But I will not have this family brought down by some little girl. You understand? I won't allow it."

I soften a bit, reaching out to touch Ida's elbow. "I know, *Momse*. I don't want the monarchy abolished either. Okay?"

That's a lie. Or at least a partial truth… when I was a kid, I used to lie in bed at night and dream about the monarchy's downfall. I wanted to do normal things like go to school or have play dates with friends.

That was a long time ago, though. I squeeze my grandmother's arm in an attempt to make her feel better. She pats my hand a few times and then pulls away.

If anything ever defined our relationship perfectly, it's that moment right there.

"Miss Keane will follow you around for a month." She goes over to the chair that she previously occupied and presses a button to summon the staff. "And you'll be on your best behavior now that you know who she is. *Ja?*"

I incline my head. "*Ja.* Sure, *Momse.*"

She narrows her eyes at me. "There are half a dozen suitable girls just waiting for you to look their way, Stellan. I've given you my list of acceptable candidates. The next time you find yourself in need of company, call whichever one you want. It's long past time that you got married."

I shoot her a scowl just as a butler sweeps into the room. He bows. "Your purse and coat, your royal highness. The car is waiting for you downstairs."

She walks stiffly over to the door, then pauses just before she hits the threshold. "I'm off to Sønderborg to try to dig your brother Finn out of whatever mess he's in. Do try to stay out of trouble while I'm gone, won't you?"

I hesitate. She doesn't wait for an answer. She just glides out of the room, patting her perfectly coiffed gray hair.

I am left alone to stare out the window and curse the luck of being born royal.

CHAPTER 10

MARGOT

The buildings in Copenhagen are a kaleidoscope of different colors: the façades are white and brown and peach and brick red, the roofs green and orange and blue and black. Gammelholm, the prestigious downtown area where the offices of *Politiken* are located, is bustling at nine in the morning.

Businesspeople going to work, tourists meandering toward the nearby art museum, a stream of teens who rush into what can only be a school next door.

Sucking in a deep breath, I look through the viewfinder of my camera at the building that houses *Politiken*'s offices. I snap a couple of photos; I've been taking photos all morning, documenting my first morning in Denmark.

I love taking photos. I love the symmetry that can be found in a perfect picture of an everyday object. I love the pungent smell of the chemicals used to develop film. I'm definitely a nerd about photography.

As I stare up at the ancient cream-colored stone of the building, Pippa gently elbows me in the ribs.

"We're already late," she says, grabbing me by the arm. "Come on."

Everything inside appears to be marble. Eschewing the ancient elevators as she tows me up the stairs, Pippa jogs down a marble hallway until we reach the doors.

Politiken, the glass of one of the doors reads. *Nyheden kommer først*.

Pippa swings the door open and pulls me inside a big room with high ceilings and about thirty people working in cubicles. A standard newsroom, it wouldn't be out of place at any paper anywhere in the world. No one even looks up at us when we rush in; the reporters are too busy typing manically or talking quietly on the phone. Against the back wall are the glass-walled offices of people in positions of power here at the newspaper as well as a well-appointed conference room.

A tall blonde woman in her fifties stands across the office, watching us with an annoyed expression. Pippa curses under her breath and tugs at her pale pink dress.

"That's Anna," she says, picking up her pace as she makes a beeline toward the woman. I do a quick scan of Anna's person and take stock of her wrinkled light gray pants suit and the stain on her white dress shirt.

A woman after my own heart. I'm wearing one of three pairs of black dress pants I own and a black Violent Femmes t-shirt paired with an oversize yellow cardigan.

Seeing Anna's disregard for dressing up bolsters my confidence.

Two seconds later, I stand in front of her and rethink my opinions.

"You two are quite late," Anna says, looking down her nose at us both. She looks at me, at the Nikon camera on its strap around my neck, and she rolls her eyes.

Pippa jumps in.

"Yes. Sorry. We had some trouble trying to leave the house." Pippa bites her lower lip, sliding her gaze to me. "But I brought Margot to you like you asked!"

Anna's gaze tightens on my face. "Yes. So you did." She spins, heading toward the back of the room. "Come to my office, both of you."

We head back to Anna's spacious office, sitting down in the chairs in front of her sleek chrome desk. She frowns as she types something into the computer at her side, then slides a drawer out.

"Margot!" she barks. I sit up, wide eyed.

"Ma'am?" I say.

She gives me a hard look before she hands over an employee badge. "This will get you in and out of the building. You'll need to fill out some tax paperwork at some point... Max will get you settled with that." She pushes back in her office chair, looking at Pippa and me. "We should talk about the story you will be covering."

I tilt my head. "Well... I came prepared with several ideas to pitch to you — "

"Enough," Anna says, cutting me off. "Your assignment has already been chosen for you."

I send Pippa a questioning glance. She shrugs and makes a quick *I don't know anything* face. Anna starts drumming her fingers on her desktop.

"You weren't aware of this already?" she asks.

It's hard to tell what she's thinking from her expression. Should I already know something?

Shaking my head, I feel my cheeks warm. "No."

Anna grunts, but I still don't have the slightest idea what she means by it. "I got the call late last night. You have been selected to work on a cover piece about Prince Stellan and his life."

My jaw drops.

No.

No way.

It's not possible.

One night together already made me flee New York. Any further contact between Stellan and me is just... a terrible, horrible, impossible idea.

Pippa, for her part, looks stunned.

"Oh, I can't do that," I blurt out, crossing my arms. "Give it to Pippa!"

Anna glares at me. "If I had my way, the most senior correspondent that usually gets her name on the most bylines would do the story. But obviously I had nothing to do with the choice, due to the fact that we had yet to meet."

My brow hunches. "Who decided that I would do the story, then?"

"Someone from the royal family, I gather." Anna scrunches up her face. "The question is, why?"

She puts her elbows on her desk, rubbing her lips. My cheeks immediately redden.

"I'm assuming that you are aware of the American tabloids and their... err... interest in me?" I tuck a strand of pink hair back behind my ear, chewing my bottom lip.

Anna glances at Pippa, then makes a show of pulling several brightly colored tabloid newspapers out of a drawer of her desk. Every single one features me on the cover, usually with an inset photo of Stellan.

She tosses them on her desk and then kicks back in her chair. "I'm familiar, yes."

I clear my throat, unwilling to be shamed. Not for this, at least.

"I think that this is a bad idea," I say. "I'm not sure why the order came from the royal family... but I have a bad feeling about it. Why sign up for something when I know out of the gate that I am going to be manipulated in some way?"

Anna glances at her watch and sighs. "This has honestly taken up more time than I care to devote to it. Either take the assignment or don't..." She smiles coolly. "But if you don't, you can kiss writing goodbye for a year. You can run research and get coffee for the office but bylines are saved for those who write whatever they are assigned."

My mouth falls open. "But... I mean..." I shoot to my feet, alarmed. "I... I don't mean to be picky..."

She stands up, folding her arms across her chest. "Yes or no?"

I quail. "Uhh..."

"Get out," she says, making a sour face. "I have to call the press office at the palace and tell them that you said no."

A gray-haired man appears in the doorway of Anna's office. He's older, maybe in his late sixties, and impeccably dressed. From the way that Anna and Pippa straighten when they see him, I gather that he's fairly important.

"Is this Margot?" he asks, smiling widely.

He sticks out his hand to me. I take it, not particularly understanding.

"Hi. Margot Keane."

"Margot, I am Emil Dall. I'm the managing editor here at *Politiken*. I was told you are going to be handling the profile of our royal prince!"

My face heats. "Well, I mean... Anna did bring it up, but I just told her that I don't want— "

He cuts me off, not even pretending to listen to my jabbering.

"Great! Anna will give you all the guidance you need. Not that we will be seeing much of you... From what I gather, you will be assigned to shadow Prince Stellan for a few weeks."

"But— "

"And did Anna tell you about what we are offering as incentive to finish this piece?"

My eyebrows go up. So do Anna's... which I think means she's as in the dark as I am.

"No..." I say slowly.

Emil smiles even more widely, showcasing his teeth. "We are looking for someone to run the arts and entertainment desk. If you take the job, you would be editing all the pieces and pitching your own ideas. It would be a huge thing for your career. You would be at the bottom of the editors food chain but above all the reporters. *Ja?*"

My eyes widen. Anna makes a choking sound, turning away and reaching for a glass of water on her desk. I glance at Pippa, who gives me a look that says *duh! take it!*

I clear my throat. "Thanks. I guess... I mean, how can I say no?"

"That's the spirit!" cheers Emil. "You will do great, I'm sure."

He turns to Anna, saying something pointed to her in Danish. Anna's face colors a little but she just nods and thanks him.

"It was nice to meet you, Margot." He smiles at everyone, puts his hands together, and bows. Then he marches out of Anna's office.

Pippa reaches out to me, her eyes wide. "He doesn't even know my name. And I've worked here for over a year!"

Anna glowers at us. "I'm glad that you changed your mind, Margot. You do realize that you will need to be *extremely* respectful when you are dealing with the royal family, *ja?*"

I wrinkle my nose. My heart still gallops against my ribs. "I know how to act. I wasn't raised by wolves or anything."

Anna's eyebrows lift a fraction. "I don't understand what you mean. What is *raised by wolves?*"

Yikes. Everyone I've encountered so far has spoken flawless English; clearly, I need to brush up on my Danish, not the other way around.

"I'm sorry, I— "

Anna flicks her hand at me impatiently. "Go set up your employee email and further instructions about this assignment will be sent soon. Now if you would kindly get out of my office, I've got an actual job to do."

She makes a shooing motion with her hands as she sits down again, pointedly looking at her computer instead of us. I beat Pippa in the rush to get out of her office and out of Anna's earshot.

Pippa pulls me over to her cubicle, still agog. "I can't believe this is happening. Emil is a *really* big deal in journalism here. There's an award with his name on it given out yearly to the best journalist."

I pull a chair over from an empty desk and sag into it. Pippa sits in her chair, biting her lip. I lean back, looking up at the ceiling as I let out a sigh.

"What in the world am I doing?" I wonder out loud. "Other than upsetting the natural order of things by getting orders from the royal palace or what the fuck ever."

Pippa sucks in a breath. "Oh god. Do you think…"

I glance at her. "What?"

"Do you think that Stellan asked for you?"

For a foolish second, my heart clatters around in my chest. Did he? Could it have been him?

Then I frown and shake that thought from my head. "I don't know. My guess would be no. But then again, I clearly have no idea who is pulling the strings around here."

"Hmm." She puffs out her cheeks. "I can try to find out whenever I talk to Lars next."

Her familiarity with the royal family makes me give her a crooked smile. "Sure, Pips."

She bites at her fingernail, swiveling toward her computer. "All right. In the meantime, let's get your email set up…"

I bob my head, sighing.

CHAPTER 11

STELLAN

"But what if instead of going to this factory and doing a tour, we all just commit suicide instead?" my little sister says, sighing as she looks out the window of the car we're being shuttled in. Annika is only eighteen and the baby of my family. She's also the weirdo.

I say that with love, as the twenty six year old black sheep of the family.

I cock a brow. "That doesn't sound particularly productive."

She brightens. "Maybe, as the royal family, we should declare that the nuclear threat to our nation is viable. And that we should, as a nation, move underground. We can all become mole people. Ooh! This factory can be the base from where we start the revolution!"

She wiggles her delicate blonde eyebrows and grins. She looks classically Danish: light blonde hair, bright blue eyes, with a smattering of freckles across the bridge of her nose. She's always full of her unique sense of humor, although it is a bit morbid.

"Mole people, huh?" I repress a sigh and look away, out the window as the city falls away behind us.

My best friend Erik looks back at both of us from the passenger seat of the SUV.

"Annika, we will be at this factory for a grand total of four hours, tops. I don't think we will have the time to overthrow the government." He runs a hand through his dirty blond, close cropped hair, shifting in the passenger seat. All six and a half feet of him is barely confined in the front seat and he doesn't look comfortable.

Coming in just an inch shorter than him, I can sympathize. Annika is tall for a girl, but when she walks between Erik and me, she looks downright dainty.

She throws Erik a grin. "You don't think that's enough time? Maybe you're just not as efficient as I am."

Erik rolls his eyes. "I'm much more efficient than any of you Løves. That's what being raised as a non-royal amongst royals does to a person."

I frown a little. "Erik, when we were growing up, you went to the same palace tutors as I did. You played the same sports. You even joined the same military regiment as me. Don't act like you're exactly a normal person."

He smiles coolly at me. "And yet… one of us will be a king and the other will not."

My neck heats. He has always had a funny knack for putting his finger right on the pulse of the issue.

Annika wrinkles her nose, looking at me. "All I know is that you both owe me big time. *Momse* wanted to send Lars or Finn along with you on this little trip, even after the disastrously bad way they handled things at the easter egg hunt. I convinced her that I am the superior choice." She grins, showing her teeth. "You're welcome."

I ignore that. Of my four siblings though, she is unquestionably my favorite. It doesn't hurt that Annika knows exactly when to put on the saccharide smile and when to keep her mouth shut.

Unlike Finn, Lars, and Anders...

"How are my little brothers doing these days?" I ask, looking at her out of the corner of my eye. "Is Anders back from Malaysia or Madagascar or wherever he went?"

"Morocco," Erik chimes in. "He's been in Casablanca."

"He's just come back." Annika looks bored. "Lars and Finn have been relatively quiet too. I think Finn is doing some survival fitness thing in the Swiss Alps... and you should know better than I where Lars is. Didn't he go to New York with you two?"

Erik chuckles, which earns him a glare from me.

"We had to leave him there in our rush to get back," I say evenly. "Duty called back here at home."

Annika smirks and rolls her eyes.

"Speaking of being the heir to the throne… I hear that we are going to meet Margot today." She purses her lips. "You remember Margot, don't you? Pink hair? An ass that won't quit? Hooked up with you and somehow *everybody* in the world found out about it?"

My eyes narrow to slits. "Yes, I remember."

Erik adjusts his mass in the front seat, sliding a look over at the driver. The driver doesn't even look at him, just keeps his eyes on the road. Erik shrugs.

"I would rather we deal with the situation like this than have some royal fixer have to go clean it up afterward."

He makes eye contact with me when he says the last bit. My neck heats again.

He's referencing the same thing that my grandmother did. The time when I was nineteen and acting out, drinking a lot and doing a lot of cocaine. I called Ida while I was strung out on drugs and desperate because I'd ended up in a motel with a girl who lost consciousness.

The royal fixers swept in and cleaned everything up. I was sent to dry out in Spain; Mathilde, a hard-core party girl and sometimes friend, ended up in a coma that lapsed into a vegetative state.

I look at the driver, my mouth twisting. There are a ton of things I feel on the topic of Mathilde, but I'm not willing to risk saying any of them out loud in front of the driver. Besides, Annika doesn't even know.

No one does, outside of my grandmother, Erik, and the royal fixers. I clear my throat and rub my temples.

"Are we almost there yet?" I grit out.

Erik sighs, looking at his phone. "*Ja*, we're only a minute away."

When we arrive at the large factory, I look up at the two-story slab of cement. I'm strangely nervous, though I would guess that has more to do with Margot being here than the public nature of my visit. "What does this place make again?"

Erik consults his phone. "Porcelain plates."

"Mole people will probably make porcelain plates their first form of currency," Annika says, straightening her aquamarine dress.

I shake my head as I stride up to the factory. I mirror her, shaking the wrinkles out from my light gray suit. Adjusting my powder blue tie, I shake hands with the owner of the plant and several other people that are deemed important.

"*God morgen.*" I smile and shake hands with another man whose name I will not remember. "*Det er godt at være her. Ja tak, hvis det ikke er til besvær.*"

Good morning. It is good to be here. Thank you so much for taking the time to show me around.

Smile, shake hands, repeat until I'm sick with it. Just part of being the crown prince, I guess.

All the while, I'm scanning the small crowd that has gathered by the front doors to meet me. Annika is all smiles and zero sarcastic comments as she shakes hands to my left. Erik is his usual brooding self as he hovers by my right side, shaking hands only when they are thrust at him.

As I am ushered inside, I spot Margot standing in the entryway there, just out of the way. Her hair is still pink and long, pulled up in a messy bun. She's still petite, her face still sweetly heart-shaped.

But this time instead of her short plaid skirt and a Hole t-shirt ripped in a dozen places, she's wearing a pair of sensible black dress pants and a black blazer. She still rocks her pink Converse and what looks like a band t-shirt under the blazer.

And looking at her still makes my heart lurch and stutter.

God, if she even hints at feeling the same way about me, I will be so completely, utterly fucked. All I have known up until now is duty.

But one look at Margot, at her beauty and her unbridled enthusiasm for life, and that all falls away. I can't ever let her know that she makes my heart race; if she has the slightest idea what is going on in my head right now, she could close her fist and crumple me like a sheet of paper.

It's time to put on my mask.

Tamping down on my facial expression, I turn my head away and pay closer attention to what the factory owner is saying to me now. Something about the plates his factory makes… something dull, no doubt.

But out of the corner of my eye, I watch Margot turn around and lay eyes on me properly. Time slows down. Her eyes widen, her breath catches.

There is something magical about the effect we have on each other, even from thirty paces away. Something *electric*. For just the briefest moment, we are the only two people in the whole world.

This, *this* is the reason that she had me teetering on the edge of falling for her.

"Stellan," Erik says, elbowing me. "The plant manager just asked if we would like a tour. I think we would, don't you?"

I pull my gaze away from Margot and zero in on the people I'm supposed to be talking to. "*Ja, ja. Hvis du venligst.*"

The plant manager beams like this is the most exciting thing that has ever happened in her whole career. She ushers us all down the hall and through a series of doors.

For the next half an hour I put on a thoughtful face, sometimes switching it up for an astonished one. Everyone's eyes are on me, making sure that I'm pleased with the porcelain plates.

I honestly couldn't give half a fuck, but I nod and smile. Annika nods and smiles too, and interjects questions where they are appropriate. We are more than just ourselves to these people, after all…

We are two members of the royal family and the rulers of Denmark. I don't even have to remind myself to keep up a cool and aloof veneer around normal people.

I think they are as alien to me as I am to them, honestly.

When we are done with the shaking hands and smiling portion of the morning, Erik wordlessly offers me a squirt of hand sanitizer. And I take it; this gesture is repeated so often on days like today that it's almost second nature for me.

Margot is at a table by herself, admiring a stack of plates. I clear my throat, adjust my tie, and walk over. When she looks up, she bites her lip. Her dark blue eyes are full of unanswered questions.

"*Haj*," I greet her.

Her eyes tighten on my face. Then she actually curtsies, a tiny smirk on her perfectly pouty lips. "Your highness."

For some reason, that throws me off balance. I frown. "I take it you survived the media vultures that circled you, looking for any little scrap of information?"

She rolls her eyes. "Yeah. I mean, they drove me out of New York City, if that's what you mean by *survived*." She tilts her head, her eerily blue eyes pinning me. "It would've been better if the whole situation hadn't ever happened though."

I push my tongue out into my cheek. Part of me wants to apologize for everything that happened. But the wiser part of me insists on being thorny. She won't get close if I am just a complete jerk to her.

"*Ja*, it would've been better. I like to keep my private life exactly that… private."

She turns to me, folding her arms across her chest. "You threw me to the wolves, Stellan. You packed up and fled New York and then I was just there, unable to leave my house." Her expression turns sour. "I guess that will teach me to go home with people who I don't know anything about."

She's right. Absolutely, completely right. But I've decided to go this direction, to throw up my walls. There is no stopping now.

I heave a silent sigh, my eyes wandering to the rest of the people at the factory. "I'm sorry. I did try to warn you…"

A laugh bubbles up from her chest. "Yeah, once the media already knew about me. You could've told me who you were when I met you."

A cold smile curls the corners of my mouth. "And you could've asked. But you didn't. And I had no choice but to turn tail and run. The paparazzi in your city are merciless. At least now that you are here, you are getting something in return for spending the night with me, *ja?*"

Her eyes widen and her mouth opens. "Are you serious? It's not like I did this for any kind of fame! And to accuse me of… of riding your coattails… it's ridiculous!" Her voice drops as she leans closer. "I made the best of a very *bad* situation. That's it."

My voice lowers. "Well, you signed a nondisclosure agreement. Which basically means that the royal family has complete control of anything you write and anything you say about me." I smirk. "So I would suggest that you keep it professional, okay?"

"Ugh!" she says, looking offended. "As if I would write about our... *fling*. You are so... so.... arrogant! And spoiled! And full of yourself to boot."

Drawing myself up to my full height, I scowl at her words. I'm not a monster, though of course she can't know that. But still... the fact that I have some sort of feelings for her only makes her barbs all the sharper.

I cock a brow, throwing it right back at her. "*Ja?* I bet you would do anything to get your name in the papers again."

Margot draws herself up to her full height, which isn't very tall at all. "You wish. I bet you have entire *fantasies* about being one of my conquests again."

She honestly has no idea how many fantasies I have that involve her.

Erik is approaching, so I just shake my head. "Keep dreaming big, Margot. That's the only way you'll ever see me naked again."

Margot's murderous expression is priceless. Turning away, I move toward Erik and raise my hands. "I think I'm ready to go. Can you have the car brought around?"

"Sure," Erik responds, his gaze sliding between me and Margot. "Come on."

Throwing a smirk over my shoulder at Margot, I stride off of the factory floor.

CHAPTER 12

MARGOT

The next morning I'm in the newsroom, leafing through the huge pile of documents the royal press secretary sent me. I signed my name to a simple two page nondisclosure agreement already, but I arrived this morning and found a whole stack of other documents and agreements on my desk.

Pippa peeks her head into my cubicle around lunch, scrunching her face up. "Hey Mags."

I shoot her a look. Mags is my nickname that only she is allowed to use; only Pippa is charming enough to outweigh the awfulness of that name. In return, I started calling her Pips, which she doesn't seem to mind a bit.

"Hey," I say.

"Almost done? I'm thinking of grabbing a kebab from the cart down the street."

I make a face at the pile of documents. Careful to dog ear at the page that I'm on, I set the papers down on top of my keyboard. "I'm not actually sure where I'm at. I think I should stay here and keep plowing through these documents, just to make sure I'm not signing my name to anything insane. Would you mind bringing me a kebab back?"

She wrinkles her nose. "Yeah, sure. But just so you know, there's a coffee cart right beside where I plan to go. And I know how you feel about coffee… but I can't carry coffee *and* a kebab back."

I brighten. "Ooh. You know I'm always in search of a decent cup of coffee."

Pippa bobs her head toward the door of the office. "I know. Come on."

"Okay, one sec." I stand up, putting the heavy sheaf of papers in a drawer of my desk and logging out on my staff computer. Then I grab my purse and hurry to catch up with Pippa.

As I'm about to leave, I hear Anna yell from her office. "Margot! Come in here, please."

I freeze in my tracks, then back up and walk to her office. "Did you want something?"

Her mouth thins. "Only for you to do your job. Will that be okay, Miss Keane?"

My eyes widen. "Yes. Of course."

She picks up a stack of papers from her desk, jogging them as she makes a sour face. "All right then. The palace press office just sent this over."

She hands me a piece of expensive card stock that is elegantly engraved with dark blue ink.

Your presence is requested tonight for a celebration honoring the 68th birthday of Her Royal Highness, The Queen Mother Josefine Ida Løve. The gathering will be held at Marselisborg Palace and require fancy dress.

No presents shall be accepted.

Kongevejen 100, 8000 Aarhus, Denmark

I look up at Anna, my eyes so wide that I'm worried about my future ability to blink. "A party?"

Anna makes a sound of disgust. "Yes. You have been given a stipend for renting dresses during your work with the palace. I really suggest you use it." Her eyes trail down my figure, taking in my clothes. "And when you get your first paycheck, I would seriously consider getting a whole new wardrobe."

My cheeks flush with embarrassment. I thought I had left the old sense of shame behind when I entered the job market… but here I am, trembling a little, trying to think of what to say.

Anna narrows her eyes at me. "You know, maybe I should do a piece about you. About how you came to be here, serving a function that no one thinks you can handle."

A look at her, puzzled. "Is that… some kind of weird threat?"

She folds her arms and surveys me. "Maybe I'm just intrigued by the flurry of excitement that followed you here from New York."

My eyebrows rise. "I'm sorry?"

"How you met Prince Stellan. I mean, you shouldn't be rubbing elbows with people of his class, *ja?* From my research, it appears that you are the kind of girl who needed several scholarships just to go to college. So how did you two meet?"

I grit my teeth. My hands ball into fists. "Are we done here? I have a thing to get ready for. You know, a royal gathering at a *palace*."

Her eyes narrow, confirming my suspicions. She's jealous. I have something that she wants, apparently.

If she only knew how tenuous my relationship with Stellan actually was…

Anna sweeps her hand out in a dismissive gesture. "Get out. And try not to horribly embarrass the paper while you're there, okay?"

"Yeah, I'll be sure to curtsy a ton when I'm off rubbing elbows with the whole royal family." I leave her office with a snort.

Bullies come in all shapes and sizes. They hang out on the playground, in cool kid cliques, in court rooms... basically anywhere that anyone can be vulnerable.

But one thing all bullies have in common? They might be able to dish it out but they can rarely take even the slightest criticism.

I make a beeline for the front door. Pippa appears at my side, wide eyed and ready for gossip. "What was that?"

Glancing back at Anna, who is still glaring at me from behind her glass-doored office, I shrug. "Not here, okay? Are you ready to go? I need to go shopping on my lunch hour."

"Yeah, sure. Just let me grab my coat."

It's less than a minute before we are bursting out of the front door of the building. I'm still processing everything, and I'm getting more annoyed by the second.

"Who does Anna think she is?" I say, grimacing.

"What happened?" Pippa asks, pushing a strand of her wild red hair out of her face. "And where are we going?"

Screwing my mouth to the side, I pull out my phone. "I need to find a place that rents fancy dresses."

"Oh! I know a place. And it's not far away. Come on. You can tell me what happened while we walk there."

I hand her the invitation while we walk and talk, doing a brief round of what happened upstairs. Pippa's eyes widen.

"Oh my god," she says, clutching her stomach. "What a bitch! She's never acted like that before."

I scrunch up my face. "She was jealous." I look at Pippa. "That's what it was, isn't it?"

She nods slowly. "That's what it sounds like, yes. I had no idea that Anna felt so strongly about getting close to the royal family."

I exhale, sliding her a glance as we rush across a crowded street. "It won't be like that with us though, will it? I mean, you know the royal family way better than I do. You've been hanging out with them for years."

She smiles at me. "No, it definitely won't. Even if you end up marrying Stellan— "

My jaw drops. "No way! That would never happen in like a million years!"

She shrugs off my protests. "We will see."

"No. No way. There are a million things about myself that I want to keep private… especially about my past run-ins with the law. The last thing that I should do is spend a hot second swooning over Stellan. Besides, he's an ass."

Pippa rolls her eyes and points across the street. "Look, there's the shop."

She points to a little display window with five elaborately dressed mannequins, each garment a totally different color, each one as fancy as the next. Pippa taps the glass over a peach taffeta ballgown with sweetheart neckline. It's embroidered with what must be a thousand pink and white and peach flowers. "That is gorgeous."

"Oh man. I was thinking of something more like… above the knee, black, and slinky." I make a face. "Come on, let's go inside."

Pippa opens the door and ushers me inside. I'm immediately overwhelmed by racks and racks of dresses in every color imaginable. Silk and taffeta and crinolines are all stuffed together in the little shop, piled so high that I can't even see to the back.

"Oh, I—" I start.

A short, balding man with the most stylish spectacles and a gray silk suit pokes his head through the stacks. *"Kan jeg hjælpe dig?"*

Pippa grabs me by the elbow, bowing her head. "English, if you please? We are here to get her a dress to wear tonight."

"Ah!" he says, waving us further in. "Come. We will find good dress." He looks at me, measuring with his gaze. "Where you go?"

"A royal function. I assume I need cocktail attire." I mimic a dress that falls above the knee. "Something black."

"Ah yes!" he cries. "Black cocktail. Black cocktail. Good, *ja*. Come, please."

He vanishes back behind a rack of dresses. When I hesitate, Pippa pushes me forward. "I've done this like a hundred times. Come on."

I shoot her a look and then wedge myself around a rack of dresses. I'm surprised to see a little changing room set up and a wooden counter holds an old fashioned cash register. A collage of brightly colored dresses cut from magazines adorns the wall behind the register.

"Hold please," the shopkeeper says, holding up a finger. While we stand there, still taking everything in the shop in, he disappears again. When he comes back, he has an armful of short black dresses.

"Black cocktail!" he cries, shooing me into the changing room. "Here, you look. You…" He thinks. "You pick."

He holds up each dress for my inspection. I wrinkle my nose. "How about… this one… this one…" I let him cycle through a couple more. "Ooh, and that one. That should be good."

"Now try." He points to the dressing room, which constructed of no more than a few pieces of dark velvet draped over a wire frame. "Then you come out, look in mirror."

He waves to a full length three way mirror that is stashed in the corner.

I step inside the little booth and strip down to try on the first dress. It's loose and unflattering, so I quickly move to the next. This one is a slinky little velvet number in a dark blue that reminds me of the cobalt sea, far from the safety of the shore.

Pulling back the curtain, I step out. Pippa squeals. "Omigosh! That dress on you is really everything."

I walk over to the mirror and my brows rise. The blue of the velvet matches my eyes perfectly. And the way the dress lays on my body is phenomenal. The neckline is a little daring, showing a hint of cleavage. But it doesn't show too much skin overall.

I do a twirl, thinking to myself that this dress fits like it was made for my body. Looking at the shopkeeper, I can't help but grin. "How much?"

"Three hundred *krone*."

Arching a brow at Pippa, I check with her. "Is that a good deal?"

She nods. "Indeed it is. It's about thirty five or forty dollars, I think. And I think I have a pair of heels to match back at the flat."

"Ah!" I turn to the shopkeeper. "You have yourself a sale."

I turn back to glance at my reflection once more. I imagine Stellan's smug face turning into wide-eyed disbelief when he sees me in this dress. Yeah, this is definitely a great choice for tonight, especially after yesterday went so poorly. Blushing a little, I retreat to the changing room.

I'm almost a little loathe to take the dress off, even though obviously I have to. When we are about to leave, the shopkeeper hands me a beautiful hair clip studded with gemstones.

"For you hair," he says with a wink. His English is a little broken, but I'm not in any position to criticize. He leans close to whisper to me. "You bring back, *ja?*"

I bow my head in gratitude. "*Ja*, of course. Thank you."

As I step outside of the shop, Pippa links arms with me. She looks more excited than I am about tonight. I wrinkle my nose.

Before I can say anything, she smiles. "We only have a few hours until it's time for you to leave. Luckily, I keep a full makeup bag at the office. Now your hair is a different matter altogether…"

She pulls me along, chattering about preparations. And I follow her, trying not to get too anxious about seeing Stellan again.

CHAPTER 13

STELLAN

I'm lost in a sea of tuxes and ballgowns. If one more old parliamentary representative comes up and orates to me about how I should fund his personal pet project the next time the parliament meets… I swear I will just open my mouth, look up, and scream *GET ME OUT OF HERE* as loud as I can.

All right, maybe not. But it's good to know I have that as a backup plan.

Erik is by my side, plucking a stray hair from the shoulder of his tux. His gaze roves around the ballroom, always on the lookout. For what exactly, I don't know.

"Are you looking for danger, political advantages, or hot girls?" I whisper out of the side of my mouth.

His eyes find me, crinkling with humor. "Who's to say I'm not looking for all three?"

"I hope for your sake that you're not expecting all three in one package…" I squint off into the corner of the ballroom. "Though I would very much like to meet her if you do manage to find someone that meets all your requirements."

He chuckles. "It's a deal."

I turn around slowly, looking for a waiter. What I spot is Prime Minister Finley bearing down on me from some distance away.

"Let's move," I say, whirling in the opposite direction.

That's when I almost trample Margot. There she is, with her heart shaped face, her pastel pink hair, and her little dark blue dress. My eyes widen a bit as I take in the flash of cleavage and the unabashed showing of her admittedly amazing legs.

With her hair pinned up, she looks like she could be a burlesque performer. God, she looks totally unlike anyone else here. And I do mean that in the best way possible.

"Margot," I say, trying not to let everyone else realize that I'm drooling over her.

She just looks at me, her steps faltering. I reach out and stabilize her, realizing that something is out of place. It's another second before it clicks.

She's underdressed for this party. Not just underdressed, but… every other lady here is puffed up in a full ballgown. Margot seems scantily clad by comparison.

And I am watching her realize it in real time. Her cheeks turn bright pink. She looks around, sucking in a breath.

"Oh. I think…" She bites her lip, swinging her dark blue gaze over to me. "I think I misjudged the dress code."

I snort. "You think?"

She flushes even further, her mouth screwing up. "How was I supposed to know? It just said fancy dress." She looks down at what she's wearing, a little shiver running down her spine. "Maybe I should go."

As she turns away, my hand snakes out and grabs her arm. I'm a little surprised at myself; it's definitely better for me if she fails and recedes into the wings of this little show we're putting on. But she looks back at me with something like suspicion in her lovely eyes, a frown making her pouty mouth turn down at the corners.

I refuse to let her just walk away from me. Even if it is cruel, considering the circumstances.

"Stay," I order her.

A mixture of uncertainty and derision is visible in Margot's eyes. It's strange; her elfin facial features show no hint of guise. Is she always so easy to read?

While she's still making up her mind, Prime Minister Finley appears, looking like a silvering, disgruntled parakeet. He takes one look at the body language between Margot and me… and a smile creeps over his face.

"Your highness, who is your companion?"

Margot stills, looking to me to explain her presence.

I swing my head around in both directions. "You already know Erik, Prime Minister Finley."

His eyes tighten on my face, which makes me happier than I can say. "I meant the young lady."

I smile indulgently. "This is Margot Keane. Margot, this is Denmark's prime minister."

She looks a bit taken aback. Pulling out of my grip, she offers Finley her hand. "A pleasure."

Finley shakes her hand for only a second. "Tell me, Margot. Was it your name that I read in the papers a few weeks ago? Something about being caught running away from Stellan's hotel, wasn't it?"

Erik clears his throat. "Prime minister, I have someone important for you to meet."

Finley looks over at him, then back at me. He frowns and smooths the bottom half of his tuxedo jacket. "Yes, all right. I'm looking forward to catching up with you later, Miss Keane."

He doesn't wait for her response. He merely waves at Erik. "Lead the way."

Margot releases the breath she's been holding loudly, looking at me. "That's the prime minister?"

"*Ja*," I answer with a sigh.

She screws up her face. "He clearly sucks."

One corner of my mouth kicks up. "*Ja*. He was raised by wolves, maybe."

She huffs a laugh. "Don't blame his lack of manners on bad parenting. I was raised by a mom who was an addict and the American foster care system. If I don't get an excuse, neither does he."

I look at her, a little surprised. "You were?"

"Yep." She looks around, as if she's already decided to leave and just needs to pick a direction. "I believe each of us gets a family of our own choosing. So maybe my mom sucked. But I've got Pippa, and she's definitely more loving and accepting than my mom could ever be."

I snag two glasses of champagne off of a passing tray. When I hand one to Margot, she gives me a glare that is instantly suspicious. I chuckle.

"It's just wine." I take a swig, nodding to the exit. "Come on."

I head for the big double doors of the ballroom, keeping my gaze slightly downcast. I've long since mastered the art of being able to leave a room without talking to anyone. When I get out of the ballroom and into the hallway, I pause for a second to let Margot catch up.

She gives me a hard look. "Do you always expect that when you snap your fingers, other people will jump?"

Raising a single eyebrow, I give her a hard stare. "Yes."

She glares at me. "Look. You clearly have a…" She waves her hand over my body. "Like a whole thing going on here. Cocky, handsome, bad boy, brooding… whatever. To each his own. But I think we can dispense with the bullshit. Don't you?"

I don't give her an inch. Instead I just roll my eyes and casually head for another set of doors on the other side of the hallway. I call back as I fling the doors open. "So you think I'm handsome?"

She makes a strangled sound, following me into a darkened parlor. There is no furniture except for one couch, which I promptly fall on. Margot looks around the room, then opts to sort of lean against the back on the sofa.

"I clearly meant that... you were going for... that sort of thing," she bites off.

I can't help but notice the outline of her ass in that velvet dress. Just looking at her right now makes me thirsty. I have to say something, something to let her know she doesn't get to me.

Even though she so clearly does. She starts pacing, from her spot behind the couch to a spot right in front of me.

God, I have never wanted her more than right now. Her color is high, her dress is slutty, and she's stalking around the room in a fit of pique.

I frown, scanning Margot from head to toe. "God, you really are underdressed. Are you even wearing panties?"

She turns bright red, standing up straight and avoiding my gaze. "Wouldn't you like to know," she snaps.

"Well... yes, actually." I smirk at her. "That's why I asked."

To my complete shock, she actually balls up her fist, moves right up to me, and smacks me on the shoulder. "You are such a jerk!"

My eyes widen.

No one other than my brothers has ever dared to breathe too hard in my direction, much less actually *hit* me. I'm surprised a second time when I burst out laughing. I throw my hands up, playing innocent. "It's strictly for scientific observation!"

Margot scrunches up her face and hits me again. Only this time I grab her small hand in mine before she can land a blow.

She glares at me, tugging at her hand. "You really are the worst. Do other people get to witness this side of your personality, or am I just the luckiest girl in the world?"

I smirk, refusing to let her go. "You're a brat. Did you know that? Every single inch of you is just a spoiled little brat."

She yanks at her hand, which makes me grip it harder. "When did I have the chance to become spoiled? Hmm? Was it when I was growing up in that group home? No, maybe it was when I was busting my ass and working two jobs to put myself through college."

The way she's looking at me makes my blood sing. My heart starts hammering a staccato beat in my chest. My cock stirs, making its needs known. I give her a dry rumble of a laugh.

"I don't know, but you are. You're also rather defiant."

She tosses her head haughtily. "You know next to nothing about me. How can you stand there and judge me?"

Margot's eyes are throwing sparks as they burn into mine. Her chest heaves.

"We are not equals. I was born to the throne… I was born to rule. What were you born to do?" I tug on her hand hard and her small hips jerk against mine. The contact sears me through.

She actually laughs at that. My eyes stray from hers down to her mouth. Her lips are bewitching. "You're crazy."

I bring my hand up to grip the back of her head, barely aware of my intentions. Before I know it, I lean forward and press my lips to her lips. She only has a split second to respond; she turns her head just a little so that my mouth ends up only catching the corner of hers.

Margot's eyes widen.

For a moment, we are frozen just like that. Me, knowing I have made a huge mistake. Her, probably wondering how to get out of my embrace.

That second seems to stretch forever… but it shatters when she raises her hands to my chest and shoves me. She's smaller than I am so in effect she pushes herself away, sputtering.

"What are you doing? Are you insane?!"

I can't help but agree with her, honestly. What was I thinking? Taking a deep breath, I try to ease some of the tension that has been building between us. I shrug my shoulders and play it cool.

"It seemed like the thing to do."

She makes a disgusted sound and backs away from me. "It wasn't."

A narrow my eyes. "I won't apologize."

Margot gives me a bitter look. "Of course not. Why would you apologize about anything at all, ever?" Straightening her dress, she turns and starts to leave the room.

I stop her with a word. "Margot."

She stills, although she doesn't turn back toward me. When she answers, her words are tart. "Yes, your highness?"

My lips twitch. "You look good in that dress."

She whips her head around and glares at me, then leaves the room with a disgusted sound on her lips. I lean my head back and close my eyes.

For just a moment, I enjoy my solitude. Then I hear Erik.

"Stellan?"

I open my eyes to find him poking his head in the room.

"*Haj*," I greet him.

"You need to meet with the French ambassador. And there are also a whole entourage of people here from Morocco to meet with you."

I sigh. "*Ja*. I'm coming."

And just like that, I'm swept up in the royal machine again.

CHAPTER 14

MARGOT

I turn a corner, hurrying along the bright streets of Copenhagen. I'm wearing a set of headphones which are plugged into an ancient iPod. Hole is playing, the angsty, screechy guitars and rollicking drums paired perfectly with Courtney Love's violent wails.

I know, it's not for everybody. But for me, it's soothing. Sometimes it's nice to hear something that really matches how I feel on the inside. I cast my gaze over the city street in front of me.

Everything seems clean here. There is no trash on the ground. There are no homeless people milling around. The buildings that rise up on each side of me are white or tan or brick. They contrast nicely with the slate gray of the street and the black and orange and green roofs.

It's early morning and fog clings to the tops of the buildings. It's hard to see more than a few blocks in front of

THE WICKED PRINCE

me, which is just as well. I try to keep my mind on the architecture as I cross the street. The second I turn a corner and the palace rises out of the mist like a graceful giant, my heart rate starts rising.

There are four buildings that make up the palace; four massive tan brick buildings all huddled in a circle, all saluting a rather large statue of a man on a horse. With their white-trimmed windows, dark roofs, and guards dressed in scarlet, the palaces definitely proudly exude *money*.

It's funny to think that the whole compound belongs to one family. Wrapping my brain around it is hard. Every single instinct I have tells me to run away screaming. The dirt poor little girl from Brooklyn who still lives inside me is terrified of all this… this *wealth*.

It's just so… *conspicuous*. I've worked so long and so hard to fight against the idea of oligarchy, that a country should be run by the rich and not by the common man. I've protested with Occupy Wall Street; when Citizens United was handed down by the supreme court I marched in the streets.

And yet… here I am, staring up at the palaces with a sourness in the pit of my stomach.

How is this place Stellan's home?

And how did I end up spending a night in his bed?

I swallow against the strange knot of anxiety that forms in my throat as I walk up to the gates. The palaces seem to frown down at me as I present my press card at the security checkpoint.

I feel like a fraud just walking through these gates, even though I'm not perpetrating any kind of deceit. A stoic guard waves me inside the gates and instructs me to walk straight ahead to the giant door of the first building on my left.

Tossing my hair back over my shoulder and smoothing my hands down my blazer, I adjust my tote bag on my shoulder.

You can do this, I tell myself.

It takes a couple of minutes and two separate skeptical looking palace servants to gain access to the palace.

I'm led down a large hallway by one of the servants. I can't help the fact that my eyes bug out a little as we walk; the echoing hallway is made entirely of dark wood, adorned with a demure dark blue carpet runner, and lined with paintings of royalty.

I feel like every painting I pass stares down at me, somberly disapproving. Telling me I don't belong here. My palms start sweating.

The servant stops by a door, motioning me inside. I'm not expecting to see Stellan; I've seen enough royal movies to know that I should be content to wait.

But there he is, extraordinarily tall in a white button up shirt and dark suit pants, standing in a room with crisp white walls. He faces away from me, contemplating a

THE WICKED PRINCE

photograph that is hung on the wall. The photograph is a black and white close up of a lion on the hunt in the savannah.

How appropriate for Stellan.

He turns a little when I approach his side. He stares down at me, brooding. The intensity in his ice blue eyes makes me repress a shiver.

Ah, yes… I forgot how compelling he is, here in the flesh.

He smirks a little. "You are a photographer, *ja?*"

My hand slides to my tote bag, where my camera rests. I raise my chin. "Yes."

He looks away, back to the photograph on the wall. It's a little like a spotlight has been taken off of me.

Why do I always feel like he is going to look right through me?

"What do you think?" he asks idly, nodding to the photo.

Frowning, I turn toward the photo in question. Tilting my head, I just stare at in for a second. "It has an interesting composition. The play of light around the lion lends the photo an intensity that I like. And the lion is very close up, and obviously fixated on something the audience can't see. It draws the audience to look just past the edge of the photograph."

"So you like it?"

Squinting, I shrug. "Yes. It's not the most interesting concept to me, but art is very subjective."

He nods, looking at the photo for another few seconds. Then he turns, pacing a few feet away to stare at the next photograph hung on the wall. I follow him, curious.

"What am I doing here, Stellan?"

He looks at me for a second, his expression telling me nothing. "I was told you were here to do an in-depth article about me. Is that not the case?"

My eyes tighten on his face. "I think you know that the reasons for the article are… well, to be polite, I would say that they are politically motivated."

One corner of his mouth curls up, making a dimple appear in his cheek. "And if you were not being polite? What would you say then?"

My mouth twists. "That buying my silence and covering your tracks by using *Politiken* is a form of government corruption."

His eyes pin me right where I stand. "I see. That's a harsh view of things, *ja?* As far as I am concerned, it just sort of…" He pauses, then shrugs. "It worked out to benefit both of us. Don't you think?"

I fold my arms across my chest. "It's just you and me here, Stellan. You don't need to lie to me. I've already signed your nondisclosure agreement. There is no illusion between the two of us."

He mirrors my gesture, wrapping his arms across his broad chest with a smirk on his face. "It's often like that when you are dealing with the aftermath of a royal scandal. Trust me. This isn't the first one I've seen."

My brow hunches. "That's it? That's your answer?"

He looks thoughtful for a moment. "That's about the scope of it, yes."

I shake my head, a little disgusted at him. "I don't know how I was ever attracted to you. Your…" I wave my hand to indicate his body. "Your body is so great, but your politics *suck*. Usually I hold myself to a higher standard than this."

His eyebrows lift in surprise. "You are saying that you learned that I'm a royal… and it made you *less* attracted to me?"

I let out a laugh. "Yes! I like to sleep with people who are actually from this planet. People who are dealing with the same kind of issues that I'm dealing with. That is…" I give another huff of laugher. "That's just not you."

He casts a skeptical gaze over me. "You're telling me that even as a little girl, you never had dreams of being Cinderella? Come on now, Margot. Be honest."

The image of me at age six flashes through my brain. A skinny, dark-haired little girl in an oversized hand-me-down dress. A little girl who had just realized that Santa wasn't real in the same month she found out what it meant when kids at school called her a welfare princess.

Bitterness threatens to overtake me. I screw up my face. "No, Stellan. You know what I dreamed of when I was a little girl?"

He pauses, his brow wrinkling. He cocks his head to the side. "No. What did you wish for?"

"I wished that my mom wasn't a junkie. I wished that the other kids in my elementary school wouldn't make fun of the old clothes that I wore. But most of all, I wished that I would always know where my next meal was going to come from."

His eyebrows rise. "Surely not. There had to be some sort of..." He splays his hand out in front of himself, gesturing. "Social safety net or something. I mean, no one in Denmark suffers that way."

My face tightens. My voice lowers. "A lot of people fall through the cracks, no matter how many safety nets there are in place. People like *me*. That's just how life is. As the future king of Denmark, I hope you know that by now."

He scowls at me. "I don't believe it."

I give him an offended look. "What, that I was starving while you were living your best life? You are the top one percent of the top one percent. You're beyond rich. And me?" I thump my chest. "I'm poor. Even with a college degree, I will never earn a fraction of what you were just... *born with*."

Stellan stares at me for a second, his ice blue gaze direct and intense. "You would correct the imbalance, I presume? Take my family wealth and distribute it differently?"

I make a face. "That's not really what I'm about. I want systematic change. Global change. The weakest and most vulnerable among us need to be taken care of. And places like this palace…" I gesture to the walls around me. "They should be repurposed. Made into museums and hospitals and schools. They shouldn't be held by one family that was chosen to rule Denmark centuries ago."

For several long seconds, Stellan actually looks like he might just leave the room. That or summon some guard to seize me. He stares at me with an icy glare.

When he finally speaks, his voice is low and gravelly, his expression stony. "The people of Denmark need their royals."

I give a soft chuckle. "Why? Why do you get to live such a lavish life just because you were born into a certain family?"

He takes a half a step forward. "We guide them in times of crisis. We celebrate when good things happen. We do a ton of charity work. But most importantly, we reflect the current state of affairs back at them. We serve as a touchstone for the entire Danish community!"

I cock a brow. "You deserve wealth because you are a mirror of the Danish people?"

He glares at me, smoothing a big hand over his stomach. "Among other things, yes."

"You keep telling yourself that, buddy. And I'll just be over here, working to right a small portion of the injustices that happen every single day." My mouth twists sourly.

He takes another step toward me, then another, then another. I gulp as he approaches, the difference in our heights never more apparent than now. Determined to show no fear, I raise my chin and glare at him, defiant.

He stops when he's almost on top of me. A hair's breadth away. The air between us seems to thin, making me drag in my breaths. Our gazes clash, him staring down at me as if I'm a bug, me giving him my best impression of the rebellious James Dean.

I can feel the heat radiating off of his big body. Scorn lights the fires raging in his ice blue eyes.

When he speaks, his voice is low and rough. "Just so you know, Margot. This little journalism assignment wasn't my idea. You being here doesn't exactly *please* me. And I am counting the days until you're out of my life forever. Do you understand?"

My gaze wanders down to his mouth for a second. I notice the dip of his cupid's bow, the press of his lips, the hint of his perfect teeth when he sneers at me. Am I stupid to bother arguing with someone that has obviously been bred for this kind of wealth?

I give my head a tiny shake. "I completely understand, *your highness*. In a month's time, I will be gone. You will move on with your life. Believe me, I fucking get that."

His laugh is deep and gravelly. "Good."

Then he moves past me, deliberately bumping my shoulder as he goes. I frown, watching Stellan stalk from the room.

That guy is definitely tightly wound.

The question is… will his behavior affect me? Because if it does, I could be well and truly fucked.

CHAPTER 15

STELLAN

My fingers are cramping up from scrawling my signature on over eight hundred letters. Not only that, but I can feel Margot just behind me. Her eyes threaten to burn a hole in my upper back. I roll my neck until it makes a satisfying pop.

Tension still simmers in the room. It has ever since Margot walked in half an hour ago.

Arrogant. Spoiled. Full of yourself.

Those words still ring in my head, thrown at me by Margot herself. I'm cantankerous today and that's a big reason why.

I turn and face the windows of my study, a room as large and dimly lit as the rest of the palace. With the same high ceilings as the rest of the palace, this room manages to be as drafty as the others. The only difference here is that the walls are predominately dark wood, the only color a hint of blue in the curtains surrounding the floor-length windows.

The light filters through a gauzy curtained layer just before the windows. Dropping my fountain pen with a sigh, I push myself up out of my chair. Instantly Margot is on her feet.

"Where are you going?" she asks, her voice low.

I walk to the window, unwilling to look back at her no matter how badly I'm tempted. I already know what will happen.

I already know that she will look at me with those deep blue eyes, her expression as cutting as a blade. She's always just on the cusp of figuring me out, or at least that's what her expression indicates.

"Nowhere," I answer, gritting my teeth. As if I could just leave when I have a mountain of letters left to sign. It's all part of the deal, being a royal. "Just stretching."

I do take a minute to stretch, raising my arms over my head. I'm half dressed for the arts event that I have to leave for in half an hour; white button up with two buttons undone, sleeves rolled up, a pair of light gray trousers.

As I stretch, I'm aware of her eyes again. Those clever, piercing eyes. I usually feel like an animal in a zoo exhibit on my best day. But having her here, in the midst of my most mundane daily tasks, is almost too much to handle.

I hear paper rustling. "Can I ask you some questions while you're stretching?"

Looking back at Margot from the window, I see her opening a little notepad. It's almost cute, the way she is deadly serious about her job. Her pink hair is curly and hangs loose. Her heart shaped face puckers a little bit as she frowns down at her notepad. As usual, she wears the same black blazer and black pants, although this time she wears an old yellow Blondie t-shirt.

I lift one shoulder casually. "If you must. I don't imagine that you actually have to write a single word if you don't want to. You know that the royal press office would gladly write the whole damn article for you, don't you?"

Her eyes narrow. Her mouth twists. "I'm writing the article. It's going to have my byline slapped on it. I might as well make something of the experience."

Shaking my head, I turn back to the window. "Suit yourself."

I move the gauzy layer blocking the window aside and peer out across the perfectly manicured lawn. A gardener moves at the far end of my view, closing a wooden gate. He has a basket of flowers on one arm and he stops, wiping his head with a cloth from the pocket of his gray coveralls.

"When you think of Denmark and its future, what do you hope for?"

Hunching my brow, I drop the curtain and turn back to face her. I know the answer to this question by heart.

"Stability, success, and growth." I give her my most deadpan expression. "Next question."

Her nose wrinkles. "You didn't even think about it."

I repress an eye roll, adjusting one of my shirt cuffs. "You do know that I'm constantly being asked the same questions, right? I'm on display a hundred percent of the time. I come prepared with the answers to fifty most commonly asked questions."

"Ah." She writes something down in her little notepad. "Well, I guess I'll have to ask a wider variety of questions, won't I?"

Instead of an answer, Margot gets a shrug in response. I return to the table where my letters are stacked, sitting down and picking up the pen once more. Dropping back into signing them is the work of ten seconds.

For fifteen minutes, I let myself fall into a trance. I relax my gaze. I think of nothing. I feel the pen moving across each piece of paper; I barely notice the fact that I have to move each piece of paper across the desk and into the finished pile. I am only barely aware of time moving.

It's not exactly a pleasant feeling to be able to lose myself so completely in a task. Nor is it bad... it simply *is*. It speaks to the fact that once a week, I do this exact same thing, in the same span of time. A thousand signatures on a thousand letters of reply. I've done it since I was old enough to hold a pen.

When I sign the last letter, I return to everyday life with a sigh. Standing, I stack all the letters neatly. Although I don't jog them; people that write me want their letters neat, without bent corners.

I do my best to give it to them.

When Margot speaks, I startle. I had forgotten that she was even here.

"What happens now?"

My head jerks to face her. I run a hand through my dark hair, standing up. "What?"

She nods to my work. "The letters. What happens to them?"

That gives me pause. "I don't know. I just leave them here when I am finished. They appear and disappear routinely." I frown. "I suppose someone in the press office comes to collect them." I shrug. "Why?"

Margot gives me a careful look. "Just trying to get a sense of what happens. There are probably a hundred thousand little tasks that get done without you ever knowing it."

My brow furrows. "I suppose so."

She flips her notebook closed. "So where do you go to now?"

I check my watch. "Oliver should be here any second to tell me I have to get ready to go. I think today I go to an art exhibit followed by a primary school."

Eyeing her, I start to roll down my sleeves. "Fetch me my tie from over by the door, will you?"

Her expression grows stormy. "Is there something keeping you from doing it?"

I raise my eyebrows. "No. You are just closer, that's all."

She folds her arms across her chest, cocking her hip. "Do it yourself."

I roll my eyes and saunter over to the tie, which has been placed on a coatrack with extreme caution by some unseen hand. As I put the tie on, I cast my eye over Margot's defiant stance.

My lips curve upward. "You're cute when you're being mutinous."

Her cheeks color, giving me a certain kind of satisfaction. She scowls. "You're a pig."

Chuckling, I nod. "I couldn't agree with you more. I'm right, though."

All that earns me is a glare.

Oliver's soft knock sounds at the door. I swing the door open, surprising him. He stands up a little straighter, his white hair and black suit looking dapper as always.

"*Deres Højhed*," he says, bowing stiffly. He always calls me *your highness*, even when I ask him not to. It's just his way. "Your car is waiting."

I start out the door behind him, only stopping about halfway down the hall. I look back with a frown. "Oliver? Hold on a second, would you?"

I walk back to the doorway that I just left, finding Margot standing at my desk. She's not touching anything. But she is staring down at the stack of letters, her brow furrowed.

"Hey," I bark.

She looks up, eyes wide. Her pink tongue darts out to wet her bottom lip. "Yes?"

I cock my head. "Aren't you coming?"

"Oh." She frowns. "Yes. I just thought— "

I turn, leaving her to hurry after me, her explanation falling on deaf ears. She has to practically run to keep up with my natural stride. I see her looking at me, trying to figure me out again. I've done something that she didn't expect and now she's trying to pin her understanding of me down again.

I hurry downstairs and up to the back seat of the waiting Audi limousine. It's considered polite to help a woman into the back of a car first. I stop and stand stiffly by the back door, motioning her in. It's more of an automatic gesture than anything else, but Margot's face flushes as she accepts and climbs in first.

Once we're in the car, I roll up the partition between the driver and us. Margot buckles her seatbelt and frowns at the partition as it rises.

"What?" I ask.

She rolls her eyes. "Nothing. I just wanted to know who was driving us."

Shrugging, I sprawl out, taking up the majority of seat. "Who cares? We'll get where we're going."

Her eyes tighten on my face. I can tell that I've somehow said the wrong thing, but I don't particularly care. "Just sit back and enjoy the ride, *skatter*."

I grin. Her cheeks flare bright pink. She frowns and shakes her head, looking away.

"What does that mean? *Skatter*," she says, sounding the word out.

"It means the one I treasure. My sweetheart."

Her eyes widen and the bright pink blush on her cheeks turns into a beat red flush. All right, that was kind of fun. It's entertaining to watch her squirm.

When she looks back at me, there is an intensity in her expression that wasn't there before. "What does the palace expect from you, exactly?"

I cock a brow. "What do you mean?"

Her lips thin for a moment. "I mean… you are supposed to be a king someday. That position comes with a lot of expectations, I'd imagine. Along with being born with a silver spoon in your mouth, there have to be downsides. Personal sacrifices. What are they?"

I furrow my brow, looking out the window thoughtfully. "Every word I say is recorded. Somewhere, somehow. Everything I do is pulled apart and searched for motives." I wrinkle my nose briefly. "That's why I liked being a nobody in New York. It's nice to set aside the political correctness and the strict guidelines and just… be anonymous for a while."

When I glance back at her, I see her scribbling in that notepad of hers again. "I can see how that would be hard," she mumbles.

My lips twist. She has no idea.

Shaking my head, I sigh. "I've never been able to just do what I wanted. When I was younger, I couldn't go to school with all the other kids. Instead, my friend Erik and I—" I stop for a second. "You know Erik, *ja?*"

She looks up at me, the blue of her eyes taking my breath away for a second. "Yes."

"Erik and I were tutored together here at the palace. He— "

"Wait, wait." She flips a page. "Okay. Is Erik a royal, then?"

I snort. "No. He's the son of the groundskeeper. My father got drunk with the groundskeeper one day; the next day, Erik was brought into my room to play." I smile wryly. "I think we were about four."

She nods. "So you weren't even allowed to choose your best friend, basically."

"Nope." I grin. "I'm lucky that he's not a fucking psychopath. And if you think that's bad, wait until you hear how my wife is being chosen for me."

That seems to actually shake her. She stops writing. "What?"

"Yep. I was presented with a list of young, eligible ladies. Each one with a pristine pedigree, each ready to produce as many heirs as I want, each one as boring as the next. I've been told to just point to one, or decide which flavor I want... a blonde, a brunette, a redhead..." I sigh. "And I'm assured that the rest will be taken care of. All I have to do is show up reasonably sober on my wedding day. Voila! Instantly, the perfect wife."

Margot scrunches up her face. "That sounds... *awful*."

"It will be!" I say. "Add to that the fact that I basically live in a fish bowl, with no expectation that any part of my life will ever be private... and you get the royal experience in a nutshell."

She chews on her lower lip, scribbling a few notes to herself. "Is it worth it?"

I tilt my head to the side. "What do you mean?"

"Everyone thinks that being a royal is amazing. It is, obviously. But it sounds more complicated than that. I guess what I'm saying is... does having everything you've ever wanted make it worth not getting to make your own choices?"

I repress a sigh, turning my face away from her. "I don't know. This is the only life I've ever had. I don't know how to live any other way."

Margot makes a soft sound, a little *mmm*. I don't know what it means. I'm not willing to ask. I'm definitely not going to look over at her to see her expression.

It's better this way. I probably shouldn't have even told her all of that. I don't know why I let it slip.

Not only that, but I find myself irritable now. Margot has a way of making me open up, but I don't want to.

I have exactly zero interest in being vulnerable around her ever again.

Leaning forward, I press the button to lower the partition. When the driver looks back at me in the rearview mirror, I catch his eye. "Could you fucking hurry it up? I have places to be."

He bows his head. "*Selvfølgelig, deres højhed.*"

Despite what I said, he doesn't drive any faster. The palace drivers never do. They always drive five kilometers under the speed limit. It's in their training. After all, they are moving precious cargo.

Sighing to myself, I lean my head back and close my eyes.

CHAPTER 16

STELLAN

I pause for a moment, making sure my weight is centered, making sure I have the right grip on the basketball. Then I jump, shooting the ball toward the hoop. It sails into the basket, runs around the rim, and then falls off the side.

"*Rend mig i røven!*" I shout, feeling sweat slide down my back.

Erik gives a bark of laughter. "You are terrible at this game, Stel."

He runs to catch the ball, dribbling it as he returns. I wipe my brow on my shirt, turning to look at Margot as I do. She sits on a set of bleachers on the other side of the gym, with her notepad open and her pen in her mouth. Her head is down, her hair spilling everywhere as she scrawls something to herself.

I can see that she's shed that terrible black blazer she usually wears, obviously feeling warm in the stifling gym.

It sits beside her, thrown carelessly on one of the lower bleacher steps like a piece of driftwood left by the sea. She has on a short black dress and leggings, the neckline of her dress tantalizingly low.

As a matter of fact, when she sits in just this position, I can almost see her nipples.

Almost.

I stare for a second too long and she looks up, catching me. Her cheeks immediately turn pink and she sits up, adjusting her dress. I lift a brow at her, just in time to get a basketball right in the stomach.

The breath leaves my lungs in a whoosh. I catch the ball and glare at Erik.

"Quit that," I command. My order is met with an eye roll.

Erik has always been my closest friend and biggest rival, all at once. He's also the only person who is completely unafraid of telling me to go fuck myself.

"Stop staring at the pretty reporter," he says, grinning. "We're supposed to be playing a game here."

I roll my eyes and forcefully chuck the basketball back at him. He catches it, dribbles, and then makes a shot. The shot goes in the basket without even touching the rim. He does a celebratory dance.

Shaking my head, I run to catch the ball. "I'm a thousand percent certain that you aren't supposed to do a dance every single time you make a basket."

His grin only widens. "Says the guy that can't dunk. Do I detect a note of jealous bullshit?"

He's right, of course. It irks me beyond measure that I'm the future king of Denmark and the soon to be ruler of everything I see… and yet I just can't manage to master basketball.

I casually stride around the court, trying not to let my ego get the better of me. We could play some sport that I actually have a chance at scoring goals, like football or handball. But Erik likes to mix up our shared workouts to allay boredom.

So today, I'm playing basketball.

I line up another shot and jump, throwing the ball. This time the ball bounces off the backboard and then bounds away from me. My eyes tighten; I hate being so intensely bad at something that should be so easy.

I swing my gaze over to Margot, who is watching my every little movement. She tucks her pink hair back behind her ear, looking at me with an unreadable expression. As she tilts her head to the side thoughtfully, she comes off as analytical.

What is she thinking?

"Seriously?" Erik asks. I turn to him, my expression innocent, but he just rolls his eyes.

He cups his hand around his mouth and calls to her. "Hey! Margot!"

I glare at him, my pulse picking up. What is he going to say?

Margot looks at him, arching a brow. "Yes?"

"You can go. Stellan needs to concentrate on his workout and then he's going to bed early. We have to get up super early tomorrow for our hunt."

Her eyebrows rise. She glances at me but I refuse to meet her eyes. Instead I just go after the ball and dribble it, shooting it toward the basket. Margot gathers her coat and stands, coming over to me.

The way she looks at me feels strange; it's the work of half a minute to realize that this is the first time I've been dressed down since New York. Usually I wear my button ups and Briony dress slacks like they are a kind of armor, keeping my shields up and everyone else out.

But just now, as she's walking over, I realize that I'm only wearing a black t-shirt and black athletic shorts. It's weird, but I feel just the tiniest bit vulnerable.

She stops a few feet from me, jogging her tote bag on her hip, her coat over her arm. She scrunches up her face. "Am I needed tomorrow?"

I keep my eye on the ball as much as I can, catching it when Erik throws it to me. "I would rather you stayed at home, if that's what you are asking."

Her eyes narrow. "It isn't. When is super early? And what are you hunting?"

Shrugging, I shoot another basket. This time it goes in the hoop. Erik whoops.

"That's what I am talking about!" he crows. Then he turns to Margot, wearing a smirk. "Five thirty. That's what time we're going. If you're going to come, wear clothes you can get dirty."

Margot scrunches up her face, her gaze sliding to me. I lock down my emotions and keep my face smooth; it's almost second nature to me, even though Erik just flat out lied to Margot about what time we start.

"All right," she says at last. "I'll see you both bright and early, then."

She turns, heading out of the gym. I can't help but watch her ass sway in that short black dress; there is a hole in her leggings on the back of her thigh that gives me all kinds of dirty thoughts.

For instance, right now I'm thinking about slipping my fingers inside that hole and ripping the thin black fabric. Revealing the rest of her pale, creamy thigh to my view…

"Stel!" Erik barks.

I straighten, my neck heating, and look at him. "What?"

He looks back at her disappearing through the gym doors, waiting until they close. Then he cocks a brow. "Once wasn't enough for you?"

I shoot him a look. "What do you mean?"

He pushes his cheek out with his tongue. "I mean, does Margot have some kind of spell cast over you? Because you can have anyone in the world… anyone but her."

I stiffen. "I know that."

"Do you want me to call some ladies over? Maybe we should have a private party."

Shaking my head, I start walking over to the wall where a cooler full of water bottles is stashed. "Have I ever in our history wanted your help to get dates? If I wanted, I could have thirty women naked in a pit, fighting over me."

He shrugs. "It's just an offer. I just saw the way you looked at her. The same way that you looked at her back in New York."

Grabbing a bottle of water, I roll my eyes. "What, like a person I find interesting?"

"No." He folds his arms over his chest. "You look at her like she's a fucking filet mignon and you're starving to death."

"As long as I don't touch her, I can look at Margot any damn way I please." I uncap the bottle, taking a long pull of the chilled water.

Erik sighs. "I just don't want the press to start investigating who you're sleeping with again. You know that one wrong look at her in front of the wrong person could spark the rumor mill to start again."

I laugh. "You think I am not aware of that? Besides, of all the women in the world…" Thinking about Margot, I shake my head. "Trust me, she is the last one I would pick to sneak around with. She's the opposite of what I want."

That isn't exactly true. Even as I say it, it sounds flat and wrong leaving my mouth. And not just to me…

Erik gives me a funny look. "You don't have to lie to me, Stel. The bullshit with the press is one thing. But here, just between us, there do not need to be any secrets."

I grin at him. "Everything is fine, Erik. You are overreacting." Taking another swig from the bottle, I set it down on top of the cooler. "Come on. Let's go for another twenty minutes, then call it a day."

His eyes narrow, but he just shakes his head and runs to get the basketball. As we dribble and shoot, he stays quiet. That doesn't mean I don't feel his eyes on me, wondering just what I'm up to though…

I'd like to know as much myself.

When we're done, we head outside, Erik regaling me with the story of last Saturday night. I'm only partially paying attention, honestly.

I admit, I am wondering about what Margot said to me earlier.

Does having everything you've ever wanted make it worth not getting to make your own choices?

That question echoes in my head for longer than I would care to admit…

CHAPTER 17

MARGOT

At eight thirty, I hear loud voices approaching me. Opening my eyes and straightening from where I was slumped over on a couch, I look up. Erik and Stellan are heading down the hallway where I'm at, both dressed in baggy paint-covered khaki shorts and scuzzy t-shirts.

And behind them is a group of maybe ten or twelve people that are all talking excitedly. Standing up, I brush off my old gray yoga pants and hole-filled Black Sabbath t-shirt. I try to school my expression to keep my annoyance off my face, but something tells me that I'm not very successful.

I showed up here before dawn and I've been waiting for three hours. A funny little prank for them to pull. It's a good thing I have slept much worse places than in this hallway on a stiff burgundy couch.

When Stellan sees me, he smirks. He strides up to me and then moves past my couch without stopping. I'm forced to gather up my tote bag and my jacket and run to catch up with him.

"So you are coming, then?" he asks casually.

I shoot him a glare. "Yup."

"Sorry we're a few minutes late," Erik chimes in, grinning like an idiot. I could smack them both in the face right this second, if they would only slow down to allow me to do it. They're both so tall; everyone in this damned country is tall, pretty much.

"You told me to be here three hours ago," I mutter. "You're just lucky that I know how to keep myself occupied."

Erik just shrugs. I speed walk down the hallway with them, taking a right down a staircase. The entire group takes a right and suddenly we are outside, queuing to load ourselves into a white passenger van.

Stellan and Erik are the first ones in. I hang back, climbing in last next to a willowy blonde young woman. She wrinkles her button nose at me.

"I'm Annika," she says, offering me her hand.

I shake it, sizing her up. "Margot."

Her delicate brows rise. My name apparently means something to her. "*Haj*. Did we already meet?"

"Yes. At the porcelain factory. It's nice to see you again." I smile, then I bite my lip, glancing back at the other people sitting in rows between us and Stellan. "How do you know everyone here?"

She laughs. "Well, I'm related to half of them. My last name is Løve."

"Oh! So you're Stellan's younger sister?" I ask. That makes sense; she has the same light-colored eyes as Stellan, and his ungodly cheekbones. I dig through my tote bag for my notepad and pen, making some quick shorthand notes.

"Yes, I'm the youngest of five kids. The only girl, too. Stellan is the oldest… and then there's Lars…"

She points out Lars, who is a dark-haired clone of Stellan's, if Stellan had two days' worth of stubble on his cheeks. I nod.

"I actually know him. He visited New York with Stellan and Erik."

"Oh, don't get me started on Erik. He is a pain in my ass… but you probably know that he's not actually related to the Løves, right?"

"I do."

She nods. "Over there, Anders is one of ours too…" She points to Anders, who wears his dark hair a bit longer and has a beard. He looks like Stellan, but he's younger and he looks as though he likes emo. "And then the rest are family friends."

"Wait, that's…" I stop, squinting as I count silently. "Yeah, that's only four Løve children."

She shrugs. "Finn is the missing link. And he's… out of town."

Her eye roll hints that there is more to the story. But before I can ask anything else, the van rolls to a stop. I crawl out, looking around what seems to be an abandoned children's playground. Jungle bars with half the bars rotted away, see saws that have seen better days, a long abandoned treehouse, and a geo-dome for climbing that appears very rusty and dangerous.

Don't get me wrong, it's all definitely overgrown and cool looking. But what exactly are we supposed to do here?

"What in the world?" I ask, wrinkling my nose.

Erik and Stellan climb out of the back of the van, sharing a grin between them. "Paintball."

My eyes widen. The driver starts handing out big airsoft guns with a few racks of various neon colored paintballs. I take one when it's handed to me, but I have zero idea how to get the paintballs in the gun.

Tilting my head at it doesn't seem to make the gun make more sense, either.

"I—" I stammer, looking around. Surely no one actually expects me to play, right?

"I'll team up with Stellan!" Erik says, grinning as he grips his gun.

"Oh, come on," Anders interjects. "Everyone here gets it, okay? You two are the ideal pairing. Why don't you make at least a little fun for the rest of us, *ja?* Spread some of that alpha male top dog bullshit around."

Stellan sighs, tugging on his t-shirt. "He's right."

"I think Stellan should be with Margot," Annika chimes in, sliding me a wink. "To help her really get a fuller picture. Erik, you can be with me."

My eyebrows rise. Erik gives her a stormy look but reluctantly agrees. "Fine."

Everybody else pairs up, heading into the middle of the playground. I tag along, watching Stellan. I thought maybe I was just drunk when I met him; I had convinced myself that it is just his usual button up and dark slacks that make him attractive.

But now I realize that I was wrong. As we all line up around the dome-shaped climbing structure, I look at Stellan's handsome features. His dark hair, his ice blue eyes, his cheekbones sent straight from heaven.

Those things are still a part of him when he's dressed down, apparently even when he wears an outfit that looks like a post-apocalyptic version of what college frat boys don.

He nods to me, leaning close. "When the driver blows the whistle, run for that big old tree right there." He nods to indicate it. "And whatever you do, do not stop."

The driver looks odd, following us in his formal black suit. He blows a little whistle. "On my signal! If you get hit, even a little, you must head back here."

I nod, trying to juggle my tote bag and my gun at the same time. The driver blows the whistle and everyone takes off in pairs; I run after Stellan as fast as I can, wondering how I'm even supposed to get the paintballs into the gun.

Surely it can't be that hard, right?

Stellan ducks behind the huge oak tree, looking around. I stop and he yanks me out of everyone else's line of sight just in time; three paintballs whiz by my head, making my heart skid to a halt.

Looking up at Stellan with wide eyes, I start to thank him. He shushes me, then takes my gun and feeds one of my tubes of paintballs into it with a loud *click*. He does the same for his gun, then holds a finger to his lips.

He leans down close. "Leave your bag here. No one will move it, I promise."

I bite my lip. The only thing in my tote bag worth stealing is my Nikon, which is worth so much that I will probably never own another like it ever again. I reach in my bag and pull out my camera, hanging it around my neck.

"Ready," I whisper.

He looks at me, his ice blue gaze seeking the answer to some question. "Why— "

Just then, a paintball whizzes by his head, landing on the tree with a hard splat. "Get down," he whispers, crouching. I mimic his movement, although I'm so much tinier than him that his version of crouching evens out with my actual height.

"Come on," he says, running full speed away from the direction that the paintball just came. I hurry after him, looking around with my senses on full alert.

One of the guys that was in the van with us pops out from behind a tree. He aims straight at me, firing but missing. I panic, shooting my gun off a couple of times. The paintballs soar into the air way over his head.

Stellan turns and sees what's going on. In one swift motion, he fires twice. The paintballs explode as they hit the man in the chest. Two giant blots of bright orange paint blossom over his heart.

"Ah, fuck!" he yells, turning to start walking toward the geo-dome.

Stellan hisses at me and I scurry over to him. He grabs my hand and pulls me behind another tree. For a few seconds, my heart rate picks up. I look up at him, at how fierce and protective he is at this moment.

I know that it's cheesy to find that appealing, but I do. Despite my resistance, I really, really do.

"You are terrible at this game," he says, scowling down at me.

Stellan releases my hand and sweeps the scope of his paintball gun in a semi-circle. I shrug a little, trying to keep the fact that I'm obviously turned on by this kind of behavior under wraps. It's just…

I can imagine that, in a scenario where the end of the world has arrived and everyone is out for their own interests, I would want to have this guy in my corner.

God, I need to say something. Anything to change the topic in my brain.

"I don't like guns!" I blurt out.

He gives me an odd look. "It's just a game, Margot."

My cheeks heat. "I know…"

Stellan's nose wrinkles. "You know what? I think you are a snob."

My jaw drops. "Me? How am I a snob? This whole thing is *your* event, your highness."

"So what? It's something new. And I think that something new totally scares you. So you turn your nose up at it without even trying it out. That makes you a snob."

I narrow my eyes at him. "Are we still talking about paintball? Or are you just taking what you feel about everything and projecting it onto this topic?"

He rolls his eyes. "Do you have to read into everything, Margot? Can this not just be about shooting people with paint?"

Adjusting my gun, I size him up. "I don't know. You tell me."

Stellan sighs, scrubbing his hand through his dark hair. "Why don't we declare a truce? Just for today. You and I will just be on the same side for long enough to dominate this game. Then we can go back to full out class warfare tomorrow. Okay?"

The corner of my mouth kicks up. I give him a sly glance. "Yeah, okay."

He looks a tiny bit surprised that I just agreed. "Okay," he repeats. "Okay, good. There's a spot that we want to get to over there." He nods. "A... I don't know the right word. Where you are protected but you can shoot at targets?"

I scrunch up my face. "Um... I think that's called a blind, maybe?"

"All right. Let's run over to it. *Ja?*"

This time, he looks to me, waiting for my reply. I can't help but nod. He bolts toward the blind and I run after him. We make it there safely and peer out from behind the trees, sniping anything that moves.

I can admit it; I have kind of a good time, shooting people and yelling when unseen people shoot through the trees. While we have this truce going on it is easy to forget that he's Prince Stellan Løve, heir to the throne of the kingdom of Denmark. I'm not a commoner that he looks down on, either.

Just now, he grins at me in a way that makes me shiver. I bite my lip and grin back at him. We even high five when I duck and roll to narrowly avoid a paintball to the chest.

His gaze roves the world in front of us again. "Come on. Everybody knows where we are. We should make a run for it. And I think there is a good hiding spot this way."

He takes off at a crouched run. I'm left trying to follow, beaming at him. We reach a large oak tree and he slows to a stop. He glances at my face, putting a finger to his lips. Then he holds up a hand, gesturing for me to wait.

Just on the other side of the tree, the earth falls away, leaving a good deal of the roots exposed. I lean over and look down as he jumps about five feet to the bottom.

He's graceful, I'll give him that.

But I'm not expecting what he does next. He just turns to me, looking up at me expectantly. "Come on. I'll help you."

He holds his hands up, waiting. I definitely don't trust him not to just drop me. Biting my lip, I take his hands. But instead of jumping into his arms, I sort of awkwardly try to hit the ground beside him.

Stellan's eyes widen as I launch myself down toward the ground. He tries to correct the course of both of our bodies with the weight of his… but he fails.

Instead, he just staggers a little, catching me as I crumple of top of him.

Shit.

My chin hits his collarbone, my knees hit the hard flesh of his thighs. The breath is knocked out of me by running into the density of his chest.

"Oof," I squeak.

He grunts. Picking my head up, I realize that I'm face to face with him, close enough to kiss. I gaze into his stunning blue eyes, gulping. My eyes drop for just the barest second to his perfect mouth.

Should we... should I...

His mouth twists with a sour expression. When he whispers, his voice is low and intense. "You make things awkward. You know that?"

I catch my bottom lip between my teeth. "I've heard that, yes."

"Let's just..." He stops, shaking his head. "We just have to get through this month, okay? Then you are free to live your life. You'll never see me in person again."

That isn't what I wanted to hear, honestly. I don't want to spend time with Stellan, but no one wants to hear that they are bad company. "Just like that, huh? When we spent the night together — "

He shoves me away, taking a full step back. "We don't have to talk about that, Margot."

My face darkens. "You know what, Stellan? You — "

I hear the paintballs being fired only a second before my thigh bursts into flame. It hurts to be shot with a paintball! Looking down, I see the spread of neon pink paint on one leg of my yoga pants.

I make a strangled noise. Whatever argument I had planned falls away. I look back up and realize that Stellan and I both got pegged by someone who likely heard our arguing.

He grits his teeth, pinning me with an annoyed glare. "Great. Just great. Come on. We should go back to the center of the game and wait until we're reset." His expression is just short of a sneer. "I definitely want a different partner next time."

I roll my eyes. "Whatever."

And just like that, our truce is ended. He starts trudging around the bottom of the tree, letting me trail in his wake.

CHAPTER 18

STELLAN

I'm sitting at my desk, looking at a stack of financial papers that are awaiting my signature. Cracking each of my knuckles in turn, I look down at the figures presented to me. Each of these documents is important because they are from charities that I patronize; nearly every single one of them is asking for a significant raise in the money that is allocated to them this year.

Money doesn't grow on trees. I know that as well as anyone. So I'm trying to ascertain what monies go to which charities. The whole thing is enough to make my temple throb.

When a footman comes into my study, I'm relieved to be able to focus on anything else for a minute.

"Her Royal Highness," the footman announces, backing out of the way with a bow.

My grandmother sweeps into the room, looking prim and proper in a white skirt suit and sensible stockings. "Hello, darling."

I raise my brow, pushing up out of my seat. "*Momse*. What brings you here?"

She glances behind her, to where the footman still stands. "Get the door on your way out, please. I would like to talk to my grandson in private."

"Your highness," he responds, bowing and seeing himself out.

As the door closes, my grandmother gestures to the love seat and chair set up by the fireplace. "Join me, Stellan."

She perches on the edge of the loveseat, crossing her ankles. I walk over and plop myself into the overstuffed leather chair, tilting my head. "To what do I owe the pleasure? I mean, it's always nice to see you, *Momse*. But I assume that you are here for a reason."

She gives me a small smile. "I don't know if you know this, but I believe I have spent more time with you than I have with any other grandchild of mine."

That gives me pause. "Perhaps."

Her lips quirk. "No, not perhaps. Definitely. I've always been here for you. Your father hasn't…" She pauses, thoughtful. "He has been quite busy, running the kingdom of Denmark. He and your mother both are always on a world tour. I've made sure to be here at your beck and call. I wanted to make sure that you were growing up with the right ideals."

THE WICKED PRINCE

I narrow my gaze at Ida. "Yes, all right."

"In addition to that, I think you know that you are my favorite." She gives me another small smile. "You look very much like my own father, after all."

What is she getting at? I squint at her, trying to puzzle out what she is trying to say to me. "Yes, Momse."

She folds her hands in her lap. "I want you to consider that when I tell you what I came here to tell you."

A sinking feeling in the pit of my stomach tells me that her announcement is not going to be good news. I frown. "You're killing me. Just tell me already."

Her brow creases. "I know it's been a while since you've seen your parents."

"Yes. They've been on a tour of Australia and Africa for almost two months."

There is hesitation on Ida's face, which is unusual. She usually just says what she has to say, feelings be damned.

"Your father... your father's health has not been good over the past year."

My heart falters. "What?"

She inclines her head. "The king has been ill several times in the past twelve months. It's enough to make me worry, honestly. And when I start to worry, I start thinking of what I can do to prepare our country for any future... changes."

My eyebrows rise. "You think that I will have to take over?"

Her lips press into a firm line. "I think that it is not outside the realm of possibility. In my opinion, it is time to start preparing you to take the crown."

For several moments, I'm too shocked to respond.

"But…" I shake my head. "No. I'm only twenty six. I shouldn't even be thinking about the line of succession."

My grandmother stops me by leaning over and putting her hand on my knee. "I'm sorry, Stellan. But I'm afraid that you will have to begin preparing for something catastrophic to happen. And the very first step is finding a wife."

I draw myself back, frowning and shaking my head. "What? No. That should be the last thing I have to worry about right now."

Ida raises her hands, trying to calm me down. "Finding a wife now will make everything much easier. If you have to step up suddenly — "

I cut her off. "No."

Her eyes narrow. "It's not just me saying this, Stellan."

It takes everything I've got to keep my words civil. "Let me guess. You have Prime Minister Finley on your side?"

She tilts her head. "Yes. And others."

"Have you noticed that two of the names on your list of marriageable girls are related to Prime Minister Finley?"

I cross my arms, my heartbeat sounding loud in my ears. "The list is only ten names long. That means, assuming that I actually go by your absurd list, I have a one out of five chance of being related to our good prime minister. Sure, I hate Prime Minister Finley and everything he stands for. But why not make him part of my family for the rest of my life? Hmm?"

She narrows her eyes at me. "There are eight other choices on that list."

I stand up, nearly trembling with repressed rage. "No. I'm not interested in having my life managed to that degree. I do everything else by the book, but I won't choose some insipid girl off a list of girls chosen by their heritage and willingness to breed. It's disgusting."

My grandmother climbs to her feet, giving me a tired look. "You have to, Stellan. Your father probably won't make it for another year in his current position."

"Well, I'll deal with that when he calls on me. And as for marriage… when it's the right time and the right girl, I'll let you know. But I don't want to hear another thing about it until I bring it up."

Her lips thin. "You can't give me orders, young man."

"And you can't dictate who and when I marry. So here we are, demanding things of the other we know will be ignored." I hold my hand out, gesturing to the door. "Now if you'll excuse me, I have this huge stack of papers to read through before my afternoon appointment at a children's hospital."

She gives her head a tiny shake and then moves gracefully toward the door. "I'm not dropping this subject, Stellan. We'll talk about it again as soon as your father is back from his trip."

I give her the most saccharine smile as I head back to my desk. "Have a nice afternoon, *Momse*."

She shoots me a glare, then opens the door and stalks out. The footman hovers at the door, looking anxious.

"Can I not be left alone?" I yell.

He goes pale, scurrying out of my sight. The throbbing headache I was getting earlier returns in full force. Rubbing my temples, I pace over to the window, looking out at the view absently.

I don't have control over so many things in my life. But this… picking a girl to marry… that is one of my few choices. I'm not insane enough to think that I will marry for love. But I'll be damned if I pick a random name off of a list that was approved by parliament.

I would rather stay unmarried forever than have marriage forced on me like that.

Turning my thoughts back to my father, I picture him in my mind's eye. He looks just like me, tall and dark haired with light blue eyes. Except there is a shock of silver in his hair, which mostly serves to make him seem even more refined.

Try as I might, I can't imagine him being ill. Distant? Sure. Quiet? Definitely.

But sick?

That thought just isn't compatible with the man I know. It just seems unlikely.

Which means that my grandmother is manipulating me. It's certainly far from the first time… but she was being honest about how much time she has devoted solely to me, to making sure I grow up as she wishes.

What would be the profit in driving me away with her endless questions of marriage unless… unless there really is something going on with my father?

A knock on the open door startles me from my morbid thoughts.

"Hey," Margot calls out softly.

I turn, narrowing my eyes. She's standing there, wearing her usual businesslike blazer and black work pants. Her pink hair is piled atop her head today, though several tendrils have already escaped to curl around her face.

Her mere presence makes my heart beat frantically against my ribs.

"Hey," I answer. I tilt my head. "Come here."

Her brows rise but she sets her ever-present tote bag down by the door and walks up to me. She stops when she's still two paces from me.

For some reason, that drives me fucking crazy.

Her tongue darts out to wet her lips as she peers up at me. Her eyes scan my face, trying to shuffle the puzzle pieces around, searching for some kind of explanation. "Are you okay?"

My lips tip up at the corners of my mouth. "I've been worse. I just had my grandmother here, reminding me of the plans she has made on my behalf."

Margot frowns. "What plans?"

I shrug. "Big life plans. It seems the closer I get to ruling this country, the less freedom I have in my own life. It's actually a bit funny."

She tucks a loose strand of her hair back behind her ear. "I see."

I give a dry chuckle. "No, I'm absolutely sure that you don't."

Her hand goes onto her hip, her eyes narrow. "There is no reason to be rude, Stellan. I thought we were getting along today."

Her posture is rebellious. There is something about the way she stands… no, the way she *is*… that calls out to me. My gaze slides down to her mouth.

A half-smile forms on my lips. "I like it when you're feisty. You know that?"

She gives a throaty laugh. "You've gone insane."

"No." I shake my head. "I'm just seeing the future in a certain light."

She gives me an odd look, wrinkling her nose. "What light? What are you— "

I stop her words by reaching a hand out and yanking her toward my body. Her eyes widen. Her palms fly up and land on my chest, resisting. Her lower body meets mine, pressing into me intimately.

It makes me crazed. I suck in a deep breath and catch her scent, honeysuckle and fresh laundry. My body responds without my brain; my cock grows hard, my skin tingles like it's about to catch fire.

"Stellan— "

I lean down, brushing my mouth against her gorgeously plump lips. I hear her sharp intake of breath, but I don't stop. No, I press my lips against hers, working my mouth in a delicate rhythm.

I can feel her heart beating beneath her skin.

For all her protests, she doesn't push me away. Quite the opposite. She pushes up onto her tiptoes and opens her mouth, letting her tongue dance with mine. She tastes so fucking good, like sugar and cinnamon and most of all, choice.

Kissing her is a kind of freedom, just in this moment. When she pulls away, her brow puckering, and looks up at me with those probing dark blue eyes…

I suddenly snap back to my senses, pushing her away roughly. "Fuck!"

"What was that?" she says, her fingertips going to trace her mouth.

I whirl, shaking my head and pacing back to the window. "Nothing. A moment of weakness."

My head pounds faintly. What exactly just happened between us?

"Should I—" she pauses, hesitating. "Maybe this is a bad time. Do you want me to come back?"

A laugh bubbles up from deep within. "I don't want anything from you, Margot."

A few seconds pass. "I should… I should come back later."

She turns and flees, her footsteps sounding as loud as gunshots on the hardwood floors. Grimacing, I rub my forehead.

Sensitivity to sound. I know all too well what that means. It's the first sign that I'm getting a migraine. Muttering a curse, I stalk from the room, heading to my private apartments to pull the shades and lie in silent misery.

CHAPTER 19

MARGOT

If this is the palace's attempt to impress me by introducing me to the glitzy, glamorous side of royalty... I have to say, it's working. I glance around the palace's garden, taking in everything: men in dark tuxedos, women in light-colored ballgowns, servants swooping by the guests with silver platters full of champagne. Everything else is a bright, vibrant green that speaks of how many hours the palace gardeners put into their upkeep.

The high hedges in the distance are immaculately maintained. The sun is just beginning to set and a million little fairy lights twinkle from where they have been hidden amongst the leaves. As I move around, the topiaries and fountains sprinkled here and there hide and reveal different groups of people.

I produce my notepad out of the secret pocket of my dress, jotting a few notes to myself.

At least three hundred people here that I can see; I wonder how many more are walking around, ducking behind the hedges, out of my line of sight.

I pause, my pen poised. Then I sigh and put my notepad away.

Ever-present, rising high in the background, is the palace. The tan brick façades and squat dark roofs look austere in comparison to the lively party fanning out in the palace's wake.

I feel more than a little out of place, even though I'm in a rented ballgown just the color of my hair. Feeling like a huge piece of salt-water taffy, I look down at my carefully beaded taffeta gown. I stand out from the crowd. Normally that's a good thing, but here…

Here I feel like even more of an outsider than usual.

A young woman in servant dress comes up to me with a tray of drinks, smiling a bit. "Champagne?"

"*Ja*, thanks." I pick up a flute off of the tray. The servant smiles and swishes off to the next group of people she sees. I sip the wine, wrinkling my nose at the tiny bubbles that burst on my tongue. It tastes awfully sweet.

I look around for a friendly face. Someone to talk to. Pippa assured me that she would be here, but as I sweep my gaze around the hedges and fountains, she's nowhere to be seen.

I do see someone I know, though. My mouth turns down at the corners. Standing on the far side of the party, chatting to a bunch of other guests in tuxes and ballgowns, is Anna. She glances my way and shoots me a wry grin.

Oh god. I have to move. Whirling away before she gets the idea to come over and bother me, I look around, lost. A large group of people catches my eye. I stalk toward them, spying a lovely statue of what appears to be a nymph playing a lyre.

As soon as I get close, I see Stellan standing apart from the large group, a slight frown on his handsome face. As I approach, he loosens his bowtie and pulls it off, stuffing it in his black tuxedo pocket. When he notices me, he smirks.

Something about that light blue gaze of his makes me blush and squirm. I hesitate.

Should I keep going? Or should I pretend that I didn't see him and just go somewhere else? Before I can make up my mind, he makes it up for me.

"Margot!" he calls. "Come here."

Making a face, I sigh and continue walking until I'm about two feet away. Then I stop; this is close enough. If I get closer, he might think that I am inviting his attentions again.

And I'm definitely not.

…right?

No, definitely not.

He gestures to the garden around us. "Welcome to our little soiree."

I chew on my lower lip and scan the garden. "Shouldn't you be talking to… well… everyone? I'm sure that almost everybody here wants some alone time with the heir to the throne."

He looks over to the big group, then shrugs. "They do. And I've given them what they wanted for the past hour. Now it's time for me to do what I want." He tilts his head. "Do you want to go on an adventure?"

I step closer, looking at him with a mixture of curiosity and skepticism. "I thought I was supposed to be here, swooning over how glamorous this whole party is?"

Stellan grins, sweeping his gaze over the garden area. "Are you impressed by this little get together? This is just a regular Thursday night."

My lips curl up at the corners. "Even if that's true, I'm not exactly dressed for an adventure."

He arches a brow, his gaze wandering down to my dress. He gives me a knowing smirk. "We'll be all right." He jerks his head toward the tall hedges. "Come."

I huff out a laugh as he turns away toward the maze. He just expects me to follow him. Then again, if I were born into royalty, wouldn't I expect the same?

I trail after him, picking up my pace when he disappears behind a tall hedge. Grabbing my dress, I jog after Stellan as best I can. As soon as I turn the corner, I stumble right into him.

My hands land on his hard abs. My eyes widen. I look up at him, my breath constricting. From this close, his ice blue eyes crackle. He bites his bottom lip, smirking a little as he grabs my upper arms to steady me.

"Careful," he says, righting me. "We wouldn't want a repeat of yesterday, would we?"

My brow wrinkles. I take step back, shaking my head. "What, when you randomly kissed me out of the blue? I had nothing to do with that, honestly."

He smiles ruefully. "You didn't exactly resist though, did you?"

I take a step back, smoothing my hands down the length of my dress. "I don't understand what's happening here. You have been cold and distant to me since I got here. Now you have done a complete one eighty and you want to talk about how we kissed yesterday?" I fold my arms across my chest. "You have to stop. You're giving me whiplash."

He turns away quickly, before I can see his expression. "I'm not trying to, Margot. Honestly." He starts moving away, deeper into the maze formed by the hedges. He glances back, but doesn't quite stop. "Are you coming?"

I swallow, then start after him. On my short legs, catching up to him actually proves quite a challenge. When I finally pull even with him, I glance up into his face. "Can I ask you some questions for my article?"

Stellan's lips thin. "Must you?"

My lips quirk. "Yes."

He slides me a look, slowing his pace. "All right."

I pull out my notepad, flipping through a couple of pages until I find the list of questions I came up with while I was doing research. Skimming the list, I choose a light topic to start.

"Your mother and father seem to be fairly busy people. Obviously." I blush. "What I mean to ask is, who did you grow up around while they were running the country?"

He frowns. "I had a whole swarm of educators and caretakers. And my grandmother was around, making a lot of the day to day decisions regarding my care. She still is, actually. Just yesterday she was here, pressing me about my private life." His lips lift at the corners. "She's bossy, but I don't mind. I think I inherited that from her."

I scrunch my face up. "That still sounds kind of lonely. Didn't you go to school?"

He sighs. "No. I was tutored privately. But once Erik was around, I never wanted for a friend."

My lips curl. "Yes, I can see that. You two are inseparable."

He stops, turning to face me. "What about you? Tell me about your childhood living in the Big Apple. Or… did you move to New York later in life?"

I give him an annoyed look. "We made it through one question about you. *One*. How am I supposed to write this article if you won't cooperate?"

He shrugs a shoulder. "You're not supposed to bore me to death, I'm pretty sure. My whole life has been documented. Photos were taken to mark each little milestone of my life. It's a part of the public record." He gives me a hard look. "I'm just trying to keep things interesting. I regurgitate sound bites about my life. You give me some of your story in return."

"What if I said that I wasn't interested in the same sound bites that you've been giving for your entire life?" I cock my head, challenging him. "I want the truth. Besides, if I write anything that is too sensitive, it will no doubt be caught by the press office."

A genuine smile plays across his mouth. "Fair enough. What I need to know is, will you be as honest in your answers as you are encouraging me to be?"

I roll my eyes. "Of course. I have nothing worth hiding."

A wrinkle of concern appears on his forehead. "So you say."

"Yes. So, to summarize: if I answer your questions, you'll answer mine."

He examines me for a moment, his eyes searching my face. "It's a deal."

Stellan holds out his hand. And I take it, shaking it firmly.

"Stellan!" a woman calls from the other side of the hedge. "Stellan, come tell everyone about your trip to Okinawa!"

He lets go of my hand and shakes his head. "I don't even know who that is." His lips curl down into a frown.

"Tomorrow, we'll go somewhere private and try to get most of your questions out of the way."

My eyebrows lift. "Okay…"

But he's heading away, already turning around a corner in the hedge maze. I frown after him. What am I supposed to make of our agreement? I have absolutely no idea.

But I do know that this is entirely new territory for me. I'm in a foreign land, at a freaking palace, trying to puzzle out a tall, dark, handsome enigma.

Nothing is familiar here, not anymore.

My office mandated cell phone buzzes in my pocket. It's a brand new iPhone, so new that I haven't even taken the plastic film off the screen yet. I slip it out of my pocket, frowning at the unknown number.

INTERNATIONAL NUMBER is splashed across the screen.

That could be anyone. An old colleague. A friend from New York. Or it could be a member of the American press. I haven't given anyone this number yet, but that doesn't mean anything in this day and age.

I let it go to voicemail, biting my lower lip. Then as soon as I get a notification of a new voice message, I press play and put it to my ear. I'm only half listening as I turn and head back to the party.

Mostly, I'm really hoping that Pippa is around. I spent an hour and a half getting myself ready for this event… I'd hate to just go back to the party and skulk around, wasting all my efforts.

When the voice mail finally plays, I almost drop my phone in surprise.

"Hi. It's your mother calling." There is a sound on the line, like the crinkling of a bag of potato chips. "I just found out that not only did you move out of the state, you frigging moved all the way across the ocean. I thought you said the last time we talked that we were going to keep in better touch with each other. Guess that doesn't matter to you though, does it?"

I break into a sweat. My mom always makes me so nervous. Even though I'm well past the age of having to worry about when and if she would ever show her face at home… it's hard to overcome a lifetime of that.

"Anyway," she continues. "Your little friend called me. What's her name? Abby? No… Something with an A. She said she had a lot of questions about you."

I pale. About me? An uneasy feeling slithers through my gut.

"I said I'd have to talk to you first." Mom smacks her lips. "I think you and me should talk, baby girl. Give me a call back quick, else I think I'm going to have to talk to that nice lady." She hangs up.

As I lower the phone, I realize that my hands are shaking. I haven't actually heard from my mom in almost a year. The last time we talked, she hit me up for money. *Again*.

And now some idiot reporter has unearthed her somehow?

Pippa's face appears around the corner of the hedge maze. "Hey! I have looked everywhere for you. Come on, there are people that I want you to meet."

Scrunching my face up, I nod. "Okay…"

I head back toward the party, but my mother looms large in the back of my mind, a specter of ill omens.

CHAPTER 20

STELLAN

I stand beside the gray gelding, petting him absently. Standing in this riding ring takes me back to my childhood days. The colors of the landscape, heather and green moss, dark colored earth and endless blue skies, all blending together seamlessly. The air here is full of strangely comforting scents: fresh cedar chips, sweet horse feed, the baser scent of horse dung.

I swear, nothing here has changed since I was a little boy, first learning to ride. The world around me back at the palace never seems to slow down. But out here, in the ivy-covered stables only a twenty minute helicopter ride from the palace?

It's just a whole different world. Time stands still. I think it's because everyone has to dress in riding gear. I'm currently wearing dark riding pants, a loose white button up, and knee-high boots almost shiny enough to see myself in.

Stroking Karl's muscular neck, I stare off into space and just... relax. Being who I am is not easy; everyone needs something from me, all the fucking time. Every minute of every day is jam-packed full of doing things to help other people.

I'm not complaining. But it's not often I get to zone out. Just... let my mind drift.

When Margot clears her throat gently, I tense up. My time is up, it seems.

I turn, eyeing her. My eyes widen a little bit. She's wearing the khaki jodhpurs and chestnut riding boots that were brought along for her... but on top, she wears a black t-shirt that reads The Smiths. Her riding pants are skintight. And her t-shirt is loose and full of holes, one especially large that shows off her neon pink bra.

God, why haven't I taken her riding before now?

She blushes under my inspection. "You are making me feel even more like an alien from another dimension than I did when I walked out of the changing room."

I shrug. "I can't help it if you look..." I pause, trying to think of how to word my thoughts diplomatically. "Eye catching."

Her eyes narrow to slits. "Cool it. Are we going riding or what?"

"*Ja, ja*. Look, the stable hand is bringing in the gentlest of our mares for you now." I point over to the fence, where a stable hand leads in a sleek-looking black horse. "Okay?"

Her expression remains full of uncertainty, especially when she's clambering on top of the horse. The stable hand helps her get into the saddle and then backs away, looking nervous. Not half as nervous as Margot looks, though…

Wide eyed, she clutches at the reins.

"You act as if you haven't ever been on a horse before," I chide her, mounting my horse.

Beneath her, the mare stands placidly. She looks at me as if I've grown a second head. "Of course I haven't!"

I raise my eyebrows. "Wait, really?"

"No! You think I'm joking about it?" Her expression darkens.

I guide my mount over to Margot, glancing over at her upright posture. "Relax your grip on the reins. Hold them like this."

I demonstrate, giving my horse a few inches of slack. She copies me, biting her lower lip. I reach over to her and correct her grip once, then smile. "There. Only pull back on the reins when you want the horse to slow or stop. And use your heels to encourage the horse to start moving. Like this."

I use my heels to nudge Karl forward. Using exaggerated motions, I demonstrate how I guide my horse. Margot's brow puckers, but she follows my movements. Soon, she guides the horse around the ring, successfully starting and stopping a few times.

"Come on." I jerk my head to the horizon. "Let's go out of the ring, into the wild. We'll go on a really easy ride, okay?"

She looks at me with terrified eyes, but she doesn't back down. She just swallows. "Okay."

Margot is clearly afraid but she's not going to let a little worry keep her from trying something new. God help me, but that's the most attractive thing she's done yet. I grin at her, nudging my horse toward the gate.

The stable hand opens the gate, standing aside to let both of us pass. I grin back at Margot as I ride. Her expression is really delightful, part suspicion, part fright, part determination. I lead her down a gentle hill, just as slow as the horses want to take it.

"Wouldn't Hunter S. Thompson be proud of you right now?" I tease.

She glances over at me, a puzzled frown on her face. "Who?"

"You know, the guy who wrote *Leaving Las Vegas*. He invented gonzo journalism. He rode with biker gangs, ran for office, and did a ton of drugs."

"Ah," she says, chuckling. "Yeah, I recognize the name now. I feel like he'd take one look at me right now and die laughing. This isn't exactly gonzo journalism."

"No?" I ask, grinning. "I don't know… You are obviously out of your element, but you're keeping your shit together."

She makes a face. "Maybe. We'll see." She looks out at the surrounding landscape, pursing her lips. "I have to say, it's quite pretty out here. What is that sort of gray plant with purplish blossoms that is growing everywhere here? It just looks like there are endless fields of it."

My lips twitch. "Heather."

Margot looks at me, her slender brows rising. "Really? It's awfully beautiful."

I nod, adjusting in my saddle. "*Ja*. There is a famous Danish song about seeing the waves of heather underneath the rolling blue skies…" Eyeing her, I shrug. "During the summer, it is so nice here."

She slides me a look. "What about during the winter?"

I wrinkle my nose. "The snow is very pretty. It can be breathtaking, in a brutal sort of way. But *ja*, the snow gets old after a few days."

"Same thing in New York. Except it is much hotter there during the summer. There's no air from July until nearly September. Stifling is the word, I think."

Pulling gently on Karl's reins, I drop back so that Margot and I can walk two abreast. She shoots me a hasty smile. "What? Am I doing something wrong?"

I shake my head. "No. I just want to be able to see your face while we're talking." I smirk. "You know that everything you are thinking is spelled out by your expressions, *ja?*"

She sends me a tiny scowl. "It is not."

"Yes, it is." I shrug. "When I was younger, maybe age seven or eight years old, I had acting classes. My instructor was a very old French man named Monsieur Bernard. And Monsieur Bernard would make us all dress up and stand in a line to be inspected." I smile, huffing a laugh. "Little kings and queens, he called us. Even Erik, though I think he knew that Erik was common. Monsieur Bernard always said that it is very important for the family of the king to learn to control their faces at all times."

Margot looks a little surprised at that. "Really? That's... interesting. Most parents would be afraid that their children might hide things from them, I would imagine."

I look out at the horizon, squinting. "You don't know my family, Margot. They are not like anyone else's family."

Her nose wrinkles a little. I fully expect her to ask when she will meet my father and mother, to say that it is an important part of her article or whatever. But she doesn't.

"No," she says, her full mouth flattening. "It would be weird to expect the royal family to function the same as everyone else, I guess."

I study her, wondering what she's thinking that makes her mouth turn down at the corners. "What about you?"

She looks up at me. "What?"

"You never answered my question yesterday. Did you grow up in New York City?"

"Ah." She looks down at the reins in her hands. "Yeah. I was born and raised in Brooklyn. It was…" She laughs to herself under her breath. "It was basically the opposite of growing up here, I think. That's what I'm gathering, anyway."

"What do you mean?" I ask casually.

Her resulting smile is a little bitter. "I didn't have anything as a kid. And I don't mean I didn't have a palace and a fleet of jets. I mean…" Her cheeks turn red. She pauses, then shakes her head. "I was just brought up differently, that's all."

I shrug. "Almost everyone grew up differently than I did."

She tilts her head, cocking an eyebrow. "Have you ever thought about finding someone who was raised in the same way? I mean, I know you are being pressured to pick someone to marry…"

Rolling my eyes, I shake my head. "Nope. Not interested."

"In talking about it, or doing it?"

I pin her with a stare. "Either. Now come on."

Digging my heels into my horse, I take off like a shot. And Margot isn't far behind, nudging her horse into a gallop and letting out a whoop of fear and excitement.

For just a moment, I let go of everything extraneous. Worries about my father's health, heavy thoughts about becoming the ruler of Denmark, constant needling about choosing a wife.

Right now, in just this moment, Margot and I are just two people flying far and fast, all the rest of Copenhagen and it's concerns be damned.

CHAPTER 21

MARGOT

"And let us not forget the children for whom we raise this money…" Stellan says, smiling into the microphone. He's in his usual dress of a richly-cut navy suit and a crisp white button up, standing behind a podium before a ballroom of people.

I'm staring at him from the sidelines, my cellphone in my hand, recording the whole thing. Still I look at him, at how he draws the attention of the entire room.

Elegant. Coiffed. Handsome.

You can say a great deal about his other attributes, including his often-oafish personality. But I look at his dark hair, his light blue eyes, his cheekbones chiseled from granite…

A person really can't find fault with his physical appearance, is what I am thinking. My cheeks warm, but I don't look away.

I watch him talking to the audience in his native tongue, something that is still foreign to me. He speaks quickly but assuredly, his voice honeyed as it glides over the alien-sounding syllables. I bite my lip, thinking to myself that I have to learn Danish sooner or later.

That is, if I stay here in Copenhagen after the article is published. All of that is a little too far into the future, murky at best.

My attention wanders: the ballroom we are in is in downtown Copenhagen, not owned by the royal family from what I can tell. The ceilings are soaring, the decoration ornate. Everything that I've seen so far in this hotel is done up in silver and black, in the style of jazz age era hotels. There's even an old gramophone; I saw it as I entered, segregated from the rest of the room with slinky red ropes.

"Thank you!" Stellan finishes his speech and the small crowd of businesspeople applaud wildly. As cameras flash, I roll my eyes just a bit.

No wonder he has such a huge ego. If everyone clapped every time I gave a speech about anything, I would probably have a big head too.

I see Stellan searching the crowd for me a second before his gaze meets mine. Blushing a little, I smooth my hands down yet another rented ballgown. This one is strapless and snow white, with a white length of taffeta meant to be worn as a wrap.

I slip my phone into my tote bag just as Stellan reaches me. He's riding high on the applause, his cheeks still pink, his smile still brilliant.

"What did you think of my speech?" he asks. His Danish accent is more pronounced just now, I suppose from speaking his mother tongue only moments ago.

I lick my lips, darting my eyes away from his face. "I think I still need to learn Danish."

He shakes his head at me, repressing an eye roll. Behind him, a five piece quartet starts playing jazz standards. "Want to see something cool?"

Clearing my throat, I manage a smile. "Always."

Stellan makes a pleased sound deep in his throat, almost a growl, but lacking the heat of anger. He grabs my elbow and starts towing me out of the ballroom. "Come. You're going to like this."

I bite my lower lip. "Am I going to be able to take notes?"

He pulls me out into the darkened marble hallway, shaking his head just a little. "I would rather you didn't. I'm celebrating tonight. You should be too."

I give a huffed laugh. "What are you celebrating, exactly?"

He shrugs. "What does it matter?"

My lips curve up. "Touché."

He guides me to the grand elevators, pressing the button to call it to our floor. I cock my head, looking at our reflection in the elevator doors. Stellan is so big and tall, so darkly handsome. I am so petite next to him; with my bubble gum pink hair and my white ball gown, I look as though I am made of marzipan candy.

What would he be, if we were both made of sugar? Perhaps some bitter black licorice, or some sort of molasses drops. Not the kind of candy most people would want to gorge themselves on, anyway...

I hear raised voices and turn my head. Stellan does too. Down the hall, Annika comes rushing out of some darkened room, her expression stormy. She says something cutting in Danish, holding her purple ball gown skirts up.

What is she running from?

My question is answered only a second later when Erik steps out into the hallway, reaching out and catching her by the arm. He spins her around to face him as if she weighs nothing.

She looks mad enough to spit at him. He leans his dirty blond head close to her ear. His words are too low to make out; from this distance, I only get the low grate of his voice.

"Erik!" Stellan shouts.

As one, Erik and Annika freeze, then turn to look at us. Annika steps away, wresting her arm from Erik's grip. Erik clears his throat and then calls down to us.

"We were just having a disagreement about…" He pauses. "Suitable choices."

Annika leans over and pushes his shoulder hard. "And I was telling him that he can't tell me what to do!"

She screws up her face and stalks away from all of us, vanishing around a corner. I see a look of concern slide between Stellan and Erik.

"Er alt i orden?" Stellan asks.

Erik shrugs. *"Ja. Vær ikke urolig."*

Before I can ask Stellan to translate, Erik takes off down the hall after Annika. I watch Stellan's face and catch a suspicious look rippling across it, but in the next second he turns back toward the elevators. He presses the button again, impatient.

"What was that all about?" I ask. The elevator doors slide open and we step inside.

He presses the button for the top floor and shakes his head. "I have no idea. My sister has always been dramatic. Erik has always been… I don't know, whatever the opposite of that is."

The doors close. Stellan runs his hand through his hair, using his reflection in the elevator doors to groom himself. I fidget nervously, wondering where we are going.

As the elevator car rises, I look at Stellan. "What are we gathered here for? Tonight, I mean. All the fancy people downstairs in the ballroom."

He swings his gaze to me. "Is it going to end up in your article?"

Sighing, I give my head a gentle shake. "Not if you don't want it to."

The elevator slows. He brushes off his tux. "We raised several million krone for my homeless youth outreach program. I am pleased, to say the least."

The surprise must be evident on my face, because he looks at me with a chuckle. "Oh, come now. If there's one thing the royal family is good at, it's fundraising for charities."

The doors roll open to a little lobby. Stepping out, I see a luxurious restaurant to the right, people in their evening attire chatting and drinking, waiters circling with refills. I start to walk that way but Stellan stops me with a hand on my inner elbow.

"No, no." He pulls me the other way. "Come on."

He walks to a stairwell and opens the door for me. I head where he directs, up the stairs to where the stairwell dead ends at a dark metal door. When I look back at him, he jerks his head to the door.

"Open it."

I push the door open and step out into a little area no bigger than a closet. To my surprise I'm greeted by the night sky full of stars overhead. I move forward just a little to a railing. Looking down, I can't keep from gaping.

"You can see the entire city from here!" I gasp. I look back at Stellan, who grins at my reaction. "I can see the palace from here. Oh! And the *Politiken* offices are right over there... which means..." I consider the cityscape, then point. "I think Pippa's apartments are that direction."

He steps forward, pressing himself against the balcony railing. "I think her apartment is over that way, actually."

I shoot him a puzzled look. "Why would you know?"

He grins at me, his eyes dancing. "Because I know. Pippa's been friends with our family for years. Does that soothe the jealous monster within?"

Yes, a little. I stick out my tongue at him. "I'm not jealous, Jealousy is for the rich. Me? I'm just trying to figure out how I'm going to scrape by."

He smirks, running his gaze up and down my body. "You're doing all right, if I had to guess. Except that your top half seems to want to be free of your ballgown..."

My mouth opens. A little sound of displeasure comes out as I quickly adjust the top of my ballgown. "It's a rented gown, okay? My boobs don't stand a chance of actually fitting in this thing." I scowl at the grin that spreads across his face. "Quit looking at my tits!"

He leans a little closer, biting his lip. Only now do I realize that he's almost close enough to touch me. My pulse starts speeding up as I look up into his face.

"And what if I don't want to stop looking?" he taunts.

My mouth goes dry. I'm suddenly aware of my hands. What should I do with them? I slip them in my pockets as my gaze slips down from his ice blue eyes to his perfect, soft-looking lips.

He breathes a little harder than usual. When I look back up to his eyes, I can tell his pupils have dilated a bit.

He wants me. I can feel it. There is something in the air, something occupying the space between us.

Say something. Tell him you want him, I think.

"I— "

The moment is shattered by his phone ringing. His eyes widen and he straightens, giving himself a shake. He reaches into his pocket and looks at the screen, then shrugs one shoulder.

"I should take this. I'll see you later, maybe."

Stellan whirls and puts the phone to his ear, pulling the door open. *"Hej ja ja - nej du forstyrre ikk."*

I sigh, looking back out over the amazing cityscape, wondering *what if?*

CHAPTER 22

STELLAN

After a record number of photo ops, meet and greets, and charity galas, I find myself fucking exhausted. Not just exhausted, actually... I feel like I'm on the verge of getting sick. I've done too much over too small of a window of time.

It's time to retreat from sight.

I text Erik letting him know that I am going to get away for the weekend. He should cancel all my plans, at least until Monday. He responds quickly.

I'll let Fredensborg Palace know that they should expect to see you. Will Margot be going with you as well?

My eyebrows rise. I hadn't thought to bring her... but I can't see the harm.

Yes, I answer. *Call her if you would. And send a car to pick her up. I'm going to drive myself.*

His response is instant. *Ja, okay.*

An hour later, when I pull up in Fredensborg's curved drive, Margot stands waiting. I take my helmet off and admire the way her pink hair looks against Fredensborg's white stucco walls and green metal roof. She gives me her most aloof look, running her hand over her short black dress.

She looks like a little pink meringue on a dessert plate. My mouth curves up. I stride over to her.

She looks less than pleased to see me. "Why am I here? I'm supposed to be having an evening off, according to the schedule your press office gave me."

I shrug. "You're here to keep me entertained."

Margot glances up at the darkening sky. "Why are we here, though? You could've asked me to come anywhere in Copenhagen. No need to drag me all the way out here." She wrinkles her nose and glances at the palace behind her. "Not that the scenery isn't majestic or anything…"

"Stop whining," I command. "Follow me."

Stalking straight ahead, I climb Fredensborg's stone steps, entering the palace itself. Two butlers and two maids await me in the grand foyer, curtsying low. I look back at Margot, who is following me with a frown.

"Hurry," I say, waving her on. "This way."

I turn right, down an echoing marble hallway. The butlers trail after Margot, as if they are unsure what I could be up to. No one will be left hanging for long, though.

I stop outside of two double doors, swinging them open to reveal my grandfather's rather large billiards room. There are three red felt pool tables by the far wall. Two long bookcases line the back wall. Standing guard by the fireplace are a taxidermized bear and panther, both posed as if they were about to attack.

As a little boy, those figures both terrified and delighted me in equal measure.

A distinguished bar made of polished cedar sits to my far left. And to my right, there are several couches and chaise recliners made out of red velvet. The walls of the room and the windows are draped in a dark green fabric.

It looks like the Great Gatsby threw up in here, but this room called my name when I thought about where I might spend some downtime. And when Margot steps inside, her eyes widen with awe.

"Oh my god," she breathes. She glances at me. "Is this place for real?"

"Yep." I take my leather jacket off and sling in onto an ottoman on my way to the bar. "Would you like a drink?"

She's not really listening. "Sure, whatever is fine," she murmurs. "God, it's like something out of a Hemingway novel in here."

She runs her hand over the smooth cedar bar top, taking it all in, her tone one of hushed awe.

Pulling a couple of glasses out from the little cabinet below the bar, I smile at her words. "I think my grandfather and Mr. Hemingway knew one another. In fact, I bet that if we went over to the library, there are some signed first editions in there."

She whirls, pinning me with a stare. "Shut. Up."

I cock a brow at her. "No."

"Ugh!" she says, throwing up her hands. As she turns away, looking at the bookshelves that are in here, I smile. She leans over and comes very close to showing me her panties. As a matter of fact, I think I catch a glimpse of them while I pop the cork on a bottle of champagne.

They're pink and lacy, just as I hoped they would be. If she knew that I could see them I doubt she would like it… so I bite my lip, not breathing a word about it. In fact, I think she'd yell at me for looking at her ass.

Why spoil such a good thing for myself?

"Who picked these books?" she asks. She straightens and turns, biting her lip as I walk over to her.

I hand her a coupe glass of champagne. "Here."

Margot accepts it, taking a sip. "Mm. Thanks."

I throw her a smile, then take my own glass of champagne over to one of the couches. I lie down on it, kicking my feet up. "I think my grandfather picked the books."

She comes over, sitting on the same couch, but at the other end. I take the liberty of putting my feet in her lap. She makes a face and slides my feet to the floor.

"Hey!" I protest. I can't suppress a grin though.

"Your grandfather had pretty strange taste. There's a whole section of transcendental poetry wedged in there."

My eyes find her face. "I have no idea what that means."

A huff of laughter escapes her. "Neither does anybody else, so don't feel bad."

I cock my head at her. "You're really smart, aren't you?"

She turns red and rolls her eyes. "Shut up."

"No. I mean it. Who the fuck has ever heard of transcendental poetry? And I've heard you call me privileged for growing up with private tutors, but you haven't exactly missed any references. You are actually, genuinely smart."

She covers her face with her hands. "Oh my god. A change of topic was needed like... *yesterday*."

Smirking, I shrug. "Okay. Tell me one thing I wouldn't guess about you just from looking at you."

Margot peeks out from behind her hands, then relents. She drops her hands, still blushing but looking thoughtful. "Umm... Ooh. I like pop music. I mean, not all pop music. But like... Billie Eilish? I know every single one of her songs by heart."

I chuckle. "I wouldn't have guessed that."

She sips her champagne, sneaking a look at me. "Now you."

I pull my feet up again, this time resting them on her thigh. She scrunches up her face but doesn't try to remove them. I consider that a win.

"I play polo."

"Ugh, I could've guessed that. I need something good."

I wag my finger at her. "You didn't let me finish. I play polo, but only because one of my charities asks me to every year. And every fucking year, I get my ass beat. I'm ridiculously bad at it."

She laughs. "All right, you win. At this game, not at polo. Because you apparently *suck* at polo."

I sigh dramatically. "You wouldn't understand. You're *common*."

Apparently, that was the wrong thing to say, because she stops laughing. Instead, she fixes me with a frown. "I don't like the way you say that. *Common*. Like there's something wrong with everyday people. Why don't you realize that we are what is normal? It's you guys, the top one percent of the one percent… you're fucking weird."

Taking several gulps out of my glass, I pin her with a stare. "Maybe. Then again, I'm not putting on airs. I'm not pretending to be something I'm not, hanging out with people I wouldn't normally meet. That's *you*."

Margot sits up straight, looking at me with a puzzled frown. "You get that I'm only here because my job told me to be, right? It's important to me that you understand that."

I roll my eyes and put my feet down on the floor. "This conversation has gotten very boring all of the sudden."

Standing up, I upend my glass of champagne into my mouth and slurp it down. When I look back at her, she has this wounded look on her face, like I'm the one who is being a bully.

I'm not.

Am I?

"Come on," I say, nodding my head to the door. "Let's explore the palace. I bet you I can count at least six blades hanging on various walls."

She wrinkles her nose but gets to her feet, following me around through room after room. She's gone quiet.

And that's no good, because I like it when she's a noisy rebel. Instead, she nods and soaks up information. No matter how I try to encourage her wild side to come out, she's retreated somewhere, put up walls that I haven't seen before.

"Come onnnnnnn," I prod her, walking down yet another marble hallway. Fat cherubs look down on me from the corners, seeming disappointed in me. "It's just a swimming pool. You don't need a suit…"

She stops in her tracks, whirling to face me. "What is your deal, Stellan?"

I pause, my mind turning over the possibilities of what she could mean. "My deal?"

"Hot or cold? Hmm? Which one do you want to be today? The friendly guy who teases me about skinny dipping in the palace pool? Or are you the jerk who likes rubbing my nose in the fact that I'm not royal?" She cocks her hip, fury written all over her face. "If you could just let me know, that would be great. It's nice to have some idea of when I should be strait-laced and when I should cut loose."

One corner of my mouth curls up. "I would love to see you cut loose. Is that an option?"

Her eyes narrow. "You know what? Hold that thought. Let's go somewhere that you don't have the home turf advantage."

I squint. "The what?"

She holds up a finger and stalks away, putting her phone out and fiddling with it.

And that's when it hits me. This big, huge wave of warmth, of happiness, of pleasure.

Oh god.

I like Margot.

I like her even more when she's a little bit cruel to me.

I *like* her when she's mean.

How did this happen to me?

She puts the phone to her ear, speaking softly into it. And all I can think is how fucked I am if she finds out how I feel. It's hard enough right now as it is…

Margot spins, her eyes lighting up. She hangs up the phone, practically bristling with excitement. "Get your coat. We're going out."

And I just nod like an idiot, trying to smash my feelings down into a hole deep inside. I can't act on them. So why does being with Margot make me so… well, *happy* isn't quite the right word, is it? I turn back toward where I left my coat, swallowing against the knot forming in my throat.

CHAPTER 23

STELLAN

As Margot leads the way past the bouncer and into the loud, crowded club, she looks back at me. The lights flash, illuminating streaks that splash across her glitter-covered face. I tug on the dark hooded sweatshirt she made me change into. She grins, reaching back and pulling my hood up a little further to better hide my distinctive features.

I grab her hand and frown. I lean close to her to make myself heard over the loud music. "Where are we?"

She pins me with her gaze. "Somewhere you won't be expected to be. Come on."

Turning, she leads me into the bar area. The bar top is made of thick plastic and lit up neon green. It casts a sickly light over all the patrons crowded around, waiting for their turn to order drinks. Ahead of us, I can see people pushing their way into what I assume is the main dance floor. The DJ booth is in the far corner; rock music plays so loudly that it reverberates through my bones.

This atmosphere is familiar to me. Grungy, underground, yet exceedingly packed with people. Just like New York, although maybe this club is a little bit cleaner.

A very little bit.

As we line up at the bar to wait for service, I brushes up against her. I leans down to her ear.

"Have you been here before?" I ask.

She shakes her head, looking up at me with a crooked smile. "Nope."

"And why are we here again?"

"The same reason you are concealing your identity. This is a neutral place. Your money doesn't mean anything here." She smirks.

I frown and open my mouth to respond, but she just turns away. The scruffy bartender comes over and she leans close to his ear, ordering drinks. He plops two beers on the counter and she pays for them.

She turns to me, plastic cups in each hand. "Here."

She hands me my beer and then heads away from the bar, elbowing her way through the crowd as she moves toward the main room. I take a sip of my beer and find it stale but cold. Shaking my head, I follow her as she weaves through the young, hip crowd. There are actually several people in this room with unnatural hair colors, but she's the only one with her unique frothy pink color.

Against her pale skin and dark little dress, it really pops.

When she finds a place that calls to her, she turns with a grin. She takes a long swig from her red solo cup, throwing up her free hand and swaying along to the insistent beat.

I take a long pull of my beer and shuffle my feet around, hoping she doesn't realize how much I feel like a fish out of water just now. She grins and grabs a fistful of my hooded sweatshirt, pulling me toward her.

I slide my free hand around the small of her back, touching my hips to hers. She bites her lip and sways against me, her eyes meeting mine. I see a teasing sort of amusement reflected there.

The song changes tempos, slowing down just a bit. I give her a smirk and lean down close to her ear.

"You are playing with fire," I tell her.

"Who, me?" she says, sliding her arms around my neck. "I don't know what you mean. Usually I'm so *cautious*."

I shake my head a little, smiling down at her. "You are dangerous."

All the while our bodies move together, almost grinding against each other, but not quite. Her small hips fit neatly against mine; my big hands splay out over her lower back. Our bellies press together but I'm hardly aware of that.

No, I'm sucked into her dark blue eyes, full of mischief and daring. We dance like that for another half a minute, then the DJ changes out music again, something faster this time.

Margot puts some space between us and rocks out, her hands going up, her movements rhythmic. Her eyes are closed, her pink hair glowing under the low light, the neckline of her dress dipping low to show off a scant quarter inch of her bright pink bra.

After another few songs, I'm staring at her like I'm a man dying of thirst and she's the only refreshing sip of water left in my canteen. I'll admit it; I'm starting to be obsessed with the way that she shakes her hips, the way that her chest rises when she breathes, the plump bow of her lips in relation to her heart shaped face. She slows down, jerking her head to the bar.

"I need another beer. Wanna come with?"

My lips lift. "Sure."

When she turns and walks away, I follow. I'm staring at her perfect ass and amazing legs as long as I can before it disappears behind other people who cross between us. Margot glances back at me, giving me a knowing smile.

God *damn*.

I find myself walking a little faster to catch up with her. She queues up, trying to pull out her wallet again. I make a face at her.

"Put your fucking wallet away," I grit out.

She wrinkles her nose. "I'm just trying to be egalitarian about getting us beers."

I lean in close, pushing the hood of my sweatshirt down off my head. "I'm the fucking crown prince of Denmark. The idea of you trying to get even with me by buying me beers is laughable."

Margot shrugs, rolling her eyes, but there is still a trace of a smile on her lips. "Whatever makes you happy, your highness."

A blonde girl in front of us overhears a little of our conversation. Turning her head, she checks out Margot, who absolutely looks like she belongs here in this club. When the blonde looks at me, her eyebrows go up. She does a double take, squinting, trying to place me.

Shit.

I turn away, raising my hood. The last thing I need tonight is getting spotted here, and with Margot to boot. Luckily, a few seconds later the bartender comes and asks for our orders. After we grab more beers, we head to an ill-lit corner away from the blaringly loud music.

There aren't any tables here as such. It's just a single long red leather booth that contours to the walls, worn and torn and covered in graffiti. Margot plops herself down on the seat beside a few young guys that look at her with wide eyes.

They probably think that their dream girl just came over to make their whole lives a little better. Shooting them a quelling glare, I find a seat beside her and stretch out my long legs.

Margot sizes me up, one corner of her mouth kicking up. She looks almost impish, sitting there so petite and so clearly amused.

"What?" I ask, sipping my beer.

She shrugs, smiling as she tastes her beer. "For an obscenely rich person, you're pretty okay, I guess."

I sputter, spitting some foam back inside my red solo cup. She grins at my reaction, wiggling her eyebrows.

"So you're saying I'm not horrible?" I laugh, wiping foam from my nose.

"I'm saying that you have your moments," she says, rolling her eyes. "You also have moments where you act like a rich spoiled brat."

"What? No way, I'm a lot more grounded than you think. I mean, considering my unique set of circumstances, the fact that I can hang out here is like… amazing."

She cocks a brow. "I admire you less for it because we're talking about it. Like I just lost maybe… five percent of the esteem that you gained in my eyes."

I chuckle. "That's good to know." I tilt my head to the side. "So not terrible and handsome. Is that all you think about me?"

She turns bright pink. "Who said I think you're handsome?"

Squinting at her, I set my beer by my feet. "Unless you've changed drastically since New York City, I would say that you did. It was implied when we fucked."

Margot shakes her head and rolls her eyes. "We didn't fuck. We did… other stuff."

I bite my lip, unprepared for the influx of mental images that spring to mind.

Margot giving me the naughtiest look as she drops to her knees. The way her hair felt against my fingers as she took me in her mouth. The way I spread her wide open and tongued her clit, over and over, soaking up every rich drop of pleasure that I could wring from her flesh.

I'm already hard for her. Leaning over, I brush her gossamer hair back. Then I lean in close so that my lips almost touch her ear.

"What, oral sex isn't fucking now?" I grate out.

She sips her beer coolly and glances away, but I can see her blush. "I stand behind my statement."

The second I lift up my hand to touch her, a static electricity starts to build in the air. Sliding my hand around to cup her jaw, I turn her to face me. I use my thumb to angle her head just so.

Margot looks back at me, her deep blue eyes pinning me in place. God, I could just look at her like this, in this moment, forever.

But her gaze slides down to my mouth. She sucks her bottom lip between her teeth, pink clashing with the white or her teeth. My ring finger slips over the pulse point in her neck.

Her heart races. I lean in, brushing my lips over hers. Her pulse jumps and she lifts her hand to my hoodie, fisting it tightly in her grip. I start to pull back, but she follows me, ghosting another kiss over my lips.

I growl into her mouth, my hands shifting Margot half out of her seat. She surges forward and I'm ready for her, kissing her. I slide my hand down between her legs, making her gasp. Then I fucking feast on her, dominating the exchange, groaning as I sweep the inside of her sweet fucking mouth with my tongue.

I groan. She tastes like stale beer laid over something indescribably delicate and sweet. Margot nips at my bottom lip when I give her the chance. I growl again, picturing exactly how she will look naked and writhing against my pillows.

God damn, she is so fucking hot.

But then she pulls back, breathing hard, her eyes darting back and forth across my face. "Stellan…" she whispers, biting her lip. "This? You and me? It's not a good idea."

I give my head a shake and try to kiss her again, but she shoves me off. "I said no. I know that's not something you're used to…"

"You want me," I say, trying to keep the accusations from my voice. I splay one big hand across her heart and pin her with my gaze. "I know you do. I can feel your heart race every time I fucking touch you."

Margot rises to her feet, surveying me as smoothly as any queen would look at a peasant groveling at her feet. "I think I'm going to go dance."

She picks up her beer from the floor and then walks off without so much as another word. I'm left sitting in the uncomfortable bench and scowling to myself.

Margot is being a total dick about this. She's probably right about it being a bad idea, but that doesn't make me feel any better.

As I lurch upward, heading after her, I catch the sneers that the young guys next to me are sending my way. I lean over, purposely using my height and sheer size.

"Fuck off," I growl.

Then I grab my beer and stomp off after Margot, my brain still doing cartwheels, trying to figure out what just happened between us.

CHAPTER 24

⚜

MARGOT

I step off the luxurious private jet onto the tarmac, pulling my sunglasses onto my face. Kristiansund spills out beneath my view like an inky puddle; I can see the coastline spreading out a couple of miles down from where I'm standing, bright green grass meeting the cobalt blue sea. In the distance, I can make out yellow and red and white cottages.

This looks like a sleepy little fishing village.

I shiver against the wind. We're so far north in Norway that the weather is quite brisk. The flight attendant is right behind me with my bags. I try to take them at the bottom of the stairs.

"Here, let me help," I offer.

I can immediately tell from the puzzled look on his face that I'm not actually supposed to take my bags. When he speaks, his English sounds clipped. He's Finnish or Norwegian, maybe.

"Let me take them over to the car for you," he says, smiling despite his bafflement. In his tidy-looking steward's uniform, he is the very picture of propriety right now.

"Right," I mutter, trailing along behind him. Raising my eyes to the limousine that awaits me, I allow myself to be ushered into the back. "Thank you!" I manage to call to the steward.

He tilts his head and a vaguely disapproving expression appears on his face. He inclines his head. "Have a pleasant journey, Miss Keane."

I never even got his name.

That's what I think about while the limo takes me down into the village, down cobbled streets as little white and yellow houses zoom by my view. That, and how I got here.

The note is still in my tote bag.

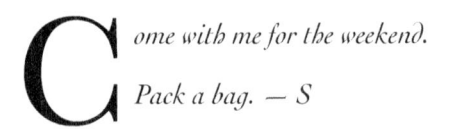

Come with me for the weekend.
Pack a bag. — S

Five hours later, feeling remarkably hassled even though I was just on a *private jet*, here I am. The limousine pulls to a halt outside of an adorable little red cottage and I get out, heaving a sigh.

Stellan called. He's my assignment.

That's the reason I came. The *only* reason. After parting ways the other night, I didn't hear from him for five days. Five interminably long days.

I wasn't entirely sure I would hear from him ever again, period. And yet here Stellan is, opening the door when I knock. He smiles coolly, stepping back and welcoming me in.

"Come on," he says, his lips carefully pursed. "Don't let all the heat out."

My nose twitches at the tone of his voice; he sounds commanding, not inviting. Heaving another sigh, I walk into a cozy, bright kitchen area. It's all done in teal and baby pink, a decorator after my own heart.

The driver leaves my bags by the door and leaves without a word. Stellan just skirts around the marble kitchen island and heads out of the room. I hate when he expects me to follow him without asking any questions.

Grinding my teeth, I trail his wake into a living area. Sunlight spills into the room from a window that stretches almost from one wall to the other. A bright white couch sits against the wall to my far right, piled high with cozy-looking afghans and soft pillows. To my left is a little table that doubles as a chess board and two chairs pulled up to it.

Straight ahead, I can see that there is a hallway, probably containing the bedrooms and the bathroom. Stellan is already throwing himself onto the couch, so I pull one of the chairs out. Sitting down, I cock my head at him. "So?"

He squints. "So what?"

A huffed laugh leaves me. "I'm here. You summoned me after putting me on the back burner for most of the week. Now what?"

He scrubs a hand through his hair. "Honestly? I don't have any plans. I just had a really busy week, so..." He shrugs one shoulder. "That's the only reason I didn't call you sooner."

I narrow my eyes and cross my arms. "So your sudden coolness has nothing to do with the fact that you kissed me last week?"

He looks tiredly out the window, sighing. "No, Margot. I don't understand you, really. You reject my advances... but still you expect me to treat you like a friend, as opposed to a nosy fucking reporter." He peers at me. "Which you are, by the way." He stands up suddenly, looking fierce. "That's what you want, isn't it? To be my friend?"

"Yes." I uncross my arms and sit forward, leaning my elbows on my knees. "Stellan..." When he looks over at me, I take a steadying breath. "You realize that I'm just trying to keep us both safe, right? I'm attracted to you. You are attracted to me. And that would be good enough if you were anyone else. But... you're not. You're the crown prince of fucking Denmark."

Stellan looks at me, his ice blue eyes threatening to pierce me through to the core. "You don't think I know that? You don't think I'm aware of that every fucking second of every single day? No one will let me forget it."

I falter. He seems to be in pain. Or maybe it's just a weariness that comes with carrying the burden of being the prince. I don't know which.

"I'm sorry, Stellan. I really am." Sitting back in the wooden chair, I watch him recompose his facial expression. He wipes away all the traces of sadness. What's left is a face I recognize all too well.

He looks remote. Withdrawn. Untouchable.

My fingers itch with the need to touch him, to tell him that things will be okay. Even though I know that saying that might just be a pretty, comforting lie.

I have less control over this situation than anybody else, honestly.

He turns to me, changing the subject as if the entire conversation before now simply never happened. "Do you want to go for a walk? Maybe we could go down by the shoreline. There is a little restaurant there that I always patronize whenever I am here."

"Are you sure you wouldn't rather stay here and talk some more?" I ask.

He pins me with his gaze. "I couldn't be more certain." He heads to the hallway in the back, leaving me to bite my lip and wonder what exactly is going on in his head. Is he still upset about the other night?

Or is he really just switching tracks like he changed subjects?

Stellan reappears, zipping a light raincoat up over his dark wool sweater. He eyes me in my dark leather jacket, short black skirt, and neon pink tights. "Are you going to be warm enough?"

I scowl at his question. "I'm fine."

"Okay." He shrugs. "Come on, then."

He strides out of the room and through the kitchen, making me scurry to keep up with him. He's out of the door and into the cool air in seconds. I follow, shivering a little at the shock of going from the warmth of the house out into the chilly atmosphere.

Stellan turns back and sees me shiver. His eyes narrow. "I told you."

I grit my teeth and stick my hands in my pockets. "It's fine. Keep leading the way, like you always do."

He squints at me, then casts a look around the cobblestone street we are on. "Yeah, all right. Whatever that means. Come on, will you?"

I start marching downhill and Stellan falls in beside me. His eyes are on the horizon as we walk. I look at the green grass and the brown shoreline, only a quarter of a mile away. They are fitted so snugly with the blue-black ocean, each affecting the other's shaping.

At length, I scrunch my face up and look at him. "So is this how it usually works? You do five intense days of hand shaking and autograph signing, then you are allowed to jet off to one of the royal family's getaways for the weekend?"

He sighs. "*Ja*, more or less. Usually Erik is with me when I escape."

I nod slowly. "And where is he this time?"

His shoulders lift in a shrug. "No idea. He said he had something he wanted to do. I didn't press him for details. Besides… it's nice to be alone once in a while."

I look at him oddly. "You're not alone, Stellan. You're with me." I scrunch up my nose. "I guess you are used to having a staff at your beck and call, Erik reminding you of appointments, a hundred people always wanting to shake hands with you. I'm starting to think that you have no real idea of what being alone is like."

He looks unamused. "Maybe I don't. Or maybe this weekend is about me, inviting you into my solitude."

My eyebrows lift. "Oh. I hadn't thought of that."

He lifts his head, nodding to a building in the distance. "I want to stop in there for a second. Wait for me."

Stellan jogs off toward it, leaving me alone to think about what he said. My mouth twists. I guess there is a wealth of things I don't understand about his life, just the same way as he can't possibly fathom every single thing about mine.

No, it's not just that, actually. It's more that I won't let him in to find out all the secrets about my past that I've buried. I don't want him to know just how poor I used to be. I don't want anyone to realize how fucking sad I am deep down either.

My cell phone beeps in the pocket of my leather coat. Shaking my head, I pull it out and read the screen. It's from an unknown number, but I have no doubt that Anna sent it.

I just got off the phone with a friend of a friend who says that you and Stellan were kissing at a club last week. That's interesting, isn't it?

Before I can respond, she sends another message.

I think that warrants a more thorough search of your background. After all, you are cozying up to the crown prince... What do you think I will find?

My face heats. I block the unknown number, furious.

How dare Anna imply that I'm out to seduce Stellan for financial reasons? The whole idea is so wrong that it takes every ounce of willpower not to throw a tantrum right here and now.

For all the good that would do...

Stellan emerges from the shop, each hand holding a little white pastry bag. He hands one to me and continues his walk down to the shore.

"Umm..." The bag is warm in my hands. I get a whiff of vanilla and sweet baked bread. "Thanks?"

I hurry to follow him, peeling away the pastry bag to reveal a sort of creamy yellow custard overflowing it's donut container. He takes a bite and moans.

"It's so good." He chews for a moment. "They are called skolebrød and they are the best thing to come out of Norway, period."

I take a small bite, managing to get custard and powdered sugar absolutely everywhere. It's yeasty and sugary, custardy but light. My eyes light up. "Oh, that is good."

He smirks at me. "Don't say I never bought you anything."

And with that comment he starts walking faster, leaving me and my short legs woefully behind. I smile ruefully at his comment, then savor another bite of the pastry.

CHAPTER 25

STELLAN

"You actually managed to make this on your own?" Margot asks. I can't tell if she's teasing or not, but I did make this popcorn on the stove with no assistance.

I roll my eyes and hand her the huge bowl, plopping myself on the couch beside her. "I can make popcorn," I say, a little defensive. "I'm not a complete idiot."

Her lips curl up at the corners. "I'll be the judge of that."

She takes a few pieces and puts them in her mouth, chewing. Then she nods. "Someone exceedingly smart made this. I can tell."

I make a face and reach for some of the popcorn. "What kind of wine do you think goes with popcorn? A chardonnay, maybe?"

Margot pulls a face. "Maybe, I'm not much of a wine drinker."

Settling back on the couch, I give her a measuring look. "You're missing out."

She grins. "Really? I don't feel like I am. I feel like I'm just fine over here, with my beer sipping and whiskey guzzling. It turns out, you don't need money to have a pretty good time."

That's the tenth time that she's brought up money since she got here. I wonder if she realizes that she wears her apparent poverty like a nationalist drapes himself in his flag. It's all she seems to want people to see when they look at her. It's almost like a suit of armor that she puts on.

Doesn't that protective shield grow heavy sometimes?

I watch her rummage around in a box of board games. "Hey, do you want to play cards or something?"

My lips twitch. "Not a chance."

Margot sighs, setting the box aside and munching on popcorn. She slides her gaze to me, smirking. "Okay. What do you want to do? Play twenty questions? Or let's go even more mature… truth or dare?"

My brow creases. "What is that?"

She rolls her eyes. "It's a game that teenagers play. I ask you to choose between answering a question truthfully, or doing something crazy that I ask of you. It's stupid, really."

Repositioning myself in a more comfortable spot, I shrug my shoulders. "It doesn't sound stupid. Let's play."

"Oh god. No," she says, shaking her head.

I cover her hand with mine, pinning her with my gaze. Her cheeks turn pink, reinforcing the idea in my mind.

I know exactly what I'm doing. Playing with Margot's feelings, pursuing her even though I know it will end up with us being in a mess.

I'm just so tired of doing what is right, what is beneficial in the long term. I don't want to make every single choice based on the specter of the future.

So I tease her a little. "*Ja*, we can play. Can I go first?"

She glances at me, then ducks her head. "If that makes you happy."

I grin at her. "Truth or dare, Margot?"

Her cheeks turn from pink to red. "Umm… truth, I guess."

Leaning forward, I snag the popcorn bowl from her and launch a few kernels into my mouth. "I was hoping that you would choose dare," I admit. "I was going to ask you to strip."

She pins me with a probing stare. "Too bad."

There is a hint of humor around her mouth, though. I squint at her, formulating my question. Mostly I'm trying to decide if I should start with something easy, or ask her something hard. I puff out my cheeks.

"Stellan, ask already!" she protests.

I tilt my head. "*Ja, ja*. Okay. When is your birthday?"

Her eyebrows rise. "October 20th. I'm a libra."

I nod. "That makes sense. Mine is April 28th."

Her lips curve upward. "That makes you... what, a Taurus? God, never in my life have I met someone who fits that bullish description so perfectly."

"I choose to take that as a compliment." I grin.

She rolls her eyes. "I've got a question. What do you like to do for fun in your downtime?"

I narrow my eyes at her. "This is my downtime. What little I get of it, anyway."

She raises her eyebrows. "Oh."

"Okay, now it's your turn, right?" When she nods, I squint at her.

Her eyes almost close for a second. "I'll go with truth. I don't want to strip down to my underwear or call the royal palace with a fake accent and demand to speak with the prime minister."

My eyebrows go up. "What?"

She blushes. "That's the kind of stupid stuff that you get dared to do in this game."

"Ah!" I chuckle. "Noted. You chose truth though, so..." I pause, thinking for a second. "In your childhood, what do you think was the most memorable experience? No, not memorable..." I struggle to translate the word. *Gribende* is what I keep thinking, but language limits me. "What could you draw a line to from the person you are now and say, that is why I am who I am?"

She gives me a funny look. "I thought for sure you were going to ask me something about sex."

I smirk. "I'm full of surprises."

She wrinkles up her face. "I see that. Umm... I have no idea, really. I just... I'll say that I do remember being maybe seven or eight years old. My mom was on a bender, she was... just off, wherever. And I was supposed to do this project at school that required me to look stuff up. So after school, I went to the public library to use their computers. And I couldn't quite figure out how to use it. You know, the New York public libraries don't exactly get funding for the latest software."

"No?" I ask.

She chuckles. "No. Anyway, when I eventually found my way to the New York Times site... I was totally blown away. Just riveted! I remember thinking that I couldn't believe that people were telling other people the news. It just... it really gave me that sort of... light bulb moment, where something lit up inside of me. I spent like three hours reading every single word I could, until one of the librarians shooed me off the computer."

I tilt my head to the side, taking in her slow smile and hand gestures as she tells the story. "Let me guess. That was the moment when you decided that you wanted to be a journalist?"

Two pink spots appear in her cheeks. "Yeah, something like that. Although I'm not actually as much of a journalist as I am a photographer."

I nod a little bit. "So you've said. Where is your camera now?"

Margot grins sheepishly. "In my tote bag, less than thirty feet away."

"You'll have to show me some of your photos sometime."

Her flush intensifies, creeping down her neck. She looks away. "Maybe some time." She clears her throat and shakes her head. "But not now. We're in the middle of a game, aren't we?"

I nod my head slowly, enjoying the nearness of her. What would it take to get her in my lap, I wonder? My head cocks to the side as I picture that particular image.

She looks at me, her lips twitching. "I have a good question. If there was no such thing as money, and you could do anything you wanted, what would you devote your life to?"

"Wait. You didn't ask me whether I prefer to tell the truth or perform a dare."

Her eyes roll. "All right. Truth or dare, I guess."

Eyeing Margot, I bite my lip. Then I move closer to her until my thigh touches hers. She looks down at the spot where our bodies meet, making some kind of calculations.

I wish I could read her mind, just for a moment.

"Truth," I say.

Her gaze flicks up to my face. She licks her lips. "I already asked you my question."

I sprawl out on the couch, laying both of my arms on the back. I'm already close enough to Margot that I could put my arm around her with ease; if I moved my right arm another half inch, I would be hugging her. I can feel the heat from her body against my skin.

Her eyes grow large. Her pupils dilate just a little.

I'm careful not to move again. After the last week of almost kissing her, of almost seducing her, I'm okay with just teasing her for a bit. It's impossible not to smirk as I answer her question.

I lean my head back, forcing myself to focus. "Hmm. If money were no object?"

She nods, leaning back. Her head rests against my arm and she doesn't jerk away.

I bite my lip, giving her another smirk. She looks at me, only a few inches away. We are so close that I can see a few faint freckles on her nose, can make out her the dark shadow of her lashes against her skimmed cream cheeks.

"I was trained as a pilot when I was in the Navy," I tell her. "I did two years there, and I have to say, I quite liked it. I enjoyed being up in the air, in charge of everything that I saw. Everything else... when the ground fell away from the plane, so did everything else."

She wrinkles her nose. "Do you think you could ever be happy living like that? I mean... not living as a royal."

I shrug, resting my head back and looking up at the ceiling again. "Who's to say? I don't plan on finding out." I suck in a deep breath. "I'm a member of the royal family, Margot. I owe certain things to my country. And one of them is my life..." I shake my head just a little. "I will always be a prince, first and foremost. I will always have my obligations. It's just... it's part of the whole package, for better or worse."

When she speaks, her voice is a mere whisper. "I know, Stellan."

I roll my head to the side, flashing her a half-hearted smile. "God, my grandmother would love to know that those words just came out of my mouth. She's always on my back about how I owe the country this and that... My honor and... whatever else." I exhale. "It's hard not to want to be different, though. It's really damned hard."

I look right in Margot's eyes as I say the last line.

The grate of her voice stirs me. "There are... there are rules you have to abide by. Right? Rules you can never, ever think about breaking?"

My throat works as I swallow my sudden burst of anger. Anger at the fact that I'm royal, anger at what is expected of me. "Yes." I reach out to cup her face, my fingers trailing over her jawline. That contact is electric, charging the air, lighting me up inside. "My life is not my own. I can't live however I want. In many ways, I have less freedom than anyone else." I suck in another breath, my gaze dipping down to her mouth. "The crown comes before all else. Especially my own wishes."

She leans in, pressing her lips ever so lightly over mine. I close my eyes, struggling not to give in. I want to kiss her back so badly that my hands are shaking.

But I know where that leads. That's the exact way that we ended up in this mess, isn't it?

Margot's hand comes up to sink into my hair. She kisses me again, her lips soft and warm. She shifts her body to touch mine; her breasts brush up against my chest, her free hand grazes my knee.

When she kisses me a third time, the touch of her lips and against mine so light and gentle that it's almost painful not to respond. I finally give in.

I kiss her back, my hand slipping from her jaw and knotting in her hair. Angling her head just so, I tease her lips with the tip of my tongue. She opens her mouth and I sweep my tongue against hers, moaning at the sweet taste. Cinnamon, mint, and a sultry hint of something deeper.

A sweet, feminine musk. I've been dreaming of that flavor; I know that I can taste more of it if I spread her thighs and feast on her damp pussy.

God, if only.

I pull away from her lips, gasping for breath. Bowing my head, I close my eyes and struggle to pull air into my lungs.

"Fucking hell," I mutter. "What the fuck is wrong with me?"

Margot doesn't say anything. She just leans her forehead against mine for a long moment. Then she kisses my cheek, the gesture perfectly chaste.

I open my eyes in time to see her stand up. I meet her deep blue eyes, which are so full of sorrow that it's almost heartbreaking to see.

"I'm sorry, Stellan," she says. She looks away and pulls at the hem of her skirt.

I stand up, straightening to my full height. That only makes the air between us crackle with some strange electricity, but I just frown. "I meant it when I said the crown comes before everything else. It comes before me. It comes before you." I shrug, feeling a sense of helplessness. "And whatever this is? This… desire? It comes before that, too."

She tosses her hair, her mouth curving into a frown to match my own. "I know."

I pause, drinking the sight of her in. Then I turn toward my bedroom, seeking solitude. "Goodnight, Margot."

If she says anything else, I don't hear it before I'm out of the room.

CHAPTER 26

MARGOT

When I get up the next morning, the late morning sun pours in through the window. Lying in bed, I think about last night. The memory of the way that Stellan looked at me, so soulful and direct, even as he told me why we shouldn't kiss… It warms me in my bed, makes my whole body tighten and flash hot.

It's funny… I think the mere illicitness of the relationship makes Stellan more desirable. I want what has been explicitly forbidden to me… the specter of what a kiss could turn into makes my desire twice as intense.

Groaning into my pillows, I know that it really doesn't matter what I want. Isn't that the point Stellan was trying to make?

I get up and go to the kitchen, looking around for him. He's nowhere to be found. So I just spend a couple of hours getting dressed and feeding myself a toasted bagel. I start a jigsaw puzzle on the floor of the living room.

That's where Stellan finds me when he comes in from his run. I look up at him as he enters the room and my eyes widen. He's wearing a t-shirt and running shorts, and his whole body is damp with sweat. He pulls out his earbuds, still out of breath.

"*Haj*," he says.

"Hey." I put my arms behind me and size him up. "Are we in a fight?"

He looks a little surprised. "I don't think so." He pauses, taking a deep breath and exhaling loudly. "Do you want to go for a walk? There's a waterfall that's only about two miles from here. I'd like to go see it, spend a little more time communing with nature before I have to return to civilization tomorrow."

My lips lift in the ghost of a smile. "Sure."

"Great. Let me get changed. We'll leave in five minutes, *ja?*"

I nod, putting the pieces of the puzzle back in the box. I toss my black leather jacket on over my dark jeans and black tank top. By the time I get my Converse on my feet, Stellan is rearing to go.

"You ready?" he asks. He seems… distracted.

"Yep." I follow him outside, zipping up my jacket against the cold.

I take a second to give him a once over. He's wearing dark jeans, an off-white Henley shirt, and a cobalt blue jacket. He's also nearly vibrating with a restless kind of energy that keeps his eyes on the horizon. They rove around the countryside as we stroll, looking everywhere but where I'm at.

Ah, that's it. He's trying not to look at me. I suppose I should do the same, then.

I stuff my hands into the pockets of my jacket, looking around me. We walk up the steep cobblestone road, emerging onto a road outside of the village pretty quickly. On either side of the road is the greenest pasture land, contrasting with the seemingly endless skies, a fat swath of white just barely tinged with blue.

We start veering left; in the distance I can see the shore of the land looming near. As we walk, the road only grows steeper. We don't have to talk; we each struggle to draw in breath as we continue to climb. I can't help but sneak looks at Stellan.

Two spots of red ride high in his cheeks. His dark hair ruffles in a gust of wind. He's handsome and brooding and everything I never thought I would want.

Stellan eventually notices me looking at him.

"It's not much farther," he says gruffly. "I promise."

I merely shrug, stuffing a quip about how he always keeps his promises deep down inside myself. He turns out to be right, though. As he leads me up a little hill, I can hear the water rushing. It gets louder with every step I take, though I can't see the source of it at all.

We are getting closer and closer to where the land drops off dramatically, ending on a cliff that overlooks the dark blue, restless sea. Close enough that I can feel the salt spray in the air, feel the rush of the air whipping around my face. By the time I see the waterfall, I'm right on top of it.

Right on the edge of the cliff.

I lean over to look at the waterfall as it spits torrents down the craggy cliff face to fall into the ocean. Stellan pulls me back, his hand gripping my upper arm. "Careful."

Frowning at him, I shake off his hold on me. "I'm fine."

Heading along the edge of the cliff, I find a spot with a full view of the waterfall. It's majestic if a little loud. Then I sit down, dangling my feet over the edge.

Stellan comes to sit beside me, squinting at the horizon. "It's beautiful out here," he murmurs.

I glance at him, at how close he is. His hand nearly touches mine; our thighs are only a few inches apart.

I wish he were closer. Why do I spend so much time longing for this man? I could pick anyone else to have this terrible crush on… but I pick the one person who can't return my affections.

What does that say about me?

He turns and looks at me, his ice blue eyes actually making my heart skip a beat. His gaze drops to my lips, then he heaves a sigh.

"What am I doing, Margot?" he asks. "Why is there this… this heat between us?"

Blushing a little, I duck my head. "I don't know," I admit. "But I feel it too."

He blows out a slow breath. "I like you."

Wrinkling up my face, I nod. "I know."

He looks at me, a little surprised. "You do?"

I roll my eyes, a smile on my lips. "Yes. Something about all the kissing tipped me off to the fact that you might have feelings of some kind for me."

He squints at me. "I am so fucking tired of all the expectations that are heaped on me. I just…"

I cut him off with a kiss. Stellan brings up his hand and cups my jaw, returning my kiss with a passion and a vigor that surprises me. I slide my hand around his neck and bury it in his short hair.

The entire time he's touching me, my whole body is awakening. Tingling, flashing hot, aching. He finds the seam of my mouth. I open to him eagerly, unable to bridle my reaction. His tongue sweeps the inside of my mouth and dances with mine.

He tastes like the way I imagine the earth feels right after a rainstorm; fresh, sharp, wet, and clean. I moan into his mouth as he pushes me down onto the ground, his mouth leaving mine to trail kisses down my jaw.

He pauses for a second, his eyes finding mine. "I want you so badly, Margot. But I won't make any promises about what the future holds—"

I kiss him again. "I don't care. Take me if you want me," I whisper against his lips. "I'm yours."

He brushes my hair away from the column of my neck, kissing and nipping the sensitive skin he finds there, sucking at my pulse point. I slip my free hand around his back, beneath his jacket and shirt. Finding a hot, smooth expanse of skin there, I rake my nails delicately across his lower back.

He growls at me, moving his mouth down to explore my collarbone, the top of my breasts. His mouth is delightfully hot and wet. Unzipping my leather jacket, he kisses my breasts through my dark tank top, shaping them with his hands. I can feel the wet heat of his mouth even through the fabric.

"Fuck," I murmur. "That feels so good."

I toss my head back and bite my lip, moving my hand around to feel the sharp lines of his hip and Adonis belt. He growls and pulls back, stripping off his jacket and pulling his shirt over his head.

My eyes widen. He is perfect, from his muscular arms and rippling abs to his clenched jaw and the sheer need in his eyes. It's like someone has just given me a hit of something strong, and now I'm in free fall.

When he starts pulling off my leather jacket and hiking my shirt up, I groan and reach for the zipper on his fly. I unzip his jeans and get my hand inside, wrapping it around his long, thick, hot cock.

Stellan groans and lets me work my hand up and down his length briefly. The skin of his cock feels velvety soft in my hand, hot and veiny. I bite my lip and watch his face, monitoring his reactions.

His eyes roll back in his skull for a minute, but soon he loses patience with my hand. He pushes me onto my back and tugs my shirt up over my head, kissing my newly bared breasts with such enthusiasm that I laugh a little, my head tipping back as I arch into his kisses. His tongue feels a little bit raspy on my nipples, as though he were part cat.

I open my legs and urge him to lie between them, guiding him with only my feet. He reaches between us and unzips my jeans, pushing them down a little.

He groans with frustration when he realizes that it's impossible for him to touch me like that. He rolls us both over so that I'm on top, then starts pushing my jeans down.

"Get these off," he orders. "Panties, too."

I'm only too happy to oblige him. It's the work of half a minute to strip myself completely. When I return to his embrace, I find him looking at me like I'm a prize fucking mare.

"God, you're so beautiful," he murmurs, running his hands down both my sides.

I blush bright pink. "Thank you," I whisper. "You're not so bad yourself."

Stellan pulls me back down to kiss me. I push down his jeans, anxious to have him inside of me. His cock touches the inside of my thigh and we both groan.

God, this needs to happen right fucking now.

Reaching down, I grab his cock and position the blunt head to press against my pussy lips. I'm more than ready for him, wet with excitement.

"Hey," he whispers, looking into my eyes. I pause, biting my lip. He moves his hand up to my face, pushing back a strand of hair that is caught against the wetness of my lips. "Go slowly for me, *skatter*. I'm close enough already and I'm not even inside of you."

I lean down, kissing him gently. At the same time, I push myself down ever so slowly, impaling myself on his cock. The fingers of one of his hands slip into my hair and knot there.

He grunts as my pussy stretches to take his whole cock. His free hand wanders down to my breasts, shaping them and pinching a nipple. Then his hand pushes me back and meanders down to my pussy, his fingers finding my clit.

"Fuck!" bursts from my lips. My pussy feels so incredibly full; his fingers tap out a rhythm against my clit that makes me writhe.

And then he starts to bounce my whole body up and down on his cock. I look up at the sky, my mouth opening, sensation blossoming. It flows from my pussy up to my tits. My whole body tightens.

Stellan stops suddenly, making me hit him with my balled up fists. "Don't stop!"

He growls and uses all his strength to flip our positions, his weight settling against my core. "Be good for a minute, *skatter*."

He starts to withdraw and plunge back inside my pussy, moving so slowly that I could scream. I writhe underneath him, needing more. "Faster, Stellan. *Please*."

He picks up my legs and puts them over his shoulders, moving faster just like I begged him to. My hand slips up around the nape of his neck into his hair.

I close my eyes, the sensations driving me ever closer toward the edge. "Stellan, yes…" I whisper. "God, that's it. Right there. Don't stop…"

He kisses me, a breathless affair. And then he starts fucking me with short, staccato movements, jackhammering his cock into my pussy.

"Oh god," I breathe. I make noises but I'm not sure what I say. I am only aware of the friction between our bodies, of the spring deep inside of me that tightens and tightens, slowly, bit by bit, until I burst.

I come without warning, shaking, screaming, gripping Stellan with my legs. Inside I'm falling off the edge of a precipice into a canyon of sensation, crashing toward the shore like a tsunami.

Stellan stiffens and cries out something I don't understand in Danish, pumping into my body, his semen feeling hot as it enters my pussy in long lashes.

"Fuck, *skatter*," he mumbles, slowing at last. "Christ."

A note of laughter bubbles to my lips. I'm high, I think; high on him. Stellan leans down and kisses my lips so passionately and forcefully that I lose my breath all over again.

When he pulls out of my pussy and lies down beside me, he's still struggling to breathe. A shiver runs up my spine and he gives me a guilty look.

"*Ja*, I know." He pulls his pants up and then starts dressing me, which is a little weird. "I should've just fucked you last night instead of dragging you out here to a waterfall to fuck."

My lips curl upward. "I didn't say anything."

He purses his lips and tries to pull my shirt down over my head. I laugh and grab the shirts from him. "I can dress myself."

Then he kisses me deeply, until I almost forget that I am cold. "Come on. Let's go back to the house."

Pulling on my pants, I arch a brow. "Are you ready to go home already?"

He pulls his shirt on over his head, wrinkling his nose at me. "No. I can think of about ten different ways I would like to fuck you, if I'm honest. I just don't want to get caught with my pants down out here."

Biting my lip, I give him a daring look. "I'll race you back to the house."

Stellan takes off without warning, apparently taking my challenge to heart. I laugh as I start running after him, feeling more playful than I have since I was a kid.

CHAPTER 27

MARGOT

We barely make it inside the house before Stellan is on me again. He stops me at the kitchen island, turns me around, and lifts me onto the smooth marble counter. Bending his head just a little, he kisses me hard, then leaves a stinging bite on my throat.

I suck in an audible breath. "Oh…"

He pauses to look at me, his eyes scanning my face to gauge my reaction. "I want to play rough."

A shiver runs down my spine. "By all means. Don't let me stop you…"

He looks at me like a kid who's just been given a lifetime supply of candy; like he can't believe that I actually gave him permission to be rough. "*Ja?*"

When I nod, he slides his hand through my hair and grips it hard, pulling my head back a fraction of an inch. "You have only to say stop, *skatter*."

I give him a slow smile. "Why would I tell you to stop doing what makes me hot?"

Stellan groans a little, pulling at my leather jacket. "We need to go somewhere with a bed so I can fuck you in it. I need your body, *skatter*."

My face heats. "Oh?"

He's already moving me backward through the house, kissing me and groping me. I love every minute of it too, getting wet just knowing that he *needs* me. He backs me into a bedroom, throwing me on the bed.

"Take your pants off. Actually, I want all of it gone. I need you bare before me."

It only takes a second for me to ditch my clothes. When I'm naked before his gaze, he looks at my mouth, my tits, the apex of my thighs.

He moves back to look at me, and I see the fire raging in his eyes. A fire that I feel too, a fire that could consume us both for all I care. His gaze drops to my lips, and I lean forward, lips parting. He moves to kiss me, his lips firm and demanding.

This is no peck on the lips. His tongue invades my mouth, sweeping and exploring. My tongue dances with his as I sigh and sink into it.

Curling my hand around the back of his neck, I reach out boldly with my free hand and grasp his hip. He allows it for a second, then breaks off the kiss and pushes me back onto the bed.

"Stay there," he orders me.

He begins to undress, taking off his shoes, pulling his tee shirt off over his head. His torso ripples as he does, and I admire his light dusting of dark chest hair. He's also got a trail of hair that leads down from his belly button and disappears into his waistband. His arms flex as he unzips his jeans, but he stops there.

I get a tantalizing peek into his unbuttoned pants as he comes closer, just for a second.

He moves onto the bed, kneeling at the end. He considers me for a moment, like he's trying to decide what to do with me. "Come here."

I shiver as I move closer, feeling like I'm under a microscope. He narrows his eyes and runs a single fingertip across my collarbone, down under the remaining strap of my slip. He draws the strap off of my shoulder, and then rolls the top of the slip down until my pink nipples are exposed to the air.

"I've imagined this a hundred times," he says absently, his eyes fixed on my nipples. "But there is no comparison to the way you actually taste."

He leans down, cupping one breast and pulling the nipple to his mouth. I immediately groan at the sensation of his hot, wet mouth on my flesh. He rolls it around with his tongue, then bites it very carefully, almost like he's testing me.

"Ahh!" I gasp. "You can do it harder."

He smirks, looking up at me. "Permission noted."

Then he elbows me aside, lying down. I look at him a little quizzically, but in the next second he lifts me onto his body, so that I'm straddling him. He angles me so that he's planted face first between my breasts, and my bare ass is in the air. I'm a little shocked at how easily he picked me up, but he clearly has other things on his mind.

He licks the skin between my breasts with his tongue, then pulls one nipple into his mouth. I moan as he bites it and sucks it, alternating pain and pleasure for me. His hands wander down to my hips, bunching up my slip. He runs his hands over my ass, groaning when he finds that I am bare underneath the slip.

He releases my breast with a wet pop, looking up at me. "*Fuck*. You're not wearing any panties. Do you know how much that turns me on?"

I blush, slowly shaking my head. "Uh uh."

He pushes my hips down until my pussy is pressed directly against his cock through his unbuttoned jeans. We both groan as he bucks up against me. He runs his hand through my hair, fisting it, and uses his hand on my hip to guide me just where he wants me.

I gasp silently as he lifts his hips and bears down on me, his denim-clad cock almost touching my clit. He starts kissing and licking my neck, using my hair as a tool to move my head to his liking. He sucks the spot where my neck meets my shoulder, bucking his hips up, and my eyes roll back into my head.

"Ahh!" I cry. "Stellan—"

He's not satisfied with that, though. He releases me, pushing me off of his lap. I'm left breathing hard. He gets up and starts to peel his jeans off.

I'm taken aback for a moment by the image of Stellan, completely naked. I've seen it before, but it's every bit as stunning to see him nude this time as it was the last. He's all muscle, his cock juts proud out… and right now, he's looking at me like he's going to consume me.

He climbs onto the bed, dragging me down to lie beneath him, and he starts kissing my neck again. I wrap my arms and legs around him, pulling him closer. I can feel his hardness against my thigh, long and hot and throbbing. He sucks at my neck, my breasts, and then he moves lower.

I don't know if I can even handle his mouth on my clit, but he passionately kisses my thighs and my knees. His scruff tickles in the best way. I open my legs wide for him, spreading my thighs. He makes a growling sound as he kisses my clit, and my whole body is suddenly alive with electric sensation.

"Oh my god!" I cry out, my hands burying in his hair.

Already, I'm bucking my hips against his mouth, desperate for more. He closed his mouth around my clit and sucks on it in long pulls, each one sending ripples of sensation up my spine. My toes curl as he brings his hand up to my pussy and introduces one thick finger. He ever so slowly pushes his finger inside as he circles my clit with his tongue.

I come suddenly, clenching and crying out. His tongue slows, helping me ride out my orgasm. Soon though, he climbs up my body, kissing me hard. I taste the faint flavor of my own juices on his tongue and shudder.

He pulls back a little bit, grasping his cock and positioning himself just so. The blunt tip of his cock presses against my pussy, and I still for just a second. I'm busy looking at his cock, trying to understand how the hell it ever fits inside me. He pushes inside the barest inch. I cry out from pleasure and pain all at once.

Stellan glances down at me, biting his lip. "You're so tight, *skatter*."

I'm honestly not sure if that's a good thing or not, judging by his face alone. He looks like he's trying to defuse a bomb or something. I wrap my legs around his hips, pulling at him a little, urging him onward.

He closes his eyes and pushes himself inside, inch by slow inch. I feel like he's stretching me out, little by little, filling me up and touching every single part of me. It's uncomfortable, even though I'm wet.

When he is finally inside me to the hilt, he opens his eyes, staring down at me with the most intense black-brown gaze I've ever experienced.

I look him right in the eye, realizing in that moment that I'm in love with him. I don't care that his dick is so big that it hurts a little; I'm too busy being stupidly, dumbly in love with Stellan.

I reach up to pull his mouth down to mine, tenderly kissing him. He kisses me back, starting to move his body, withdrawing his cock and then thrusting back in.

"Ahhh, that's so good," he mutters, raising himself up so that he can see our bodies joined together. "Fuck, Margot. God, you're so damned beautiful."

He grabs my wrists and pulls them up above my head, working his thick cock in and out. I dig my heels into his upper back as he starts kissing and biting my neck again. I start to forget the discomfort, focusing instead on the pleasure of his lips on my skin, the wonderful weight of his body against mine.

I moan as he releases my hands in order to palm my breasts. It feels natural to wrap my arms around him to lightly rake my fingernails down his back.

Stellan suddenly withdraws from me, flipping me over. He guides me to my hands and knees, positioning his cock at my entrance before he plunges back inside.

"Ohhh!" I cry out, feeling my innermost muscles clench.

"Your pussy feels so good," he grits out. He takes my hand and guides it down to my clit, rubbing it in gentle circles. "I want you to come again. Show me what a good girl you are. Make yourself come for me."

His words send a shudder of pleasure down my spine. He lets go of my hand and grabs my hips, thrusting his cock into me again and again, as hard as he can. I call out, an insensible sound, as I start to touch myself.

The way he is fucking me now is rougher, coarser than before… but for some reason I like it more. A lot more. I close my eyes, rubbing my clit, and feeling the brutal way he handles me, ramming into me over and over again.

An invisible spring tightens deep inside me with every thrust, feeding my craving. My fingers help me along, but it's really Stellan's cock that makes little ripples of pleasure swell and burst across my body.

He's touching some spot deep inside me, a spot that I seem to be able to angle my body just so to encourage him to hit over and over again.

"Yes," I groan desperately. "Yes, right there… I…"

And then I'm calling out his name, screaming it, as I go over the edge, falling into a deep ocean of pleasure. He stiffens and growls, filling me with three single, brutal thrusts. I can feel him pulsing inside my pussy.

He slows at last, half-collapsing on the bed with me. He turns me over, kissing me tenderly. I cling to him, feeling…

Loved? Freshly fucked? Overwhelmed?

I lay on his chest, listening to his rapid heartbeat as it begins to slow. My eyelids begin to droop, and my breathing evens out. I'm not asleep per se, but I'm not far from it. When he speaks, it startles me.

"Ready to go again?" he asks, his voice barely more than a rumble in his chest.

I open my eyes and squint at him. "Again?"

He chuckles, brushing my hair back from my neck. He places a long, lazy kiss on my bare skin. "You want me, don't you?"

I bite my lip, but we both already know my answer.

It's yes. It will always be yes, for him.

CHAPTER 28

STELLAN

Going back to real life after a full weekend of Margot seems like the world twisting a cruel knife in my gut. And yet here I am, back in the palace, going through my schedule for the next month with Erik and a young woman from the royal press office.

I try not to look completely disinterested as Nora pushes a piece of paper to me across the dining room table.

"These are the schools you are engaged to speak at this month," she says, looking down at the stack of papers on the table in front of her.

"Mm," I say vaguely.

Erik clears his throat, looking up from where he's seated beside me. "Is that a *'mm, I approve'* or a *'mm, I don't approve'*? Send a smoke signal. Help us out here."

I consider him, frowning. Then I look at Nora. "I approve of everything you have to present me with today. I think we should wrap this up, don't you?"

Nora flushes, rising and clearing her throat. She gathers her papers and bobs me a curtsy. "Your highness."

I follow her to the door of the dining room, peeking my head out into the hall to make sure that no one is lurking around. Then I close the door.

Erik kicks his feet up on the table, scanning me critically. "What's up with you? You usually tell the press office to cancel at least half of your engagements."

I walk to the window, looking out over the gardens. "I'm distracted today, I guess."

He's quiet for a few beats. "Does this have to do with Margot?"

I swivel my head toward him, shooting him a glare. "What?"

He looks unruffled. "I know that you flew her up to meet you in Norway over the weekend. People talk."

I look back out the window, my face contorting. "*Pis*," I curse. I heave a sigh.

Erik stands up, stretching. "So? Did you two finally fuck?"

"*Ja*," I admit. Then I think about what he just said and turn to give him a hard stare. "And what do you mean, finally?"

He rolls his eyes. "Please. You two were always going to fuck. I saw the future written all over your face when you first told me that Margot was going to be coming here."

I snort. "You can't have known that."

"We've been best friends for twenty years. I've never seen you as far gone for a girl as you were when we left New York. If you think I didn't pick up on the sparks between you two, you're crazy."

I consider that for a second and then nod slowly. "You're right. I won't deny it. We did fuck like two rabbits. On every surface, multiple times. Four times in the shower."

A grin spreads across his face. "I knew it!"

"*Ja, ja*. You're psychic." I screw up my face. "I'm not sure what is wrong with me, though. Usually after I fuck a girl, I don't think about her again. Margot is still in my system, I guess."

I crack my knuckles, brooding. Erik walks over to where I'm standing, leaning his shoulder against the window's frame. He looks at me carefully.

"Are you in love with her?"

Shooting him a dark look, I cross my arms. "What? No. I only recently decided that I don't hate her, honestly."

He smirks at me. "You know what they say about there only being a thin line between love and hate…"

I scowl at him, opening my mouth to retort. But I don't get a chance. The heavy door to the room flies open, a butler hurrying to get inside the room.

"We're having a private conversation," Erik starts calling.

That's when my grandmother steps into the room, her eyes narrowing at us. She looks as polished as ever in her white woolen skirt suit. "Mr. Moen. Your services are no longer needed. Take the rest of the day off."

Erik's eyebrows fly upward. He understands that my grandmother has way more power than he does; he bows to her, sliding a quick look my way. "Your majesty."

"I'll catch up with you tonight," I tell him, waving him away. Then I turn to my grandmother. "You look lovely today, *Momse*."

She gives me a look that is nothing short of withering. "Get your jacket. We both have an engagement at the *Rigshospitalet*, the children's hospital."

My eyebrows rise slightly. "I think I'm supposed to be at some kind of children's puppetry thing in an hour."

Ida stares at me coolly. "Meet me downstairs at the car in five minutes. Don't keep me waiting."

"*Ja*, of course" I say, but she's already turned and is marching out of the room.

As I gather my dark suit jacket and add a dark blue tie, I try to figure out just what she wants with me. My fingers freeze as a stray thought crossed my mind: what if Ida somehow knows about Margot and I fucking?

Surely not... right? I mean, she would have to have spies everywhere for that to be the case. Trying to recount to myself the handful of people who would know *and* could've told her, I head down to the limo that is pulled up downstairs.

My palms are a little sweaty as I reach the car. She's already inside. She's small and frail, and yet... she carries herself with the kind of poise that a supermodel would kill for.

When I slide in, Ida waits until we start moving to eye me. "May I be frank with you, Stellan?"

I incline my head. "Please, *Momse*."

She looks away, out her window. "Your grandfather was a mighty king. He was fair and just, but he was first and foremost Denmark's king. Before me. Before his children." She pauses, drawing a breath and pushing it out. "Having such a remote father figure had an undesirable effect on his children."

My eyebrows rise. "On my father?"

Ida clears her throat, swinging her gaze around to me. "It was a personal failing, as I see it. I felt responsible. And I was determined that the next generation... that's you, dear... I was determined that you should grow up with a strong sense of duty. And I hoped that your grandfather would be able to carry the crown until you were ready for it. But... that obviously wasn't meant to be."

I am more than a little surprised that my grandmother is being so forthcoming.

"I'm sorry about grandad passing." I reach out and touch her forearm. She gives me a resigned smile and pats my hand a few times.

"Thank you. But that's not really the point I am trying to make. I am trying to say that I am not omniscient. I don't see everything. I can't always catch every little mistake and correct it before other people see it."

Fuck. So she does want to talk about Margot. A solid mass of angst rises in the pit of my stomach.

"*Momse*..." I begin, trying to decide. Should I deny the allegations she's about to lay against me? Or maybe it would be better to explain. "Let me—"

She cuts me off. "Stop." She draws a line in the air with her hand. "Listen to what I'm saying."

I settle back, looking at her with a blank expression.

"I need you to really take what I'm telling you seriously." She pauses. "It's time that you settled on a wife."

I shake my head. "I don't—"

"Stop talking for a moment!" she cries, her hands balling into fists. "You are not listening! We are out of time. Your father is not well. Do you hear me? He's ill. He may need to be replaced at any time."

My mouth opens and closes. My eyes are fixed on her small figure. "…what?"

"Your father is ill, Stellan. The doctors aren't sure what is wrong with him, but he's been forgetting things for a long time. And then last week he just fainted. We revived him but he had trouble with his vision… He was blind for almost a day." She draws in a shaky breath. "I learned about it from a phone call. Gorän says it wasn't a big deal, but I know he is wrong."

A million questions race around my head, half of which Ida probably doesn't have the answer to. I try to marshal my thoughts.

"Where is he? When are my parents arriving back home?"

My grandmother looks upset. "Your father is insistent that he and your mother continue on their world tour. I tried every argument I could think of… he will not hear anything different."

"That's…" I search for the word. "That's *absurd*. He needs to come home and be checked into the hospital."

Ida shrugs. "I quite agree. Do you think I would be here with you if I had the option of being by my own son's bedside? But it's not in your father's nature to be told what to do or where to go. That leaves me in the rather precarious position of getting you ready for coronation. And the first step of that process is to find a suitable marriage partner."

"It's not like I have to be married," I fire back.

She glares at me. "It's what has always been done."

"So?" I ask, defensive.

I blow out a breath, looking out the window. We're driving through downtown Copenhagen and many beautiful multicolored building fly past my view. But I can't even take that in; I'm just floored by my father's illness and my grandmother's demands.

"Stellan," she says sharply. I look at her, trying like all hell to keep my emotions off my face. The last thing I need right now is for all my secrets to come out. And I swear, Ida has a way of just looking at me and knowing what is in my soul.

It's time to chance the subject.

"I'm worried about father," I say, hedging a little. Yes, I am worried about him… but there are other things, bigger secrets, that are in the forefront of my mind just now.

"Are you going to make me pick a girl for you?"

Startled, I frown at her. "Do you really think I would let you do that?"

She folds her hands in her lap and favors me with a hard look. "It's not really an issue of what you'll allow. I don't want to select a mate for you. But if you don't, I will."

"Momse," I say, my voice gone to grit. She looks at me, her eyes tightening. "I'm telling you right now. If you do that, if you so much as bring a single girl around with the purpose of getting me engaged, I will freeze you out. Don't make me do that."

We pull up to the children's hospital just then. My grandmother doesn't take her eyes off of me, though.

"Decide for yourself if you want to. You've got a month. Then I will start to make plans on your behalf." The driver opens her door and helps her out, leaving me scowling after her.

"Your highness?" the driver says, looking in the car.

I don't want to go inside, not after what Ida just said. But I'm finding that what I want rarely factors into any decisions when it comes to the royal family. So I just get out of the limo, rearranging my scowl into a pleasant smile.

There are a few photographers, and I raise my hand to them, waving politely. But inside, I'm a seething mass of anger.

CHAPTER 29

MARGOT

"I'm sorry, madame." The butler bows his head. "His royal highness Prince Stellan has stepped out rather unexpectedly."

I wrinkle my nose, unsurprised. Of course Stellan doesn't show up the day after we fucked each other's brains out. *Of course.*

"Ah. Thank you." I lift my camera from my tote bag. "Would it be okay with you guys if I just took some photographs? Just you know, the dining room and the salons…"

"Of course, madame. We have been instructed by the press office that you are to be given full access to the upper half of the palace. Will you need anything else?"

"No, no." I shake my head and give him a halfhearted smile. "I'm fine."

The butler bows and retreats, leaving me alone in the corridor just outside Stellan's study. Biting my lip, I look around. I try the study... but of course, it is locked.

What could I have hoped to find in there anyway? Stellan's private diary with all his innermost thoughts jotted down just for me?

Unlikely.

Besides, he's made enough of a statement by just not showing up than anything I could've read.

I just wander the halls, opening doors at random. Mostly I find the rooms empty or filled with the ghostly shapes of furniture with the dust covers on. Climbing the stairs, I am drawn to the elegantly draped window that dominates the end of the hall.

I snap a few photos of it, and then draw the see-through curtain aside. Aiming my camera lens down onto the street, I catch an unexpected sight.

A flash of a familiar hair color. It's bright red, like a candy apple.

Yeah, that's got to be Pippa. And she's wearing a loose white romper and beaming at a man. She says something and he picks her up, whirling her around. When he stops, she kisses him. Then he glances my way, laughing.

My eyebrows fly up. It's Lars Løve, Stellan's younger brother.

Whoa. That is a hell of a secret to keep, especially for someone as chatty as Pippa.

Pippa bats at his arm. He puts her down and then heads off at a loping run. Pippa turns like she is going to walk somewhere, maybe to our apartment or the offices of *Politiken*.

I stuff my camera in my bag and sprint downstairs, catching up with her in less than a minute. She looks at me, her blue eyes widening.

"Margot!" she squeaks. "I haven't even seen you since Thursday night. Where have you been?"

I chuckle. "Do you really think you're just going to distract me with a question like that?"

A hint of pink lights up her cheeks. "What?"

"Did I just see you kiss Lars on the lips just a minute ago? You two looked pretty comfortable…"

She tosses her fiery hair, glancing around. The blush spreads further across her cheeks and darkens to a red hue. "Shh." She pulls me further away from the palace. "It was just a one time thing. No need to announce it, okay?"

I grin at her. "Umm, wow. I had no idea that you were sucked into the royal family like *that*."

She throws up her hands in front of her face, hiding. "It's… complicated. Lars and I go way, way back."

My eyebrows rise. "What? Tell me everything!"

She peeks at me from behind her hands. "How about I tell you everything over a cup of coffee? I haven't had any caffeine today and I'm dying."

"It's a deal," I say, putting my arm around her. "There's a coffee shop around the corner. Come on, let's hurry so you can spill your guts all over the place."

Pippa rolls her eyes but doesn't resist as I pull her along. I wasn't kidding about the cafe being really close; when we turn a corner, there it is, all glass and pastel colors inside. We order and then take our seats outside.

I lean forward eagerly. "Tell me everything," I demand.

Pippa wrinkles her nose. "I met Lars when I went to St. Malo, a prestigious boarding school in Switzerland. And before you even start, I want you to know that I only went to a school that the Danish royal family would send their child to because I was offered a full scholarship."

I shrug. "I wasn't judging."

Her shoulders relax a fraction. "Oh. Well… yeah. I've known Lars since we were both just kids. He was a year older than me at school… and he was also my first kiss."

"Whoa. That sounds like a relationship."

She glances at me sharply. "It is definitely *not* a relationship. It's just… a friendship that has lasted a long time. It's complicated."

I stare her down. Is she for real? It seems like she really believes it, but I'm not sure where I stand.

The barista brings our drinks out and Pippa makes a big deal of thanking her and sipping her latte. I level her with a long look.

"So if you're just friends, what happened between you last night?"

She flushes. "Too much wine. We just… fell into old patterns."

"Old patterns like sleeping together?" I ask, scoffing.

Pippa looks down at her latte, running her finger over the white cup's handle. Her mouth twists with humor, but I see a faint echo of sadness on her face too. "Yes."

I take a sip of my latte, savoring the creaminess of it while I look at her. "Why are you two not dating?"

She looks up, a little bit of alarm on her face. "Well, for one thing, neither of us is interested in being tied down. Also, not to put too fine a point on it, but there are a million expectations of anyone who openly dates a royal. Not the least of them being the you are well bred and well behaved… and looking for a ring."

I swallow, looking down at my latte. "That does sound like a sticky wicket."

She smirks at me. "You are actually the only person who probably knows better than I do, Margot. Tell me, has anything come of your insane crush on Stellan yet?"

My eyes widen. I blush furiously. "I'm not sure what you mean."

She shakes her head at me. "Oh, please. Ever since the second you laid eyes on him, you've been making this face at him. Like this."

She angles her face and flutters her lashes. I make a disgruntled sound.

"Uh! No. I am not like that!" I protest.

"Oooh, you are too!" she cries, laughing. "Talk about a couple that just seems like they are bound to slip up and end up banging the hell out of each other…"

I feel my face heat. "Pippa…"

She studies me for a second, then grins. "Oh. Oh! I think you already did slip up! You did, didn't you?" She throws her head back and cackles. "I was right!"

"Oh my god," I say, rolling my eyes. "Okay, so Stellan and I finally did it. So what?"

"Umm… yeah, that's not good enough. I'm going to need details. Was it great? Where did you do it? And how did you guys leave things?" She spreads her hands out over the table. "Tell me everything."

I groan. "Please don't make me."

She snots. "Dish."

"Ugh." I run my fingers through the curls in my hair. "Okay. Umm… yes, it was great. We went to a little coastal house in Norway for the weekend and we…" I pause, screwing up my face. "We did everything we wanted to do for a full twenty four hours, on every conceivable surface. And then…" I shake my head. "I thought we left things on a good note, but then he just stood me up today, so…"

I throw my hands up in the air. "Who knows?"

Pippa leans forward. "Do you think he got in his own head? In my experience with Stellan, duty is his weakness. If he spends too long thinking about how he wants to do something but is duty bound to do something else… he ends up doing the un-fun thing. It's just how he is."

"Well… it doesn't really matter. I am not exactly chomping at the bit to get involved with all the crap that comes along with trying to date Stellan. He is great, but…" I shake my head. "The whole 'requirements to date a royal' thing doesn't sound like I'll like it. I'm all about smashing the patriarchy and breaking through glass ceilings, not reinforcing them."

Pippa gives me a look. "You might say that. But what does your heart have to say?"

I give a humorless chuckle. "My heart says what I tell it to say, period. End of story."

"Does it? Tell me, how do you get your heart to listen? That's one of the things that I struggle with constantly." She pouts.

I shift in my seat, not entirely comfortable. "I don't know. You just do."

Her lips lift. She raises her latte to her lips, sipping it coolly. When she sets it down, she eyes me.

"I think you are full of shit."

"What? Why?"

She shrugs. "I think you just haven't given yourself enough time to consider whether you are a complete lovesick fool or whether you're just dabbling. Dipping a toe into Stellan's pool to test the waters." She smirks. "I'm willing to bet you're the former."

"Well, I call bullshit on you not being in love with Lars! It's complicated? I just bet it is, Miss Welch. I think you love him and you're just not willing to say it out loud."

"Ah!" she says, making an outraged sound. "I could say the same for you!"

"No, no. You and Lars share a history. Stellan and I were born under two totally different moons in two completely different solar systems. Okay?"

Pippa's eyes narrow. "I don't think so."

My phone buzzes. I reach for it, checking the screen. Then a warm feeling rushes over me when I read the words.

Sorry about today. Got held up. Meet me at seven tonight? Wear cocktail attire.

There is no signature, but I know who it's from. I smile as I respond.

. . .

Just give me an address.

When I look up, Pippa is surveying me knowingly.

I turn red. "What?" I ask, putting my phone away.

She rolls her eyes. "Don't pretend like that wasn't Stellan. You are so easy to read, it's crazy."

I sigh. "All right, it was Stellan. Happy?"

She reaches across the table, catching my hand. She looks me in the eye. "Yes. I am."

I pull a face. "Do you want to walk with me back to that dress shop? I need something to wear tonight."

She grins. "I can't think of anything that would make me happier. We need to put you in something that is so hot, it'll melt Stellan's tie right off his body."

Giggling at Pippa's description, I down the rest of my latte and then head to do some shopping.

CHAPTER 30

STELLAN

I pull at my tie, wishing like anything that I could loosen it. But this little gallery opening is as fancy as they come. My black suit and tie just make me one of the crowd.

I take a sip of the old fashioned I ordered at the bar earlier, scanning the gallery for the hundredth time. Margot is running late.

If she's coming at all, that is.

And I'm standing here, uncomfortable in my suit jacket, fending off the general public. I sigh aloud and make myself focus on a large framed photo photograph that's displayed on the wall.

Somehow she sneaks up to stand beside me. When I notice her standing there, looking thoughtfully at the art, I take a step back.

"Jesus christ," I mumble. "You look…"

I trail off. She's wearing a short-sleeved, floor-length dress that is just a shade or two darker than her neon pink hair. Although the dress doesn't show any cleavage or legs, it's so tight that it looks like she was sewn into the damn dress.

She runs a hand through her hair, giving me an uncertain smile. "I hope that sentence ends well."

I nod slowly, trying to unglue my eyes from her tits and ass. "Uh huh."

She cocks her head. "I'm guessing you're not secretly mad at me, then?"

"What?" I glance up and meet her deep blue eyes, puzzled. "Why would I be?"

She shrugs one shoulder, coming close to me. One corner of her mouth turns up. "I didn't know what to think when you didn't show up today."

Casting my gaze out over the gallery, I squint. "*Ja*. My grandmother changed my itinerary unexpectedly. Apparently, no one thought to inform the press office."

"Ah. Is everything okay?"

Her eyes are on me. Probing me. I glance down.

"*Ja*. My grandmother is just reminding me of my duty to the country, I guess. Nothing for you to be concerned about, Margot." I sigh, smoothing my face into a pleasant expression. "Let us talk about other things. The art, for example. I thought you would like the exhibition."

She arches a brow, then swings her gaze to the wall. A large photo of a busy Bombay market hangs in front of us, the image colorful and busy. While she looks at it, taking a little step toward the canvas, I look at her.

Margot really does look beautiful this evening. Her dress rustles a little as she leans forward, then she looks at me, her dark blue eyes crinkling with humor.

"Do you have any idea who this photographer is?"

I screw up my face. "No. This is a benefit for the Copenhagen Contemporary Museum. I just thought that you would appreciate this particular room, that's all. You know. It's the same kind of art that you do."

Her lips curve up. "It's very nice."

I cock a brow. "There seems to be a *but* waiting in the wings."

"But nothing." She comes closer, standing beside me and sliding her hand into the crook of my arm. "Is this okay?"

I look down into her face, my mouth kicking up. I hope that no one looks at the two of us standing so close and assumes that we are guilty of exactly what we are doing… but then again, I don't really care. Not when she's so close.

"*Ja*," I say softly. Bending down, I whisper in her ear. "Your dress is really killing me right now. I'm imagining that it would look so nice on my bedroom floor."

"Stellan!" she admonishes me. Then her lips twitch. "I guess you really aren't mad at me."

"You wouldn't be here if I was." I straighten up as one of my father's cabinet comes into view. "Ah, shit. There is a man over there that I would rather avoid, if I can. Let's keep moving."

Margot lets me guide her into the next room, which is just more of the same thing. Light gray walls, with photographs centered ten feet apart. I flag down a waitress and get her a glass of champagne.

For her part, she seems to pay less attention to the art hanging on the walls than the glamorous people in fancy dresses and swanky suits strolling around. She's unusually closemouthed, which makes me even more curious.

"I can't help but wonder what you're thinking," I say.

She breaks away from her hawk-eyed gaze over the gallery patrons and flushes. "I guess I'm just… absorbing. I had never considered before today that maybe people just live like this. The parties and galas, the freshly pressed suits and fancy dresses…"

"You realize that you are wearing a ballgown, do you not? You're actually a little bit better dressed than almost everyone else here."

She gives me a tiny glare. "This is a rented dress, Stellan. I'm definitely Cinderella in this scenario, trying to fit in at the ball."

I smirk. "Do you have singing mice to dress you?"

"No, but I've got Pippa." She rolls her eyes. "I just... I'm wondering if all billionaires and millionaires are so... hands off. That's what I was thinking, to answer your question."

"Ah. Well... in my family, the answer is definitely no. My mother is very active in her charitable work, most of which involves spending a lot of time with HIV and AIDS patients. My sister Annika is really devoted to working with the NATO peacekeepers. She's gone for a month at a time, advocating on their behalf. Finn spends a good deal of time working with refugees in Spain and Portugal. Anders is worried about feeding the entire world..." I shake my head. "Everyone that I know has their causes that they support and work toward."

She frowns. "But not you?"

"Uhh, no. I mean, I have events like this. I'm a major patron of so many museums and I sit on the board of tons of charities... but when it comes down to it, I just have the crown to worry about. Trust me, it's plenty."

Her eyes meet mine briefly before she glances away. "I see."

I tilt my head to the side. "Do you?"

She nods, screwing up her face briefly. "Actually, yeah. I can imagine that it's an all-encompassing thing. As it should be, I guess. I mean... in the United States, we have the president. And they have to be on call twenty four hours a day, seven days a week while they're in office. I can't imagine that being the king of Denmark is any different... and that's *for life*."

Making a face, I nod. "*Ja*, that's about the size of it."

She squeezes my arm. "Wanna get out of here for a while? I mean, as long as you are avoiding people…"

I smirk. "I can give you about half an hour. Then people will start to notice my absence, I think."

She grins, mischief lighting her eyes. "Take a walk on the wild side, Prince Stellan. Be bad."

I roll my eyes. "Please. Nobody does bad the way royals do it, okay?"

"Mm." Her eyes dart around the room, spying a partially hidden door. "Let's see where that one goes."

I let her pull me along after her, slipping out the door and into the shadows of the museum after nightfall. Margot slides her small hand into mine and pulls me down the hall.

I would be lying if I said that feeling her warm skin against mine wasn't as exciting as our escape from the gallery benefit. I try to remind myself that I can't actually like this girl… I shouldn't even be here, letting her pull me into a darkened gallery.

But I don't do anything to stop her. I'm not entirely sure I could if I wanted to. She turns the light switches on, a spotlight falling on her and throwing her into profile.

She glances at me, her eyes sparkling with mischief. "Pick a painting." She motions to a couple of paintings. "And look at it for a minute. Then tell me how it makes you *feel*."

"You had me sneak away from the party to critique art?" I ask.

Margot cocks her head, tugging at my elbow. "It's important to look at things and process how we feel about them. Art is all about making that process happen in a safe space. Sometimes what you see intentionally invokes emotion; sometimes it's a more…" She pauses to find the right word. "Internal process, I guess."

She pulls me over to one painting. It looks vaguely familiar. It's small, probably only two feet by three. Hanging in a simple silver frame, it's an enormous field of what looks like wheat, all in oranges and yellows. There is a lone figure cutting the wheat in the far corner. Overhead, a light green sky overshadows the mountains.

"It's… nice, I guess?" I say, tilting my head to take it in from another angle.

Her lips curve upward. "I recognize the painting. It's called *Wheat Field With Reaper*. Look, look how everything is yellow, yellow-green, orange-yellow, gold… There is a man working over here. And he is just surrounded by these dry, *thirsty* colors. I look at all that and I wonder at how hot it is… I can't quite make out the detail of the man's face, but I see him laboring all alone. It's sort of serene, I think."

I nod slowly, glancing down at her. "I can see that."

She gives me a half smile. "It's by Van Gogh, for what it's worth. He said it was about death and how he wasn't scared of dying."

"Ah! For some reason, I find that sort of worrisome."

Margot shrugs a slender shoulder. "I think the next painting is a Van Gogh too. I don't know what it's called, though."

We walk over to look at the painting, which is several trees painted against a field of little white flowers. In the back, a river or a road meanders past.

"Hm." I study the painting.

"What does it make you feel?" she asks delicately. "The mishmash of colors on the trees. The oddly... sort of curvy and pointy bark of the trees. The white and yellow and green of this field of flowers... Back here, you see some blue flowers as well."

She gestures, wiggling her fingers over the painting. I make a face.

"I'm really terrible at this game."

"Just look for another minute. Let that particular bright shade of green soak into your senses. What does it make you think?"

I give her a long look, then glance at the painting. "I don't know. The green is... fresh? Sort of... it has an energy?"

She lights up. "Yes! It definitely does."

Scrunching half my face up, I sigh. "It's spring, obviously. So it kind of makes me wonder what the same place would be like in other seasons."

"It most certainly does." She grins. "That wasn't so bad, was it?"

She looks up at me, her eyes so deep blue, her hair so perfectly pink. Grabbing her by the waist, I pull her against my body and kiss her. I pull in deep lungfuls of her scent, making me horny as fuck and plastering a stupid smile over my face.

When I release her, she turns pink and bites her lip. "Thanks." She giggles. "For the kiss, I mean."

"Oh, that was strictly for my personal pleasure."

Margot rolls her eyes but she has a grin on her lips. "Should we get back?"

I let her go, following her back into the darkened hallway. But as I go, there's something in the pit of my stomach… a sensation I can't quite name.

It sticks with me for the rest of the night, floating around in my head. I don't want to name it, so I pretend it isn't there.

But it definitely is…

CHAPTER 31

MARGOT

I have a long week. At the newspaper, I have to explain to Anna why I'm not almost done with my article… I haven't even started writing it, but she doesn't need to know that.

Add that to the monotony of the royal routine finally setting in. I arrive in the morning. I spend an hour with Stellan at the palace, more likely than not having intense, gymnastic sex. And then we spend a full day visiting factories, schools, children's hospitals…

It's fun for a few days. And then… it's *work*. By the time I get home at night, I'm dead on my feet.

I can see Stellan getting tired as the week winds down. To myself, I can admit that I'm fairly exhausted too. And yet this is only my third full week of keeping pace with the royal schedule.

I have no idea how all the Løve family do it forever.

Luckily, Stellan proposes the perfect antidote to my exhaustion. A whole weekend at a house on the coast, a two hour drive from Copenhagen. We'll be by ourselves in a mansion...

Yeah, it doesn't sound too shabby. I just have to shove down all my *working class girl* judgments to enjoy it. Without really taking any time to think it through, I tell Stellan yes.

Two hours later, we are so close to the ocean that I can actually smell the salt in the air. As we pull through the trees, the ocean is just right there, down a sandy beach. I sit up as we pull around to a gray, three story mansion house.

The second we stop, Stellan is out of the driver's side. "Look at it!" He points to the gray sea, grinning as he opens the car's trunk. "I could stare at that all day."

I climb out of the car, squinting at the coastline. A gust of wind takes me by surprise and blows up the back of my short black dress. I squeal and smooth my dress down.

Stellan grins at me. "You might as well get naked, because I plan on being au naturel all weekend."

A shiver of excitement runs down my spine at his words. I don't want him to just assume that I am game for anything, although I mostly am. I shoot him a look. "We'll see."

He grabs me and hauls me up against his frame, kissing me hard until I'm just a little breathless. Then he lets me go and picks up the suitcases. "Come on. Wait until you see the inside of this house."

I follow Stellan up the neatly manicured tan brick path into the house. As I step inside, my eyes widen. I look around at the foyer, which is painted with the most amazing mural of a river with nymphs playing around it. There is no furniture here, just this delicate and detailed portrayal painted on the walls.

"What… what is this?" I say, noticing something new every second I keep staring around.

He grins. "Apparently one of my relatives holed themselves up in this house for several years. This was the result."

"Whoa." I move closer to the wall, squinting to make out the detail in one of the nymphs. "This is amazing."

"Wait until you see the living room," he says, nodding his head toward it. "I'm going to go upstairs and drop our things in the master bedroom."

He heads off up a staircase. Nodding absently, I follow the hallway back, taking the first doorway that opens to the left. Inside I find no furniture to speak of. Instead there is light that pours in from the floor length windows, illuminating another breathtakingly detailed painting.

It depicts a plain-looking building, maybe Greek or Roman in design. A robed woman who carries a basket of bread is in the center of the painting. A burst of sunlight shines down on her, signifying that perhaps she is chosen by god. She hands pieces of bread to a flock of ratty looking children, some of whom are crying upon receiving their ration. And the look on the woman's gently lined face… it is so sorrowful, it actually makes my chest seize up.

Stellan comes to lean against the doorframe, ducking a little as he enters the room. "Amazing, isn't it?"

I move closer to the wall, in awe. "It's so lifelike. And her expression… you can tell that whoever did this has felt exactly that kind of sadness before."

"*Ja*. Apparently it is St. Agathe, feeding the children of Carthage." He wrinkles up his face. "After the museum, I got the idea to come here. There are loads more paintings in every room. But this one is really good."

"Who did this painting?" I murmur.

He shrugs. "I think a great aunt, several times removed? I don't know. Someone crazy."

I frown at him over my shoulder. "That's a cruel thing to say."

He rolls his eyes just a little and shrugs again. "Come. Let's go into the kitchen. There is a happier painting in there. It's gold and jeweled, apparently inspired by a Fabergé egg."

He turns and heads down the hallway, expecting me to follow. And I do… but I cast a glance over my shoulder as I leave the room. St. Agathe looks back at me, her eyes so full of sadness that it makes my heart break.

That will stay with me for a good long while, I think.

Stellan shows me a few more paintings, then takes me upstairs to the master bedroom. To my surprise there is no mural waiting for us in here. The walls are robin's egg blue, the room dominated by a giant four poster bed with crisp linens.

He pulls me onto the bed, his blue eyes lit with lust and hunger. He kisses me passionately, already tugging my dress up and over my head. He tosses it to the side without a second thought. I toe my shoes off, sighing as he kisses my neck.

"Fuck," he mutters, sliding his gaze up to meet my own. "Do you realize how fucking beautiful you are, *skatter?*"

My cheeks turn pink. Under his relentless gaze, I feel so *seen*, the opposite of invisible.

"No," I breathe. His look is so direct and frank, so honest. It sears me from the inside out.

When he speaks again, it's as much a worshipful promise as it is a compliment.

"I do." He sucks in a ragged breath. "You are so damn beautiful. And I don't just mean physically."

My eyes widen at that. He means… he likes my personality? It's a little hard to believe him, but it's even harder not to counter that with the earnestness written across his face.

In the next second, Stellan buries his face in the space between my breasts. I'm not wearing a bra, so I'm bare before him.

"Fuck," he mutters again, looking at my breasts. My hard pink nipples demand attention. My whole body tingles in anticipation of his mouth on my skin.

"Yes," I moan. "Touch me. Taste me. You can have all of me."

He puts his hands on my breasts, pushing them together, licking and kissing them both. My back bows, thrusting my nipples out and pushing my head back. This is too much, the sensations are so pleasurable that I fear for my sanity.

I feel that familiar connection in my body, between my neck and my breasts, my nipples and my pussy. He touches my breasts and I feel it in my pussy, feel my body readying itself, feel myself growing wetter. I roll my hips against his, my mouth opening to release a soft moan.

I need more. This is everything. This moment, these sensations, that passionate expression on his face. But I can't wait until he's inside me.

"Stellan..." I whisper. "I need you. *All* of you."

I push eagerly onward, rolling my hips again. Stellan has what I lack. He is going to fuck me, filling a chasm deep inside of me that I never even knew was there with his magnificent cock.

Burying my fingers in the short hair at his nape, I gasp as he kisses me. There's an impatient moment where he tries to get his shirt off. But as soon as he does I run my hands over his abs and sides, my breath catching as I look at the skin he exposes.

"You're so *hot*," I marvel.

"I can't wait anymore." He groans, looking at me. "It's not enough, *skatter*. It's never enough. I want you naked, wet, and ready for me," he grits out.

His gaze is direct and scorching. He is a ravenous fire, threatening to burn me alive. And I am the kindling, stacked and ready, welcoming his

spark to my dry tinder. We are so very close to combusting, all we need is a match to light our fire and raze us to the ground.

"I'm ready," I whisper, tugging on his jeans. "I need you, Stellan. I need you to fuck me."

He presses his kiss down on me like he's drowning and I'm the only oxygen in the whole entire world.

I work at the zipper on his jeans, undoing it and then sliding my hands around to his ass. His skin is hot and smooth under my touch. I slip my hands down the strong muscles I find there, pulling him against my body again. I slide his jeans down his hips, kissing him again.

Our tongues dance for several beats, as if we are fighting one another. God, yes.

He frames my breasts with his touch, skating one of his hands down my

ribs, down my belly, to the fine thatch of dark hair that grows between my legs. I close my eyes and moan as his fingers trace the lips of my pussy. It's all I can do not to spread my legs and beg for him to touch me. I'm like a bitch in heat, out of control, only for him. And I don't care at all.

I'm shameless and needy and wanting what only he can give me.

In the next second though, he nips at my earlobe and lays me down on the bed.

"Scoot back," he urges, voice gone to gravel. "Open your legs for me, *skatter*. Let me see your creamy pussy. Let me see what is *mine* for the taking."

Dropping my head and moving a couple of inches further back on the bed, I obey, opening my legs a little. My thighs shake with need and excitement; I can feel myself creaming at the very idea of him tasting me. I moan as his clever fingers find my clit.

"That's it," he coaxes, looking down. He puts a little space between our bodies, urging me onto my back. He repositions himself, rubbing his long, hard cock when it pops out of his jeans. "Spread your knees wide for me, skatter. I want to see all of you."

Feeling a weird combination of shameless and embarrassed, I spread my legs as far as they will go, knowing that he could crush me or reject me.

If he did that right now, I swear I would die. If anybody else saw me like this, so naked and utterly desperate, I would cry. But I look at Stellan and the desire in his ice blue eyes emboldens me.

I want to be wanton with him, to show him how hungry I am for whatever he will give me. I've waited for this moment for what feels like forever, so I might as well be brazen right now.

"Looking at you like this, spread out and waiting for me to touch you... it's the hottest thing I've ever seen." Stellan puts two fingers in his mouth, then drops those fingers down to massage my clit. I stiffen at his touch. It feels so good and all he's doing is gently massaging my clit.

I am not a choir girl; I've definitely rubbed my clit before. But when he does it, it feels wholly different. It feels so damned good, like I'm stretching and reaching for something explosive that is just outside of my grasp.

I suck in a breath. He kisses my lips, looking deep in my eyes and controls me with his touch. I'm spread open and wet, my heart pounding, my blood singing in my veins.

"It feels so good," I whimper.

He massages my breast with his free hand, shaping the nipple with clever fingers. I lean back a little, biting my lip and staring at him. I want to remember this moment, this moment of being connected to him so intimately.

Stellan gets this little smirk on his lips as he looks at me.

"What?" I ask, flushing at his probing gaze.

His smirk becomes a sly grin. His fingers dip from my clit to my core, circling and teasing. Bringing some of the moisture from my slit up to massage my aching clit in slow movements. I gasp and arch my back.

"I'm just watching you. Waiting to see you come apart." He slides one finger into my core, making my pussy ache to be filled.

I shiver against the sensation, desperate for more. "Stellan..." I gasp.

He sinks down to his knees. My thighs tense and my knees start to close, but he tuts at me. "What are you going to do? Are you going to stop me from tasting you? You want this, I promise you."

Biting my lip, I relax my thighs.

Pulling both hands out to push my knees wide again, Stellan starts kissing the inside of my thigh, making his way down to my pussy. I squirm, aching for what I know is coming. He's gone down on me before and I remember exactly how fucking good it felt. I can feel the excitement building, feel myself growing hotter and wetter every second.

His nose tickles the inside of my thigh, just an inch from my soaking wet slit. I can't help the moan that escapes my lips when he parts my pussy lips with two fingers, blowing delicately on the glistening pink flesh he finds there.

Stellan glances up at me, still smirking. "Make noise for me, *skatter*. I need to hear it."

My breath leaves me all at once, like someone punched me in the stomach. I nod slowly. "Yes, Stellan," I whisper.

As he teases me with slow kisses to my pussy, I hold my breath and bury my fingers in his hair. When his tongue circles my clit, a moan bursts from my throat.

"Oh god," I gasp. "Oh, please don't stop... *please...* "

He chuckles against my flesh. It seems natural to voice what I'm feeling, so I just go for it. As he sucks on my clit, I writhe against his mouth.

"Stellan, please! You make me so hot... I can barely look at you eating my pussy..."

He sets up a rhythm, licking and sucking, making me as hot as fire. It feels good to rock my hips against his mouth, to whisper *yes* when he hits the right spot, to throw my head back and let soft sounds leave my throat.

All the while, he keeps leading me down a path, driving me wilder and wilder with desire. He makes me crazy, playing my body like a violin, driving me insane with want.

"Please, baby..." I moan, my eyes closing. "I'm right there..."

I climax suddenly, violently. Choking, I feel the vibrations deep within my body ripple out to my breasts, my collarbone, my legs, my fingertips, my toes. God, it feels so amazing. I never want it to end.

Stellan is already kissing his way up my body, getting to his feet. I can't speak so I just turn my flushed face up to him, offering him my mouth.

He takes it greedily, kissing me hard, his mouth tasting deep and earthy and charged, the flavor a little like putting my tongue on a battery. It's my taste, I realize with a start.

How could I not have known that I have a flavor of my very own? I gasp, finding it unspeakably sexy that he still tastes like me.

His hands are everywhere, sliding from my shoulders down to grab my ass, then back up to my breasts. Although I just orgasmed, already I can feel my body preparing for more. There is no question; I still want him.

I cling to his shoulders with one arm as I begin to fumble with his jeans with the other, smoothing my fingers down his back, clutching at his bare ass. I've lost some of my shyness, exploring the shape of his ass, the way his lower back and legs feed into it. It's dense muscle, lean and smooth just like every other place on his body that I've touched. I slide my touch down the back of his legs, finding the exact spot that hair begins to grow.

He doesn't seem to mind my explorations or my curiosity in the least.

Stellan moves back an inch, pushing his jeans down to reveal his cock. Thick and long and gloriously pink, it jumps at my touch. His cock has a number of veins that seem worth exploring. I trail my fingers down his length, shuddering when it feels like hot velvet. Curious, I feel the weight of it in my palm, looking at his face.

He bites his lower lip, his eyes hooded, and allows my inquisitive touch for a moment. When I curl my fingers around his cock and give it an experimental stroke, he groans and reaches out to stop my hand.

"Not this time, *skatter*," he manages, looking a little strangled. "I've waited too long. If you keep touching me, and keep looking at me with those innocent eyes, I'm going to come right away." Stellan leans down and kisses me passionately. "I really want to know what it feels like to come inside that pretty pussy of yours."

My eyes widen and I lick my lips. "I want that too."

He pushes me back on the bed and eases his cock out of my grip, pressing the blunt tip against the inside of my thigh. I pull him in with my legs, making him readjust a little until he settles the tip of his length against my soaking wet slit.

Stellan closes his eyes, his breathing growing heavy.

"Fuck me," I plead with him. "Please, Stellan. Don't make me wait any more."

We both groan in unison as he pushes inside, stretching me out with each inch. My whole body is alive with sensation, my breasts tingling.

"You're so big," I whisper.

I grip his shoulders, my nails digging into his flesh. His brow furrows in concentration as he works his length all the way in. It's a little uncomfortable for me, if I'm honest. Having so much weight crushed against me and being so intimately stretched out is awkward and almost painful.

But I trust Stellan; he has only brought me pleasure so far.

"God *damn*," he murmurs. He closes his eyes for a moment, then opens them and pins me with his icy gaze. "You are so fucking tight, Margot."

The reverent look on his face excites me, makes me squirm, grinding on his cock.

"Keep going," I urge him. "You told me you would fuck me, so do it."

He looks up at me, a sheen of sweat beginning to break across his forehead. He moves then, slowly pumping his cock in and out of me. I start to feel ripples of pleasure, tentative at first, then more and more certain.

I moan, loving the feel of him, of his big body smacking against mine. I run my hands down his muscular back, feeling the power that coils within him. It's addictive.

Stellan takes my breast in one hand, pinching the nipple. I start to move in time with him, rolling my hips. Little licks of flame start to unfurl themselves deep inside of me, stealing my breath away.

"Ohh," I moan. "More," I beg. Tossing my head back, I meet his cautious thrusts by snapping my hips again and again. He's being careful with me, but I don't want that. I want him to have all of me; I want to feel scorched by him, ruined by his every movement. "Stop being careful. I want... *more*. Fuck me harder, Stellan. Do it like you mean it."

He stiffens for just a moment, then grabs my hips and pulls me up a few inches. He forgets his hesitant rhythm and starts hammering himself in and out of my pussy. My eyes widen for a second.

"Shit," I swear. My pussy clamps down on his cock in the position we are in. Suddenly, I feel everything a thousand times more, every single nerve ending on fire. "Oh god. Yes. Yes!"

He starts sweating in earnest, his sweat mixing with my own. Looking at his fierce expression, I'm unsure what I've unleashed in him, more beast than man. He looms over me, his thrusts nearly violent, every single one of his muscles working toward one goal.

Fucking me. I know I can touch myself, make this come to an end for me. I don't want to, though. It's so good, feeling stretched out by his giant cock, his sweat dripping off his face and landing on my chest. But at the same time, the ripples of my inner pond are growing in size, becoming chaotic.

I can't hold it in forever.

It feels unbelievably good to move my hips in time with each thrust. I focus on that, squeezing my eyes closed, my fingers grasping my own nipple. Stellan groans, slowing his pace down and slipping his hand down between us.

"I need you to focus," he whispers. "I can't come until you do and I'm getting close."

He brushes my clit, the sensation like a live wire. I suddenly feel electrified, moaning and clutching at his shoulders.

"Yes," I breathe. "Yes! Faster!"

He speeds up his thrusts and punctuates each one by thrumming my clit. Sounds pour from my throat; I clutch at his shoulders, ready to burst. "Come for me," he whispers, his words a plea and a command at once.

I clench my eyes shut, stretching, reaching for what I know is about to happen. I can feel the strings of desire tightening... I just need them to break. "Stellan... I..."

I reach a sudden cliff, running up one side and launching myself off. I howl my pleasure skyward. That's what coming feels like — falling down a

deep, dark crevasse. My lungs seizing up, my whole body shaking and clamping down. My pussy spasms, clenching his cock. A million tiny jolts of sensation overwhelm my entire system, all at once, threatening to burn me alive.

Stellan doesn't need to ask if I climaxed. He seems to know my body already, that all I need right now is for him to finally come. I open my eyes and keep my hips moving, trying desperately to breathe. He hammers his cock home at a blistering pace, his movements freezes as he approaches his own peak.

"God damn," he whispers, pumping his hips madly. He pushes me back down, his fingers tightening around my throat. Not actually choking me, just dominating me completely.

And I love every second of it.

I raise my chin, sliding my fingers over his and pressing down. "I'm yours, Stellan. I'm fucking yours."

That seems to trigger his orgasm. His eyes widen, his thrusts growing erratic. He slams his body against me, filling me with his cock. "Fuck, Margot, you're making me come..."

Then he roars, thrusting hard and raggedly a half dozen times. I feel him coming, feel his semen fill me in hot pulses. He closes his eyes and shudders as he comes, gasping in breaths. I can only turn my lips up to his once more.

CHAPTER 32

STELLAN

When I wake up late the next morning, I find myself alone in the big bed. We fucked four times, each time a little different. The first time was about exploration, the second time I dominated her, the third time was sort of breathless and quick. And the fourth time... the fourth time lasted all fucking night into the early morning.

Margot drained all the energy from my body and I fell asleep with her head on my chest.

And yet here I am, waking with my cock already hard for her. There is some kind of spell she has woven around me, with her sly smiles and breathy moans. She tugs the ends close so that I'm stuck in a strait jacket of my own desire; I can't help but want her.

Only her.

My chest feels tight as I get up and throw on my jeans. I pad downstairs to the kitchen, where I drink water straight from the tap and then put a pot of coffee on to brew.

I lean against the kitchen counter, closing my eyes and thinking of the last couple of weeks. The main bright spots were times when I got to sneak away with Margot.

Time we spent together, alone.

It feels like that means something, but I'm unsure what. Scrubbing a hand over my face, I sigh. A delicious aroma fills the kitchen and draws a sleepy looking Margot in.

"Hey," she says.

"*Haj*," I greet her.

She wears one of my dark t-shirts and presumably nothing else. That idea excites me, although I should probably at least refill my body's energy supply before I strip that shirt off her body. Sliding her phone onto the marble countertop that stands between us, she gives me a feeble smile.

Fuck. Now that I look at her face, she looks as though she's been crying. Her eyes are puffy and her nose reddened. My hands curl into angry fists.

"What happened?" I ask.

She glances at me and shakes her head. "Nothing."

"That's bullshit." I place a mug of coffee before her, then start filling my own mug. "Tell me."

She wrinkles her face. "I just talked to my mom, that's all. We argued. It has nothing to do with you."

I lift my mug with a frown. "I'm assuming this is the same mother who caused you to be put into the foster care system?"

She looks up at me, startled. For a second I think she's about to fire back a retort. I cock a brow as she stares at me with those gorgeous dark blue eyes.

And then her face crumples. She whirls and takes off through the house, a sob escaping her as she flees.

My eyes widen. What just happened, exactly?

"Fuck," I mutter, putting down my mug. I hurry around the kitchen island and go after her, calling her name. "Margot! Margot, wait…"

Chasing her into a small room crowded with dust cloth-draped couches, I watch as she falls onto one of them and curls into a ball. The room is lit only by a window at one end. I follow her to the couch, watching as she buries her head and stifles another sob.

Royal life prepared me for so many things, but this is just not one of them. I sit down on the couch as gingerly as I can, reaching out a hand to touch her shoulder. She shudders under my touch but doesn't look at me.

"Margot," I say, feeling helpless. "What's going on?"

She inhales a shaky breath and then turns her head toward me. I frown as I take in her red-rimmed eyes and the tears on her cheeks. She studies me, sucking her pink lower lip between the whiteness of her teeth.

God, that look of hers skewers me, sears me right through.

"*Skatter*," I murmur, reaching out to cup her tear stained face. "Talk to me."

She sits up, wiping at her face. When she responds, her voice is watery and tight. "I wasn't supposed to cry in front of you. That is definitely not how I saw the weekend going."

I shrug lightly. "A month ago, I didn't plan to be here with you at all. Things change."

Margot bites her lip, looking at me carefully. "Back there, in the kitchen? The way that you talked about my mom and my time in the foster system. You were just so casual about something that you have no way of knowing anything about. And that… that *hurt*."

My brows rise. For a moment, I am genuinely without words. I made her cry? Her tears were my doing?

How do I even respond to that? I'm so out of my depth here and drowning quickly. She frowns a bit as she watches me.

"I… I'm sorry," I say, looking at her earnestly. "I didn't mean to hurt you."

She nods and looks down to her lap, wiping her cheeks again. "I know," she mumbles.

I move closer to her, putting my arm around her. It feels a little awkward but I do it anyway. Cupping her jaw, I tilt her face up to look at me. Then I sweep my thumb across her cheek, collecting the remnants of moisture I find there.

"I really am sorry," I say, my eyes darting back and forth as I try to read her face. "You always mention it so casually. I just thought... I mean... I never realized that you were sensitive about your mother."

She gives me a watery smile. "It probably doesn't help that I just got off the phone with her. She had the usual horrible things to say."

"Like what?"

Her cheeks stain pink. "She's been talking to several reporters about me. More like baiting them, it sounds like. She hasn't decided which reporter she wants to spill my life story to..." Her mouth twists bitterly. "Which means, I assume, that no one has said that they will pay her as much as she thinks she deserves." She wrinkles her nose. "My mom has always been that way."

"She's going to sell your story to some paparazzo?" I ask, baffled. "Why on earth would she do that?"

Margot sighs, shaking her head. "According to her, I still owe her big time. If she hadn't gotten pregnant with me, she says she would've quote 'been a real beauty'. Having me ruined her body I guess."

I squint. "What? You didn't choose to be born. How could any of that be your fault?"

She shrugs a shoulder. "That's only the beginning of what mom says I owe her. My mom has a running tally of my debts that goes all the way back to when she had to buy me diapers and pacifiers." She bites her lower lip for a second. "Don't even get her started about how I drained her resources anytime that I lived with her. Funny, because any time I was in foster care, she railed and ranted about how the government shouldn't interfere in our lives."

I glance away, struggling to keep a lid on my temper. "Your mother sounds…" I trail off, searching for the right word. I don't want to upset Margot, but it's clear that her mother has some mental issues that predate Margot's birth.

She sniffs, breaking my hold. Putting a few inches between us, she looks down at her hands. "Go ahead. You know you want to say it."

Her voice is distant. I think I almost made a very bad misstep, twice in a row.

"She sounds hard to deal with," I finish, touching Margot's knee. "It sounds like you had a lot of stuff piled on top of being… financially unstable. That's what I am hearing you say."

She looks up at me, sucking in a shaky breath. "Yeah. That's just the very surface of it, honestly. The tip of the iceberg."

Standing, I pull her to her feet. She comes naturally into the shelter of my arms, looking up into my face. I don't have the words to describe how it feels, just holding her like this. "I want you to tell me more. You say I don't know about it. So I want you to tell me. But… not in here. This room is weird and creepy."

Margot pushes up on her tiptoes and cups my jaw, then kisses me lightly on the lips. My heart thuds painfully against my ribs; I'm relieved at the fact that I finally did something right, but it's more than that.

Her scent is in my nose. Her warmth seems to invade me, my whole being. My fingers curl around her waist, digging into her skin. What is this feeling?

Possession. That's it. This is the first time I've really ever felt like she was *mine*. And for the life of me, I can't see how I'm just going to let her go. Not yet.

She lets me go and steps back, turning around and leaving. I trail after her, trying to get a firm hold on what I'm feeling. But of course, she doesn't give me the chance.

She walks into the kitchen, bites her lower lip, and gives me a once over. "You don't really want to hear about my background, do you?"

I stop a few inches away from her, looking at her sweetly curved face. "I meant what I said."

Margot wrinkles her nose and presses up on her tiptoes to kiss me. Then she takes a seat at the kitchen bar and inhales slowly. "Okay." She grabs her mug of coffee, running a finger around the rim. "I was born in Brooklyn. Which sounds like it was hip and funky… but it wasn't. My mom was a stripper for most of my childhood, and that job… well, I don't know if it led her to drugs or if drugs led to her stripping. Either way, my mom was too busy living her life to give me much thought."

THE WICKED PRINCE

She smiles sadly at her coffee mug. "Yeah. It's always been just my mom and me, no dad in the picture. As soon as I was out of diapers, she stopped paying for a babysitter. She just left me for days on end. So I found ways to keep myself busy... like the story I told you about discovering my passion for journalism at the library." She sucks in a deep breath. "But there were other things that I did, too. Bad things. I ran with a really awful crowd for a while."

My eyebrows lift. "I was wondering where you got your sense of style."

She looks up at me, smiling sheepishly. "Yeah, I guess I always idolized the punks of the 1980s. They just seemed so cool. Like they were living their grubby little lives out loud and not shutting up about how miserable and downtrodden they were." She makes a face. "Plus their music was just noisy and riotous and fun to dance to."

"No disagreement here." I slide my mug of coffee across the counter, taking a sip. It's tepid, but it's still coffee. "So... your mother didn't always take care of you."

"She did what she could do, I guess." Margot shrugs a shoulder. "I was in and out of foster care, usually in group homes. I did really well in school, but I was an outcast for sure. Nobody wanted to be friend with the weird kid who wore the same clothes all the time and never brought any cake on their birthday."

I nod. "Yeah, children can be cruel-hearted."

She sighs. "Yeah. Luckily, I got myself into NYU. And that's where I met Pippa." She drums her fingers against the counter. "That was a huge turning point for me. She was also into journalism and she sort of opened a doorway to that world."

Tilting my head, I try to imagine Pippa and Margot back then. Margot looks at my expression and laughs.

"What?" she asks.

"Nothing. I'm just trying to imagine a world without this rebellious, punk rock-loving version of you in it." I shake my head. "I think I'm glad that you are you."

Her lips curve upward and she rolls her eyes a little. "Thanks, I guess."

Standing up, I drag her chair towards me. Then I bend down and kiss her. Margot turns her head up, digging her fingers into the short hair at the back of my head.

When I pull back, I lean my forehead against hers. I whisper lulling words to Margot. "Thank you for opening up to me."

Her smile turns into a slow grin. "Of course." She twists and pushes the chair she is sitting on away and leans her small frame against mine, hips touching hips, her breasts against the hardness of my chest. "Take me to bed, Stellan."

I've never wanted anything more. I sweep her up in my arms and carry her toward the bedroom, my lips on her lips, my heart beating in time with hers.

CHAPTER 33

STELLAN

I rise early, the habit ingrained from my time in the military. After I shower and dress myself, Margot is still soundly asleep. I sit down on the bed beside her, looking down at her. Some women I've spent the night with have been like sleeping beauty in their slumber; placid and peaceful, unresisting and serene.

Margot isn't like that. She hugs a pillow to her bare chest, a tiny pucker of emotion creasing her brow, her mouth set in the echo of a frown. Her cotton candy curls spill backwards from her head like a dash of ink spilled in water. Her hands are tight little fists, looking like she's ready to fight.

And yet, I still find her incredibly beautiful. Not despite.

Because she is rebellious to her very core. Even in sleep, she doesn't lose her edge.

But the best thing is when I lean over, dropping a kiss to her bare shoulder. She stirs, opening her sapphire eyes a crack. And then she smiles at me. Big and bright, sleepy but all the more meaningful for it.

"Hey," she rasps.

One corner of my mouth lifts. "*Haj*."

She wrinkles her nose. "Were you watching me sleep?"

I shrug a shoulder. "Just for a second. I was actually coming to wake you up."

She sits up, stretching and yawning. "What for?"

"A surprise. Come on." I stand up. "And wear a bathing suit. There should be a bunch in the closet. We're going somewhere that I want you to see."

She makes a face at me but gets out of bed. An hour later, she joins me in the kitchen. I'm leaning against the island, sipping my coffee.

One look at her makes me do a double take and choke on my coffee just a bit. She's wearing nothing but a tiny black bikini under a filmy white robe. And her Converse, as per the usual.

I bite my lip. "You look…" I search for the right word. "*Edible*. Maybe we shouldn't even leave the house."

That earns me a scornful sound from her lips.

"This bathing suit is scandalous," she complains, indicating her outfit. "There were so many of them hanging in the closet, but this is the only one that was my size."

I give her a smirk. "You are just lucky that we carry sizes suitable for tiny people. You are elf-sized."

She rolls her eyes. "Are we going out to the beach or what?"

"We are. Here, I made you a coffee to go."

Her eyes widen with glee as she accepts the mug. "You're really getting to the core of who I am as a person," she jokes. "Coffee first, then literally everything else."

The beach is only a short walk from the house. As soon as we step outside into the salty air, I take a huge breath. The sun beams down on us as we stroll to the beach. I came out here earlier and set things up, so my footprints are already in the sand.

Margot makes a silly face as she steps in one of my footprints. "A giant has already been here, apparently."

That makes me grin. "He's giant all over, if you know what I mean." I lean close to stage whisper. "I'm saying that I have a huge cock."

That makes her cackle. "Yes, I'm aware. It's not for nothing that I'm walking a little stiff-legged today."

Pure male satisfaction fills me. "If you're lucky, I'll show it to you again later."

She shakes her head at me but she can't stop grinning. "Shut up."

We walk down to the pebble-strewn shore, sand clinging to our feet. I've left two paddle boards there, their matching paddles sticking up out of the sand.

"What is this?" Margot asks, pulling her hair back into a bun.

"Paddle boarding." I wiggle my eyebrows at her. "I've done it before. I'm *practiced*, you could say. So I'll mostly just be here to watch you fail at it." I arch my brows. "It should be a good diversion."

She squints at me, then turns her gaze out to the green-blue sea. "Twenty dollars says I'll be good at it by the time we finish." She pauses. "No, wait. Money doesn't matter to you. How about you pose for my camera tomorrow if I can get good today. And if I don't..."

I grin wickedly. "If you don't, I get to put my cock anywhere I want tonight."

Her brows fly up and she turns red as a beet. "You want to do *anal?*"

"*Ja*. Of course. I have just been waiting until the moment is right."

Her eyes tighten a little. "Well, it doesn't matter anyway. Because I'm going to win."

I rub my hands together and lick my lower lip. "I really hope you lose, *skatter*."

She flushes and looks down at the paddle boards. "You're going to get your ass kicked. Let's go."

I hold up my hands. "Slow down. First I need to know if you've ever surfed."

Margot's brows knit. "I'm from the city. And even though the water is right by us, it's safe to say that I have never surfed anywhere."

"Okay. Starting from the end of the board, yeah?" I point to the end of one of the surf boards. "You grab the sides, and then move onto your stomach. Then you lift yourself upward…"

"Oh, right." She moves onto the board. "Like this?"

"*Ja*. Then you sort of turn your leg…" I show her on my board. "And slide your other foot forward. Then the hard part, which is having enough balance to stand on the paddle board."

"Right. Got it." She scrunches her face up. "I mean, I think I do."

"Good. Let's paddle out, then."

We pad out to the sea, the sand stiff and crunchy, breaking away under our feet. When I step into the ocean and feel it swirl around my feet, I suck in a deep lungful of salty air.

Glancing at Margot to make sure she's still with me, I put my paddle board down on the water.

"Don't forget to attach your leash to your ankle," I say. Balancing awkwardly for a second, I do as I said.

I look at her as she does the same, biting her lip as she attaches the leash. I can't help the way my eyes dip down to her lush mouth, or the way they slide down to her tits. She's taken off her cover up and is just wearing that little black bikini now.

I realize that I am as bad as a horny fucking teenager, filling in what I can't see. But I don't bother to jerk my gaze away this time.

She looks up and colors when she sees me looking at her. She tucks a strand of hair behind her ear. "What?"

I grin. "Nothing. Are you ready to try to surf?"

She starts to move out into the water. "Ahhh. The water is cold!"

She jumps back, glaring at me like I've just endangered her well being somehow.

I pull a face. "It's warmer than room temperature."

"It's so cold!" she disagrees. "You should've warned me."

"So you give up, then? Because I count that as a forfeit."

She wrinkles her nose at me. "No."

She stomps back into the water, her movements obviously irritated. She likes to win; I should make a note of that. I wade out after her, carrying the paddles, and watch as her body disappears into the ocean. I shiver a little as I submerge myself up to my shoulders.

We both paddle out a little ways. The wind picks up a bit. I can feel the ocean sweeping us aside, which is unusual. When I have paddle boarded before, the sea was calm and placid.

That doesn't stop us from trying to paddle board today, though. She flounders a little bit trying to get on top of the board and then pops up... only to fall back into the water. When she resurfaces, gasping, I can't help but grin.

"You can give up any time you feel like it, you know."

She splashes me and I laugh. She grabs her board. "I'm ready to go again. But I want to see you do it."

A wave crashes just behind us, distracting me. I look over my shoulder and see dark gray clouds on the horizon. "Shit. Those weren't there before, were they?"

When I turn back to look at Margot, she's eyeing me suspiciously. "I don't think you can do it."

I roll my eyes. "Of course I can. We'll do it at the same time, *ja*?" And look over my shoulder again. "I'd say we have about thirty minutes before we probably should get off the beach."

She jerks her chin up at me. "Bring it on, Hagrid."

"Who is Hagrid?"

"Less talking, more paddle boarding." She grabs her board and steadies herself, struggling to get on the board.

I balance my own board, climbing on and standing up. I use the paddles that I'm holding to help keep myself from tipping over either way. Grinning, I turn to Margot.

Just in time to see her fall again, hitting the water with a loud smack. I make a face; that had to hurt. A wave crashes right on top of where we are swimming, distracting me for a second.

When she doesn't resurface immediately, I look around for her board.

Fuck.

I can't see it anywhere.

Turning myself around, I keep looking.

Fuck, where can he have gone?

"Margot?" I call, panicking.

I sense movement about ten feet away. I see a flash of pink right before she surfaces in a spray of white water, coughing and choking. She flails a little bit, pushing the wet hair out of her eyes, going under for another second.

I don't think. I start swimming towards her, calling out her name. "Margot!"

She comes back up just as I reach her. We make eye contact but she looks like she's a little confused and disconcerted.

"You're okay," I promise. "You're okay. Come with me." I tug her into my arms and swim for shore, although it is a struggle to hold onto her and swim with one arm. When my feet hit the sandy bottom of the ocean, I feel a strange sense of relief.

Margot coughs a few more times as I pull her onto the shore and put her down just out of the water's reach. "Hey. Are you okay? Look at me."

She nods, sucking in deep breaths. Her voice is pure gravel. "Yeah."

Untethering myself from my board, I sit down beside her and pull her into my arms. She's cold, much colder than me. She barely weighs anything. I press a kiss to her forehead, only just now feeling the weight of the adrenaline that kicked in.

My heart pounds. I'm sweating even though I'm not hot.

But Margot is safe. She's right here, in my arms

"Fuck," I mutter into her hair. "Jesus, that was scary."

She raises her head and I see tears in her eyes. She clears her throat. "Sorry."

I shake my head. "There is nothing to apologize for. It's just… for a second, I thought I had lost you. And that thought almost killed me."

Her eyes well up and she nods, falling against my chest. "Sorry."

"We need to get you warmed up. You're freezing." Pulling back from her, I stand up and help her to her feet. "Let's go back to the house."

Above us, the first lick of lightning splits the sky in two. A few fat droplets of rain fall onto us. Margot covers her face and takes off toward the house at a run.

I follow a little slower, weighed down by my thoughts.

What if something bad had happened to her?

What would I have done?

My chest tightens.

I realize, in that moment, that I'm in love with Margot. I love her so, so much. I can't even think about all the things that could have happened to her today.

Fuck. Just considering what almost happened makes my heart wrench in my chest.

She stops just before she reaches the door, shivering and looking back at me. And I pick up my pace without thinking about it, because she might need me.

And that's more important to me just now.

CHAPTER 34

MARGOT

After making sure that I'm okay, Stellan kisses me with so much passion that it leaves me shaking. I want more, so I kiss him again.

We quickly devolve into two creatures born of need. The kissing turns to fucking, the fucking turns to shouting each other's names as we come. And then we do the whole thing again and again, until we are exhausted.

Stellan is splayed out on the bed, his eyes closed. I'm lying beside him, my leg thrown over his. I delicately trace the lines of his chest with my fingertips.

Looking up at his face, his dark hair all askew, his five o'clock shadow becoming more pronounced, I sigh silently. He is so damned beautiful, with a strength of character that drives me to distraction.

In the early evening light, shadows cling to his face in a way that I think is perfect. If I don't get a picture of this moment, I'll regret it. I want to suspend us in this moment in time, so that I can always return back to it.

Even after he's gone. Even after I don't have any right to touch him.

"Are you awake?" I whisper.

Stellan opens his eyes a crack. When he speaks, it's a gravelly purr. "Sort of."

"I want to get my camera and take some photos of you. The light is just perfect."

He closes his eyes again and raises his fingers to press the bridge of his nose for a moment. "Photographs for your article?"

"No. Just... photos for me. I want to remember this exact moment. I swear to you, I'm the only one that will ever see them."

His eyes open a slit and focus on me. I get the feeling that he's trying to decide if I'm being truthful or not. My cheeks heat.

But he just closes his eyes again. "Sure, *ja*."

I let out a squeak of excitement, bouncing up to retrieve my Nikon from inside my tote bag. I lie back down, a little farther back this time, and take the lens cap off. After fiddling with the camera setting for a second, I look through the viewfinder.

There Stellan is, seeming so much larger than life. His naked torso makes my mouth water. He shifts a little, putting his arm behind his head.

God, does he even realize how tantalizing he is in this moment? He's a perfect specimen. He's not just rich. Not just obscenely privileged. Not just attractive. Not just well-endowed.

He is all those things. And yet, there's so much more underneath. Compassion, kindness, curiosity about the world around him... all supported by a backbone made of steel.

I squint and snap several photos, then move to my knees and try for a different angle. For a few minutes the room is silent except for the sound of my shutter clicking.

Stellan opens his eyes and gives me a knowing look. "Did you capture the perfect image of me?"

My lips curve upward and I wrinkle my nose. "Want to see?"

He arches a brow. "If you are offering, yes."

I flip a switch on my camera and the screen below the viewfinder comes to life. Moving over to Stellan's side, I show him the first photo. His brow draws down and he frowns ever so slightly, but he doesn't say a word.

I silently toggle through the thirty or so shots I've taken. His face never changes; he shows a little interest and an equal amount of skepticism.

"Well?" I ask gently. "What do you think?"

He purses his lips and shrugs. "I understand why the outside world is so fascinated with me. I'm a member of the royal family. A curiosity. A zoo animal, at times." He screws up his face. "But I don't quite understand why you are interested in capturing me like this."

Tilting my head a fraction, I turn the camera off. "Like what?"

He hesitates then shrugs. "Naked. Resting." He squints. "Why would anyone want to see that particular side of me?"

"Do you mean while you are vulnerable?" I ask.

Stellan frowns and shrugs again. "Sort of. Maybe."

I take half a minute before I respond. "Doesn't everyone want to catch a glimpse of Atlas at rest?"

He huffs out a chuckle. "Is that who I am now? Do I carry the weight of the world on my shoulders?"

My answer is instantaneous. "Yes. In my opinion, a large part of who you are is wrapped up in your duty."

He seems to give that some thought. "I guess you are right. It's sort of impossible to be anything other than the king-to-be. I don't... if my life changed suddenly, I wouldn't know who to *be*."

I smile at that. "Oh, I don't know. I think you would figure it out very quickly. Your personality is more than your sense of honor." I turn my head to the side. "I could see you as a royal air force pilot. You'd eventually become... a commander, or whatever. And you'd live in a very fancy house downtown with your perfect wife and three gorgeous children."

His lips lift at the corners. "Sometimes I really, really wish that was possible. I wish I could have an ordinary life. My brothers have a normal life. My sister has one too, sort of." He sighs. "I'm not the only one who has to worry about appearances, but…"

I scrunch up my face, finishing his sentence. "But you're the only one that will be inheriting the crown. So everything really counts for you, and you alone."

He chuckles. "Basically, yes."

Putting my camera aside, I lay down beside Stellan once more. Running my hand across the smooth skin of his chest, I bite my lip. "I know that this is the only time we'll ever really get together. I just…" I lower my gaze, unable to meet his eyes. "I want you to know that I am trying to make the most of it. To… to cherish it, I guess. It means a lot to me."

His hand comes down to cover mine, pressing my fingers against the wall of his chest. "It means a lot to me too."

My eyes threaten to fill with tears. Suddenly, all I can think about is next week. "My article is supposed to be done by now. I haven't even started it, but… how will I… how do I begin to write it?"

He tips my chin up so that I'm looking at him. "I don't have an answer for that. But…" He hesitates. "I don't want this to end."

My lips tremble. I blink away a sheen of tears. "No?"

He shakes his head slowly. He has never looked so serious before this moment. "No. Do you?"

I blurt out every dumb thing in my mind without even thinking it through. "I love you, Stellan."

As soon as I say it, my eyes go wide and my cheeks turn bright red. The reaction is instantaneous; I close my eyes, my heart lurching in my chest.

What the fuck did I just say?

Did I admit to being in love with him *out loud?*

Am I a fucking idiot?

"I shouldn't—" I start, but he cuts me off.

"You do?"

I open my eyes, cringing. "Yes. I didn't mean to... I mean, I just blurted it out. It wasn't very elegant— "

He cuts me off again with a press of his lips against mine. Crushing, insistent, I hear him take a breath against my mouth. "I love you too, *skatter*."

I freeze. Surely I didn't hear that right. "What?"

Stellan cups my jaw with his hand, his ice blue eyes burning into mine. "I'm in love with you. I know it's only been a little over a month. I know it feels like it's too soon. But I've never felt this way about anyone before in my life."

My brain feels like it's tumbling down a set of stairs. My mouth opens and words fall out. "You... you feel this way too?"

He draws my hand up over his heart and laces his fingers with mine. "Yes, *skatter*."

"Oh." I stare at him for a second, giving him time to tell me he's joking. But he doesn't.

I scramble up onto all fours, climbing on top of his body and kissing him so fiercely that I can't quite think straight. He groans and sinks his fingers into my hair. His cock is already hard for me, long and thick and stiff as steel.

I reach down between us and position his cock so that it is flush with my entrance. Already I can feel my pussy growing slick with my excitement. When I push the crown of his cock inside me, he murmurs my name.

"Margot."

I bite my lip and look down into his face, already feeling stretched out by his cock. He draws my head down and kisses me slowly as I push my body down to meet his, taking him in inch by inch. When he releases me again, he moans.

"Look at me," he says. "Keep your eyes on me."

We fuck slowly, my hips working to raise me up and down on his hot cock, his hands roving all over my body. He tweaks one of my nipples and I cry out, increasing my pace.

The whole while our gazes are locked.

"I really fucking love you," he grits out.

I smile, breathless. "I love you too."

His hands anchor my hips in place as he starts to thrust up. When he moves like that his cock touches a spot deep inside me that makes my eyes roll up in my head and my toes curl. I can feel tendrils of excitement reaching through my body, up from where we are joined to my tits, my neck, my mouth.

It's like he's touching me everywhere at once.

"Look at me!" he commands.

I open my eyes and focus on his face as he thrusts up into me again and again, his movements growing rougher with every passing second. And I love it; I would take him any way I can get him, but when he's rough it's just that much better.

"Touch your clit for me. I want to watch you unravel," he whispers, ramming me with his rapid-fire thrusts.

I bite my lip and slip my hand down, two fingers searching for my clit. The second I find it and begin to circle it with slow strokes, my eyes drift closed.

"Open your eyes, *skatter*," he says, his voice gone to gravel. "Let me watch you fall apart."

I force my eyelids open just as I start to peak. "Oh my god. Oh my god... Stellan..."

My hips jerk as I climb the last few steps to plummet over the edge. As I watch his beautiful face, I come harder than ever, my pussy spasming, my hips lurching, my entire body on fire.

"Fuck," he whispers. He comes all at once, his cock filling my pussy with long lashes of his seed. I can feel him twitching inside my body and right now, it's the sexiest thing I think I've ever experienced.

Stellan reaches up and cups my face in his hands, tugging me down for a breathless kiss. I collapse on top of him, kissing him lazily and loving the damp, hot skin of his naked torso pressed against mine.

He gives a husky chuckle. "Damn."

I give him an exhausted grin. "I know. I didn't think that the sex could get any hotter between us… and then there was *this*."

He kisses the corner of my lips, then my cheek, then my jaw, working his way down to my neck. I inhale suddenly, still sensitive on every inch of my body.

"What are you doing?" I ask, giggling and squirming.

"I want you to remember this day forever," he murmurs, pressing lips against my throat. "And I'll use every tool at my disposal to do it."

He finds a spot just at the juncture of my throat and neck. Then he bites down pretty hard, hard enough to make me gasp. Just when I start to react, to push him away, he releases me and kisses away the pain.

"Why did you do that?" I protest.

Stellan's lips curve upward. He looks me dead in the eye. "Because now I can be sure that you'll remember. Every time you look in the mirror. Every time something touches your skin just here." He traces a light touch over the bite mark. "You'll remember that I said I loved you, won't you?"

The rush of tears that fill my eyes are unexpected. I nod slowly. "Yes, Stellan. I will."

He smirks. "Good."

Then he kisses me on the lips again, distracting me. But I will never forget that stinging pain at the base of my neck or the man that caused it. He is right. I will always remember why he did it, too.

Shivering, I embrace him and open my mouth against his, ready for more.

CHAPTER 35

STELLAN

The next day, I push the morning's plan of packing up and leaving for Copenhagen into the evening. I'm a little desperate for more time before I have to be Prince Stellan again.

More time to spend with her, time I can be free. Time I can be *myself*.

Margot accepts the news of the extra day with a slow smile. "I agree to it on the condition that we leave this bed. I swear, you take me to these little coastal retreats and we hardly do anything but have sex. Not that I'm complaining about the sex, but…" She wrinkles her nose. "My body is pretty sore from fucking for like twelve hours in a row yesterday."

I smirk. "I like pushing your boundaries. How else will I know what the limit is?"

She rolls her eyes. "In hindsight, it was about two times less than we fucked yesterday. I should've had some more water or something because my arms and legs and abdominal muscles are a hot mess today. And that's not even talking about how much you..." She pauses, blushing. "Stretched me out."

I give her a wicked grin. "Good to know. I'll admit to being pretty sore myself. Maybe next time we should be prepared with bananas and coconut water."

She scrunches up her face. "Next time? What next time? My excuse for being in your life was officially over at the start of business today."

My heart starts hammering in my chest. God, I hadn't even thought of that. Tiny blades of turmoil slide through my gut and slice me to ribbons.

I don't know how I'm supposed to answer, so I just play it off like her question was no big deal. Even though in reality the thought of not seeing Margot again kills me.

I smile as if nothing happened. "The idea that we're not going to absolutely ruin each other's bodies later today is pretty laughable. But... I think there is a restaurant within walking distance. Do you fancy a stroll down the beach?"

She wrinkles her nose at my awkward phrasing. "Sure."

We get dressed, me in dark jeans and a white t-shirt, her in the short black dress that she wears so often. And then we walk down to the beach.

It's beautiful and sunny out, though windy enough that the day is pleasant rather than burning. I offer her my hand and she takes it, sliding her small palm against my own. She glances up at me, tucking a wild curl of her pink hair behind her ear. In the wind it's pointless though.

She sticks her tongue out at me and I laugh. "What is that for?"

She shrugs. "When you get too in your head, you get like... physically locked up. Your muscles are noticeably tighter, you're just all..."

She playacts jerky, blocky movements.

I shake my head. "Who says I'm in my head?"

She puffs out her cheeks. "You've been awkward ever since I said that we might not be able to see each other anymore."

I stumble in the sand and her eyes widen. "See? You are in your head."

I roll my eyes and shake my head. She's completely right, but she could at least do me the courtesy of ignoring it like I'm doing.

"So get my mind off of it," I challenge her. "Tell me a story."

"No." She wrinkles her nose. "We spent time on my story yesterday. I want to hear more about you, Stellan. And not the junk that you tell every other newspaper." Margot pulls my hand to her chest, holding it against her heart. "I want to know more about who you are as a person."

I make a face. "Like what? You want to hear my favorite bands?"

She shrugs a shoulder. "If that's what you want me to know, then sure. Who is your favorite band?"

Grinning, I slow our walking pace to a crawl. "The Rolling Stones."

Her eyebrows rise. "That... is not what I expected you to say."

"I live to surprise you, Margot," I tease.

"You just seem too buttoned up for that." Color springs forth in her cheeks. "No offense."

"*Ja?* Well. I'll have you know that I was once arrested."

Her eyes widen. "Wait, you were? What happened?"

"It was... I'll call it a youthful lapse. I partied a little too hard, did too many drugs. Got sick all over myself. Resisted the police when they were only trying to help. You know, all the usual embarrassing things."

She winces. "You didn't!"

"Oh, I really did."

"Oh, your parents must have been so angry!"

I exhale a slow breath. "Sort of. They knew, they were just... busy. My grandmother kept a keen eye out for all of her grandchildren, so she got the call instead of my father." I chuckle, shaking my head. "If you think I am stoic, wait until you see my grandmother receive bad news. But that night when the police brought me to the palace... the door shut, and it was just the two of us... It was the only time I can ever remember her being openly furious."

"That sounds terrifying."

"What, my grandmother? *Ja*, it wasn't great. You have to imagine someone about your size wagging her finger in my face and telling me how I wasn't living up to the family name. My grandmother was worried that her voice would carry and so she whispered and yelled at me, all at once. After about four hours of that, most people would go crazy."

She cracks a smile. "She sounds intimidating."

I squint off toward the place where the sky, sea, and land all seem to blend together. "You should meet her."

Margot pulls a face. "Uh... yeah, right."

My heart pounds in my chest. "No, I'm serious."

She stops, pulling her hand from my grip. I turn and look at her, my eyebrows lifting. She shoots me a confused look. "What?"

"I love you. You love me. So— "

"So we should *get married?!*" she says, horrified.

I give her a funny look. "No. I'm just saying... maybe we should... I don't know... *date*."

She crosses her arms and cocks her hips. "Stellan... we both know that's a terrible idea. You have a list of girls to choose from— "

I reach out and grab her by the waist, tugging her up against my hips. Then I cup her heart-shaped face, tucking a strand of those pink cotton candy curls behind her ear. "But I am not in love with any of them. I'm in love with *you*."

She bites her full lower lip and pins me with her intensely blue gaze. When she speaks, her voice is a mere whisper. "I know."

"So? I want you here. Stay with me." I draw in a deep breath, feeling more naked before her than ever before. "I've never felt like this about anyone before. And I'm not willing to just throw that away because it might upset some people."

She shakes her head, taking in what I said. Her brow hunches. "I don't even know how we would make that happen. Are you going to come up with a lie to tell your family? Am I going to lie to my editor?"

I take her hand, pulling it against my chest and trapping in beneath mine. "Is that what you want?"

Margot looks at me for a moment, as if trying to decide something. Then she shakes her head again. "No," she replies softly.

"So date me. We'll just show up holding hands and let everyone else deal with the fallout."

One corner of her mouth turns down. "That's not the best attitude to have, Stellan. Besides… dating you… I would assume that it comes with certain… *expectations*."

"It doesn't have to." I mean the words, but even as they leave my lips, I sense that they're not the fullest truth. "Look. I'm saying… this is all new to me. It's all new to you. Let's just… forge a path together."

She sighs, looking away. For several moments, I can hear nothing but the sea in the background and the hammering of my own heart.

Is she really going to turn me down?

When she swings her gaze back to my face, I can see the torment that is going on behind those beautiful blue eyes. "I want to say yes. I really do, Stellan."

My lips curl upward. "So do it, *skatter*."

Margot presses up onto her tiptoes, seeking out my mouth. I lean down and kiss her, pressing my lips to hers. She drops back down, biting her lower lip.

"Okay," she whispers. "I won't go anywhere, as long as you still want me to stay."

Wrapping my arms around her, I hug her. She settles against my chest, her arms slipping around my waist to hold me tightly.

I close my eyes and try to memorize every detail of this moment. To store this memory, keep it safe for a rainy day. Because I won't always be this happy. She won't always get to say yes.

But just now, it's enough.

CHAPTER 36

STELLAN

In the driver's seat of my car, I look over at Margot. She looks anxious, chewing her lip and bouncing her knee.

"We are almost back to the palace," I say. "Have you thought of what you're going to say to your bosses?"

She looks over at me with a worried smile. "It's all I've thought about since we got in the car. Yet I haven't come up with anything good. What do I say? *Sorry about the story, but I've decided to date the crown prince?*"

I shrug. "Tell them the truth. They can't be mad at you for that."

She gives a huff of laughter. "Yes they can. They have every right to fire me. If I lose my job, I might get a call from immigration, wondering what I'm still doing here."

I fix her with a long look. "You won't. I'll have Erik make some calls."

Sighing, she looks away. "I wish I didn't need you to call in any favors. But thank you for doing it."

I pull the car up the long driveway in front of the palace, putting it in park. Glancing over at Margot, I tug her hand into my lap. She turns her head toward me, biting her lip.

I reach up and tuck a strand of her hair back behind her ear. "I have to go in and tell my grandmother that I'm defying her. You have to go tell your editor the same thing, basically." I inhale deeply. "If it helps, I'm still in love with you."

She laughs. "It definitely doesn't hurt."

I pull her in, kissing her fully on the mouth. Then I turn her loose with a sigh. "All right. I'm ready to face the firing squad."

Margot nods, opening the car door. "Yeah. Text me later and let me know how it went."

I climb out of the car and lean against the roof briefly. As she stands and grabs her bag, I stand there, looking at her ass and her bare legs in her super short dress.

God damn. After a weekend like we just had, where we fucked until we were too exhausted to move every single day... I should have found the saturation point with Margot. I should be content and fulfilled. And yet... I'm not.

I don't know that I'll ever be, to be completely honest.

I bite my lip, smiling. "I will."

She wrinkles her nose and then walks away, heading for the *Politiken* offices. I take a deep breath and look up at the palace. Then I stride toward the main entrance, jogging up the steps.

As I enter a few people are waiting for me. A butler, several maids… and Erik, standing tall, looking especially Scandinavian with his blond hair and enormous stature.

"Erik," I greet him. "How are things?"

Just from the way his lips thin, I can tell that he is irritated with me. He just turns and heads toward the carpeted stairs in front of us. "You were missed yesterday."

I follow him up the stairs and into the grand hall, heading toward my study. He bursts through the door and strides past the leather armchairs and the fireplace, throwing himself down in the leather couch with a loud sigh.

"Well?" he demands. I close the door and sit on a corner of my oak desk, crossing my arms and pursing my lips.

"Well what?" I ask.

"You cancelled your appearances yesterday."

Cocking my head, I squint at him. "So?"

"So… you missed the board meeting regarding the children's cancer center to be named after Anton. You knew that was important to me!"

That gives me pause. Anton was Erik's little brother; he died of childhood lymphoma. The board meeting was a meeting of the royal family, in which they voted on which projects to fund.

"Ahh. Shit." I wince. "Did the family really vote against a children's cancer center?"

"It got funded, but barely. That's not really the point, Stellan. You promised me that you would be there to champion Anton's name!"

I blow out a breath. In the back of my mind, I knew that coming back to Copenhagen was going to be like this. I knew that I would be disappointing someone and letting someone down. I always am, I guess.

It's just usually not Erik.

"I'm sorry."

"That's it? That's all you have to say?"

Puffing out my cheeks, I sigh. "I spent the weekend with Margot."

Erik stills, his eyes tightening on my face. "What do you mean, you spent the weekend with her?"

At that moment, the door to the study swings open. I turn and watch as my grandmother glides in wearing a light gray pantsuit.

I paste on my coolest smile. "Ah, *Momse*. Good, I can tell both of you at once."

My grandmother arches a brow. "I hope you are about to tell me why you felt like shirking your duties yesterday. It was very difficult to get enough royals to cover all your engagements."

I want to roll my eyes, but instead I just continue to smile. "I'm dating Margot Keane."

Her nostrils flare. Erik shakes his head, glaring at me.

"That's a bad idea," he mutters.

I shoot him a glare.

Ida raises her chin and looks me square in the eye. "Is that the journalist from America?"

"Yes."

She brushes a bit of invisible lint from her jacket sleeve. "You know that you can't marry her."

I hold up a hand. "No one said anything about marriage. I haven't even looked into that possibility yet."

She eyes me. "Stellan, you were raised to hold yourself to high standards. Certainly higher than a poor American reporter. I mean, really! I'm not even sure that our constitution will allow the crown prince to marry a foreigner, much less someone of such a different class than our family."

My lips thin. I draw myself up to my full height. "I know that Margot isn't your choice, *Momse*. But for now, she is mine. So you can either deal with it or you can find someone else to be your well-behaved little pet prince."

Ida's hand goes to her chest. She opens her mouth to retort, but I'm already turning my attention to Erik.

"And you." I glare at him. "I am sorry that I missed the vote yesterday. That was wrong of me. But I'll tell you now... I won't tolerate anyone telling me how to live my life. You need to get comfortable with the fact that I'm dating Margot." I look at Ida. "Both of you do."

Erik looks angry. "You don't even know any of her past, Stel. Trust me, she has plenty to hide."

"Really?" I ask, crossing my arms. "Tell me. Go ahead. Get it out of your system now."

Ida clears her throat. "I had someone look into her background. It isn't pretty."

I make a disgusted sound. "So what? Unless one of you is willing to tell me what kind of mysterious things Margot has done that I don't know about..."

There is a silent moment where Ida and Erik look at each other, their frowns heavy. I shake my head.

"I didn't think so," I say.

A butler hovers in the doorway and clears his throat. "Pardon me, but the crown prince has a number of engagements to prepare for today..."

"Thank you," I say to the butler. Swinging back to Erik and Ida, I shrug one shoulder. "Being the prince never ends."

Then I turn and stride out of the room, following the butler.

CHAPTER 37

MARGOT

Getting out of the limo with twenty pounds of ballerina pink tulle zippered snugly around my body is a real struggle. I push myself up against the doorframe, cursing my own decision to wear this delicate, strapless ballgown. When I finally find my feet, I pat my hair discretely.

Are we really about to do this? My heart pounds. I look up at the fancy hotel we are at, praying that I don't sweat in this dress.

Stellan is right by my side, offering his arm. He's at his most dazzling dressed in a dapper tuxedo and his smile as he looks me up and down gives me chills.

"You look amazing in that dress," he intones, his eyes taking me in. "You're going to be perfect tonight."

I place my hand on the inner elbow of his tuxedo jacket, exhaling. "Thank you. I won't even bother to compliment you, because you always look perfect."

He smirks. "Come on, then."

He leads me past the bowing bellhops and valets, through the perfect pink granite lobby, and up a gorgeous pink granite grand staircase. We emerge onto the second floor and hear the party before we see it; strains of a string quartet escape from the ballroom to our right. He sweeps right past the people crowded around a set of wide double doors. I try to play it cool, lifting my head high like I belong here, but I don't.

I am just pulled along with *him*.

As we enter the ballroom, I notice people bowing. They're definitely bowing to Stellan and not to me, but it still makes me uncomfortable. The party is already in full swing, the women in extravagant gowns, the men stunning in their tuxes.

It's a Wednesday night, for god's sake. Don't these rich people have better places to be than here? Especially tonight, the night that Stellan and I are stepping out together as a couple.

My heartbeat gallops away in my chest. I suck in a breath.

"There's Pippa," Stellan says, nudging me.

I glance in the direction he nods. Pippa is right there, wearing the most amazing bright pink ballgown topped with an enormous bow. She turns and spots me, grinning.

I look up at Stellan, then go still. I want to go see Pippa, but I definitely don't want to let Stellan down.

He leans in so close to my ear that his words are a kind of tease. "I'm afraid we have to say hello to a number of important people first. I promise you, the second we are through, you can go see Pippa."

I grin, slipping my hand down to find his. "Is this okay?"

His lips twitch. "Very." He kisses me on the lips and tucks a strand of hair behind my ear. I can feel the gazes of the people around us turning curious.

I blush red as a ripe summer strawberry, straightening his lapel. "You can take me around to as many people as you want. At the end of the day, I get to be here with you."

He smirks then leans down to whisper in my ear again. "Good girls get rewarded. Just something for you to think about."

My blush deepens, going all the way down my neck. "You are wicked. A truly wicked prince."

He winks. "You're fucking right I am."

Stellan guides me over to an older couple. He says hello, chats with them for a moment, then introduces me.

"This is Margot Keane, my girlfriend."

My eyes widen a little. I glance at him with a startled look. We definitely didn't talk about labeling this thing between us. The older couple look at me curiously as we shake hands.

"Hi," I say, because I have no idea what else to say.

"You're American!" the woman says, a little taken back. "How… interesting!"

My cheeks burn sixteen shades of red. She just made it clear as day that I am the weirdo, standing here in a dress I don't own, on the arm of a man who isn't mine. I nod dumbly, feeling like I want to crawl under a rock and never come out again.

This was such a bad idea. I watch Stellan's face anxiously, trying to figure out when he's going to pull the ripcord and bail out of this disaster.

It's only a minute before Stellan excuses us, pulling me by the elbow as he moves away. He looks down at me, but never stops moving. "If we keep circling, it will look like we are on the way to talk to someone," he confides.

"Should I leave?" I whisper.

That causes him to stop. "What? Why?" Then he glances back where we just were. "Oh, because of the Eldins? God no. I picked them as the first people because they will hate you no matter what you do. They hate me, to be perfectly honest."

My jaw drops. "What?"

"*Ja.* I just wanted you to cut your teeth on them. Because it doesn't matter if you are the most charming person ever or if you're a nervous wreck… they are so old and so conservative that they won't approve of you either way." He slides his palm up my back, his smile genuine. "It wasn't that bad, actually."

A surprised huff of laughter leaves my lips. "It was terrible! Not to mention the fact that you sprang the whole girlfriend thing on me…"

He smirks. "What? You're going to say that you don't desperately want to be my girlfriend?"

I blush and roll my eyes. "You know what I mean."

"I do." His eyes shine with a mischievous light. "Are you ready to meet people who aren't an absolute waste of space?"

I suck in a deep breath. "Okay. I'm ready."

For the first ten people I am introduced to — as Stellan's girlfriend, no less — I'm nervous. The next thirty or so go by in a blur. And after the next thirty, my head starts to spin.

"I need a break," I whisper to Stellan.

He raises his brow. "Now? We are almost done." he wrinkles his nose. "We just have to greet my grandmother and Prime Minister Finley. Don't worry, they are almost always together at these things. My grandmother thrives when she feels like she's important. Finley does his part by following her around and kissing her ass."

I color faintly. "Okay. I just… I don't know how you do it. Smile for everybody, remember mundane details about their lives…"

He shrugs. "I've had years of practice. Trust me, you get better at it the longer you do it."

Taking a deep breath, I close my eyes briefly. "Okay. I can do one more."

When I open my eyes, I find him looking around the ballroom. "I think my grandmother and Prime Minister Finley are holding court all the way over there."

He takes my hand and leads me through the densely crowded ballroom. It's weird to watch people realize that they are in the path that Stellan intends to take. They jump out of the way, apologizing profusely for having done exactly nothing.

We pass Pippa again, who is slow dancing with Lars. Her head is on his shoulder, her eyes are tightly closed. He holds her as carefully as if she were made of the most delicate glass. As if he is afraid to shatter her.

I tug on Stellan's hand. When he looks back, I nod at them.

He doesn't look the least bit surprised. "That's been going on for years. They're best friends. Or maybe they are lovers. Who can keep track anymore?"

He turns away and keeps going, and I force myself to turn my gaze toward the far corner of the ballroom. We pass by more people and then the path we are on clears. There in the corner of the room is a huddle of people, centered around the most petite figure, that of Stellan's grandmother.

She is elegance personified. She's wearing a dress made of ivory silk and she looks as perfect as a wedding cake topper.

"What do I call your grandmother?" I whisper.

"Her Royal Highness," Stellan whispers.

He leads me right up to the people gathered in the circle. Without a word, the circle widens, leaving a gap for us to step through. Her Royal Highness is just finishing a story and several people laugh.

She looks right at me, her face creasing ever so slightly. I can feel her gaze as it traces down to where I cling to her grandson's hand. She cocks an eyebrow, looking at Stellan.

"Should we go somewhere more private?" she asks him.

Stellan grips my hand harder. "Why would we? I just wanted to introduce you all formally." He turns to me. "Margot Keane, this is Her Royal Highness, the Queen Dowager. And right beside her is Prime Minister Finley, the Prime Minster." They each lower their heads for the barest second. "Everyone, this is Margot. My girlfriend."

Every pair of eyes within hearing distance is suddenly on me. Every drop of blood in my whole body rushes to my cheeks.

"Hello," I say softly. "It's a pleasure."

Prime Minister Finley clears his throat. "Girlfriend, you say?"

Her Royal Highness fastens her gaze on me. "I suggest we withdraw to somewhere we can speak alone, Stellan."

Stellan gives everyone a bland smile. "We are perfectly fine, *Momse*. Thank you. Actually, I promised Margot that we could head to another engagement as soon as she had formally met you."

The expression of astonishment mixed with a frosty anger looks right at home on her face. "I would speak with you in private— "

That's the moment that I hear the first angry shout. I whip my head around and see a few of people wearing all red coming into the ballroom.

"*Danmark ønsker frihed!*" one cries, raising a fist in the air. The others shout in support.

"*Frihed fra tyranni!*"

"*Frihed!*"

My eyes widen and my jaw drops. They are protesting. Worse, they are protesting *us*.

I look at Stellan, who instinctively steps in front of me. "What are they saying?"

"*Afskaffe monarkiet!*" another one screams.

Stellan's face is stony as he watches the protestors as a swarm of security guards moves in to surround them. "They're calling for freedom from tyranny. I assume that they are Red-Green Party protestors, calling for the abolishment of the monarchy."

I turn back and look at the protestors, my face going beet red. Though I've been too wrapped up in Stellan lately to be a rabble-rouser, I have been in their shoes. I've even been to Red-Green Party meetings.

How am I on the other side of the issue now? My heart starts beating at a frenzied pace.

Am I turning my back on the issues I once so cared about?

A bodyguard materializes out of nowhere. *"Vi må flytte dig et andet sted, Prins Stellan."*

He starts to corral Stellan, who has a good four inches on him. *"Vi tager afsted,"* Stellan says. "Come on, Margot."

I allow myself to be hustled out of the ballroom while the protestors are being herded out the opposite side. One of the protestors throws a balloon filled with red paint, which bursts against the doorway just as I pass under it.

Red paint falls on my head and the back of my dress, but Stellan shelters me from most of the fallout.

"Rend mig i røven!" he mutters. "Fuck! We have to go. Come on, let's get out of here before the press gets wind of the protest."

Still stunned, I let him lead me down the back stairway and to a waiting car.

CHAPTER 38

STELLAN

A few days later, I'm escorting Margot down a long hallway at Winthrop Manor, the house in which my parents have finally come home to rest. I slow my pace, stopping her for a second. She looks up at me, her face worried.

"What?" she asks. "Did you forget something?"

My brow creases. "Are you okay?"

She nods slowly, pressing her hands down over the full skirts of her light blue ballgown. "Why wouldn't I be?"

I shrug. "You've been quiet ever since we went to that ball."

She bites her lip, her face heating. "I know. Just… I'm still a little shaken by the fact that the protestors were protesting you. I'm trying to figure out how to feel about being a part of the problem and not part of the solution."

My eyebrows rise. "I didn't realize you felt that way."

She bows her head and shrugs. "It's just… stuff I need to get over, I guess. I'll figure it out. Don't worry."

I reach out, grabbing her hand and hauling it against my chest. "Are you sure you're still okay with meeting my parents? It's a big step, I know." I pause. "Is it too soon?"

There is a moment of hesitation. I see in her eyes that she's still not a thousand percent sure. But Margot raises her chin, looking at me proudly.

"I'm ready," she affirms. "I promise."

I lean down and kiss her, reassuring myself as much as her. She tastes sweet and perfect, just like she did the last ten thousand times I've kissed her. I squeeze her hand, then lead her to the doorway of the dining room.

"Your highness," the servant at the door says, bowing low. "Please."

He waves us into the room. Everyone else in my family is already here, and my late joining doesn't exactly go unnoticed. The entire table turns to me, as if they are collectively waiting for something.

I reach behind myself and find Margot's hand. She's gone pale as we approach the two empty seats, situated between my father and my little sister Annika.

"Speak of the devil," my brother Lars announces.

"Yes, we were waiting for you two," Annika says, looking amused. "Join the party."

My father looks jovial as usual, a huge dark-haired giant with bright red cheeks. "Ah, our firstborn has finally deigned to join us."

My mother gets to her feet, rushing over to hug me. She's a tiny person, and when she embraces me tightly, several strands of her dark hair escape the chignon at her nape. "Ach, *min son!*"

I let myself be hugged for a second, then chuckle. "Okay, okay." My mother lets go and I draw Margot closer. "Mother. Father… this is Margot. Margot, meet the king and queen."

Margot curtsies awkwardly. "Your highnesses."

"Oh!" my mother says, beaming at Margot. "Please, call me Thora. And that's Göran."

My mother then proceeds to be her charming self, embracing Margot and pulling out her chair. Margot turns red and hurries to sit down. I see Annika tug on her arm and whisper something into her ear. Judging by the smile that appears on Margot's lips, I would guess that Annika just told her something whimsical.

"Sit, sit," my father says. "Join the rest of us."

I take my seat next to him, looking around the table. Lars and Finn are in attendance, though Finn looks bored.

"Where's Anders?" I wonder.

My mother clears her throat. "We should talk about that later," she says, smiling. "We are all here to meet your new friend, Stellan."

I reach for Margot's hand under the table, glancing at her. "Girlfriend. She's my girlfriend."

My father looks surprised. "You didn't tell my mother that, I hope? She would have a stroke."

"Oh, quit," my mother answers, rolling her eyes. "She'll be just fine. Your mother gets so hysterical over everything."

I look at my siblings to gauge their reactions to that. Annika wrinkles her nose, Finn looks at his glass of red wine, and Lars looks somber. No help there, I guess.

Not that I really expected it.

"I did tell her," I reply. "In fact…" I grip Margot's hand. "I was hoping that you could give me guidance about announcing the relationship to the cabinet and the parliament."

Margot squeezes my hand. I glance at her and she gives me a wide-eyed look that says *we didn't talk about that!*

I wink at her. "When the time is right, I mean."

Annika interjects. "Isn't that like… a step away from announcing that you're engaged?"

Between us, Margot goes pale and shrinks down in her seat an inch. My father sizes us up, then gives his head a shake. "Your sister is right. Telling parliament is quite serious."

My mother actually tears up. "I'm so happy for both of you! Now Margot… I learned you are from New York City. Is that correct?"

Clearing her throat, Margot nods. "Yes, ma'am. Born and raised."

"That's fascinating." My mother looks at my father. "Isn't it?"

"Very," he says. "Tell me though, aren't you a journalist?"

Margot goes red as a beet. "Yes, sir."

He waves his hand. "Göran, please. And you realize that being my son's girlfriend will probably mean you won't get the best stories assigned to you any longer, correct?"

Margot looks at me, wetting her lower lip with her tongue. "Yes sir… I mean… yes, Göran."

I sit forward, eager to defend her. "Margot isn't dating me for access to the royal family."

"Oh! Göran is not suggesting that!" my mother says, eying my father. "Is he?"

My father, ever the wise man, knows when he should stop talking. So he just smiles. "No, of course not."

I sit back and let Margot take over the answering, making eye contact with my father once more. His lips tip upward and he gives me a nearly imperceptible head tilt.

I take that to mean that he approves of Margot. Then again, how could anyone not be pro-Margot when my mother is so obviously over the moon about her?

We get through dinner just fine. Between Annika and my mother peppering her with questions, Margot talks almost the entire time. She is bashful at first but in the end, I feel like she charmed the hell out of my parents.

Now there is just the rest of the fucking world to go, I guess.

When it's time to go, my mother hugs both me and Margot so hard that it's almost painful.

I shake hands with my father, who is still seated at the table. "Talk soon?"

His lips tip upward. "Yes."

There's something hanging between us, a moment of hesitation on my part. Should I bring up what my grandmother told me? "I'm glad you are doing well."

He frowns but says nothing. He just nods his head.

Then I squire a talked-out Margot down to the waiting limo, where she crawls in the back seat and closes her eyes.

"Oh my god," she moans as I climb in beside her. "I'm so tired! How do you do that all day, every day and manage not to go insane?"

I give her a look. "That was just my family. That was the easy part."

She wrinkles her nose. "The easy part of what?"

"You have to know that being my girlfriend is..." I stop, trying to decide what I'm going to say. My mouth turns down at the corners. "My sister wasn't wrong. Let's say our next step is declaring our relationship to parliament. That's as good as telling everyone that they should expect a royal wedding in the next year."

Her eyes widen. Her throat works as she swallows. "I didn't realize that."

I puff out my cheeks, exhaling slowly. "Well... now you do. What do you think?"

She screws up her mouth. "I think that's asking a lot of us."

"So you would say no?" I ask, my brow descending.

Margot pins me with a surprised gaze. "What are you asking, exactly?"

I rake a hand through my hair, growing agitated. "I'm not asking you to marry me yet. But... are you at least open to getting married? I mean, you had to give this *some* thought when you agreed to date me."

She sucks her lower lip in between her teeth, her gaze lowering. "A little. I..." She pauses, taking a deep breath. "I'm not against getting married. I just didn't think... I mean... I thought we would have more time to get comfortable with the idea."

"Royals are born ready to marry. It's one of our duties to the country." I exhale, waiting a beat. "Historically, the royal family marries people who are wealthy and titled. People who may or may not be royals in their own right. People with the same expectations that my family has." I reach out for her hand, holding it gently. "I thought… I just thought that we were lucky, because we happen to be in love with each other."

She looks at me, grasping my hand. "I do love you, Stellan. You know that. I just wasn't prepared for all the bullshit that other people are forcing on us. But I realize that you don't really have a choice in the matter, do you?"

My mouth lifts at that corners. "No, I don't have a choice. In the grand scheme of things though… I can imagine much worse things than having you as my wife."

She gives me a tiny smile. "I feel the same as you do. It's just a lot at once. I have so many questions… Where would we live? What would happen to my job?"

I push my cheek out with my tongue. "There's only one question that matters, in my opinion. When I ask, will you say yes? Because everything else is flexible."

She blushes six shades of red, but she doesn't look away. "Yes. When you ask me someday, I will say yes?"

I shrug, a smile tugging at my lips. "Then that's settled."

Margot slides her palm along my jaw, drawing me close for a tender kiss. I let my eyes sink closed, let my thoughts only hover on this moment.

This moment in which she said *yes*.

CHAPTER 39

MARGOT

I wake so early that dawn has yet to break. I'm still not used to sleeping beside Stellan, especially not here in the palace. His bedroom here is beyond ridiculous, featuring a massive four poster bed and floor length windows wrapped in gauzy white.

I settle on my side and watch him in his sleep. Without his piercing ice blue gaze he seems softer, though his body is still every bit as rugged. My fingers itch to reach out and touch him.

I love him so, so much. My heart twists in my chest. I shouldn't wake him, but it is hard.

Rolling onto my back, I repress a sigh. My mind goes back to yesterday evening, to the all but proposal he sprung on me in the backseat of the car.

Honestly, I haven't really thought of much else since he asked me.

When I ask, will you say yes?

I thought I had died then and there when he asked, and I wasn't sure if I was in heaven or hell.

I mean, on one hand… Stellan and I have just fallen in love. It feels real… but there is so much more that's yet to be seen. Why rush into things?

And then on the other hand… he just basically asked me to be his *princess*.

Never in a million years did I ever actually think that someone as hot as Stellan would ever look at me like he does. Like we're in the desert, and I'm the only glass of cool water for a hundred miles around.

I've never felt that kind of connection with anyone else. And I never expected to, either. I think that what Stellan and I have is so special.

But the whole royal thing really ratchets up our mutual expectations like a million degrees.

I'm not just agreeing to be his girlfriend. I'm agreeing to be the future queen.

And that thought terrifies me to the depths of my soul.

Heaving a silent sigh, I realize that there's no way I'm going to go back to sleep. I get up, moving stealthily to grab my pink silk robe from where it's hanging by the door. Then I pad out of the bedroom and into the adjoining living room.

A footman is just pulling back the drapes on the windows, revealing the new dawn just now breaking. I see the table, on which he has already laid out an assortment of waters and juices with fresh croissants and jam.

He bows to me and leaves without saying a word. Something I'm trying to get used to still.

I suck in a breath and wander over to the table, pausing when I see the newspapers spread out beside our breakfast. My own young face stares back at me, shell-shocked.

My mugshot.

Oh fuck.

PRINCE STELLAN'S LOVER HAS DARK PAST

My heart starts hammering in my ears. I snatch the paper up with trembling fingers and unfold it. I only have to scan the first few lines to realize that my own mother ratted me out.

Not only that, but she somehow dug up this old photo of me and gave it to the newspaper.

Fuck!

I stare at the picture. At sixteen years old, I was nothing but trouble. My hair is dark brown, I'm wearing oversized men's clothes, and worst of all… I hold my hand down low, but you can clearly tell that I am flipping off the camera.

I ball up the paper in my hands and release a scream. "Fuck! Where is my phone?"

"What's going on?"

I whirl and find a sleepy Stellan standing in the doorway, completely unashamed of his nudity. My eyes widen and my heart seizes. I can feel myself turning red.

I wasn't even thinking about him yet… What will he think about my teenage lawbreaking?

"I… I…"

He walks over to where I dropped the crumpled piece of newspaper, smoothing it out. His eyes widen and he looks up at me expectantly.

"What the fuck is this?"

The boom of his voice makes me jump out of my skin. I can't even look at him when I answer.

"I had two arrests when I was only sixteen. One for criminal trespassing and one for shoplifting. I guess… I guess that The New York Post must have paid my mother a lot for this story, because they have pictures and everything."

He points to a chair next to the table, his voice shaking. "Sit. Tell me everything that happened." His eyes pin me in place. "Do not leave anything out this time, Margot."

I scurry over to the chair, taking a seat. Stellan sits across from me, folding his arms across his chest and scowling at me in a way that makes my stomach do flips.

"Um. So…" I blow out a breath. "When I was sixteen, I ran with a bad crowd. There were a bunch of us, guys and girls, all about the same age. All homeless or in-between homes at the time. All angry. I didn't actually think my mom remembered any of this because she was on a bender at the time..."

"Margot!" he growls. "What happened?"

I suck in a breath. "Right. Sorry. I got arrested twice, like I said. Once for criminal trespass, because a bunch of us were squatting in a house together. And then I got busted like three weeks later for trying to shoplift stuff to eat."

I'm so humiliated at saying it out loud. My face is red, my ears are ringing, and I can't sit still.

"Why didn't you think to tell me about this when I asked about your background?" he asks, seeming mystified.

I glance at Stellan, biting my lip. "I didn't realize that you were looking for anything in particular. I was just... trying to tell you about my life," I say, growing defensive. "I didn't realize that you were asking for a full background check. I usually don't tell people I date about it for the first six months, if ever."

He looks so confused and angry. "Why not?"

"Because it isn't really anyone's business!" I shout. I shake my head. "When I got arrested the second time, I did a diversion program. When I turned eighteen without getting arrested again, my record was expunged. And I happen to think that my being a reformed bad girl isn't really the most interesting thing about me, if we're being perfectly honest."

Stellan shakes his head slowly, exhaling as he scrubs a hand over his face. "This is fucked up, Margot." He glances at me. "I mean, I won't lie. I was attracted to your rebellious streak. I love it sometimes, but other times… like now for example…"

I take a deep breath. "I wasn't trying to keep it from you Stellan. Honestly, I wasn't. It just didn't occur to me."

He studies me for a long moment, then nods. "I believe you."

My heart starts thrashing around in my chest. "You do?"

His face creases. "*Ja*. I don't think you are a dishonest person, Margot."

I launch myself on top on him, surprising him with a hug. Burrowing my head down against his chest, I let out a joyful sound. His arms close around me. He brushes my hair back, kissing the top of my head.

I've never been loved like this. Not ever.

My tiny brain gets totally overloaded and my eyes tear up. I hug him hard, blinking back tears.

"I'm sorry, Stellan." My voice breaks.

"Oh, *skatter*," he murmurs. "What am I going to do with you, huh?"

Wiping at my face, I lean back and look at him. "Will we have to tell your family?"

He looks at me like I might be simple. "Yes. My grandmother will have heart palpitations."

Ducking my head, I hide against the solid wall of his chest. "I'm so embarrassed."

"Mm. Not only that, but you have to tell me everything else. Any dirt, any secrets you have… spill them right now. It's better just to know where you might be vulnerable."

I frown. There isn't anything… is there?

"Well… I don't think that I have any other secrets…" I say.

"Really? Nothing else the press will get their hands on? Nothing that would make them salivate? Because I'm basically going to introduce you to the world as my better half. Soon to be a princess, one day to be queen."

That thought makes me heart seize. "Hearing you say that… it seems unreal."

Stellan pushes me back a couple of inches, his ice blue eyes pinning me. "I'm sorry to bring this back around to the point, but… what is the press going to find, Margot?"

An image swims up from deep down. "The only thing I can think of…" I wince. "There may be some footage of me protesting."

He frowns deeply. "Protesting what?"

My face heats. Occupy Wall Street. The Dakota Access Pipeline. The Red-Green party had a demonstration…"

Stellan makes a displeased noise. "Tell me you didn't sneak off and protest with the Red-Green party while you were here. Please, Margot."

I put a calming hand on his chest. "I didn't. They might be an actual political force over here, but in New York they are just people making noise. I went to one of their protests originally because a band I liked was going to be there."

He squints at me. "Has anyone ever told you that you are lucky you're beautiful, Margot?"

My blush deepens. "I've heard that before, yes."

He cups my jaw and pulls me in for a deep kiss. When we break apart again, he sighs. "You are trouble, you know."

I wrinkle my nose. "I know. I don't want to be troublesome to you, though."

He cracks his knuckles. "I know, *skatter*. I really do."

I bite my lower lip. "Is there any way to contain this news story? Like… do you have any pull with the royal press office?"

He glances off at the window, through which the dawn has finally broken. "Some. It kind of depends." He hesitates. "You're probably going to have to apologize to someone about something."

My eyes widen. "To who? About what?"

Stellan shrugs. "I have no idea. But as soon as I tell the press office, I can bet you that they are going to tell you to apologize to everyone for everything." He scrunches up his face. "It's their advice about every scandal."

I make a face. "Do I have to?"

He smirks. "No. But it will make things easier if you intend to eventually make this your home and make me your husband."

I wince. "I love you so much, Stellan. I really do. That's the only reason that I'm okay with this."

He pulls me close for one last kiss, then sighs. "I had better get dressed. I'm going to have to try to get out in front of this."

I get up, biting my lip. "I'm just going to tell you this one more time. I'm sorry, Stellan."

The ghost of a smile crosses his face. "I know, *skatter*."

Then he leaves the living room, heading into the bedroom to get dressed. And I'm left standing in my silken robe, hugging myself and feeling bereft.

CHAPTER 40

STELLAN

Just as I finish getting dressed to go over to Marselisborg Palace to see Ida, my phone buzzes. It's a message from Erik.

Your grandmother is here to see you and she is in a mood.

Fuck! Running out into the living room, I find Margot there, frowning at her phone.

"Come get dressed," I say, my eyes skating over her little silk robe. "My grandmother is on her way up here."

She stands up, slipping her phone into her pocket and swallowing. "Oh!"

She rushes past me into the bedroom and I close the door to give her privacy. A butler knocks on the living room door and I clear my throat. I won't lie, I'm a little nervous, going to bat for my girl.

"Come in!" I call out.

The door swings open and the butler steps in. "Her royal highness," he says, bowing as he escorts my grandmother in the room. Impeccably put together as always, my grandmother is wearing a light blue linen skirt and a modest white silk top.

"*Momse*," I greet her. "I was just coming to see you."

Ida looks at me strangely and then turns to dismiss the butler. "Please make sure we are not disturbed."

The butler bows and closes the door. Ida hesitates, then walks over to the sofas. She perches on one. "Take a seat, my dear."

Shit. What does she know? Could there be more in Margot's past that she wasn't honest about?

The thought is like an icy knife twisting in my gut. Composing myself sternly, I take a seat on the couch opposite her.

"It really isn't that big of a deal," I say.

Ida's eyes narrow on my face. "I don't know what you are talking about, Stellan. It doesn't matter." She clears her throat, looking me in the eye. "Your father has had an accident."

That news, completely unexpected, comes out of nowhere and hits me like a freight train.

"What?" I blink repeatedly.

"He is fine. He just walked off the middle of a stage yesterday. But I asked him what happened... and he admitted that he felt confused right before it happened."

My eyebrows lift. "What?"

Ida makes a conciliatory expression. "I've been telling you to be ready for this, Stellan. And now it's here."

"Wait." I shake my head, trying to understand. "Is my father hurt?"

She exhales, picking at a loose thread on her skirt. "Just some bruises and scrapes. But after talking to your father and several doctors, it has been decided that Gorän needs to step down."

I have to lean back, letting that sink in. My father has always been so big and so strong. To think of him as... a confused man who fell off a stage...

"Stellan." My grandmother crosses her ankles, looking concerned. "You realize what I'm saying, do you not? Your father has to give up the crown. And you will have to step up and take it from him."

My eyes widen. "I'm sorry?"

"You are going to be coronated. And I'm afraid it will be soon." A wrinkle appears on her forehead. "Your father is ill. I'm sorry to put this so bluntly, but it's time to dispense with your little girlfriend and bring your focus back where it ought to be. On your country, my dear. Your life is about to become extremely complicated and I don't think you will have time for any… distractions."

I hear Margot gasp from behind me. I whirl, finding her in the doorway. She looks prim and proper in an expensive ivory silk dress, but her face has lost all its color.

"Is the king okay?" she asks, neatly ignoring her part in my grandmother's wishes. She looks at me, imploring.

My heart flip flops. I reach out my hand and Margot instantly picks up her dress and runs to sit down beside me, taking my hand. She looks at my grandmother.

"Please tell me he's going to be okay," she says again.

Ida clears her throat and narrows her gaze on where Margot touches me. "My son will be fine, thank you. It's my grandson I have to worry about, it seems."

Twining my fingers with Margot's, I pull her hand into my lap. "Tell me what you need, *Momse*. I will do what I can."

Her look of displeasure is cold as ice. "Very well." She lifts her head. "After I leave here, you will never be without protection again. Your guard will be right outside your door for the rest of your life."

I swallow. When I speak, it sounds as nervous as I feel. This is just a lot to take in. First my father, then the loss of my last little bit of freedom.

"Okay." I pause a beat. "What else?"

My grandmother looks at Margot, then purses her lips. "You're the heir to the throne, Stellan. You can't be dating. You can't let everyone see how vulnerable you are, especially not right now." She smiles coolly. "You have to either declare your intentions publicly or stop seeing one another."

I tighten my grip on Margot's hand. "Let me worry about dealing with my relationship, Momse."

Ida arches a brow and gives me a chilling look. "Fine." She stands up. "There are a thousand different documents for you to sign before you ascend to the throne. There's a ceremony to be planned out. You'll have to meet with all the lords and ladies that support us, and parliament besides. You'll have to decide who's going to be in your cabinet, who stays, who goes."

"I'll do what is needed," I promise her.

She levels a glare at Margot. "And you might want to see your father, because I'm sure that he will have thoughts on…" She waves her hand at me and Margot. "Whatever is going on here."

I rise, bringing myself to my full height and peering down at my grandmother. "That's enough. I've heard you."

Ida looks back at me, nothing on her face but sincerity. "I really hope you have, Stellan. The time for playing at being king has come and gone. Now you must show the entire world who you really are. I can only hope I've prepared you for the role."

She reaches out for me, touching my face briefly. Then she spins and heads out of the room, her head held high. I stare after her, trying desperately to take all the things she said in.

"Stellan?"

I look back and realize that I'm still gripping Margot's hand so hard that it's probably painful for her. I drop it apologetically. "Sorry, *skatter*. I'm just…"

She steps in front of me, pressing me down with two gentle hands on my shoulders. "It's okay. Sit down, Stellan."

I bury my face in my hands, feeling like a fool. "God damn it."

"I'll be right back. I'm just going to get your phone, okay?"

She disappears and then reappears, holding my phone up. "Here. When you're ready, you can text somebody to get in touch with your father."

"Thanks." I exhale, pushing myself backward into the pillows. "Fuck!"

Margot doesn't say anything. She just sits down beside me and runs her hand over my knee, looking distraught.

After a minute, I look at her.

"My grandmother was right about one thing."

She arches a brow. "Which thing? She said several."

I pin her in place with my gaze. "My life is about to become very complicated, Margot."

"I know," she says softly.

I stare into her dark blue eyes. "Are you still willing to run the gamut with me?"

"Of course," she says. "I'll do whatever you want."

"But what do *you* want? That's what I am really asking here."

She nods a little, taking a deep breath. "We should keep seeing each other, obviously. And I don't have any real objection toward you making things between us more…" She pauses and takes another gulp of air. "More official. I just want to be in the background."

I sigh. "I don't think that the press will let you just hang out in the background, Margot."

She nods again, looking down. "I know. But you asked what I wanted, not what's realistic."

She looks so sad that I can't help but pull her closer, pressing her small body against my larger one. My head rests on hers. My heart beat drums against my chest.

I close my eyes, inhaling. The sweet scent of Margot fills my nose.

"I want that too," I admit.

My heart aches. For my father, who I have yet to see. For my grandmother, who is just trying her best, though it may not seem that way.

For Margot, who is coping with the change in my status way better than I am.

And for this, this closeness. I have a very real sense that these moments are under threat now… though I swear I will do what I can to protect them.

My phone chirps. I open my eyes, sighing before I even read the words on the screen. They're from Lars.

He wants to see all of us right away.

I shoot off a reply before flinging my phone down.

Be there soon.

Then I look at Margot. She looks so anxious; I almost can't stand to look into her sweetly heart shaped face.

"I really fucking love you," I tell her.

She grabs my hand, pulling it over her heart. "I love you too. I always will."

Giving her a kiss, I reluctantly let her go and rise from the couch. "I'm going to go see my father."

She gives me a small smile. "I'll be here, waiting for you when you get back."

With a heavy heart, I turn and start moving away. When I step into the hallway, three suited guards turn to look at me.

"*Prime Ministerr*," I say, nodding to them. "*Lad os gå.*"

I head down the hall, feeling my invisible golden collar tighten just that much more.

CHAPTER 41

MARGOT

I stand in the darkness, silhouetted by the enormous palace windows, just staring out into the moonlit night. I'm wearing a beautiful light gray ballgown but my shoes are abandoned by the door of the living room. I press my hands to my face, feeling the heat that rushed to my cheeks a few minutes ago.

I snuck away from the rest of the dinner party and ran up here as soon as I could. That's only after I made a complete fool of myself by talking over Stellan, though.

It didn't seem like that big of a deal to me. It's just a normal part of the conversational flow, at least in America. But apparently it was enough to stop every other conversation and draw all eyes my way.

My cheeks still burn just thinking about it.

"*Haj.*"

I turn a little, seeing Stellan standing there, filling up the doorframe. His face is mostly in shadow but I would recognize his tall frame anywhere. My mouth turns up at the corners.

"Think his name and he shall appear."

Stellan moves forward, his face emerging from the shadows. "I noticed that you were gone and I came to check on you."

I walk across the room to the couches, falling onto one of them. Keeping my tone light, I look at him as he walks over. "You found me. Hiding upstairs from my own shame."

His lips twitch. "It wasn't that bad."

I roll my eyes. "Everyone at the dinner thought I was raised in a barn."

He gives me a funny look as he sits across from me. "What?"

"They thought I was lacking in manners."

"Ah! I wouldn't worry about what they think, honestly." He sits back, steeling his fingers.

"Well, I am worried. I'm worried from the second I wake up until the second I'm asleep. I don't want to embarrass myself… but more importantly, I don't want to embarrass you."

Stellan shrugs a shoulder. "I wouldn't worry about it."

I squint off toward the window. "I wasn't cut out for this... this caring about what everyone thinks. I just want to be able to wear my ratty old t-shirts and listen to my loud punk music and walk around taking photos. I don't want everyone else's opinions about how I walk funny and who I should be associating with."

I stick out my tongue to make a disgusted face. My expectation is that he will laugh, or make some funny remark. But to my surprise he leans forward, his face looking serious as the original sin.

"Margot. If you don't want this lifestyle, please tell me right now. There is still time to turn the car around."

My eyes widen. "I'm sorry. I didn't mean to complain..."

He shakes his head. "No, I'm serious. Can you be a royal? Can you deal with the invasion of privacy and the world judging your every move?" He stops, then exhales a long breath. "I know it isn't very romantic to have this conversation. But I really need you to think about your answer. You'd have to give up any kind of job. You'd have to put down roots here. I will move heaven and earth to make you my wife... but you have to meet me halfway."

For a second, I can only blink. For Stellan to say these things to me, so bluntly and without pretense or the disguise of humor... it's unusual, to say the least.

"Stellan— "

He holds up a hand. "I want you to consider what I am saying, Margot. There is an escape option for you... but that window is growing smaller by the day. Do you understand?"

I flush, sitting up and looking at my hands in my lap. "I do."

He put my conundrum into words, which is more than I have been willing or able to do. As I sit there, his words swirl against me and wash over me again and again.

Can I be the queen that Stellan needs? Am I dignified enough? Humble enough? Resilient enough?

Simply put, do I have what it takes?

Half a minute of silence lapses before I realize that he's waiting for an answer. I glance up at his darkly handsome face, biting my lower lip.

"I don't know," I confess. "I'm sorry. I wish I did."

Stellan sits back on the couch, looking upset. "I thought that you wanted this."

"I love you. That part has never been in doubt. But… you're asking me to make a major decision that will affect the rest of my life. And it's just… it's hard." Screwing up my face, I sigh. "If you were anyone else, I would just say yes right now. But… your honor, your sense of duty… they are a part of you. And I'm trying to figure out whether I can put honor and duty first like you do."

He frowns. "You make me sound selfless. I'm anything but that. If I really only cared about duty, I would've just picked a wealthy Danish girl to marry and sired an heir by now."

I wrinkle my nose. In my head, I can just picture Stellan and some willowy blonde standing in a royal portrait, holding a baby. The question is, can I put myself in the place of the blonde?

"I know," I say with a shrug. "I'm trying my best to figure out whether I can commit to the royal lifestyle. You already know that I'd commit to you in a heartbeat."

His smile is a little heartbreaking. "I know, *skatter*. We are just running out of time. A decision has to be made."

I suck in a breath and nod. "I know."

Stellan stands up, holding out his hand to me. "Come."

Getting to my feet, I slip my hand into his, relishing how warm his skin is. "Back to the dinner?"

His mouth curves up. "No. It's been two days since I've even seen you naked. I'm starving for your body, *skatter*."

My heart beat drums a staccato rhythm against my ribs. Pressing myself closer to Stellan, I pull his head down, kissing his mouth. He growls and sweeps me off my feet, carrying me to his bedroom.

He strips me naked and tosses me on the bed, then undresses himself. When he comes after me, his touch tender and brutal, I can't get enough.

He takes me from behind, pulling my hair and caging my body in with his. He fucks me, slowly at first, his thrusts growing more and more rough. He soon has me calling out his name, panting breathlessly, as he drives me closer and closer to the brink. And I've never felt so free as I do in the midst of our sweaty, mind-blowing sex.

Trapped under him, pinned like this, is exactly where I want to be. It's all the rest that has me questioning whether I can commit to being his.

Later, when we are done, our sweat cooling as we suck in hasty breaths, I cling to Stellan.

"I love you so much," I whisper against his chest. "I always will."

He just pulls me closer, still struggling to pull air into his lungs. The way he holds me, like I'm some fragile thing that is too precious to break… it almost makes me cry.

As I drift off to sleep, the last thing on my mind is a question.

Am I really going to let this wonderful man slip away just because I can't stand being scrutinized by strangers?

I really, really hope not.

CHAPTER 42

STELLAN

A couple of days later, it is clear that word of my relationship with Margot has gotten to the press. Normally I am not bothered by a few reporters that might turn up here and there. But they've been growing in number over the last few days, showing up at every event I have, elbowing each other in order to get to within earshot of me.

"Prince Stellan! Is Margot your lover?"

"Stellan! Stellan! Will you marry her?"

"Will the wedding be soon?"

I ignore them as I get out of the back of the limo and hurry into the palace. Looking back at the swarm of reporters and paparazzi, I'm nearly blinded by a flashbulb going off to the right of the palace doorway.

Shaking my head to clear my vision, I turn and trot inside the darkened palace. Running up the grand staircase, I make my way down the echoing hallway to my living room.

When I open the door to find Margot wiping away a tear and trying to hide that she's been crying, I feel my heart twist in my chest. She sniffles and sits up straighter in the hard backed chair by the table, running her hand over her black cotton dress.

"*Haj*," she greets me.

My heart twists again. She's trying to learn Danish for me.

"*Haj*," I say, walking over and giving her a hug. "I am guessing that you saw the reporters?"

Margot wipes at her face bashfully. "Yeah. I was going to go out to meet the personal shopper you suggested for me… but I couldn't even manage to leave the palace."

She sucks in a deep breath. "It's especially hard because I don't even have any answers for them."

I pull away, shaking my head. "That isn't anything I can help with, Margot."

Pulling out the chair opposite her, I sit down and glance out the window. She wrinkles her nose delicately.

"I know," she says. "I was just… telling you how I feel."

I drum my fingertips on the table. When I speak, my words come out sharper than I intended. "The prime minister came to see me today. He asked about you. How do you think I felt, telling him I don't have any more answers about our current predicament than you?"

I can actually hear her inhale. She narrows her eyes at me. "I'm sorry that you are feeling the pressure. It must be terrible to feel like you don't have much control of things."

I shoot her a glare. "It's not that hard to make up your mind, Margot. You either want me, and can accept all that comes along with me… or you can't."

She ducks her head, her jaw tensing. "You make it sound so easy."

I grind my teeth. "It might not be easy for you. For me, there was never a choice. I didn't get that kind of freedom."

She shoots to her feet, pacing over to the window. "Yes. I know that you had a hard childhood, Stellan. Just like you know that mine wasn't any easier." She hisses out a breath. "I feel like we could go around and around in circles over this for a thousand more years."

I try to take a calming breath. "We're out of time, Margot. I think you know that."

She leans against the window, scrunching up her face. "I just need more time."

"Time for what?" I ask, raising my hands. "What will a few more days get you that you don't already have?"

"I don't know," she says mournfully, her gaze still fixed on something out the window. "Clarity?"

I try a different tack. "When I came in here, you were crying."

Margot glances at me, uncertain. "So?"

"So… you had one run in with the press. And you… you cracked under the pressure! Not even very much pressure, I might add." I pin her with my gaze. "If that's the way you handle a tense moment, I worry about you being able to handle the everyday scrutinies that accompany royal life. Like… if you can't cope with this, how are you going to handle it when the paparazzi find out that we're engaged? How are you going to deal with being pregnant?"

Margot's eyes go wide. Her retort is immediate and biting. "I don't know, Stellan! This is all new to me! I can't fathom how I'll deal with anything, let alone being pregnant with your child!"

There has been a tenuous thread between her and me. But her outraged tone, her angry gestures… they cause me to pull on that thread until it snaps.

I get to my feet, my voice gone to gravel. "Maybe we should both do ourselves a favor and stop trying. Maybe we are just not suited."

She stares at me for a second, her mouth opening. "What are you saying, Stellan? Are you saying that this…" She gestures to the air between us both. "Isn't worth it?"

"Maybe I am," I say, my gut twisting.

A fresh sheen of tears in her eyes tells me that I've hit her in a soft spot. "I've been daydreaming. I've been living a lie. Pretending… pretending that if I tried hard enough, I could make people forget that I'm a foreigner. Make them forget that I come from nothing." She looks deathly serious, her little hands forming fists. When she speaks again, her voice is watery and rough. "I thought that I could make you forget. But that's not quite possible, is it?"

I spread my hands wide. "Maybe not, Margot. Maybe we are just... two people that should have been together. Maybe in another life, if we were a little more similar..."

A tear breaks loose and runs down her face. She swipes at it angrily. "We are fundamentally different, Stellan. That's what makes us... us."

I close my eyes for a second. "So... what? We're different. I'm still a royal. I'll always be a royal."

She crosses her arms. "And I'll always be common, no matter if you marry me or not. You could bestow a thousand titles on me and I'll still be..."

She trails off, unable to finish her thought. She looks down, ducking her head and wiping at her face.

My fingers itch to touch her. I ball my hands into fists. "All you have to do is leave," I grate out. "All you have to say is that you can't do it. If you don't want me to chase after you, I won't. I love you, but..."

Margot looks up at me, her dark blue eyes agonized. Her words leave her in a huff of breath. "But maybe love isn't enough."

Her words ring out, settling between us like shattered glass. I suck in a breath.

"Margot— "

"No!" she says, shaking her head fiercely. "No. I won't ever be the perfect, quiet, submissive little wife you all expect me to be! You want me to quit my job… and be just… completely dependent on you…"

She breaks down in tears, a silent sob rippling through her whole body.

I don't know what to say. I don't know how to make this better. My heart is frozen in my chest; my lungs feel brittle when I draw a breath.

"So go then," I utter. Margot looks up at me, tears running down her face. "Go!" I yell.

A final twist of the knife, cutting both of us to the bone. Her face goes white.

"If I leave— " she whispers.

"Fucking go. Be done with it already," I toss the words out, turning away from her. "This is over."

I start to walk away. Behind me, I hear her gasped breath. And then she lets a sob escape her as she turns and runs away, out the door faster than I can draw a breath.

When I turn back to look, all I see is an empty doorframe.

"Fuck!" I shout, reaching out blindly to overturn a plain wooden chair. Then I angrily tip the whole table on its side, making a noise that isn't half of the fury that I feel.

I storm toward the bedroom, needing to brood in silence.

CHAPTER 43

STELLAN

Five days.

It has been five days since Margot and I fell apart. Four sleepless nights, five agonizing, drudgery-filled days.

I sit in the backseat of another limo, my eyes closed, wishing... well, I don't know exactly what I want. I want Margot to reappear, to explain why she was so wrong before when she said she couldn't live like I do.

"Stellan."

I crack open my eyes, sliding a look at Erik. He's sitting beside my against the black leather seats, looking concerned.

"I'm here," I say, adjusting my big body in the car.

He looks at me, scrubbing a hand through his blond hair. "We're almost back at the palace."

I loosen my tie, feeling miserable. "*Ja*, okay."

Glancing out the window as Copenhagen flies by, I flutter my eyes closed again. Erik clears his throat.

"What can I do to make you less…" He pauses. "Whatever you are right now? It's hard to watch you be so… listless. Is this still about Margot?"

I laugh and look at him again. "It's about everything and nothing, all at once."

He cocks his head. "Who rejected whom?"

His question puts a scowl on my lips. "That's unclear. I laid out an ultimatum… and she backed away from it." I sigh, shaking my head. "I just want to move on already. I want to be done with all of this."

Erik squints. "You look like you haven't slept in weeks. Maybe you need to talk to a doctor or something."

I shoot him a glare. "It's not that bad."

"Today you kept calling the minister of health Prime Minister Kelley, even after you had been corrected numerous times. Yesterday, at the gala, you were totally distracted and got drunk in public. I could go on."

I roll my eyes. "So?"

"So, you need to shake this off. You're the fucking crown prince of Denmark. If you want to drown your sorrows in women, all you have to do is say so. If you want to do something daring and dangerous, I have like five activities up my sleeve, waiting for you to say the word. But you've got to pull it together."

I clamp my mouth shut, glaring at the front of limo. When I don't respond, Erik shifts his weight.

"I'm sorry that Margot hurt you."

I look at him funny. My heart squeezes in my chest. "She didn't hurt me."

He slides me a skeptical look. "No? You wouldn't call this behavior you've been displaying heartbreak?"

If I could kill with a look, Erik would be bleeding out right now. "No. It's not heartbreak. It's... disappointment. It turns out that all my initial biases about Margot were right on target... I just allowed myself to get distracted by the nice ass and pretty blue eyes that those things accompanied."

He doesn't seem to know what to say to that. Furrowing his brow, he shakes his head. "It still sucks to go through a breakup. I mean... you've never really had to go through one before. Because of who you are, girls just flock to you. And you've never really spent any time with a girl who didn't want the crown."

I roll my eyes. He's right about one thing: Margot definitely didn't want the crown or anything attached to it.

Outside my window, the palace looms close. The second we stop, I bolt out of the back seat, not waiting around for Erik. He has to jog to catch up with me as I head inside, taking the stairs two by two.

I come to a halt when I reach the landing, squinting at the circus that awaits me there. No less than twenty young girls stroll up and down the hall, which is set up with a runway like a fashion show. The girls model barely-there dresses for my little sister, who sits at one end of the runway, her head cocked. Loud, upbeat music blares from a single speaker.

As soon as Erik and I walk over, suddenly the models are far more interested at making sexy faces in our direction than whatever Annika has them doing.

Annika turns around, spots us, and heaves a sigh.

"Girls, please!" Annika says, clapping her hands to get the models. "Take a five minute break, then we are all going again."

"What are you doing?" I ask her, annoyed. "This is my private hallway, Nika."

She scrunches up her face, standing up. I realize now that she's also wearing a sparkly silver dress similar to those the models have on; if Momse saw Annika right now, she would have a heart attack.

Annika gives me a cool smile. "Hello, big brother. It's nice to see you too." She wrinkles her nose. "This hallway has the best light. I need tons of good natural light for the fashion show I'm working on. Don't worry, it's for charity."

I grit my teeth. "Annika, take your models and your… party… somewhere else. I'm not in the mood."

Annika pulls a face. "You suck." She turns, cupping her hands to her mouth. "Turn the music off! We're moving to another floor!"

I glance at Erik, who is staring at Annika's barely covered ass so hard that it's a miracle it's not on fire. The look of longing on his face is an emotion I know all too well. It's the exact look I used to give Margot, before we fell into bed together.

I reach out and shove him. "What the fuck is wrong with you?"

He glances at me, his eyes widening. "Nothing. Let's go."

Erik starts pushing his way past the models and the runway, trying to get to the door of my study. I'm right on his heels, shoving him again once we make it into the study.

"On top of all the shit that I'm dealing with right now, the breakup with Margot and the upcoming coronation... I have to worry about you trying to fuck Annika?"

He pins me with a hard gaze. "Jesus. No. I swear. It's just been too long since I've gotten any pussy, that's all."

I glare at him. "That had better be all. You know better than to fuck around with Annika. She's only eighteen. Barely an adult."

"Stel, come on. Even if I was tempted — and I'm not saying that I am — I'm not stupid. Our friendship is more important than any crazy ideas my libido might have."

Getting very close to Erik's face, I stare him down. "It has better be. Twenty years we've been friends. Longer than Annika has even been alive."

"*Ja*. I know. I wouldn't do anything to mess that up, okay?"

I scan his face for signs of deception, but I come up empty handed. Shaking my head, I push past him. "You'd better remember that."

He gives me an odd look. "You really are fucked up right now, you know that? You should be more focused on making some kind of decision."

I throw myself down into one of the overstuffed leather chairs. "A decision about what, Erik?"

He takes a seat on the corner of my highly polished desk. looking down his nose at me. "It seems like you either need to call Margot, or you need to find some other way to deal with the breakup."

I scowl at him. "I'm not calling Margot. Things between us are done and dusted."

He shrugs a shoulder. "Okay. So let me throw a party. I'll invite a ton of girls and we'll all have a great time. You can have this weekend to party and recover, then be on your feet again by Monday."

This idea of throwing a huge party leaves a bad taste in my mouth. "I'll pass."

Erik checks his watch, then stands and wanders over to the bar setup that we always have on hand. He pours two glasses of whiskey, sauntering over to hand one to me.

I take a sip, though it can't be past two in the afternoon.

He drinks a little, looking at me. "You need to relax."

"I don't want to relax," I fire back, feeling prickly.

"What do you want to do, then? Huh? You can't spend any more time brooding."

Sitting back, I stare at the whiskey in my glass. "I don't know. I just don't want to feel like this anymore," I admit to him.

"Great." He walks over to my desk and sets his tumbler down, pulling out his phone. I watch him texting for a minute.

"Who are you texting?" I ask.

He looks up at me. "You said you don't want a huge party. So I am arranging for something more private and intimate. You, me, a couple of girls, a discreet evening."

Draining the contents of my glass, I stand and put the glass next to his. "Just give me a few days by myself, okay? I just… I need time."

His eyes narrow on my face. "To heal?"

"One more comment about how Margot broke my heart and I am going to punch you right in the nose."

He grins. "That's the spirit. No woman can keep you down!"

Rubbing my temple, I turn toward the door. "You are impossible. And on that note, I'm going to go lie down."

Leaving my study, I head down the hall toward my bedroom. But Erik's voice still echoes in my head.

And that's not heartbreak you're experiencing?

I don't know what it is, but I'm ready for it to be over, and soon.

CHAPTER 44

MARGOT

My least favorite place to be in the whole entire world has got to be my current one: in Anna's office at *Politiken*, listening to her vent about how useless I am.

"I got a call early this morning," she shouts, pacing back and forth over the small office's length. "And would you believe it, it was from His Majesty's Press Office, calling to officially axe the article that you were apparently, supposedly, theoretically writing for us."

I slide an inch lower in my chair, my face turning neon pink. My input is not required for Anne's critique so I just swallow and try to ride it out.

As if I need another reminder that Stellan and I are over. Just thinking about it makes my eyes watery — and I swore that today, six days after we broke up, I wouldn't dissolve into tears in front of everybody.

Anne turns, pinning me with her dark gaze. "Well? Do you have anything to say for yourself, Margot?"

I suck my lower lip between my teeth and bite down. "No, ma'am."

She paces the tiny space for a half a minute, her face contorting with anger. "Of course not. You know, the press office refused to explain why they pulled the plug on this project… but the young woman that called said it was not their idea." She stops, turning to glare at me again. "That means that it was your idea, Margot. Is that right?"

I look down at my lap. "It's very complicated, Anna."

She laughs coldly. "You know what? Get out of my office before I fire you. As a matter of fact, take some time before you even think about coming back here."

I think she expects me to stay, to fight with her over my job. But I'm up and out of her office as soon as she says that. I can feel her eyes burning holes in my body as I gather my things.

As I barrel out of the front door, I repress a sob.

No Stellan.

No job.

Paparazzi mobbing the doorway of Pippa's apartment.

Will I even last here in Copenhagen? Because it sure feels like I have ruined Denmark for myself. Aside from Pippa, I'm essentially alone in a foreign country.

My eyes well up and I dash away my tears as I head toward the river.

"Margot! Wait!"

I turn to see Pippa rushing toward me, looking concerned. She catches up to me and throws her arms around me as I try not to cry.

"This place sucks!" I moan into her hair.

"Oh." She pets me as one would a cherished dog, caressing my hair. "I'm sorry. You should know that Guy asked me to come down and fetch you. Apparently, he didn't like the way that Anna handled you at all."

I allow myself one more whimper, then put some space between us. Pippa offers me a leather satchel, smiling a bit.

"It's a laptop. He thought you might have an interesting perspective on the royal family, if you feel up to it."

I take the satchel, adding it to the burden I already carry on my shoulder, including my tote bag. "Thanks."

She cocks her head, rubbing my shoulder. "Have you eaten anything?"

I nod. "A whole pint of gelato, straight from the container." My cheeks go pink. "And a cupcake." I pause. "And a whole loaf of French bread with butter."

She arches a brow. "I see. Heartbreak apparently makes you eat."

I nod. "I couldn't sleep again last night so I just stared at the ceiling and ate a whole block of cheese."

She grins. "Sadness-induced insomnia coupled with a little fridge binge. Got it. Honestly, I've heard of worse things."

I scrunch up my face. "My stomach hurts."

"Come over here," she says, marching me over to a bench and sitting me down. She sits beside me, squinting up into the bright blue sky. "Have you heard anything from him?"

Her question knocks the breath out of my lungs, so I just shake my head. She heaves a sigh.

"Stellan is quick tempered, as I'm sure you've found out. But he's also fair minded. I'm sure if you called him, he would take you back in a heartbeat."

I pucker up my face like I'm tasting something sour. "That will solve exactly nothing."

Pippa looks at me out of the corner of an eye, pushing her cheek out with her tongue. "Can I be really blunt?"

I raise my eyebrows. "I thought you already were."

She makes a face. "I think that this was your first fight."

I give her my most dubious look. "We fought all the time when I first moved to Copenhagen, Pippa."

She rolls her eyes. "That doesn't count at all. Since you guys have been all lovey dovey, you haven't been cross with each other. Then when you did get frustrated with each other, there was so much pressure on him to settle down… and on you to say yes to being a royal…" She wrinkles her nose. "It was a powder keg, just waiting for a match to be struck."

I suck a deep breath in, struggling not to start crying again. "I love him, Pippa. I really do."

Her hand lands on my knee, rubbing little comforting circles in my flesh. "I know, Mags. I know."

"It was just an insane amount of pressure," I admit, putting my bags down on the ground. "I wanted to say yes to him. I really did. But the timeline was all kinds of fucked up."

"Yes," Pippa says with a nod. "I think if you two didn't have to face his upcoming coronation so soon…"

"God!" I cry out, looking heavenward. "That really put a rush on things. I was trying to tell him to slow down… that things were going too fast for me… but I think that he just had so much pressure from his grandmother and his family that he couldn't hear what I was saying."

She sighs. "You're not going to like what I'm about to say."

I look at her for several long beats. "What?"

"If you really love Stellan, I think you should try to reach out to him."

"What?" My cheeks heat. "No way! No. He told me not to come back."

She rolls her shoulders. "Call it the heat of the moment. Wouldn't it just be tragic if he feels the same way and you never know because you're both so damn stubborn?"

I make a disgruntled sound. "What if I were to show up at the palace and he doesn't want to see me? That would be so embarrassing, I don't even have the words."

She smirks. "So you do want to try?"

"I didn't say that!" I protest.

"Okay, but let's just say that you decide you are willing to give it a go." She puts up a hand to stop my complaint. "We are just brainstorming here. No harm, no foul. Yes?"

I tuck a strand of hair behind my ear. "Just brainstorming," I reiterate. "Just… in case."

A dimple flashes in Pippa's cheek. "What if you made like… a grand romantic gesture?"

I scoff. "Like showing up at the airport at the last moment? Isn't the guy supposed to do that?"

Pippa shrugs a shoulder. "Maybe for other people, yeah. But you? You're Margot Keane. You're a rebel. You live by your own rules. And if you want to make a grand gesture, then by god, you can do it!"

I stare at Pippa for a second. "I just realized that you actually believe in me. You are a really good friend, you know that?"

She beams at me. "Duh. I've always believed in you, Mags."

I hug her, sudden and hard. She makes a funny noise at first, but then she relaxes and claps me on the back. When I pull back, Pippa arches a brow.

"So. Shall we make a list of romantic grand gesture ideas?"

I shake my head slowly. "No."

Her eyebrows rise. "No?"

"I just realized that we work at the main newspaper in the country. Millions of people see whatever gets onto our front page."

Pippa looks shocked for a second. "Are you suggesting what I think you are?"

I squint at her. "Maybe. I mean, my words will almost definitely reach Stellan. And if it works, I am sure the *Politiken* editors will forgive me." I wrinkle my nose. "Right?"

She looks a little unsure. "If it doesn't work, Margot… if you publish a personal letter addressed to Stellan in a public paper…"

I wince. "I would have to leave the country."

"Yeah, that would be the least of your worries."

"So… I'll have to make my letter really good," I say, taking a deep breath. "Oh god. Am I really going to do this? Agh! Where would I even begin?"

Pippa's lips curve upward and she slides me a knowing glance. "Start at the beginning."

She picks up the leather satchel, opening it to reveal the laptop inside. Then she stands, tucking her glorious red hair behind her ears.

"I should get back to my own work," she says with a sigh. "Good luck. Call me when you need help."

"Thank you, Pippa." I crack open the laptop and open a blank word processing document. "Start at the beginning. I can do that…"

Typing out the first line, I start the scariest letter I will probably ever write.

CHAPTER 45

STELLAN

My father clears his throat and adjusts his seat at the table. We're having breakfast on the vast veranda of Gråsten Palace, where he and my mother are currently staying.

He pushes his mostly full plate away. I want to ply him with a million questions about how he is feeling, but I have a feeling that he won't like that. It's normally fairly awkward between us, but today... it's tense.

"So. Have you heard anything conclusive from the doctors?"

My father scratches his dark beard. "No."

I sigh silently. "May I speak openly?"

"I wish you would." He looks off into the distance at the verdant gardens below the terrace. I can't read him; I think I know exactly where I inherited my remoteness.

I take a deep breath. "Are you still stepping down? Because if not... I have a number of loose ends still that need to be tied up. If you are going to keep the throne—"

"No. You are still on track to be king."

My expression tightens. "Ah."

My father looks at me for several long beats. "You don't desire the crown?"

I give a dry chuckle. "No."

"Mm. I didn't either." He looks down at the glass of orange juice in front of him, turning it slowly by the rim. "What would you do if you had more time?"

Margot's face flashes in my mind. Frowning, I shake my head. "I don't know. I made some decisions recently that may have been hasty..."

I trail off and drum my fingers on the tabletop. My father spears me with his frosty blue gaze.

"You are talking about Margot?"

I can feel my neck heat. "Among other things. But yes, I would do things differently if I had more time." I scrunch my face up. "And if I had a time machine, I guess."

My father's eyebrows lift slightly. "How so?"

I shrug, uncomfortable. "I don't know. I would put less pressure on her to accept my marriage proposal, I guess."

He looks surprised. "I didn't realize that you had asked."

Pursing my lips, I shrug again. "I didn't ask her officially. I asked her what her answer would be… and she took weeks to reply to it."

He looks dubious. "Her reply was no?"

Heat creeps up my neck, coloring my cheeks. "Her reply was just that she needed more time."

"And you felt that you were running out of that resource," he comments, fixing his gaze on his orange juice glass again.

"Well… yes," I admit. "If I had it to do over again, I would do it differently."

My father sighs. "Stellan. Let me give you some advice. If you find a woman to share your life with, and you're sure that she's the one, you don't halfway ask her to marry you. You grab onto her and you don't ever let go." He coughs. "I consider myself insanely lucky to have found your mother. She is passionate. She is loyal. She fights for the causes she believes in. But most of all, I know that she'll stick by my side. No matter what. That's worth more than all the gold in the world."

I'm a little taken back by his words. My father and mother obviously love each other, but I have never heard my father talk about her for any length of time.

Letting that sink in, I take a deep breath. "I'm glad that you found Maman."

He snorts. "You'd better be. I never planned on having a bunch of children. That was all your mother. She wanted a big brood. And what your mother wants, she tends to get."

"That's... bordering on being too much information." I wrinkle my nose.

My father rolls his eyes. "That is neither here nor there. What is certain is that you need to contact Margot. If she is your great love, she will be glad to hear from you."

I give him a skeptical look. "Has Erik been talking to you about this? Because he said exactly the same thing."

My father sighs. "No. But there must be something there if we both have the same advice for you, Stellan."

Sitting back in my chair, I shrug. "I don't know."

"Do you love her?" My father cocks his head.

"Of course."

His gaze narrows on my face. "I don't understand. What is the issue?"

I grow embraced. "I don't know. What if she can't accept my lifestyle? I mean, the media scrutiny is already intense and we aren't even publicly a couple. What if she says yes and then changes her mind in a couple of months?"

He shakes his head. "If that happens, you can deal with it together. Don't be a fool. Take this risk, son."

I look down at my lap. He's right, of course. I have been a fucking idiot. I love Margot so deeply that she haunts my dreams.

"It's a big risk," I say, my voice growing rough. "But you are right... I have to put it all on the line. Otherwise she might leave Denmark altogether. And that... that would just crush me."

My father smiles. "Good. In that case... I think you are ready to read today's issue of *Politiken*." He pushes his chair back and stands, gesturing to a servant. "Bring him the newspaper, will you?"

The servant scuttles forward, offering me the newspaper on a platter. I frown and accept it, noticing the photo on the main page a few seconds later.

It's a gorgeous portrait of Margot, her expression sad. A tear tracks down her face as she contemplates her hands.

The headline is simple. Dear Stellan, I love you.

My heart starts pounding. "What is this?"

My father touches my shoulder as he heads inside. "I'll leave you to read it by yourself."

"Thanks," I murmur, unfolding the newspaper. Margot's letter is printed just below the fold. Not quite believing what I'm seeing, I start to read.

D*ear Stellan,*

We met one warm summer night in New York City. The attraction was instant, the chemistry between us so potent that a few sparks grew into a raging, untenable fire.

I knew from that moment — you were special somehow.

When I arrived in Copenhagen, I hated you. Or at least I thought I did. The news of us being tied together — me as the journalist, you as the subject of my research — hit us both hard.

I come from nothing. You come from the kind of privilege and wealth that makes my head spin. And yet... we found common ground.

You let me in. I dropped my shields, became vulnerable with you.

And somewhere deep inside, a begrudging respect turned into a breathless, wild, restless kind of love. It wasn't my choice.

I couldn't help but fall in love with you, my wicked prince. The world tried to turn us against each other... wanted us to dance to its beat.

I thought I couldn't do it. I ran, I hid. But in my heart of hearts, I know one thing is absolutely true: I will move mountains for you. I will walk across endless deserts, dive into the deepest oceans.

My love for you knows no bounds.

Now I stand here waiting, holding my breath, hoping desperately that you will read this... and you will meet me at Fredericksberg Gardens today. I'll be there at three in the afternoon, and I'll wait all day for you.

I hope to see you there, Stellan.

With undying love,

Margot

. . .

I sit back, floored. If there was ever a doubt about anything related to Margot, now I know exactly how she feels. She's assumed so much of the risk without realizing that I was only steps behind her.

God, I love her so much, it makes me feel sick. It is almost overwhelming in the entirety of it, hitting me like a tidal wave on an otherwise perfectly calm day at the beach.

I stand up, tucking the newspaper by my side.

"Well?"

I turn to find my father and my mother standing at the doorway of the terrace, looking expectant. My neck heats.

"I didn't realize you were there."

My mother stomps her foot. "Tell me your reaction to reading Margot's letter! I am dying over here."

"I... I'm going to go meet her," I say, swallowing. "Papa was right... no half measures this time. I'm going to the gardens alone and leaving with a fiancée, come what may."

My mother throws her hands up, squealing with glee, and bounds over to me for a hug. "That's so wonderful, Stellan!"

My father digs in his pocket and pulls out a ring box. "You will probably need one of these."

My eyebrows fly up. "A ring?"

He coughs. "Your mother dragged me along to the Copenhagen treasury after we met Margot for the first time. Your mother knew that you would need a ring."

"Ohh, and it's so perfect! It was your great grandmother's ring. Sparkly and pretty. It will look great on her delicate little hand, *ja?*"

Pulling me over to my father, my mother opens the ring box. I look at the ring with wide eyes.

"This is really happening," I say.

"Yes!" my mother sings, beaming so wide that it's hard not to get caught up in her happiness. "I'm so happy for you, my Stellan."

She cups my face, kissing me on the cheek. I smile, rolling my eyes a little.

"She hasn't said yes yet."

My father smiles softly. "I think we all know just what she'll say."

Shaking my head, I tuck the ring box in my pocket and wish my parents goodbye.

CHAPTER 46

MARGOT

There is something tranquil about standing just where I am with my eyes tightly closed. The scent of gently blooming jasmine rises to my nose. Birds chirp from the perfectly manicured greenery all around me.

I exhale slowly, my hands still trembling. Opening my eyes, I take in the beauty of the romantic gardens with the soft pink wild roses growing up and around the natural wood gazebo.

I'm so nervous that I can't think straight. What if Stellan never saw my letter? Worse, what if he did and still doesn't show up?

This whole idea was really romantic in my head, but now… standing here in the same outfit I was wearing when we met, sweating through my clothes…

It seems destined to fail. Biting at my thumbnail, I pace the gazebo. Eight steps one way, eight steps the other.

This plan was not well thought through.

I hear a rustle and whirl around. The rose garden just beyond the gazebo is still. The tree lined path leading away is long, empty, and all but silent.

I check the time on my phone. 3:15.

God, Stellan isn't coming. I signed myself up for waiting all night for him... but I am as sure that he's not coming now than I have been about anything in my whole entire life.

I head to the steps, sitting down and burying my face in my hands. I suck in a shaky breath.

"What are you doing on the ground, *skatter*?"

My heart pounds. I look up and my eyes widen. Stellan strolls down the path, looking as dapper as he's ever looked in a tuxedo and a crisp white shirt.

One of my hands clutches my chest over my heart. "You came," I whisper.

He covers the last few steps, stopping right in front of me. "I saw your letter. You asked me to meet you. How could I say no to you?"

His eyes sparkle with humor. I'm still petrified. I make a promise to myself that I wouldn't cry.

Instead, I climb to my feet, looking up at him. "I should've written a speech. I didn't get past the point of you showing up."

He smirks. "I think we'll manage."

Reaching out a hand, he gently touches my shoulder. I don't know what comes over me, but I jump onto him, climbing his big body like a tree.

Stellan chuckles, the reverberations vibrating his chest. "I guess it wouldn't be real if you didn't make it awkward, would it?"

He slides his hand along my cheek and cups the back of my head, lowering his mouth to mine. I make a soft sound as his lips touch mine; he tastes sweet and clean, like fresh mint. When his mouth opens and his tongue touches mine, sweeping the inside of my mouth, I put my arms around his neck and plow my hands into the back of his hair.

I've missed this so badly.

He groans against my mouth. "I've missed your scent."

My lips curve upwards. "Is that all?"

He pulls back, brushing a stray strand of hair from my face. "No," he says quietly. "I've missed everything about you. Your smile. Your sense of humor. Your moral outrage. My body craves yours, *skatter*."

I'm left breathless and wide eyed at his openness, his vulnerability in this moment. His ice blue eyes are so earnest that it almost makes me cry.

"Stellan…" I whisper, my voice breaking. "I love you so fucking much."

He presses his lips to mine with such passion and intensity that I feel stunned. "I love you too, Margot. I know that my life is complicated, but I don't think I can go on without you."

I draw in a breath that turns into a hiccup. "I meant what I wrote to you. If you need me to, I'll move heaven and earth to be yours."

He exhales a shaky breath. "I think you know what I have to do, right?"

I arch a brow. "What?"

Pushing me back a step with gentle hands, he clears his throat and digs in his pocket. Then he kneels down on one knee. My hands fly up to my mouth.

He pauses for a second, lowering his dark head. When Stellan looks up at me, he gives me a tense smile.

"Fuck, I'm so nervous," he admits.

My eyes well up at that. I brush my hand against his shoulder. "Don't be."

He bites his lip and holds up his offering, a small dark blue velvet box. When he cracks it open, a dazzling diamond and sapphire ring sits cushioned there.

Oh god. Is this really happening?

Stellan reaches for my hand. "Margot Keane. You are the most challenging, most wonderful, most amazing woman I've ever met. When I think of the future, the only one I can see clearly is one with you by my side. Will you please do me the enormous honor of being my wife?"

My heart beat drums its rhythm in my ears. I dash away tears from my eyes, nodding. "I will."

His expression is glorious. He beams as he pries the ring from the box. Setting the box aside, he takes my hand and slides the ring onto my finger.

I reach down for him as he stands up. He kisses me and slips his arms around me, lifting me up in his arms. He's marking me for the whole world to see: I'm his now.

His, and his alone, until the end of time.

I finally pull away with a giggle. "Is this real?" I wonder. "I feel like I'm high on something."

He sets me on my feet, grinning. "I was just thinking the same thing."

My cheeks hurt from how hard I grin. I definitely look like a lunatic but I don't care. I glance at my hand and the ring takes my breath away again.

"Who do we tell first?" I wonder aloud.

He scrunches up his face. "My parents already know that I was planning to propose. They encouraged it, actually."

A hand flies up to cover my heart. "They did?"

He nods. "*Ja*. And Erik told me to quit being so stubborn and call you." He squints. "Everyone in my circle is very pro-Margot, it seems."

I smile at that, but I suck in a breath. "Everyone but your grandmother."

Stellan shrugs. "When she finds out that I have proposed to you and you said yes, she will change her mind. She wants the best for me. And you are what's best for me, *skatter*."

I grin. "Yeah?"

He pulls me against his hard body, smirking. "*Ja*."

I put my arms around his neck and press my lips to his again, inhaling that clean masculine scent that is purely him. When he finally pulls away, he takes me by the hand.

"Are you ready to be my princess now? Because the second we leave this spot, the press will be all over us. The Gardens kept them outside just because I asked but you know they'll be waiting just past the gates. They'll have a million questions and generally be pretty invasive."

I smile up at him. "As long as you're by my side, I can face them. I can face anything."

He twines his fingers with mine, kissing my hand. "Okay. I promise not to leave your side. You have my word on that, *skatter*."

I blush. "I love you, Stellan."

He gives me a wicked grin. "I love you too. Just wait until we get back to the palace, where I can show you just how much…"

My heartbeat thrums. "I can't wait."

Stellan winks at me, leading me out of the gazebo and down the tree lined path toward our future.

CHAPTER 47

MARGOT

My feet ache in these staggeringly tall high heels. But that's what you get when you give your own fabulous designer free reign. I'm wearing what has to be the biggest, goofiest strapless ball gown ever created, dressed in head to toe pink crinoline. I looked in the mirror and gasped about how I look like Barbie threw up everywhere...

But when Stellan saw me in this dress, the way his eyes lit up told me I was wrong.

I lift my head, trying to look poised. A thousand faces stare back at me from the ballroom floor, making me want to squirm. I shift my weight onto one foot, prompting Stellan to look down at me.

"What are you doing?" he whispers. "You're thinking of running away, are you? This whole engagement party was your idea."

I wrinkle my nose at him. "You're stuck with me now. Sorry."

Even though we are on a dais, with probably a thousand people looking right at us, Stellan kisses me on the lips. Several cameras flash and I blush.

There is really no way of getting used to being watched every second that we are in public. At least I have Stellan here to keep me from lunging at reporters who ask me obnoxious questions.

Prime Minister Finley, who is front and center at the podium, clears his throat. "So I am quite proud to be here at the announcement of the engagement of our own Prince Stellan and his bride-to-be, Margot Keane. After the Prince's coronation next week, Miss Keane will officially set to marry the king…"

It's the hardest thing ever not to look down and hide my face from the cameras that go absolutely mad just now, flashing brightly for a full minute. I put my hand into Stellan's and he gives it a squeeze. Prime Minister Finley drones on for another minute but I don't hear much of what he has to say.

I'm being tested. And by god, I will pass muster.

"And lastly, I would like to make an announcement that comes straight from Prince Stellan and the future Duchess herself. This gala is open to the public. Everyone is welcome, of every race, sexuality, ability, and economic status. The couple hopes…"

He pauses, frowning ever so briefly. "That everyone will mix, mingle, and find their next charitable cause right here tonight. And toast the happy couple as they…" Finley fights a disdainful look. "Begin their lives in an act of service, forming a line of people serving hot food to all who come." Prime Minister Finley looks up, clearing his throat. "Hear hear."

The audience applauds, some more wildly than others. I look up at my husband-to-be.

"That's our cue," I say, wiggling my eyebrows. "Let's stop by the bathroom on the way downstairs so I can take off these heels, okay?"

His smile is warm. "As you wish, Princess Margot."

Turning around, I am immediately brought up short by the Queen Mother, Lady Ida. I almost trample her and then step back so fast that Stellan has to catch me to keep my balance.

"Queen Mother!" I blurt. "It's a pleasure to see you again, ma'am."

She smiles wanly. "Hello, Margot." She looks between me and Stellan. "I hope you two are doing well?"

Stellan slides his arm around my waist. "We are, thank you."

The Queen Mother seems pleased. "Wonderful. Margot, I wanted to borrow you sometime this week to talk about the wedding. There are so many Danish royal traditions to consider. Would you mind if my secretary reached out to…" She pauses, cocking her head. "Well, whomever is in charge of your schedule."

My heart thuds against my ribs. "Of course. I would be honored, ma'am."

She gives me an odd little smile. "You are going to treat Stellan well, won't you?"

Blushing, I nod. "I will, ma'am."

She nods back, looking at Stellan.

"Very well. Run along now, the press are probably foaming at the mouth to ask you questions."

She turns and heads off toward the prime minister. Stellan guides me toward the door, but of course his grandmother was right.

It's an absolute mob scene. Flashes go off. Questions are hurled at us.

"Margot! Margot!"

"Stellan, when is the wedding?"

"Margot, who are you wearing?"

"Are you two happy to be engaged?"

I close one eye, raising my hand against the bright camera lights. "We're thrilled."

A young man steps close to me, thrusting a microphone is my face. "Margot, your letter in *Politiken* has made you insanely popular with the whole of Denmark. How does it feel to be so universally loved?"

I burst out laughing. "Are you planted by the royal press office?"

He looks a little confused. "No. I'm from the Daily Tribune."

Stellan steps in. "Alright, alright. Move back a little and give us some space. Margot is unused to being so popular, *ja*? She is adjusting quite well."

His answer makes me want to kiss him. Instead I just pull at his hand. "Everyone, could we all start to move downstairs? You can ask your questions while we serve everyone food."

With a little bit of tussling, we make it down off the dais and into the hallway. A nameless assistant is there to hand me a change of shoes. I slip away from Stellan and push the door of the bathroom open.

There is no one inside, so I hurry into the fancy bathroom. As I sink onto the embroidered, overstuffed ottoman, I let out a sigh.

It's blissfully silent.

Taking off my heels with a clatter, I rub my feet for a second. "God damned beautiful heels. You are absolute murder on my feet but you look so pretty."

The bathroom door opens and I look up, a little startled. There is Anna, looking sleek and sophisticated in her knee-length black cocktail dress.

"Ah. There you are, Margot. I was hoping to catch you alone."

My eyes narrow. "What? Don't tell me you've come to yell at me some more about the newspaper? I don't know if anyone told you, but I quit two weeks ago."

Anna cocks her head and gives me the most saccharide smile. "I came to apologize."

I squint at her. "What?" I look around. "Who made you do that?"

Her smile widens and when she talks, it's through her teeth. "No one. I just realized... that I was wrong. And I should have been much nicer to you. If I had realized who you were— "

Standing up, I shake my head. "No. No way."

Her smile goes flat. "I think you should listen, Margot."

I slip my flats on my feet, picking up my heels. "You shouldn't treat people the way you treated me, Anna. And you definitely shouldn't be here apologizing to me now."

Anna clears her throat. "Yes, I am coming to understand that. I was hoping that we could work together because... you know, I know you..."

I give her a funny look. "And you don't think Pippa knows me better?"

She looks down at her hands. "Well, I just thought since I am an editor and Pippa is a bottom level journalist, you would want to speak with me."

I let out a sharp bark of laughter. "Yeah. No thanks. It was... interesting... running into you. I'm due to serve food to whoever wants it." I pause. "Maybe you should do some shelter work. It teaches you to be humble and kind. That would be my advice to you, take it or leave it."

Striding out of the room has never felt quite so good. To my surprise, Stellan is standing just beyond, waiting.

When he sees me, his smile lights me up inside.

"Ready?" he asks, offering me his arm.

I surprise him with a kiss. "I really, really love you. Don't forget that."

He kisses me, smoothing his hand down my back. "I love you too, *skatter*. That's what my ring on your finger symbolizes. It means that I will love you until the end of my days."

My lips curl up. "Forever?"

He chuckles. "Forever."

I link hands with him and let him lead me downstairs, toward whatever lies ahead. I know in my heart that I will get through anything as long as he holds my hand.

THE END

Want to get a little more of Stellan and Margot? You are cordially invited to their private wedding ceremony... sign up for my mailing list and get this exclusive scene right now.

CHAPTER 48

ANNIKA

Dusk has just fallen over the beach, coating everything in sight in a dusting of shadow. The ocean looks dark and intense as the last rays of light disappear over the horizon. Our enormous beach house is the only structure around for miles and its back patio spills right out onto the dunes of sand that lead down to the water.

Other than the twinkle of tea lights on the patio, it's quickly growing dark. I open my arms to the unbelievable spread of the night sky. The stars wink down at me.

Maybe tonight is the night.

My best friend Kalindi looks over at me from her beach blanket, looking beautiful as ever. She has light brown skin and dark eyes, with hair as thick and lustrous as a raven's wing. She leans back, adjusting her pink bikini.

"What would you think about me snagging your brother?" she asks. Her accent is a mix of British and Indian influences, and her voice is melodic. But her words make me pull a face.

"Which one?" I ask. "Don't say Stellan. All my life, my friends have been asking me whether he is single."

She shakes her head with a soft smile. "No, Annika. I'm talking about Finn."

My eyebrows rise. "Finn?" I glance back toward the house, at the picnic tables where the older guys and their friends are sitting, Finn included. "Are you sure you mean him and not Anders?"

Kalindi wrinkles her nose. "What's wrong with Finn?"

I scrunch my face up. "Nothing. He's just... odd. Remote. You are a beautiful ray of sunlight and I wouldn't want him to dim your vibrancy, that's all."

She rolls her eyes. "I just mean a casual make out, nothing serious." She turns and looks at the group again, wrinkling her nose as they get up and head for the house. "I think I'm going to go inside and change my clothes. This bathing suit is cute but itchy."

"Okay." I sit back, noticing that a lone figure walks by us out toward where the water laps at the beach. With his ruggedly good looks and his blond hair, I can spot Erik easily though it's dark. "I'm going to stay for a while."

Kalindi shakes her head. "You shouldn't like him, Nika. He's almost ten years older than us."

Pouting, I look down at my sun-kissed skin in my tiny black bikini. "Erik is only eight years older than me, first of all. And second of all…" I look up at her. "It's just snagging, as you say."

She shakes her head. "You are crazy. He doesn't even know you're alive."

That stings. I make a face. "I know."

She smiles. "Okay. As long as you realize. I'll be inside, scavenging for food."

I nod, letting her leave. My eyes find Erik again, silhouetted against the darkened beach. He wears jeans and a plain white t-shirt, his sleeves rolled up in a way that shows his bulging biceps. He bends over and rolls his jeans up to mid-calf. He keeps walking down a little further, submerging his bare feet in the foam left by the lapping sea. Without realizing it, I stand up, brushing myself off. It's only when I've pulled my shorts and black t-shirt on that I realize that I'm going to go talk to him.

I shiver. Maybe tonight will really be the night. The night that I'll remember for the rest of my life… The night that Erik takes my virginity.

I've only been waiting for him for five whole years. It's time.

Brushing my blonde hair back, I take a deep breath. As I pad barefoot through the sand, I give myself a mini-pep talk.

Just be casual.

Don't be an awkward weirdo.

Play it cool!

A few feet away, Erik turns and notices me. His expression hardens for a split second and then he turns away.

"What do you want, Annika?"

I freeze. This is not the reception I anticipated. Far from it, actually.

Walking forward to pull even with him, I take a deep breath. But when I speak, my tone is petulant.

"I didn't realize that you had the whole entire beach booked up," I say, gesturing to the vast darkness surrounding us.

He looks at me sharply, but doesn't respond right away. I take a moment to drink him in. He's extremely tall, taller even than my older brother Stellan's massive height. His body is perfect and muscular without being too bulky. He has a face that is made for movies, with high cheekbones and long eyelashes, and these deep hazel eyes that make me melt.

Erik grunts. "Stellan is a fucking asshole."

I squint, wrinkle my whole face. "It must be hard to be best friends with the future king of Denmark. Especially when it means you basically get a free ride, wherever you go."

As soon as I say it, I wish I could take it back. There is something about Erik that makes me mean and petty when I really want to be sweet.

He lets out a bark of laughter. "You are a brat, Annika. A spoiled little brat. You know that?"

My face heats. Of course I know that.

"No," I say, sticking my tongue out at him.

He scans me head to toe and then shakes his head. "Yes. You are."

He turns around, walking back toward the house. My heart wrenches; this was my chance to finally tell Erik that I've wanted him for longer than he could possibly know. Now that chance is ruined.

I curse my mouth, which operates on its own sometimes. When Erik stops a few feet away and picks up a bottle of liquor, I raise my brows.

He uncaps it and takes a long pull, letting out a gasping sound when he's done. He turns back to me, holding the bottle out to me.

"Whiskey?"

A breeze blows, making me shiver as I jog the couple of steps toward him, taking the bottle from his hand. He casts another glance at me as I uncork the bottle.

"You should be inside," he murmurs. "Where it's warm and safe."

I take a sip of the whiskey and wince as it burns its way down my esophagus. It's half a minute before I can speak. "Safe? Safe from what?"

Erik looks at me, smirking a little and shrugging. "I don't know. Give me the bottle back, brat."

I narrow my eyes at him, handing it over. Our fingers brush, our gazes collide. His hazel eyes are shadowed so I can't read his expression exactly, but for a split-second I swear there is a carnal interest there.

That, or I'm just imagining what I want to see.

Erik's eyes dart away. He takes another long slug from the bottle. "This whiskey is bullshit."

I wipe a couple of drops from the corner of my mouth, not really knowing how to respond. I'm eighteen; it's not like I have a ton of whiskey tasting experience.

"It's better than some," I come up with at last.

He eyes me skeptically. "*Ja*. It will get you drunk, which I guess is what counts."

I study him. "Are you? Drunk, I mean."

He turns to stare stonily out at the waves. "Maybe." He squints. "I'm on vacation. I almost never get to relax."

He sounds defensive. I shrug my shoulders.

"I'm not judging. I was just curious. I don't think I've ever seen you drunk."

He looks at me again, screwing his handsome face up. "*Ja*, okay."

When he offers me the bottle again, I shake my head. "No. I like champagne, not whiskey."

He lifts a shoulder. "Suit yourself." Tipping his head back, he drinks.

I watch his neck as he gulps the liquor down. I notice his lips then, looking plump and perfectly kissable. Licking my own lips, I let my gaze wander down his body. His arms are both bare and impressively muscular. I can see the definition of his abs in his tight white t-shirt.

Before I realize it, words are leaving my mouth. "I changed my mind. I want some."

Erik raises his brow. "All right."

He takes a step toward me, handing me the bottle. I let the bottle drop to the ground, putting my arms around his neck. He gives me a startled look.

"Wait— "

I am too close to finding out what his lips taste like to stop now. I push up on my tiptoes and press my mouth against his, hesitating once my lips touch his. He seems frozen for a second, his brain taking a moment to catch up to reality. His eyes sink closed.

Then his hands find my lower back, drawing me against the firmness of his body. At the same time Erik deepens the kiss. No more peck on the mouth; his kiss is rough and dominant, his lips working against mine.

I open my mouth to him and he takes every inch I give him, sweeping his tongue inside my mouth like a man staking his claim on unchartered territory for the very first time.

A rugged rumble leaves his chest. If I weren't kissing him, I would have missed it. But it spurs me on, makes my hands spear into the back of his short blond hair.

That's all it takes to make him push me back a step. His eyes fly open, shocked.

"Fuck," he says. "Oh, fuck. That… that should not have happened."

My cheeks go pink. "Erik — "

He shakes his head, cutting me off. "No no no. That… I mean, you're barely eighteen! You're my best friend's baby sister."

I shrug. "So?"

He looks horrified. "So? So, your brother will kill me if he ever finds out. It doesn't matter that I'm drunk…"

I bite my lower lip, looking at him. "I won't tell. It'll be just between us."

Erik shakes his head. "This is bad. This… this can't happen again."

And with that, he picks up the whiskey bottle and starts running back to our beach house. I stare after him, touching my still-warm lips with my fingers.

Despite everything that Erik just said, my lips still curve upward.

He may think that he can resist me. But I haven't even tried anything yet. Not really.

I stand amongst the sand dunes, as the moon comes out to light the night with its soft glow, and make a silent resolution to myself.

Erik will be the one to take my virginity. I just have to convince him that he wants to fuck me as badly as I want him.

A smile plays on my lips. It shouldn't be that hard.

Shivering against the breeze, I stroll back toward the house, plotting my next move.

WANT TO FIND OUT WHAT HAPPENS NEXT? OF COURSE YOU DO! FIND OUT IN HIS FORBIDDEN PRINCESS!

ABOUT VIVIAN WOOD

Vivian likes to write about troubled, deeply flawed alpha males and the fiery, kick-ass women who bring them to their knees.

Vivian's lasting motto in romance is a quote from a favorite song: "Soulmates never die."

Be sure to follow Vivian through her Facebook page or join her email list to keep up with all the awesome giveaways, author videos, ARC opportunities, and more!

VIVIAN'S WORKS

THE PRINCE AND HIS REBEL
THE WICKED PRINCE
HIS FORBIDDEN PRINCESS (SEPTEMBER 2020)
ROYAL'S FAKE FIANCÉ (NOVEMBER 2020)
THE ROYAL REBEL
THE RECKLESS PRINCE

SAME WORLD, DIFFERENT CHARACTERS...
SINFUL FLING
SINFUL ENEMY
SINFUL BOSS
SINFUL CHANCE
SINFUL TEACHER (A NEWSLETTER EXCLUSIVE)

WILD HEARTS

ADDICTION
OBSESSION

HER OFF LIMITS DIRTY BOSS
HIS BEST FRIEND'S LITTLE SISTER
HIS INNOCENT FAKE FIANCÉE
HER OFF LIMITS BEST FRIEND

For more information....
vivian-wood.com
info@vivian-wood.com

Printed in Great Britain
by Amazon